THE NAMING OF THE BEASTS

Praise for Mike Carey:

'Entertaining, well-paced, intelligently plotted and full of memorable characters'   *The Times*

'Imagine an unholy cross between Buffy, Jonathan Creek and hardboiled noir, set it in the sleazier bits of London . . . Fast, fun and furious'   *Guardian*

'Witty, deadpan and shudderingly noir . . . You've heard the rumour that Londoners are never more than a few feet from a rat – Carey will persuade the same is true of the undead.'   *Daily Express*

'Extremely impressive – entertaining and assured. You're left with the eerie feeling that Felix Castor will be haunting us for a long time to come.'   *SFX*

'Simply brilliant novels . . . One of the best books series around right now'   *Forbidden Planet International*

'Carey's writing is nimble and witty, his dialogue believable . . . quirky, dark and imaginative'   *Kirkus*

BY MIKE CAREY

MIKE CAREY

THE NAMING OF THE BEASTS

www.orbitbooks.net

ORBIT

First published in Great Britain in 2009 by Orbit
Reprinted 2009, 2010 (twice)

A CIP catalogue record for this book
is available from the British Library.

ISBN 978-1-84149-655-9

Typeset in Garamond 3 by Palimpsest Book Production Limited,
Grangemouth, Stirlingshire
Printed in the UK by CPI Mackays, Chatham ME5 8TD

Papers used by Orbit are natural, renewable and
recyclable products sourced from well-managed forests and certified
in accordance with the rules of the Forest Stewardship Council.

Mixed Sources
Product group from well-managed
forests and other controlled sources
www.fsc.org Cert no. SGS-COC-004081
© 1996 Forest Stewardship Council

FSC

Orbit
An imprint of
Little, Brown Book Group
100 Victoria Embankment
London EC4Y 0DY

An Hachette UK Company
www.hachette.co.uk

www.orbitbooks.net

*To Ade – for music, Brick Lane curries,
Bunhill Fields, Masonic temples, Old Brewery
and attendant conversations*

Acknowledgements

All my knowledge of the Rickety Twins comes from my wife, Lin, and from the Theatrelands section of the London Metropolitan Archive's website. I'm grateful to both. For the internal geography of the Paterson Building, and my own visualisation of Jenna-Jane Mulbridge's little empire, I have to thank Ade Brown: he took the time and trouble to give me a guided tour, and fed me background information as I needed it. Castor's comments on alcoholism carry echoes from the same source. Thanks also to my agent, Meg, for unfailing support, and to my editor, Darren, for a Spiro Agnew joke that's better than the one I used.

1

It's strange how other people's deaths can take you, some-times. You can build up as much scar tissue as you like – and I'd say I've got more than the average allocation, one way and another – but death can still sneak up on you from an unexpected angle and twist your guts.

The murdered woman had been trying to get out of her tiny little studio flat by means of the window. She'd prob-ably been surprised in bed: woken from sleep to find the intruder already in her room. At any rate, the sheets and the duvet had spilled onto the floor, spread out along a more or less straight line between the bed and the point where she'd died.

A lot of the woman had spilled onto the floor, too. A crude wooden javelin of some kind – most likely the broken-off leg of a table – had passed through her lower abdomen with enough force to drive itself several inches into the plaster of the wall below the window. She remained impaled on it, slumped forward against the glass, one hand dangling at her side. The other hand was raised as though to reach for the latch, but it had come to rest on the sill instead.

A carpet of blood spread out from the body on all sides across the cheap yellow linoleum, setting off the death scene from the rest of the room.

She was a Caucasian woman, as the papers would no

doubt put it, in her thirties, with a consciously retro-styled white Afro: tall but very slender of build, to the point where some of her friends might have worried that she was anorexic. The tabloids would probably add, with their usual eye for salacious detail, that she was naked except for a pink baby-doll nightie too short to hide her modesty. She looked vulnerable and pathetic, transformed into a tableau in the course of her undignified flight, brought down from behind by whatever it was she was running from.

Apart from that disconcerting centrepiece, the room was pretty forgettable. The decor was of the kind that says in many subtle ways, 'I rent this room and I couldn't give a toss what it looks like.' The Georgian-green paint was okay, if you like goose turds, but the dirty, smudged aureoles around the light switches and plug sockets gave a reliable measure of how long ago the paint job had been done, and how many indifferent tenants had passed this way since. The only picture on the wall was a washed-out sub-Constable landscape of haystacks at harvest time, standing underneath a cloudless blue sky. A handsome young farmer walked away from the viewer, his pitchfork resting lightly on his shoulder, the muscles of his bare arms artlessly exaggerated. Give him a pair of chaps, pull his pants down a notch to show some arse cleavage and it could be gay porn.

Police forensics officers wearing white plastic disposables over their street clothes, white gloves on their hands and white masks on their faces were measuring, sampling, dusting, scraping, labelling, correlating, flower-arranging: the room was a hive of activity, as though the dead woman was hosting a party where all the guests were pallid ghosts.

I turned away from the corpse, set my back to it resolutely, although that didn't still the toxic stew of contradictory emotions that was slopping around inside me. It was a hot, moist armpit of a night, from which the heat of the day had barely begun to fade, and the small room was filled like a cup with the stink of spilled blood and split bowels.

Gary Coldwood, a copper to his fingertips, fixed me with an expectant glance. I shook my head. I knew what it was that he was expecting and I wasn't up to it just yet.

'Who found her?' I asked him.

'Bloke in the flat below,' Gary said. 'Nervous type. Highly strung. The call-in was mainly him screaming for the best part of a minute before the switchboard operator could get the address out of him. We've got him downstairs now. The Basilisk is taking his statement.'

The Basilisk. That would be Coldwood's sometime partner, sometime nemesis, Ruth Basquiat: Miss Blonde Ambition. Not the first person I'd have chosen to take a statement from a poor sod who was still traumatised from seeing his upstairs neighbour crucified against her own bedroom wall.

'Anyone see anything?' I pursued. 'Hear anything?'

Gary breathed out loudly: it was almost a snort. 'Welcome to Brixton,' he said. 'Home of the three wise monkeys: see no evil, hear no evil and I fought the law. Even the gent downstairs didn't pick up the phone until the blood started dripping through his ceiling.'

'So who was she?'

Gary consulted his notes. He knew I was stalling, but he also knew when to push and when it was best just to lead me to water and wait for me to drink. He was looking tired, his bristling unibrow wilting on his forehead like a caterpillar caught on bare scrub. There was a downward set to his broad, muscular frame, as though the local gravity where he was standing was two or three times Earth normal. I guessed it had already been a long night, and wasn't likely to end any time soon.

'Ginny Parris,' he said, reading aloud, 'with two Rs. She was a hooker who worked the backstreets off Atlantic Road. Bit of a local landmark, by all accounts. "She didn't use nothing any more – she was clean for six months now. She used to work for Red Paul, but since he went down she looks after herself, doesn't she? She's not stupid." That ringing endorsement brought to you courtesy of Pauline "Exotique" O'Malley, Miss Parris's former colleague, at her business address behind the Mercury cab rank on the Brixton Road.'

He put the notebook back in his pocket, his sombre face contrasting with the flippant tone of his summary.

'It wasn't a man who did this,' I said, stating the obvious.

'No,' Gary agreed. 'It wasn't. Not unless he put that thing through her with a siege catapult.' He was momentarily distracted by a uniformed constable who was about to move a table out of the way of a bunch of white-coated lab-rats. The table was probably the source of the murder weapon, because one of its legs had been broken off. It lay at an oblique angle, reminding me faintly of a dying horse in a Sam Peckinpah Western. 'Oi!' Gary yelled at the plod. 'Don't touch a bloody thing until it's been dusted and logged. Didn't your mum teach you anything, you plukey little gobshite?'

The constable blanched, mumbled an apology and backed hurriedly out of Gary's line of sight, where he probably relieved his feelings with an obscene gesture or two.

'No,' Gary said again, returning his attention to me. 'The working hypothesis is a *loup-garou*. Which is one reason why you're here, Castor. If whoever did this was undead, you can presumably tell us what size, brand and flavour it was. And then you can toddle off home to bed, which is obviously where you've come from.'

I put a hand up defensively to my stubbled chin. Okay, so I looked like I'd been rolled up wet and put away dry. But I wasn't on the force, I was just a civilian adviser, so Gary could go fuck himself. He couldn't exactly put me on a charge for letting the side down.

'Didn't have to be were-kin,' I mused aloud. 'Could be a geist, or a zombie.' Neither of those options sounded right, though. A poltergeist powerful enough to do something like this would have left the air saturated with its presence. Even the Thomases — exorcist hate-speak for rationalist sceptics — on the Met would feel like they were breathing cold shit soup. And most zombies are weaker than humans, not stronger: they can push themselves a little harder, because their pain–pleasure wiring collapses after a while, along with the rest of their nervous system, but this was way outside the normal range of activity for a dead-man-walking.

At that point, belatedly, I registered something else that Gary had said. 'One reason why I'm here?' I echoed. 'Why? What's the other?'

'All in good time,' Coldwood said, his expression studiously neutral. 'There's another wrinkle to this one, but I don't want to prejudice your findings. Now are you going to do that voodoo that you do tolerably well, or shall we all stand around while you carry on throwing guesses at the fucking wall?'

'Oh, handle me roughly, Detective Sergeant,' I said in a bored drawl. Gary and me have a certain amount of history now: we're even friends, in a way, although it's a friendship with arcane rules about when we cut each other slack and when we don't. We have default roles and positions that we tend to fall into when we meet. Right now, that was a useful bulwark against the splatter-shot blood-red reality behind me.

I looked round at the busy-bee forensics team, who were still doing their labour-intensive thing on all sides of us, and the small herd of uniformed constables loitering around the doorway.

'You'll need to clear the room,' I told Gary. 'I won't be able to pick up a blind thing with this lot going on.'

Gary hesitated, then nodded. 'Mandatory fag break,' he called out to his team. 'Collins, work on the stairwell for a bit. Webb, get some of your mob taking statements from the neighbours. I can see them all rubbernecking out there, so we might as well use them while we've got them.' He pointed towards the door. 'Everybody out.'

They left in dribs and drabs, the forensics guys packing up their kit with finicky care and looking glumly frustrated, as though they'd been smacked in the head with a wet fish in the middle of some promising sexual foreplay. A case like this doesn't come along every day: although as far as that goes, they probably only had to wait. Things were changing around us, faster and faster. The world wasn't a sphere any more, or at least it didn't feel that way a lot of the time; it felt like an inclined plane.

Gary was the last to leave, and he lingered in the doorway. 'I don't have to tell you not to touch anything, do I, Fix?' he asked, his expression hovering somewhere between wary and apologetic.

I looked him squarely in the eyes. I knew what he was thinking. I used to work for the detective branch in an official capacity, under Coldwood's tutelage: consulting exorcist, by appointment, with all the privileges a civilian informant gets from the boys in blue. Then twice in the last two years I'd been the main suspect in a murder investigation, and Gary had had to bend over so far backwards to keep me out of jail that he could have won a limbo competition in Queenstown, Jamaica. It reflected badly on his judgement that I kept landing up to my neck in shit.

'I know the drill,' I said.

'Yeah, I'm sure you do.' He gave up the point. 'Give me a shout when you're done.'

He left at last, and I was alone with the body. I circled the broken table and stared down at her sombrely, feeling compromised and shamed in some indefinable way by her vulnerability, her violation.

But I had a job to do, and Gary would already be looking at his watch. 'Meter's running,' as he liked to say, still searching for that Hollywood tough-guy persona that always eluded him because he could never quite bring himself to be a big enough bastard.

In the lining of the Russian army greatcoat which is my work uniform there's a sewn-in pocket just big enough to house my tin whistle within easy reach of my left hand.

I put my hand in now and drew it out. Putting it to my lips I played a few random notes as place-holders for a tune that didn't exist yet.

The room darkened around me. The world of flesh and blood and words and meanings went away.

Exorcism is a peculiar way to earn a living. The pay is shit, the hours are appalling, there's no career structure and the work itself can shade from same old same old to lethally dangerous inside of a heartbeat. But I'll say this for it: it's a vocation. To do it at all, you've got to be born to it.

It's got nothing to do with religious faith. If it did, I'd be out of a job because, despite my Catholic upbringing, me and God haven't been on speaking terms since I was six. It's just an extra sense, or maybe an extra set of senses. An exorcist knows when the dead are around, and he can reach out and touch them in various ways: specifically, he can bind them and he can banish them.

And the dead are *always* around. You've probably noticed yourself how bad it's got just lately. Chances are, some time in the last few years you bought a house or rented a flat and found that it was haunted; or else someone you knew clawed their way up out of the grave and decided to renew an old acquaintance; or, God help you, maybe you had a run-in with a *loup-garou* – werewolf, to use the vernacular – or one of the lesser Hell-kin. In which case, you can be thankful that you're even alive to read this.

Maybe the huge spike in the supernatural population created its own Darwinian pressures. Or maybe not. It seems just as likely to me that the potentiality for exorcism as an innate skill was always part of the human genome, but most people who had it lived and died without ever finding out that it was there. These days . . . well, you tend to find out pretty fast.

We've all got our own ways of doing the job. Some people do it the old-fashioned way, with the traditional props: a bell, a book and a candle, a dagger and a chalice, maybe a bit of an incantation in hacked-up medieval Latin. I've even done it that way myself on occasion, but only to impress the mug punters. Any kind of pattern will do to hold a ghost: a sequence of words or sounds, lines on a piece of paper, the movements of a dance, even a hand of playing cards. If you've got the knack, you can choose your own tools, your own gimmick. Although in my experience it's closer to the truth to say that it chooses you.

I do it with music. My second sight is more like second hearing, which means that I experience ghosts, demons and the undead as tunes. With my trusty tin whistle (Clarke's Original, key of D) I can reproduce the tune, and tangle the ghost up in the music so it can't get free. When I stop playing, it goes to wherever music goes when it's not being played. Problem solved. It's not so straightforward with demons, because they tend to fight back, but that's the basis of what I do right there: a natural talent that I've turned into a steady job.

The word 'steady' in that sentence was meant as sarcasm.

The first part of an exorcism is the summoning, where you make a connection with the ghost and call it to you, but before you can even do that, you've got to learn its nature, its unique *this-ness*, so you know what it is you're calling to. A general invitation usually doesn't work.

I sat to one side of the dead woman, just outside the wide circle of spilled blood, and played a halting, broken-backed tune that was more like a question than a command. I was fishing: sending out feelers through the heights and depths of some vast volume that wasn't air or water or even space, an infinity that fitted comfortably into this pokey little rented room.

Nothing. My hook was out there, but nothing bit.

It wasn't that there was nothing there. Any building that's more than a few years old develops a sort of emotional patina, a set of resonances that an exorcist will pick up at once if he opens himself to it. There were plenty of echoes in this room: the joys and sorrows and bumps and grinds of ordinary existence lingering in the air, in the brick-work, like the unstilled vibrations of a sound that had passed outside the range of human hearing.

But the ghost of Ginny Parris refused to come on down.

She was there. On some level, in some form, I was aware of a presence in the room. Diffuse and weak and scattered, it hung in the ether like Morse code, discontinuous but replete with meaning: a dot of misery here, a dash of fear and confusion there, and way over here an incongruous flash-silence-flash of hope. I went on playing, a little encouraged. Normally this stage of the game is kind of a cumulative thing. You start off slow, with only the barest sense of the ghost's presence, but you zero in on it with your talent, with whatever interface you use to make your talent work for you. You describe and define and delimit it, bring it in closer, sharpen the signal. It can come fast or it can come slow, but sooner or later you reach a tipping point where it becomes inevitable. The pattern of the ghost is imprinted on your mind, and after that it can't get away from you. You can make it come to you, bind it to your will. You can question it, and it has to answer you if it's able. Or you can make it go away and never come back.

That wasn't what was happening here, though; if anything, this was the exact opposite. The sense of Ginny's presence got weaker rather than stronger: those vestigial traces effaced themselves more and more, faded away gradually and inexorably, until it seemed like it was only the music that was keeping them there at all.

I kept on playing. Typically, by this time, the random notes would have modulated into a recognisable tune. But they didn't. They remained fragmented and formless, just as she was.

I suddenly had the terrifying conviction that a piece of Ginny Parris was clinging to the lifeline of my tune to keep from tumbling off into the abyss of whatever-comes-next. So I kept the lifeline going for as long as I could, feeling her getting further and further away from me in some direction that doesn't really have a name. It was a strain now to maintain that contact. I felt a trickle of sweat on my forehead, and my heart was racing.

I played her until she was gone.

And in her absence, in the spaces through which her soul had trickled away, I sensed a second presence. It was even fainter than hers had been, but for very different reasons.

Dogs hunt in packs, bark their lungs out and stink the place up like a roomful of wet carpets. Cats hunt alone, in silence; crouch low to let no silhouette show above the skyline; bury their droppings so the prey won't know where they've been hunting. The scariest predators are the ones you don't see until their jaws snap shut on your throat, and so it is too with the predators of the spirit world.

I sat in the silent room, breathing in the stench of death, and waited for my heartbeat to slow back to a sustainable seventy-some beats a minute. It took a long time.

When I felt up to it, I climbed to my feet and went to the door. There was no sign of Gary on the narrow landing or in the stairwell, but a copper at the bottom of the stairs, by the street door, had obviously been briefed to give him a shout when I surfaced. He looked out into the street and called something that I didn't hear.

Gary appeared shortly after and came up to join me.

'What did you get?' he asked bluntly. Then before I could answer he raised a hand to shush me, fished in his pocket and came up with a digital voice recorder – an Olympus DS-50, his favourite toy from last year. He clicked the record button, held it to his mouth like a telephone. 'Witness name is Felix Castor,' he said. 'Time . . .' consulting his watch '. . . 1.17 a.m. Place, flat 3C, 129 Cadogan Terrace, SW2. Witness – a practising exorcist – was called in by investigating officer in CI capacity.'

He held the recorder out in my direction.

'Talk me through it, Castor.'

'You can forget your *loup-garou* hypothesis,' I muttered, pushing the device away again.

Gary's interest quickened. He shot me a stare that would have cost him plenty at the poker table.

'Go on,' he said.

'She didn't answer the summoning. There were . . . pieces of her all over the place, but they didn't add up to anything. She hadn't just been killed, she'd been shredded.'

Gary's eyes flicked involuntarily to the corpse.

'Fuck,' I said impatiently. 'Not her body, Gary. Her soul. Whatever killed her got her soul as well. It was a demon. She was killed by a demon.'

Even a couple of years ago, if I'd told him that, he would have laughed in my face. Now he took it calmly, too calmly in fact. He seemed almost to have been expecting it.

'Did you pick up anything else?' he asked.

'She didn't die quickly,' I said. 'Or at least . . . she did, in the end, obviously. But the thing was in here with her for a while before that. She had long enough to go through a lot of different emotions. At one point, I reckon . . . she thought it might let her live. I don't know why that would be.'

'Yeah,' said Gary. 'I do. Maybe.'

He turned the tape recorder off and put it back in his pocket.

'Something you're not telling me,' I said. It was a state-ment, not a question. This whole situation was screaming set-up at me in three-part harmony.

'Yeah,' Gary admitted. 'The other reason why I came to you with this. I mean, you're not really on the books any more, and your friend Juliet has it all over you in the eye-candy department. But I think this one's yours, Fix.'

I waited, but he didn't seem in any hurry to spit it out.

'Well?' I demanded. 'What?'

'The name didn't mean anything to you?'

'Ginny,' I murmured. 'Ginny Parris.' Maybe it did at that. The memory wouldn't come clear, but alarm bells started to ring, way down in my subconscious.

'Not her real name. Birth certificate has Jane, but she liked to call herself Guinevere. When that wouldn't fly, she shortened it to Ginny.'

My heart took a ride down to my stomach, in the express elevator.

'Oh Jesus,' I said. 'She was . . .'

Gary waited for a few seconds in case I finished the sentence myself. When I didn't, he finished it for me. 'Yeah,' he confirmed. 'Rafi Ditko's old girlfriend.'

2

I went to pieces for a while back there. It wasn't pretty.

It began about three months ago, after the demon Asmodeus, wearing my friend Rafi's body, broke out of the bespoke prison cell I'd run up for him at the house of the Ice-Maker, Imelda Probert, killing Imelda herself and three other people along the way, and walked out into the world to see what was new.

That was enough of a catastrophe in itself: Imelda left a teenaged daughter, Lisa, who as far as I knew had no other living relatives. Asmodeus was a monster, and his tenancy of Rafi's flesh was an abomination. And demons being demons, I had to assume that those first four murders were only a foretaste of things to come. But what made the whole thing infinitely worse was that it was mostly my fault.

Okay, it wasn't me who had freed Asmodeus from captivity. The honours for that fiasco went to a little-known and technically excommunicate Catholic sect known as the Anathemata and their priest-slash-general Thomas Gwillam. Gwillam wanted to exorcise Asmodeus, but the people he put on that work detail weren't up to it. They went in half-cocked, got themselves cut to pieces, and in the process freed the demon from the psychic straitjacket I'd put him in.

But I was the reason he was there in the first place:

I'd taken him to Peckham, to Imelda's house, from the Charles Stanger Care Home in Muswell Hill, in a desperate attempt to keep him from falling into even worse hands. I was also the reason why he was strong enough to get free and fight back, because I'd allowed him to feed on part of another demon. It had all seemed to make sense at the time: feeding Asmodeus had set a young boy free from a possession that would eventually have killed him.

But then the Anathemata had stuck their oar in, everything had gone to Hell in a hand basket, and Imelda had died.

I honestly didn't give a tinker's fuck about Gwillam's three exorcists. Like Rosencrantz and Gildenstern, they'd made love to their employment, and they'd only got what they'd been asking for. But Imelda . . .

Christ Jesus and all his angels. Imelda.

'*Don't make me regret this*,' she'd said when she finally gave in to my undignified begging and let me land Rafi on her. And then when I suggested waking Asmodeus to let him feed on one of his homeys, she was horrified and enraged. She'd only agreed because she loved her own kid so much, and she couldn't stand by and watch someone else's kid dragged down to Hell when she had it in her power to do something about it.

I drew up the plan of attack. I led the charge. She was the Light Brigade and I was Lord fucking Cardigan.

So yeah. I took it hard. And yeah, I suppose I took the coward's road.

I stayed with Imelda's daughter, Lisa, until the ambulance arrived. She hadn't said a word the whole time; just sat with her mother's head in her lap, rocking her back and forth as though she was asleep. The only time she showed any animation at all was when the paramedics tried to separate her from the blood-boltered corpse. Even then, she didn't fight them or cry or swear at them; she just held on tightly to Imelda's chest, forcing them to pry her fingers loose one by one. And after that she stopped moving altogether.

I watched the ambulance go.

Then I found an off-licence, bought a bottle of whatever whisky came readiest to hand, took it to one of the wooden benches at Elephant and Castle and drank it dry.

My memories of the days and weeks that followed are a little patchy, but I know that that bottle was only the first of many. I would have taken other drugs, probably, if any had been kicking around, but booze has always been my sledgehammer of choice when I want to throw a tarp over the day and pass out fast.

Only now it wasn't just a day I wanted to blot out. I wanted to forget I'd ever been born. I wanted to erase Felix Castor and rewind. Someone else might do a better job of taking up the space he used to occupy.

So I did my best to turn my brain into half-congealed soup, but in spite of my best efforts, a few scraps of sense input from that time manage to stand out fairly distinctly.

I remember being carried home one night by my good friend Juliet – who, being a succubus, didn't even break a sweat – and propped up against the door like a sack of coal. She would have taken me all the way to my bed, I'm sure, except that my landlady, Pen, doesn't allow her in the house: Pen has a 'no succubi' rule that's fairly strict.

I remember Pen standing in the doorway of my room,

cursing me out. 'You selfish, self-pitying bastard!' she was saying. 'He's out there. He's out there on the streets right now, and all you're doing about it is lying here in your own vomit! Well fuck you, Fix! I'll find him myself, if you won't help.'

I remember crawling on my hands and knees on the floor of my room, groping under my bed for a bottle that had fallen and rolled. When I found it, most of the contents had spilled out. Heartbroken from the loss, I cried. Then drank what was left in a single gulp, and coughed and hacked and wheezed for five minutes because the neck of the bottle had attracted enough dust and fluff to choke a horse.

I remember being called to the hospital to talk about Lisa's condition. I'd given myself as next of kin because I didn't know any other name to put down. So I had to go, wishing all the while that I'd given the paramedics a false name and address. She was still completely unresponsive, and the doctors wanted to know if she had any history of catatonia or neural disorders. They also wanted me to sign a shit-load of papers. I started in blithely enough, until my eyes came briefly into focus and I realised what some of the consent forms were for. Anti-psychotics. Electro-shock. Surgical interventions. I fled, pursued by shouted assurances that most of the permissions were 'just in case'.

I remember sitting in a car park late at night, my back up against the rear tyre of a truck, playing my whistle. I was trying to reproduce a note I'd never heard before. Something totally new: an *ostinato* that had sneaked its way into the world without my noticing, and that only my legless, almost mindless state was allowing me to hear right then. As I moved my fingers to half-block the stops and hit painfully elided semitones, ribbons of nearly invisible nothingness like the ghosts of tapeworms drifted past me and through me, seeking the music as though it was a form of sustenance.

I remember lying with my cheek pressed against cold stone, thinking with something like relief that it might all be over at last. This might be a mortuary slab that I was sprawled out on. But it wasn't. It was just another stinking, sticky pavement strewn with broken glass, just another station of the booze-hound's cross.

Alcohol is a curious thing: an arcane and complex thing that opens up its mysteries to you in successive layers. At the very heart of its cruelty, there's a dark and terrible compassion, which is this: after it's poisoned you, you can take it as medicine. You can get into a cycle where you're drinking to carry your body through the pains and wrenches of withdrawal, and in the short term it actually works.

I rode that horse for a while. Then I fell off it and it trampled me. Then it pissed on me as I lay in the gutter.

Coming back was slow, and at first almost accidental. I woke up in my lightless room, stewed in my own sweat and feeling like someone had magically transformed my tongue into a size-10 army boot. I was on fire with the ague of chemical need, alternately too hot and too cold inside my skin, on which salamanders were crawling with hooked claws, and snakes with rasping scales.

I couldn't find the light switch, couldn't even remember the layout of my own room. I staggered to the bathroom in the dark, filled the bath with cold water and fell into it, fully clothed. Well, the clothes smelled like they needed a wash in any case, so it counted as economy of effort.

By the time the sun came up, I'd ridden out the worst of the shakes. I stood up on wobbly legs, stripped the sodden clothes from my body and washed properly. Shaving was harder, because my hands were still about as steady as the plastic mule in the game of Buckaroo, but I persevered.

I staggered downstairs about an hour later, wearing a pair of clean underpants that I'd providentially found down the back of a radiator and one of Pen's 200 or so T-shirts with Celtic knot designs on them. On the table in the hall there was a stack of mail for me, including a brown enve-lope in legal quarto size which had come recorded delivery and had bad news written all over it. I ignored it for now. First things first.

I rehydrated myself with a couple of litres of water, and zapped my nervous system with about the same amount of strong black coffee. I still felt like the walking dead, but I'm not prejudiced: some of my best friends belong to that fraternity. And at least my brain was starting to work again.

The first thing it did was play me back those few snip-pets of memory, like answerphone messages. The worrying one was Pen saying, 'I'll find him myself.' I needed to have a word with her about that, but she wasn't in her base-ment sitting room when I went down there to check.

The rats were, though, prowling restlessly round their rat-habitat. So were the ravens, Edgar and Arthur, one of them sitting on an actual perch, the other on Pen's computer monitor. They clacked their beaks when I entered, and Arthur cawed intimidatingly.

I make a point of feeding the ravens whenever I see them, because it doesn't make sense to piss off birds whose beaks are strong enough to open tin cans, but it's occurred to me recently that I'm only making a Pavlovian connection in their minds between Castor and food which may one day come back to bite me in the arse, either figuratively or literally. I took some frozen liver from Pen's fridge, thawed it out in the microwave and split it between the two of them. They fell on it like a pair of blood-crazed maniacs. It looked like they hadn't been fed in a while. To be on the safe side, I fed the rats too. Then I went upstairs and fed myself, saved from the agonies of indecision by the fact that the kitchen was empty except for a tin of baked beans and a packet of Ryvita crackers. Well, okay, there was a half-finished bottle of Janneau Armagnac too, but I made myself look away. I didn't want to go on another bender until I was sure Pen was okay.

So I fixed myself some weight-conscious beans on toast and ate them slowly with Radio 4 playing in the background. That told me what day of the week it was and who was prime minister; the fine detail I could fill in for myself later.

In the meantime, that bottle of brandy was still making indecent suggestions to me from the kitchen. I decided to get some distance from it before I found myself in a compromising situation.

I went back upstairs to my room with the vague but virtuous intention of clearing up some of the shit that had accumulated during my spectacular drunk. But the scale of the task daunted me. There was broken glass trodden into the carpet, a sour stink of stale, spilled booze in the air, and the lurking likelihood that picking up any one item of dirty laundry or overturned furniture would reveal greater horrors underneath. I gave up on the idea before I'd even started. I was able to assemble myself a less ridiculous outfit, though: a black shirt, dark grey cargo pants and a pair of low-heel boots that have proved over the years to be as durable as Permian granite.

After that I just waited for a while: in the back garden until the sun got too high, then in the basement with the ravens. Morning shaded into afternoon, with no sign of Pen. She couldn't know that I'd wake up and feed the birds, so her absence was doubly hard to explain.

I was on the rack again by this time: sweating like a warthog, with a sick, hollow feeling in my stomach that only alcohol could fill. My head throbbed as though it was a blood-filled pimple that would burst at a touch. And the physical symptoms fed off my disquietude about Pen, and vice versa, until I couldn't even sit still, but had to walk around the room like a prisoner in solitary taking the only exercise that was on offer.

How long did someone have to be off the scene before they counted as an official missing person? A lot longer than half a day, surely. But it might be worth calling Pen's sister Antonia, and seeing if she'd showed round there. The only thing that made me hesitate was the fact that Tony hates my guts and would curse me out loudly down the phone. She shouts a lot. Really, a whole lot; and I felt right then as though the wrong harmonic would just shatter me.

But I steeled myself to do it in the end, and I was actually dialling when the key turned in the lock upstairs.

I put the phone down and headed up to ground level. Edgar and Arthur glided over my head, keen to get their word in first. They didn't need to worry: I was fighting another bout of the shakes, and they could have beaten me at an easy walk.

When I got to the top of the basement stairs, Pen was bespeaking the door: talking to it in guttural undertones while touching the wood at the four cardinal points. Pretty much everyone puts wards on their doors and windows these days, to prevent unwanted visits from the recently deceased. Mostly they buy them in ready-made, though: photocopied stay-nots and tied-up sprigs of flowering herbs from the Camden Market spiritualist stalls, crucifixes and vials of holy water from the local church, mezuzahs and salats and cunningly modified Mani scrolls and every other flavour of religious prophylactic all readily available now by weight or piecemeal. Pen, though, makes up her own. She's a pagan, and a priestess in an indie church that doesn't even have a name. She keeps that side of her life very much to herself though, and I've learned not to ask.

The ward laid, she turned to look at me. It was a searching look that lingered speculatively on the clean shirt and the freshly sliced, mostly stubble-free chin.

'Hey,' I said, crossing over to her. 'I was starting to get worried.'

She submitted to a kiss on the cheek, but I heard her sniff the air as I leaned in, so I knew she was still trawling for information on my sobriety and soundness of mind.

'I'm sober,' I assured her.

'Yeah,' she agreed dryly. 'I'm sure that will last.'

She walked past me into the living room, threw her

handbag down on the sofa, then threw herself down after it. I hadn't really registered it until now, but she was in disguise. Instead of her usual flamboyant colours, she was wearing a suit in a subdued mid-brown, and she'd tied her hair back in a tight bun. In short, she'd done her best to avoid a second glance. Not easy for Pen: she stands five foot nothing in her cotton socks, but has intensely green eyes like chunks of radioactive kryptonite, flame-red hair and a general air – which is pretty much accurate – of being a compact container for a lot of dangerous energy. I'd had a serious thing for her once, but it was a long time ago, back when she and I and Rafi were all at college together. It might even have gone somewhere if Rafi hadn't been an item in that list, but the chemical bond that developed between the two of them reduced the two of us, by some mysterious alchemy, into just-good-friends, which is where we've been ever since.

All the same, I must have looked a little like a suspicious husband as I stood over her now, arms folded and face solemnly set. 'Where have you been?' I demanded. 'The birds were starving.'

'Looking for Rafi,' she answered shortly.

'Overnight?'

'He's got a demon inside him, Fix. I don't think demons keep office hours.'

She closed her eyes to deter further questions, so I waited to see if she was going to volunteer any more information on her own.

'I suppose it's too much to hope that you might have left me some of that brandy?' she asked after a while.

I went and got her the bottle and a glass. Just the one

glass, although my palms prickled at the proximity of the booze. A single medium-to-large-sized shot would set me up so right.

But that way lay madness, and another lost weekend that might easily last until the middle of next week.

Pen poured herself a generous shot, then as an after-thought she offered me the bottle. I shook my head and she grunted in what sounded like surprise but could have been approval. She emptied the glass in three swigs: not the most respectful way to treat the fruit of Monsieur Janneau's labour of love.

'I take it you struck out,' I said, after a carefully judged pause.

'Can't hide a thing from your rapier intellect,' Pen muttered bitterly.

'Where did you look?'

'Everywhere.'

'I mean, were you working to a plan? Following any concrete leads? Or were you just thinking you'd recognise Rafi's aftershave if you got close to him?'

Pen poured herself another. 'He never wore it,' she said, staring into the glass. 'Even back when he was . . .' a perceptible pause '. . . himself.'

And doesn't that seem like a long time ago, I thought glumly.

'I asked myself what *you'd* do,' Pen said, returning un-expectedly to my last question. She shot me a look of the kind that's usually called old-fashioned. 'What you'd do if you weren't totally stewed, I mean.'

I took both the compliment and the insult on the chin. 'And?' I prompted.

'I decided you might try a bit of lateral thinking. Who'd know about demons?'

'Other demons?'

'And users. And people who want to be users. I've been going round the two-finger clubs, blagging my way into other people's conversations. And the reason I stayed out all night is because I got an invite back to a house party down in Surrey where they were meant to be doing a summoning. Only it turned out it was just a bunch of ponced-up ovates who couldn't find their arses with a map and a photofit picture.'

She stopped, registering my shocked expression. 'What?' she asked defensively.

I was both impressed with her grasp of the lingo and appalled at what she'd been doing. Only exorcists apply the term 'user' primarily to people who summon demons rather than people who ingest chemicals to get happy. The two-finger clubs, in the same trade-specific argot, are satanist dives – so called because the satanists like to draw their pentagrams with two arms pointing upwards and three down – symbolically rejecting the Holy Trinity. An ovate is the lowest rank in the Druidic Gorsedd, but when applied to the satanist churches it also means a wanker who can't draw a magic circle without making it look like an Easter egg – which if you're a demon-worshipper sends entirely the wrong kind of message.

'You don't want to mess with those people,' I told Pen, meaning it. 'In among the harmless tosspots there are some real nasty pieces of work. People who've hung around with Hell-kin long enough to go native.'

'Those were the ones I was hoping to meet,' Pen

answered impatiently. 'Don't baby me, Fix. I know what I'm doing.' She took a sip of her brandy and scowled at the glass as if it had done her some mortal hurt. 'In any case,' she said, 'it didn't work. I didn't get to meet any of the big operators. Oh, there are rumours everywhere. The infernal messiah has been born at last, and he's incubating inside the Centrepoint tower. Someone's drawing a socking great magic circle around the whole of London by joining up the white lines on the M25. The bishops of all the satanist churches are meeting over in Kensington Palace for the biggest summoning ever seen. But you could tell when you tried to pin them down to specifics that it was all bollocks. Most of the people I was talking to knew less about what was really going on than I did.'

'What is going on?' I asked her. 'I've been out of the loop for a few days.'

Pen snorted derisively. 'Try two weeks,' she suggested. 'Time flies when you're enjoying yourself, doesn't it?'

I wouldn't describe the mill I'd just been through — was still going through — as 'enjoying myself', but I didn't bother to argue. 'Are the police looking for Rafi too?' I asked, calling a spade a spade.

Pen shrugged. 'They must be,' she said bleakly. 'His fingerprints were all over Imelda's house. Mostly in other people's blood.' Her face crumpled momentarily, and tears welled up in her eyes. I moved forward to hug her, but she warded me off with one hand, not ready or willing to take comfort from me. 'I don't know how this can end now,' she said, her voice trembling. 'He killed her, Fix. He killed Imelda.'

'Asmodeus killed Imelda,' I amended.

'And Rafi did too. It was his hands that Asmodeus used. It doesn't matter that he didn't want to do it. When they catch him, they'll lock him away for life.' She wiped away the tears with furious energy before they could fall.

I couldn't think of anything consoling to say. Everything she'd said was true, and she hadn't said the worst of it. Even if London's finest dropped the ball, and Rafi somehow got away without being had up for murder, being welded to Asmodeus was a life sentence in itself.

Back when I first met Rafael Ditko, at college in Oxford, I really didn't know what the hell to make of him: he was a bum, essentially, but a bum with his own inimitable style. A mature student from the Czech Republic, he was older than the rest of our little circle by three years and some small change, and he had a spectacular impact on all of us: on Pen more than anyone, because she'd fallen in love with him more or less at first sight, and then had to watch while he bedded every other girl we knew, weaving his way in and out between their official boyfriends with no call-out charge and no waiting.

He was the sort of guy who never paid for a round, never cleaned up his own messes, always called the tune but left someone else to settle accounts with the piper. By rights we should probably have hated him, but he had that knack – that mix of rakish good looks, ineffable charm and perfectly faked sincerity – that makes other people love you and want to carry your burdens for you. He was destined for a happy, directionless life probably full of other people's sofas and other people's wives: nature had adapted and equipped him for that evolutionary niche.

But that was until he met me. I was falling fast at that time – a fall that had begun when my death-sense kicked in at full power, around my thirteenth birthday. Rafi was rising like an ego-propelled rocket, and we ricocheted off each other in a perfect example of Brownian motion. Rafi's exuberant hedonism and the cool, arrogant way he handled the world's slings and arrows helped me to pull out of the self-destructive anomie that I was drowning in. My effect on him was less wholesome: I triggered a fascination in him, an obsession with the dead. Rafi being Rafi, the obsession expressed itself in competition. He wanted to outdo me in delivering the necromantic goods: to go on expeditions to the undiscovered country and bring back souvenirs.

It destroyed him, in the end. By some route I've never been able to reconstruct, he fell into the orbit of one Anton Fanke, the founder and leader and prophet-in-residence of the so-called Satanist Church of the Americas. The SCA seems to model itself on the Moonies in some respects: its deacons use total-environment conditioning, surrounding you with their own people so that the only truths you hear are theirs. Rafi dropped his old acquaintances and disappeared from our radar, much to Pen's dismay. Ginny, his girlfriend at that time, was an SCA plant who fed Rafi's addiction with badly photocopied grimoires, mountains of steganographic horse shit and a few nuggets of lethal, undeniable fact.

I don't know why they chose Rafi. What I do know is that Fanke had a lot of arcane and complex ideas about how magical ritual should work, and he'd come to the conclusion that in magic the practitioner is part of the system.

For some reason, that meant that when he attempted his biggest ever summoning, raising one of the most powerful demons in Hell by means of an adjuration spell adapted from Honorius' *Liber Iuratus*, he decided it should be Rafi Ditko rather than himself who drew the circle and intoned the needful words.

The summoning went wrong, and Rafi ended up possessed by Asmodeus instead of commanding him. Then I sealed his fate by trying to carry out an exorcism without knowing what it was I was trying to cast out. I'd never met a demon back in those days. I was armed for bear, but I found myself drawing a bead on Leviathan.

I've tried many times since that night to reconstruct what it was I did, with a view to reverse-engineering my own tune and finding a way to put things right. It's not easy, for a lot of reasons. The scene was one of violent chaos: in the bathroom of Rafi's flat in the Seven Sisters Road, with Rafi thrashing and raving in a bathtub full of boiling water right beside me. That water had been ice about a minute and a half before, but the fierce heat that was burning Rafi up from the inside had made short work of it.

I found what I thought was the intruding spirit, and I started to weave a tune around it. The notes came quickly and fluently. I was expecting this thing, whatever it was, to put up more of a fight, but despite Rafi's cursing and convulsions, the binding wasn't too hard at all.

But as I was about to move on to the banishing, Rafi had a moment of lucidity. He stared at me with absolute terror in his eyes. 'Fix . . .' he whispered. 'Please! Please don't . . .' In an instant he'd vanished again, going down for the third time in the lightless wells of his own hind brain. Asmodeus surfaced in his place, tenting the skin of Rafi's face with the ridge poles of his own inhuman physiognomy, and blistering my ears with a curse from the arse-end of Tartarus.

I twigged it then, all of it. I knew what it was that was possessing Rafi, and I knew what I'd caught in the tightening coils of my tune. I was about to exorcise my best friend's spirit from his own body, and leave the demon standing alone on the field.

I couldn't just stop playing; that would destroy Rafi for sure. So I did the only thing I could think of, which was to change the tune into something else. I modulated key and pitch and tempo, trying to ground the binding power of the music in something else besides Rafi. And the demon, seeing what I was doing, fought back.

It was like being in a tug of war in which the rope is a frayed mains cable with a million volts flowing through it. I couldn't stop, couldn't let go, couldn't let my concentration slacken for a moment. We wrestled for hours, the demon writhing inside my friend's flesh, me hunched over the bathtub with the whistle jammed to my mouth, playing a skirling, nightmare arabesque.

And I won. Kind of. I bound the demon.

Only I bound it to Rafi, and I couldn't untie them again.

It was the opposite of an exorcism: the man and the monster were welded so tightly and inextricably that they'd almost become one being. It wasn't exactly a Jekyll and Hyde deal, though; it was worse than that. Asmodeus was calling the shots from day one. Rafi's personality remained totally submerged, except when I was able to bring it to the surface again with another summoning.

And Rafi's body was locked up in a silver-lined cell at the Charles Stanger Care Home in Muswell Hill, silver being a good specific against demons as well as the undead. The official diagnosis was schizophrenia, but the Stanger knew what they were dealing with and took no chances. They kept the demon down with wards and charms and neuroleptic drugs, administered in industrial quantities.

That was how things stayed for the next three years. I tried a hundred times to recreate the tune that had turned Rafi and Asmodeus into spiritual Siamese twins, but I never even got close. And without that starting point to work from, I didn't have a bastard clue how to separate them out again. There's no sieve in the world with a mesh fine enough for souls.

And now I'd run out of time. Asmodeus was walking the streets, leaving a trail of dead bodies in his wake. Something had to be done, and now that I'd sobered up long enough to string two thoughts together, I knew that it was me who had to do it. It was either that or stay smashed out of my skull for the rest of my life.

Thus conscience does make cowards of us all. It's a bitch.

After finishing her second brandy, Pen tried to re-establish an air of normality by mucking out the rats' cage. I left her to it and went back up to my room to make another pass at the mess: a parallel process really, except that my room smelled a lot worse than rat shit.

I worked with more of a will this time, and made some inroads into the chaos. Just having something to do was therapeutic, although I still felt fragile from the heroic abuses of the past few days and I had to take things slow.

Every so often random flashes of memory would play across my inner eye. I let them come and go again without trying to force them, intriguing though some of them were. As with birds, chasing after them would be the surest way to make them scatter.

I remembered sitting on cooling asphalt and trying to find a new note on my whistle, convinced that I was hearing the note in the air all around me. I could almost hear it again now, but it remained tantalisingly just out of reach, like a dream that's already started to evaporate as you wake up piecemeal from a troubled sleep.

The withdrawal pangs hit me again, harder than ever, prickling my skin and covering me in an instant with cold sweat. I hardly even noticed. That note, that elusive ostinato, remained wedged in the doorway of my mind like an overlarge piece of furniture that couldn't be pulled or pushed. It wouldn't come into clear focus and it wouldn't leave me alone.

I took out my whistle, put it to my mouth and blew a few random chords. A, C and then G took me by a sort of natural progression into 'Henry Martin', a wholesome little tune about murder, exploitation and the irreversible loss of innocence.

There were three brothers in merry Scotland,
In merry Scotland there were three,
And they did cast lots as to which one should go
To turn robber all on the salt sea.

When Henry Martin was swinging from the gallows tree, I moved on to another equally pleasant ditty, and then another after that. The evening wore on into night as I played, and an unsettling feeling crept over me by degrees: a solid conviction based on the most fleeting and ephemeral of impressions.

Imagine you woke up to find yourself a prisoner in an unfamiliar room, in total darkness, with your hands and feet tied. Unable to move, unable to see, you'd have no way of finding out what kind of place you were in. But when you shouted for help, the echoes of your own voice would come back to you, and give you some sense of the size of the room: the extent and maybe even the shape of the volume of air that surrounded you.

That was kind of what I felt right then: playing the whistle woke up my death-sense, and my death-sense told me that the world had changed. The echoes of the simple, dolorous tune described a space that was subtly, infinitesimally altered from what I knew, what I'd expected. I wondered what in Hell that might mean.

Disconcerted, I lowered the whistle. I was about to try another tune when I saw Pen standing in the doorway, staring in at me. There was a tension in her pose and in her expression. 'You're upsetting the birds,' she said.

I put the whistle down on the table beside my bed. 'Everyone's a critic,' I deadpanned.

She stared at the whistle for a moment, then shook her head, visibly giving it up. She turned away, towards the stairs, but an afterthought struck her and she stopped on the top step, looking back at me over her shoulder. 'You had some calls,' she said.

'When I was . . . out?'

'Exactly.'

'Anything I should know about?'

'Some woman named Pax. She called lots of times. She said she had some news for you.'

Trudie could keep on stewing. There was nothing she could tell me that I wanted to hear. Her heart belonged to Mother Church, and I wasn't interested in the rest of her, shapely though it undoubtedly was.

'What else?'

'Someone from the Brent Library Service. A woman . . .'

'Susan Book.'

'Sounds about right.'

That was more interesting. Susan is married to Juliet, and Juliet is always interesting, just by virtue of being Juliet.

'And Gary Coldwood,' Pen finished up. 'He rang just now, but he couldn't stay on.'

'How come?'

'He said he was on his way to a murder scene. And he wanted you to read it for him.'

3

Which brings me back around to where I was, more or less: standing in Ginny Parris's drying blood and swallowing the bitter pill of her true identity with a growing sense of dread.

'Rafi's girlfriend.' I repeated the words.

'Yeah,' Coldwood confirmed with a laconic nod. 'I note the pained emphasis, Castor. I know Pen Bruckner is the only woman who deserves that label in your book, but this is all ancient history now. Ginny Parris was named on the incident sheet when Ditko was first brought into the Stanger for psych evaluation. Her statement was still there in the paperwork, and that's how she described herself. Relationship to patient: girlfriend.'

He stared at me for a moment, as if he was expecting me to argue the point. It was the last thing on my mind.

'So,' I said, my casual tone sounding hollow even to me, 'did your forensics boys come up with anything?'

Gary shrugged with his eyebrows. 'They took prints,' he said.

'From where?'

'The door. The broken table. The light. Even a good virtual from the dead woman's throat. Whoever it was didn't go out of his way to be discreet.'

'Whoever it was?' I must have sounded like I was clutching at straws.

Coldwood's eyebrows rose and fell in a virtual shrug. 'We haven't had a chance to match them yet,' he said. 'That's what we're doing now. Ditko's prints are on file. If it was him, we should get a positive in the next couple of minutes.'

He looked past me towards the door. 'So he comes in through the door,' he said didactically. 'We'll assume it's a he. He doesn't force it. Doesn't have to. Left hand on the knob, which is consistent with using a key. Smeared print on the lintel above the door, which we're taking to mean . . .'

'That's where she kept the spare,' I said.

Coldwood smiled dryly. 'You've got a larcenous mind, Fix.'

'I keep the wrong company. Coppers, mainly.'

Gary let the insult slide, turning his head as his gaze travelled from the door to the broken table and then on to the bed. 'She hasn't heard him yet. Most likely she's asleep. He walks towards her. Maybe he smashes the table then, to wake her up, to get her attention. Maybe he just says her name. But she hears something anyway, and she reaches out for the light.' He glanced down at the bedside lamp lying on its side on the floor: its feeble little pool of radiance reminded me of a votive candle in a funeral chapel. 'She turns the lamp on, but her hand slips – probably she's panicking a little. The lamp falls but doesn't break. She can see him now. Her gentleman caller – again, just for the sake of argument. He doesn't touch the lamp himself. No prints of his anywhere around there. So evidently he doesn't mind being seen.'

Coldwood turned again, to look at the window. My gaze

followed his, and a little bile rose in my throat as I stared at Ginny's broken body.

'The fingerprints on the throat were a telling little detail,' Coldwood ruminated. 'I mean, given that the cause of death wasn't strangulation. It ties in with what you said about him being in here with her for a long time. He held her by the throat, but he wasn't trying to kill her. Not straight away.'

'You don't know that.'

Gary was measuring angles with his eye, his head turning to the bed, to the window, back to the bed. 'Yes, we do,' he said absently. 'Well, if it's Ditko we do. Because he could have snapped her neck one-handed in half a second. He might have been giving her a shiatsu massage, or intimidating her, or feeling for a pulse, or doing pretty much anything else, but the one thing he wasn't doing right then was killing her. So . . .'

He paced out the distance from the corpse to the bed, walking around the tangle of bedclothes.

'So there was something else,' I finished. 'Something he did first. Or tried to do.'

'Makes sense, doesn't it?' Gary knelt at the head of the bed, staring at the headboard. I'd only just noticed that there was blood on it, and on the pillows beneath it. 'What do you make of this?' he asked, pointing.

I thought of the emotions – recent, strong – that hung in the air of the room like a visible fog. Fear had been the most vivid of all, but hope had been in the mix too. Ginny Parris knew what Rafi was now: who he bunked with. But at least once after she woke up and realised she wasn't alone in the room, she had thought she might make it out of this alive. What did that mean? That she saw Rafi, as well as Asmodeus? Spoke to him?

I tried to piece it together in my mind.

'He was holding her still,' I said tentatively. 'Maybe while he talked to her.'

'About what?'

'No idea. Maybe I'm barking up the wrong tree. But whatever they were doing, he started to get angry. The blood on the headboard means she was injured here, right?'

'Lesion to the back of the head. Lots of superimposed lacerations.' Gary smacked the back of one hand into the palm of the other. 'Bang, bang, bang. Then he lets go of her, and she runs. But for the window. Why not the door?'

I ignored the question because I was still thinking about the previous one. If it *was* Rafi – Asmodeus – then what would he want to talk to Ginny about? Would she still have connections among Fanke's all-American satanists? Fanke himself was dead, but did she still subscribe to the newsletter? Attend the AGM? Was he shaking her down for a phone number or an address? That didn't feel right, somehow. Surely Asmodeus would have better ways of making contact with the necromantic fraternity than dropping in on Rafi's ex? And if he wanted to send a message, he'd probably have had enough self-control not to shoot the messenger.

'She runs,' I agreed. 'And he kills her. Without a second thought. So either he's already got what he came for by this time, or else he knows it's not here. Or maybe he's lost interest. Anyway, for whatever reason, it's game over now. He . . .' I didn't finish the sentence. I just nodded toward the broken table.

'We're three storeys up,' Gary persisted. 'I don't know why she didn't head for the door.'

'He was between her and the door,' I pointed out, but that was only half the answer. She knew she couldn't fall forty feet to the ground and walk away. She didn't care. She had to get out of this room, and away from the thing that had come for her. Even death must have seemed better than the alternative right then. No, cancel that: death was on the cards either way. She just wanted to meet it on her own terms, without any help from the thing that was wearing her former lover like a glove puppet.

The opening bars of Beethoven's 'Für Elise' sounded in the room. Gary fished about in his pocket and came up with his mobile.

'Hello?' he said into the phone, and then, 'Right. Thanks. Keep me posted.' The voice at the other end of the line gabbled, sounding – as voices at the other end of the line always do – like a sound effect from a 1940s *Looney Tunes* cartoon. Gary frowned. 'What? What's that supposed to mean? Well put him on then. No. No, I'm still at the effing crime scene. I'll come in when I'm done here, not before.'

He lowered the phone and put it back where it came from. 'That was the lab,' he said. 'It's Ditko all right.'

'Asmodeus,' I corrected automatically. I was already so sure it was him that I felt no surprise, just a faint sense of increased pressure weighing down on me, as though my invisible bathysphere had descended another hundred feet or so into the shit soup that now surrounded us.

'Listen, I've got to get back to Uxbridge Road nick,' Gary said. 'Some tosspot from SOCA has popped up and started throwing his weight around. Says he wants to review the case. I've got to slap the cheeky sod down before he gets his feet under the table.'

He headed for the door, and I followed him.

'You want a lift?' he asked.

I thought about that. It was a long way home, and the last Tube train had gone more than an hour ago. It would have been easy to say yes. But I had a lot to think about, and I wanted to shake off the atmosphere of that room by walking in the clean air.

'No thanks,' I said. 'I'm good. Gary, keep me in the loop, yeah? I know Asmodeus better than anyone. If you get a lead on where he is, count me in.'

'Makes sense to me,' Gary answered as we went down the stairs. 'No offence, Castor, but I'd rather have you face this bastard than any of my lads – or me, for that matter. At least you know what you're letting yourself in for. If we get anything, I'll call you. But keep your bloody phone turned on for once, all right?'

We parted company at the door and I walked away through the thinning crowd of onlookers. Nothing to see now: just the dead woman's arm up at the window, raised as if she was waving to us. Gary's hard-working boys and girls were packing up their circus and the novelty had all worn off. Tomorrow was another working day.

As I walked back up Brixton Hill, I tried my best to think about the circumstances of Ginny's death without letting the image of her body, sprawled on the floor like a broken toy, intrude into my mind. I didn't manage it.

What had Asmodeus come back for? Why had he taken the trouble to find her, and then to talk to her before he murdered her? Had he come there with bloody execution already on his mind, or had his gleefully sadistic nature, which I knew only too well, simply got the better of him?

The night was hot and sticky, with the smell of tarmac-adam rolling in from somewhere on a lethargic wind. It drowned out the more enticing smells of cooking from closer at hand: someone was having a very late supper of jerk chicken, and it wasn't going to be me.

Perhaps because I'd been playing my whistle such a short time ago, my death-sense was fully awake. I saw a ghost sitting in the middle of the road, its knees drawn up to its chest and its head bowed. Hard to tell if it had been a man or a woman; after a while, unless you had an unshake-able self-image when you were alive, the fact of being dead tends to erode you at the edges. Little by little, you start to dissolve – unless someone like me gets to you first and wipes the slate clean all at once.

There was a much more recent ghost standing in the mouth of an alley just before the junction with Porden Road: a young man in a faded blue shell suit, conducting one half of the conversation he'd probably been having just before he died. The sound reached me as a thin mosquito whine. In his chest there was a deeply shadowed hole about the size of a grapefruit.

In a doorway a little further on, an old woman sat clutching a Tesco carrier bag like a baby in her arms. I could tell without looking that she was dead: not a ghost this time, but risen in the body, a zombie. The smell of putrefaction hung around her, as solid as a curtain.

There was nothing unusual about these sights. London, like the rest of the world, had been playing host to the walking, waking dead for about a decade now; and London, like the rest of the world, had adapted pretty well, all things considered. If a ghost minded its own business, you ignored it; if it became a nuisance, you hired an exorcist to drive it away. You steered clear of zombies unless they were family or close friends, and you put wards on the doors of your house because you knew there were other things abroad in the night that had never been alive in the conventional sense, and an ounce of prevention is worth a metric ton of cure.

So, yeah, this was the new status quo. And for me it's a living, so it would be a bit hypocritical if I complained about it. But I couldn't shake the suspicion — the fear — that the status quo was changing. Maybe it was just that drunk-dream about the new note I couldn't make my whistle play, or maybe it was the stuff I'd learned on the Salisbury estate about how human souls — given the right conditions — can metastatise into demons, in much the same way that axolotls can become salamanders. What with one thing and another, the ground didn't feel too solid under my feet right then.

And being preoccupied with weighty metaphysical questions, I let my guard down like a total fuckwit.

I was walking past the high wall of someone's backyard, which was topped with an ornamental layer of broken glass to deter casual visitors. That gave me the only warning I got. Something moved — the merest flick of dark-on-dark at the very limit of my vision — and there was a faint, brittle sound from above my head as one of the shards of glass was broken off clean. Then a great weight hit me squarely between the shoulder blades and I pitched forward, the pavement coming up to meet me.

I managed to turn a little as I fell, meeting the cracked grey paving slabs with my shoulder rather than my face. That was the most I could manage though. I still got the wind knocked clean out of me, and a second later a boot hammered into my midriff to seal the deal. I lay there on the ground, curled around my pain, trying to pull my scattered wits together enough to move.

There was the sound of a footstep right beside my head. 'You see? You see that?' a harsh voice grated. Actually it didn't sound like a voice at all; it sounded like someone trying to scrape up a tune by sliding one saw blade across another. 'Even in this fucking weather, he wears the coat. I think the concept of mercy killing applies here.'

Booted feet walked into my line of sight. One of them drew back for another kick, which gave me time to throw my arms up and catch it as it came forward again. I twisted and pulled, hoping to throw my attacker off balance, but he tore loose from my grip before that could happen. I completed the roll anyway, came up facing him on one knee with my hands raised *en garde*.

Asmodeus threw back his head and laughed, which isn't a sound you want to hear with a full stomach. He stared at me with contemptuous amusement. But when he spoke again, the words were so much at odds with the expression on his face that I felt an eerie sense of unreality.

'Run, Fix,' he said. 'For Christ's sake, run. Don't try to fight him!'

This time it wasn't Asmodeus's voice; it was Rafi's. It came as something of a jolt because Rafi had almost never managed to surface by himself, without the help my whistle could provide. Asmodeus was the dominant partner in their forced marriage, with all the rights and privileges that entailed.

He was dressed very differently than when I'd seen him last. He'd have to be, of course: you can't walk around Brixton dressed in Marks and Spencer pyjamas and hope to avoid public notice. From somewhere he'd dredged up an all-black ensemble – boots, trousers and an overlarge shirt open to the waist over a string vest of the kind our American cousins call a wife-beater. Or maybe these things had been some other colour to start with, and had turned black after the demon put them on.

He walked around me, taking his time. The face was still Asmodeus: the black-on-black eyes, like holes in the world, would have told me that even without the mocking, bestial expression. If he was surprised that Rafi had taken momentary control of the communal vocal cords, he didn't show it.

'Think he'll make a fight of it?' he growled. 'Or will he turn and run? I don't mind either way; I'm just asking. As his friend, which way do you think he'll jump?'

Asmodeus was talking to Rafi, over my head. If I hadn't been preoccupied with the matter of my imminent death, I might have been offended. My hand went to my tin whistle by automatic reflex, but there was no help there. I'd never managed to work out a full exorcism for Asmodeus, though I'd tried a hundred times. Oh, I could have come up with a tune that would have have changed the balance of power between Asmodeus and Rafael Ditko, but there was no way I'd get beyond the first few bars before the demon made me eat my whistle.

He smiled, interpreting the gesture correctly and

obviously being of much the same opinion as me with regard to my chances.

'He's funny, isn't he?' he grated, continuing his conversation with his internal audience. 'He makes me laugh. He's got that Dunkirk spirit. Eat as much shit as God wants to cram into your throat, but never say die.'

He took a step towards me. I threw a punch, but it didn't connect. Asmodeus moved, faster than a snake, and batted my hand aside. 'Count backwards,' he said, 'down to zero.' Then his arm came back, and he smacked me open-handed across the face.

The force of the blow spun me round as a DJ spins a record. I hit the pavement again, tasting blood in my mouth, my head ringing. I looked up blearily as Asmodeus, in no particular hurry, walked across to join me. Behind him, headlights stabbed out of the darkness, turning the demon momentarily into a silver-edged silhouette.

I had to force myself to move. Knowing that it was either move or die helped, but the ringing in my ears distracted me and my fingers didn't want to do what they were told. I reached for my whistle again and drew it out as the bright red double-decker bus loomed up behind the demon's shoulder.

Asmodeus stared down at me, shaking his head in pitying wonder. 'It's like people say,' he snickered. 'If all you've got is a hammer, everything looks like a nail. And if all you've got is a whistle, the whole of life is one big fucking show tune.'

He leaned down, his hands reaching for my throat. 'Opera,' I corrected. '*Götterdämmerung*, you smug bastard.' I plunged the whistle a couple of inches deep into his left eye, and as he bellowed in pain and rage I slammed my foot into his stomach with all the force I could muster.

The timing was almost perfect. Asmodeus took two steps back, but regained his balance almost immediately and didn't actually fall. That didn't matter though, because the two steps had taken him off the edge of the pavement. He went under the nearside wheel of the bus and vanished from my sight.

The bus went into a skidding stop, slewing round in the road. A body like a shapeless sack was dragged along with it, trapped in the wheel arch in some way and dispersing itself in red-black smears of pulped flesh across the rough dry asphalt.

I was up and running by this time. One glance back over my shoulder showed me that Asmodeus was moving again already, his arms weakly twitching as he tried to lever his ruined body up off the road surface. I knew from past experience that no amount of purely physical damage would keep a demon down for long. Flesh is like an item of clothing to the Hell-kin, and they're used to making running repairs. It would take Asmodeus a few minutes to replace his lost body mass though, and I could use that time to get clear.

I was sorry that Rafi had had to suffer along with Asmodeus, sorrier still for the poor sod of a bus driver, whose trauma at running down a pedestrian was now about to be compounded by seeing the man in question get back on his feet looking like a couple of hundred pounds of rough-chopped chuck steak. But needs must when the devil drives, and the pushy bastard has been my chauffeur for as long as I can remember.

I ran with my head down and my arms pumping, putting the adrenalin that had flooded my system during the fight to good use. God help me when I crashed, but at least now I had a fifty-fifty chance of living long enough to do it.

I risked a single glance behind me. Asmodeus was already up and running. His gait was drunken and asymmetrical, but he had more than human stamina and he seemed to be at least matching me for speed. Further back, a thin scattering of shrieks rose raggedly into the air as the passengers on the bus saw what had risen from under its wheels. They had nothing to complain about: the demon was heading away from them.

At Baytree Road, where the one-way system kicks in, God decided to smile on me – although with most of the street lights down it was a miracle he could find me in the first place. A black cab with its flag up was coming slowly into the bend. The cabbie must have been lost: you don't go wandering around Brixton Hill at two in the morning just to take the air, and it's not a salubrious place to fish for fares. Not unless you're prepared to do a Teddy Roosevelt and kerb-crawl lightly while carrying an apocalyptically big stick.

I leapt into his path, throwing my arms into the air like some idiot at a Neil Diamond concert. He slammed on the brakes, started to curse me out and then thought better of it as I brandished a twenty-quid note under his nose and shouted, 'North of the river. Anywhere.' He waved me in with a long-suffering shake of the head, and we picked up speed as we headed west.

In the cab's rear window, Asmodeus receded into the distance. I was safe. Even so, it took the better part of ten minutes before I stopped trembling. I've looked death in the face before but it's a little different when he's wearing your best friend's face. It gets you on a whole other level. I had to fight to get my breathing back under control, and to stop the window-shutter slamming of my ribs against my heart. I was like a marathon runner hitting his twentieth mile, and the stink of the cab's upholstery, unleashed by the long hot evening and compounded of equal parts sweat, cigarette smoke and crappy perfume, didn't help one bit.

But tonight's events, whichever angle you looked at them from, stank worse than anything the cab had to offer.

After we crossed Father Thames at Vauxhall I got the cabbie to fork right onto Millbank, where New Labour used to keep shop in the good old days before they availed themselves – with no sense of irony – of the cheaper work-force available in North Shields. There were lights on in the decaying tower block, shining pale and a little baleful across the restless night: the ghosts of Tony Blair and Gordon Brown, maybe, pursuing their old disagreements like the boarhound and the boar through the rifts of some low-rent eternity.

The cab dropped me off at the western end of the Strand, near Cockspur Street. There was eighteen quid on the clock and the cabbie took the twenty with bad grace, no doubt believing that a pick-up in Brixton at that hour of the morning deserved something special in the way of a tip. I was inclined to agree, but that was all I had on me so the argument was purely academic. He muttered something under his breath as he drove away: probably, in the circumstances, something more or less accurate.

The walk from the centre of town back up to Turnpike Lane took me over an hour. I felt like I needed the time to think, even if my thoughts kept circling around the same drain. Asmodeus had killed Ginny, and then he'd hung around the scene long enough to pick up my scent and take a crack at me. What the Hell was he up to? We'd had a sort of love-hate thing going for most of the time Rafi was at the Stanger. Asmodeus knew who he had to thank for his human ball and chain, and would have liked nothing better than to rip my head off and spit down my throat. But he knew that killing me would close a possible escape route, so for the most part he contented himself with more subtle forms of revenge. The only time he'd ever seriously tried to kill me was when he was sure Fanke's satanists were going to cut him loose again with a ritual involving human sacrifice.

Was that the link? Ginny. Fanke. The Satanist Church. Was Asmodeus demob-happy again, looking for an early remission on his life sentence? Or had he just given up hoping that I'd find a musical sieve that would strain out the demon from the man? Either way, it was bad news for me.

In Somers Town I passed a small group of zombies sitting huddled around a fire they'd made in the eternally closed doorway of an abandoned parking garage. It was a pathetic sight, because there was no way the fire could warm them: the nerves in the dermal layers of the skin are the first to go. And the night was still clinging onto the day's heat like a lover keen for one last sweaty embrace, so surely this was the only campfire burning in London tonight. Comfort food for the dead.

Zombies get a lousy press in movies, horror novels and comic books, but I've always found them pretty easy to get on with. Ghosts, now they can be bad news. A poltergeist is a ghost that's made of nothing but pent and pissed-off feelings, and they can do real harm unless you bring in someone like me to cut the feelings off at the source. But the poor bastards who come back in the flesh have put all their fortunes in a sinking ship, and with a few notable exceptions they're as docile as lambs. Who wants trouble when your body's falling apart anyway and can't repair itself from damage? It's better to sit tight: to think good and hard about that last shallow ledge you're about to fall off, and what you're going to do when it gets too narrow to hold on to.

These guys didn't look like they were going to be any trouble. There were around a dozen or so, and I'm using 'guys' in the inclusive sense: it was a mixed gathering. In the hot, humid air they smelled like a fridge on the third day after a power cut, but that was the only offence they were capable of giving.

'Spare a quid, guvnor?' one of the women said, holding up her hand as I passed.

If I'd had one I would have flicked it over my shoulder and kept on going. But the cab had taken the last of my liquid funds, so I was denied that easy out.

'Sorry, love,' I said, slowing involuntarily. 'I'm boracic.'

She stared at me with one eye, the other socket being full of some milky-white goo that I was trying not to examine too closely. 'All right, sweetheart,' she said, resignedly. 'Have a good night.' She looked down and away suddenly, as though staring at my face hurt too much.

One of the other walking dead took up the slack, favouring me with a truly hideous grin. 'What about plastic, mate? We take everything except American Express.' A hollow snicker went through the ranks of the undead, like a breeze through dry grass.

I turned out my pockets theatrically. 'Only thing between me and you lot is a pulse,' I said. 'But I come through this way a lot. When I'm in funds, I'll stop by again.'

'Course you will,' one of the zombies agreed sardonically.

I'd stopped walking now, which in purely social terms was a mistake: once you've stopped, how do you start again without looking like a selfish, blood-warm bastard who thinks of the dead in the way racists think of people with a different skin colour, as belonging to an alien species?

'What do you spend the money on?' I asked, by way of small talk. The walking dead can't eat or drink: they don't have any stomach enzymes to break food down, or any blood to carry the disassembled feast through the light-less chambers of their bodies.

'Wards.' It was the woman who'd asked me for money in the first place. She spoke bluntly, tersely, her face – still averted from mine – expressionless. 'Wards and stay-nots.'

I laughed politely. 'Right,' I said. 'Scared of ghosts, are we?'

Now she looked up at me again, and the others did too. 'Not ghosts, mate,' one of the men said.

'*Loup-garous*?' That did make a kind of sense, although it would be a pretty desperate werewolf that fed on this meat.

I was still the focus for all eyes. The woman put her hands out towards the fire, the gesture forlorn and futile, like a bereaved mother singing a lullaby to her dead child's doll. The fire was only a memory of something she'd had once and would never have again.

'There's other things besides the hairy men,' she muttered. 'More all the time, from what I can see. They come in the night, wriggling all around you. Shining, some of them. Don't know what they are, or where they came from, but I don't want them crawling over me in the dark, that's for bloody sure.'

There were murmurs of agreement from all sides. I flashed on a memory: the tapeworm-like ribbons of nothingness that had drifted around me as I sat on the pavement, drunk out of my mind, and tried to play the new note I was hearing in the night.

'World's changing,' said another of the zombies, his voice a horrendously prolonged death rattle. 'It don't want us no more.'

'Never fucking did, mate,' said another man gloomily. 'Cold leftovers is what we are. Shoved to the side of the plate.'

'Something always turns up though, doesn't it?' I pointed out with impeccable banality. I fished in another of my coat's many and capacious pockets and came up with something that might cheer them up – a half-bottle of blended Scotch. I handed it to the woman, who looked at it with solemn approval. Although I said that the dead couldn't eat or drink, some of them do anyway, even though they know it will sit in their stomach and rot, giving the vectors of decay something extra to work on. Others, like my friend Nicky, drink the wine-breath and take some attenuated comfort from that.

'Thanks, mister,' the dead woman said. 'You're a diamond.'

'Take care of yourself,' I said, probably at least a month or so too late, and went on my less-than-merry way.

Pen was not only still up, she was actually outside the house, prowling around the floral border underneath the ground-floor windows in a state of simmering rage.

'Look at this,' she said as I came up, as though we were already in the middle of a conversation. 'I only planted these tulips yesterday, and something's trampled right through them. You can't keep anything. Not a thing.'

The sheer ordinariness of the topic was welcome right then. 'You could put a circle of salt down,' I said. 'That's what my dad used to do, to stop cats shitting in our coal bunker.'

Pen breathed out hard and audibly. She hates the way I elide the fragile boundary between folk magic and bullshit.

'Seriously?' I said. 'You're standing in the garden in the middle of the night because something broke your tulips?'

Pen looked at me and shook her head. 'No,' she admitted. 'I'm laying down some more wards.' She showed me the lump of white chalk in her hand.

'The ones on the doors and windows aren't enough?'

'They always have been. Now . . . I don't know. It's weird, Fix. This is a warm night, isn't it?'

'Very.'

'But I can't stop shivering. Everything feels wrong, somehow. It has done ever since . . .' She didn't have to finish the sentence. By tacit assumption, all unfinished sentences could be taken to refer back to the night of

Asmodeus' escape. She might have had some more to say about how she felt, but it was then that I stepped into the light from the open doorway. Pen gave an audible gasp as she stared at my damaged face.

'Oh my God,' she said, dismayed and solicitous. 'What happened? Don't just stand there, you twerp. Come on inside and let me put something on those cuts.' She shoved me toward the house, leaving chalk marks on the sleeve of my coat.

'I was in a fight,' I said, putting up only a token resistance.

'With what? A combine harvester?'

I hesitated. Sooner or later, I'd have to tell Pen what had happened tonight but, given the mood she was in, if I did it right then and there I'd be guaranteeing her a sleepless night.

'It was just an argument that got out of hand,' I said.

'At Coldwood's crime scene?' Pen didn't sound convinced.

'Well, some of these grass-green constables still need the rough edges knocking off of them . . .'

She let the lie stand, but since she knew that was what it was, she reneged on her promise of a hot poultice. She handed me a yellow Post-it note instead. *Sue Book,* it read. *10.30. Get back to her tonight if you can.*

But I couldn't. Not now. Sue might be shacking up with a sex-demon, but she was a humble librarian and she worked nine to five like most ordinary, decent people. If I called her up at three in the morning and interrupted her beauty sleep, I might get a tongue-lashing from Juliet. And pleasant though that sounds, Juliet's tongue can strip rivets off steel.

'She sounded like she'd been crying,' Pen said, as Arthur the raven came swooping down from the banister to take up his station on her left shoulder.

Sue? Crying? That was unnerving.

'Anyone else?' I asked.

Pen shook her head.

'Then I guess I'll turn in,' I said. 'Unless you want to draw some more stay-nots. I'm good for that if you've got another piece of chalk.'

Pen snorted. 'As if I'd trust a ward you'd written,' Pen said. 'I know mine work: all I know about yours is that they'd be spelled wrong. Goodnight, Fix.'

It wasn't, particularly. I couldn't get to sleep for a long while. The night was a furnace and the booze-craving was still churning sourly in my stomach and sending static through my nerves.

When I did sleep, it was a shallow doze punctuated with disconnected, rambling dreams. A dog scratched at a dry crumbling fence; a butcher sharpened an overlarge knife on a leather strap, accidentally slashing his own arms every so often with the tip of the unwieldy blade; an old gramophone played all by itself in a dark empty room, the horn echoing with nothing but scraping static because the song had finished.

Some time before dawn I opened my eyes, still half-adrift on the tides of sleep. What was the sound now? I wondered dully. But this was the waking world, and the intermittent scratching that had accompanied me along all the avenues of my dreams was now sounding from directly over my head.

Something was up on the roof.

My room is under the eaves, with nothing but a skin of plasterboard and another of slate between me and the outside world. Whatever it was that was moving up there, it was close enough to register on my death-sense as a synesthetic thicket of jangling, discordant notes. This wasn't a cat out for a night on the tiles. It was one of the dead, or the undead, or the never-born.

I responded instinctively, whistling a few of those spiky notes between my teeth. I know damn well that the tin whistle I carry is just an amplifier for something inside me: I can work unplugged when I need to, and that was what I did now.

The scratching stopped. There was a single muffled thump and then a skitter of movement. I jumped out of bed, tracking it, moving with it across the room, around the chair where I'd dumped my clothes to the open window.

The dead thing got there before me. It dropped down from the roof onto the broad window ledge, man-sized and man-shaped, outlined in silhouette for the briefest of seconds before it bunched the muscles in its legs and kicked off backwards, somersaulting out of my field of vision.

In that second I'd been staring into Rafi's face – twisted into something like agony, his mouth straining open as though he was emptying a continuous scream into some fold of the night I didn't have access to.

4

'Why didn't you tell me?' Pen shouted, for about the fourth or fifth time.

'I was going to,' I protested. 'Seriously, Pen, I was going to. But . . . you were tired, and you were upset, and I just thought—'

'Don't spare my feelings, Fix!' She stood before me, rigid with fury, her fists clenching as though she wanted to hit me. 'Don't ever hide things from me and think you're sparing my feelings, because you don't know what they bloody well are!'

It was four in the morning by the kitchen clock, and only ten or fifteen minutes after my brief encounter with Asmodeus, so we couldn't expect the sun to come up for a couple of hours yet. The night seemed unfairly, impossibly prolonged. Its twisted events were taking on some of the flavour of those heart-hammering nightmares that start to lose coherence even as you're waking up from them, but that still manage to leave their mouldering fingerprints all across your day.

'Fair enough,' I said, rubbing my eyes with the heel of my hand. They felt like they'd been boiled and peeled in their sockets. I leaned against the wall for some much-needed support, but I didn't feel as though I could sit down right then, with every nerve in my body still trying to opt for either fight or flight and arguing the toss with its neighbours. 'You're right. I know you're right. I'm sorry.'

The soft answer is meant to get you out of corners like this, and it generally works pretty well for me because I use it sparingly. Now, though, Pen seemed to take my throwing in the towel as an insult on a par with the original offence. She needed to fight someone, and I wasn't helping. 'You . . . ratbag!' she exploded, and punched me hard on the shoulder. My shoulder had seen a fair amount of rough handling when I danced with the devil down in Brixton, and Pen packs more beef than you'd think, given her petite frame, but I gritted my teeth and took it like a man.

She stomped away to the sink and threw stuff around for a while. I thought she might have been making coffee, or maybe running up a tasty and nourishing meal out of Ryvita crumbs and bloody-mindedness, but there were no visible results: just pots and pans and dishes and items of cutlery being moved from A to B, and in some cases from B back to A again.

After a few minutes they weren't moving so fast or so frequently, then they stopped altogether, but Pen still kept her back to me and didn't speak for a while.

'How did he look?' she asked at last, her voice barely audible.

'He was . . . mostly Asmodeus,' I answered, choosing my words very carefully. 'I mean, Rafi was in there, but Asmodeus was driving. And, you know . . . the first time he was attacking me. The second time I only saw him for a moment. We didn't get the chance to talk much.'

It's hard to fob someone off when they know you as

well as Pen knows me. She turned to stare at me grimly, hands clasping the sink's stainless steel rim, like a boxer in his corner waiting for the bell to ring for the next round.

'He looked unhappy,' I temporised.

'Go on.'

'He looked as though he was awake and aware but completely under Asmodeus' thumb.'

Pen flinched visibly. It was a worst-case scenario: for Rafi, it meant not just seeing but experiencing everything that the demon did. But there was worse, and I had to say it now, because if I let it roll until the morning she'd be even less likely to accept it.

'Pen,' I said, 'you've got to get out of here.'

Her eyes widened and she gasped out loud. 'What?'

'Just for a while.' I raised my hand placatingly, thought about putting it on her shoulder and then thought again. 'Just for a few days, until this is all over. Until we've managed to get him back.' Those last three words sounded exactly like the shameless fudge they were, eliding the whole process of subduing the demon, capturing him without harming Rafi, and getting him back into some place where he could actually be contained. I had no ideas, currently, as to how any of that was going to be done, but it didn't change the situation, and I ploughed on doggedly, trying to make her understand.

'He's trying to kill us,' I said. 'I don't know why, when he's walked the thin red line for so long, but he's out for blood, and we're all in danger until he's locked up again.'

'You don't know that,' Pen snapped back angrily. 'He came after you. Twice. That doesn't mean he wants to hurt me.'

I took a deep breath, wincing because my ribs were bruised too and it bloody well hurt. 'The woman he killed in south London,' I said. 'Her name was Ginny Parris. She was involved with Rafi around about the time he was getting into all the black magic stuff. She helped him with it, because she was part of that scene. But they were lovers too, Pen. And for one of those reasons or the other, or maybe both, he went to her flat tonight, had a little chat about old times, and then murdered her with the leg of a table.'

Pen looked me squarely in the eyes, unimpressed. 'Then the connection's obvious, isn't it?' she said. 'This woman helped Rafi to perform his summoning. You tried to exorcise Asmodeus afterwards. It's the people who were there on that night – that's who he's going after.'

'No,' I said flatly, 'it's not.' This was the hardest part to explain, but I tried anyway. 'Asmodeus was talking all the while we were fighting. Taunting. Making jokes.'

'He does that, Fix.'

'I know. But he said one thing that stuck in my mind because I didn't get it at first. He said, "Count backwards, down to zero." It felt weird. Sort of abstract, when you put it next to the "I'm going to feed you your own intestines" stuff. I thought . . . maybe he was thinking of a surgical operation, where the anaesthetist tells you to count down from ten, and you fall asleep when you get to seven. That kind of black humour would be in Asmodeus' style.'

Pen carried on staring at me, not speaking. She knew there was more.

'But just now, after he came here – after I saw him jumping off your roof – I realised something else. Something

I probably should have clicked on earlier. When we fought, Asmodeus wasn't talking to me. Rafi was – he told me to run. But when Asmodeus referred to me, he used the third person every time. "He's funny. He makes me laugh." He never spoke to me once; he was just talking to Rafi the whole time. So he was telling Rafi to count backwards, not me. To count down to zero. And I'm nearly certain he meant it as a threat, or a promise.'

I did put my hand on her shoulder now, leaning forward until our faces were almost touching. I had to make her understand this. 'He meant, "You're going to lose your friends, one by one. I'm going to take out everyone who ever meant anything to you, until there's no one left." Pen, who's to say he even started with Ginny? He could have been busy on this ever since he broke free from Imelda's. He's had time to work his way through Rafi's entire address book by now. I don't want to think about what we're going to find when we start looking into this properly. And I don't want you to be next.'

Pen swatted my hand away and put the tips of her fingers lightly, momentarily, to my chest: not pushing, but warning me to keep my distance. 'I don't care,' she said. 'I'm staying here.'

'I'm telling you, he didn't just come for me. He was hanging around here before, that's obvious. He was probably the one who trampled your tulips. If he decides to—'

Pen cut across my words. 'I didn't say I didn't believe you, Fix. I just said I'm staying.' Well, I'd known before I weighed in that this was going to be tough. I opened my mouth to hit her with a fresh wave of eloquence, but she hadn't finished. 'If Asmodeus *was* after me, then why

was he up on the roof when I live in the bloody basement?
You know the answer as well as I do. It's because I've put
wards on every window and door and wall of this place.
They're strongest at ground level, because that's where I
cast them, but they work all the way up to the chimney
stacks – otherwise you'd have woken up to find Asmodeus
sitting in your lap. Today I'll do the upstairs rooms and
the eaves. And I'll work outwards from the house through
the drive and the garden, planting stay-nots every four or
five feet. He won't be able to get within a hundred yards
of us.'

'Pen, you can't live like a hermit,' I pointed out. 'You've
got to come out some time.'

'You said it would just take a couple of days. I can stay
at home for a couple of days. I work over the phone mostly
anyway, so it's no hardship.'

'A couple of days was a guess,' I protested. 'It could be
weeks, or months. We just don't know.'

'I'm staying,' Pen repeated. 'Don't try to argue me out
of it, Fix. If Rafi needs me, I want him to know where to
find me. And if Asmodeus comes round, I'm not scared
of him.'

Not scared? I was fucking terrified, and I didn't care
who knew it. I'd seen what the bastard could do.

When the sun came up I climbed up onto the roof using
an extending ladder that I'd half-inched from a building
site down the street. I was pretty sure I could get it back
before anyone clocked on for the day.

Sitting precariously on the ridge, I inspected the damage.
It made interesting reading. The demon had raked the
slates with his fingernails, snapping several and scoring

deep gouges in others, but he hadn't punched at them or tried to tear them free. Pen was certainly right when she said that if it was a matter of strength alone he could have smashed his way in without even working up a sweat. So whatever had kept him at bay, it had nothing to do with the physical properties of slate and wood and lead flashing. Pen's wards had taken the strength out of his hands and the will out of his cold, clammy heart.

That made them something special in the way of stay-nots. In St Albans, when I'd gone after the leader of the Anathemata, Father Thomas Gwillam, with Juliet riding shotgun, I'd seen my favourite succubus walk through a door that had a dozen different wards on it. They hurt her, but they didn't slow her down. I'd seen her walk through Pen's wards too, for that matter, seen it a dozen times, most recently when she'd brought me home after one of my epic drunks. The only thing different this time was that the demon Pen was keeping out was a passenger inside the body of her ex-lover. Food for thought. Maybe not all magical prophylactics were created equal; maybe, as in quantum physics, the observer was part of the system.

After I came down, I made up a list of people I should call: people who'd known Rafi at college and might possibly be on Asmodeus' hit list now, and people he'd introduced me to later when we met up for one of our infrequent reunions. Some I didn't have numbers for, and the numbers I did have, when I finally picked up the phone and tried, weren't always live any more. But I put the word out (lie low, lock your doors and windows and don't talk to strangers), and I asked everyone I could reach to call anyone else they knew who might have counted as a friend or acquaintance of Rafi's either in Oxford or in London.

But Rafi had been born in Pilsen, in the Czech Republic, and for all I knew he had an entire extended family out there. Would Asmodeus go after them? He might be disinclined to try. Demons are chthonic powers, and they don't respond well to air travel: the one time Juliet had tried it, it had knocked her out for days. Asmodeus could take a bus or a train, but it was a long trip and most of the demons I've met have tended to have a hard time with the concept of deferred gratification. Hopefully – assuming I was right in the first place about what he was doing – Asmodeus would start with the targets that were closest to hand.

All the same, I could ask Nicky Heath, my go-to dead guy, to pull up whatever family records he could find and maybe shake loose a few phone numbers for me. I had to try, anyway: the karmic weight I was carrying already from this fucking fiasco was heavy enough to stave half my ribs in, and I seriously didn't want to add to it.

Nicky doesn't like talking specifics over the phone. He has a paranoid streak wider than the Thames at Deptford, and prefers to take commissions on a face-to-face basis. That meant a pilgrimage out to Walthamstow, to the abandoned cinema he'd lovingly restored and re-equipped for an audience of one. It wasn't a place I liked to linger: the decor is great, but being of the zombie persuasion, Nicky finds a temperature of three degrees Celsius a little on the warm side.

I called Gary Coldwood first, and told him about my late-night bare-knuckle fight with Asmodeus. He was solicitous for my health but oddly vague about the progress he'd made on the case.

'I talked to about fifteen or twenty people,' I said. 'To tell them what had happened to Rafi if they didn't already know, and to warn them that they might get a visit. But some of them must have thought I was just a crank. It might sound better coming from a copper – and you could probably get updated numbers for some of these other names. Do you want the list?'

'Where are you now?' Coldwood asked instead of answering me.

'I'm at Pen's, but I won't be staying here for long. Sue Book has been trying to get hold of me for the past few days, so I need to go see her.'

'Sue Book?'

'Juliet's lady love.'

Gary gave an involuntary exhalation, somewhere between a sigh and a grunt. It was the same sound he always makes when he's forcibly reminded of Juliet's sexual orientation. He's not homophobic; it just hurts him, fairly viscerally, that she's not available.

'Well where will you be in a couple of hours?' he asked me.

'Willesden Green, most likely. Sue works in the library over there.'

'Okay. You know the Costella Café on Dudden Hill Lane?'

'I can find it.'

'Call me when you're done. I'll meet you there. If Asmodeus didn't leave enough of your face for me to recognise, wear a red carnation in your buttonhole.'

I made a comment in which both buttonholes and arseholes figured largely, and hung up on the cheeky sod.

As I walked up Pen's crazy-paved garden path, something in the semi-tamed undergrowh next to it caught my eye. Maybe the trampled tulips were still in my mind, or maybe I was catching some death-sense echo from what was hidden there. Either way, before I really thought about what I was doing I knelt down and parted the blades of elephant grass.

There was a flat piece of stone lying on the ground, right beside the path. It was the neutral grey of granite, but it had a slightly polished sheen. On the upper face of it someone had painted, in red, a pentagram.

I picked it up and examined it. The work was very fine: thin lines, perfectly straight and uniformly thick. The whole thing was only about four or five inches across, so the lettering around the outside was very tiny, but still perfectly legible: the names of Samael and Lilith figured there, along with the names of three of their kissing cousins. In the centre was a single word consisting of four Aramaic symbols:

$$\text{ץ ⌐ ⌐ ρ}$$

I ducked out of seeing *The Passion of the Christ* because someone spoiled the ending for me, so my Aramaic is pretty rusty these days. If it had been Greek, I could probably have made shift, but I can't get along with these proto-Hebraic alphabets that have about seven different shapes for each letter depending on where they appear in the sentence: they give me migraines. Some things though, I could tell just from a superficial inspection.

There are two kinds of necromantic contraption exorcists regularly run into. The first is a ward, also called a stay-not or occasionally a foad (short for 'Fuck off and die'). They're basically magical prophylactics, setting up boundaries the dead and undead can't pass. Some of them aren't necromantic at all: they're pure nature magic, using flowering herbs and twigs cut, bound and blessed by priests or adepts – life and faith as a bulwark against death and its dominion. Others are incantations, like the ones that Pen uses to bless the walls of her house. Often though, they're devices just like the one I was holding in my hand right then: collections of visual symbols tied together in intricate patternings that somehow trap a tiny potent piece of reality in their folds. I suppose it's something like the way my music works. In the centre of the circle there's a command aimed directly at the dead soul to show it how unwelcome it is: *Hoc fugere* is the commonest – Latin for 'Get out of town' – closely followed by *Apoloio*, which means 'Don't let the sun go down on you here' in Ancient Greek.

The other kind of magic circle is the exact opposite of a ward: it's a summoning. The design is similar in almost every respect, but the word in the centre of the pentagram will usually be the name of the entity you're trying to call up or get on the right side of.

I didn't know what it was I had here, because I had no idea what that four-letter word meant. I could see at a glance though, that it was a meticulous piece of work: someone had put a lot of time into it, even if they hadn't bothered with the incantations that usually go with the design. You didn't make a ward like this and then throw it over your right shoulder for luck.

Something of Pen's, then, set down here to supplement the organic wards she normally used. It was straying a bit further into Dennis Wheatley territory than she normally liked to go – her magic being of the 'Hello birds, hello sky, hello trees' variety – and for a moment I thought about asking her what it was for. Second thoughts prevailed: given the mood she was in right then, it could wait.

In any case, there's always more than one way to skin a cat, especially in the digital age. I took out my phone and used its crappy little built-in camera to take a picture of the stone, right up close, then put it back where I'd found it.

Willesden is within spitting distance of my walk-up office in Harlesden, but I try not to spend a lot of time over there in case someone tries to employ me. It's been known to happen in the past, and it usually leads to unfortunate consquences.

I'd tried calling Sue Book to tell her I was coming, but I only got her voicemail. And at Willesden Green Library, what I got was short shrift. 'She's not in,' the man at the desk told me. 'She took the day off sick.' He was a slim, vaguely Goth-looking twenty-something with a festive sprinkling of acne across his forehead and a *Love Will Tear Us Apart* T-shirt which I was willing to bet he'd bought on the strength of hearing the track once on YouTube. He looked me up and down with what he probably thought was withering scorn. But I've been withered by the best, and this kid left my foliage intact.

'Is she okay?' I asked him.

'Depends what you mean by okay.'

'Well let's say I mean what everyone else means by okay. Is she sick? Unhappy? Has she been hurt in some way.'

'You should probably ask her.'

I gave it up. The unfriendly vibe was puzzling: the kid was making some assumption about me, but I just didn't have the leisure time to tease it out. I grabbed a 297 bus over to Wembley, where Sue and Juliet live together in the house Sue inherited from her mother and walked the last half-mile through the day's uncompromising heat, feeling slightly out of place and disadvantaged in the sunshine as nocturnal creatures usually do.

There was no answer to my knock. The windows were closed in spite of the heat, and the curtains drawn. It didn't look promising. I knocked again, then took a few steps back from the door, positioning myself so that if anyone looked out from behind the living-room or bedroom curtains they'd see me standing there.

I waited for about two minutes. It occurred to me to pick the lock and go inside – my misspent youth has left me with the best set of cat-burgling tools in the Home Counties and a relaxed attitude to using them – but what would I say if Sue was in there, laid up with flu, and I walked in on her in her smalls? It was the sort of thing that might be hard to explain to Juliet, even on the grounds of neighbourly concern.

But unless my night-adapted eyes deceived me, there was indeed a twitching at the corner of an upstairs curtain. And then, after another short interval, the scratching sound of a door chain being disengaged.

The door opened a crack, and Sue peered out at me, a fuzzy-edged silhouette in the twilight of her hall.

'Felix,' she said, in a slightly bewildered tone.

I walked back to the porch, giving her a reassuring wave. 'You called,' I said.

'Yes.' If anything, the crack got a little narrower. 'But . . . it's all right now. I'm fine. I just wanted to ask you something, but . . . it got sorted.'

To get a less convincing tone of voice, you'd have to go to the court recordings of Adolf Eichmann saying, 'I was only following orders.' Lying didn't come easy to Sue. I suspected that very few things did. Timid, self-effacing, uncomplaining and with lower self-esteem than a readers' wives centrefold, she'd spent most of her life being the sort of willing drudge that props up half the organisations in the UK, quietly holding the fort while their colleagues ascend the ziggurat. But then she'd met Juliet, and her life had veered off in a new and wondrous direction.

'I'm fine,' Sue said again, with even less conviction. 'I shouldn't have bothered you.'

'Well that's what friends are for,' I pointed out. 'Listen, it was a long walk over here, and I'm feeling permanently dehydrated right now because I spent most of the last three weeks pickling my internal organs in Johnnie Walker, so could I come in for a quick drink? Of water, I mean.'

There was an awkward pause. 'Well . . .' Sue faltered. 'I'm not dressed, and . . . I'm off sick, Felix. I . . . I haven't been . . .'

Enough with the bullshit. I put a hand on the door and pushed it gently, not forcing my way in but forcing the point. Sue gave a sound that was almost a whimper and stepped away, averting her face, as the door swung open.

She was dressed in a slightly tatty blue silk dressing

gown with a motif of ukiyo-e storks flying over the perfectly unruffled surface of a lake. She folded her arms across the front of it as if she was afraid it might fall open, even though it was tied with tassels at waist and hem.

With her head turned away from me, the side of her neck was fully exposed. There was a mark like a bruise there, wide and dark: a blue core surrounded by an irregular yellow halo.

'Sue . . .' I said.

Slowly, reluctantly, she raised her head and stared at me with wide, unhappy eyes.

'She didn't mean it,' she said. 'She just . . . I said something stupid and she got angry.'

The bruising continued up the left side of her face, an irregular archipelago of blue-black islets in malarial yellow waters. Her right eye was swollen closed.

'Got angry?' I repeated, incredulously. 'Sue . . . I mean . . . fuck!'

'It was me,' Sue said flatly. 'It was my fault.'

Juliet is a succubus, a demon whose specific modality is sex. That makes her one of the most perfectly adapted predators ever to emerge in any ecosystem. She makes men desire her – using a bag of tools that only starts with her stunning beauty and hypnotic scent – and then, when they're at the highest pitch of sexual frenzy, vibrating like tuning forks, she devours them, body and soul.

I know all this because I was one of her victims. Gabriel McClennan, a fellow exorcist and part-time necromancer in the pay of an eastern European master-pimp named Lucasz Damjohn, had raised the demon Ajulutsikael and set her on my tail, figuring that a lethally close encounter with a demon would look like an occupational hazard for someone in my line of work. But I survived, against the odds. I managed to talk the succubus out of finishing me off (an experience which bore the same relationship to normal coitus interruptus as an exploding supernova does to a Bic lighter), and then she talked herself into sticking around on Earth. She changed her name to Juliet Salazar, met a nice girl, got married and settled down. A happy ending for everyone except me: part of my soul still has a hard-on for her that doesn't look like dying down any time soon.

The phrase 'drop-dead gorgeous' gets bandied around a lot, with 'drop-dead' functioning as an over-intense intensifier. Juliet is drop-dead gorgeous in a very specific and literal sense. The bone-white skin, the black eyes that are almost entirely without whites – these things might seem too odd to be attractive if you met them anywhere else, but as soon as you see Juliet you want her. Her tall, generously curved body becomes the image of the ideal for you, the incarnation of desire. And if you get in close enough to inhale her perfume – her earthy natural musk – then you're lost.

There was a time, back when she was just starting out in the business, when we used to share a lot of our cases. You could say that I showed her the ropes, or at least taught her some knots that she didn't already know, but if I'm honest, what I was mainly doing was trying to domesticate a big, scary jungle predator into behaving like a house cat. It was a bumpy process, with a number of very memorable upsets along the way.

As I stared at Sue's battered face, one of them flashed across my memory with sudden and unsettling vividness.

Juliet and I were mooching our way through a disused factory somewhere out past Gants Hill. It had changed hands at a bankruptcy auction, and the new owners were concerned about the complaints they were getting from residents in the area. People had seen lights and heard noises in the dead of night when it wasn't Christmas and they weren't even drunk. So the outfit that had taken possession hired me to give the place a prayer and a sing-song, and I took Juliet in with me because at that point I was still pretending to be her sensei.

We'd been all through the building once and found nothing more suspicious than some obscene graffiti. It was half past one in the morning, nothing was moving, and we were pretty sure that we were in for a quiet night. So we sat down on a lathe, or maybe a steam press, and I started to rummage through my pockets for a hip-flask full of liquid sunshine which by rights ought to be there.

But Juliet caught the edge of a scent that shouldn't be there, and before I could even get comfortable she was off – across two shop floors and a storage hangar the size of the Hatfield Galleria, out onto the yard and in among some prefab packing sheds at the far end of a desolate asphalt apron where a fleet of a hundred vans had once been parked.

Seven of these sheds were empty. The eighth . . . well, that was empty too, but there was a trapdoor in the floor and Juliet made a beeline straight for it. It was locked, but it didn't fit all that tightly. She got her fingers in around the edge on one side of the lock plate and started to pull. I went looking for a crowbar, and found one eventually. I also found some stuff I wished I hadn't, including an inspection pit full of gnawed bones. I had a bit of an inkling now what it was that had been giving the neighbours disturbed nights.

I took the crowbar back to the trapdoor and started to use it to good effect on the opposite side from where Juliet was tugging, but I think she'd have got there without my help. After thirty or forty seconds the wood of the trap gave a series of gunshot-sharp cracks and she lifted two thirds of it free. The rest stayed attached to the hinges.

From the bottom of the lightless well we'd opened came a weak, despairing wail, and then another.

I'd brought a torch with me. I switched it on now and pointed it down into the dark. It lit up a small, terrified face – just for a second, before a hand came up to shield those wide eyes from the sudden, unaccustomed light. I moved the beam to right and left: wherever the spotlight fell, whimpering children ducked and scurried away from it.

We'd stumbled across a *loup-garou*'s larder.

We looked for a ladder or a rope, but found nothing. The kids, meanwhile, cried and shrieked at the bottom of the hole. I shouted a few reassurances down to them, but clearly this was a conditioned reflex: they knew by now that when the trapdoor opened, someone's number was up.

After a terse parley, we agreed that Juliet would stay at the mouth of the pit and keep guard while I went and found some means of getting down into it. I headed for the door, but I was still a few steps short of it when two unsettlingly tall shapes filled it, blocking my path.

Not one *loup-garou* then; this was a team effort.

I eyed their muscular frames to get an inkling of what I'd be up against. They weren't overly broad at the shoulder, but they were so tall that they easily outmassed me anyway. The one on the left looked unremarkable except that when he grinned – as he did then – his teeth showed as a spiked forest of razor-sharp incisors with not a molar in sight. The other had a face that was a mass of old scar tissue so deep and rucked that I could barely see his eyes. They were both dressed in blue overalls, presumably so that from a distance – or to a trusting or myopic observer – they'd look as though they had some reason to be here.

They came inside and closed the heavy steel door with an echoing clang.

I took a step back, reaching into my coat and unshipping my whistle. Then I changed my mind, let it slide back again and picked up a heavy cast-iron pulley block from a pile of packing cases instead. Werewolves, you've got to hate them. They're mostly old souls because it's a difficult trick to pull off, and to pry the spirit loose from the animal flesh that it's shaped and sculpted . . . well, that's even harder. In fact it's like pulling buckshot out of a tiger's hide while the tiger is trying to eat your head. Given the fact that the pair of them were going to be on me inside a second, I was probably going to have better luck with the pulley block than the whistle – a cat in Hell's chance, say, rather than a snowball's.

They moved forward in unconscious synchrony, and I swung with the block. I timed it right, catching the scar-faced one off balance as he moved in, but it made no difference: he was too damn fast. His arm flicked out and swatted the thing out of my hand before it could touch him. On the backswing he pounded his closed fist into the side of my head and I staggered back a step, seeing stars. Then I backed away again, quickly, out of instinct, and his extended claws whipped past so close that if I'd been wearing a tie it would have been reduced to comical confetti.

The two of them tensed to leap, and I went for my whistle again because it was all I had left. But then Juliet pushed me firmly aside and strode past. I caught my breath. I had to, because it was so thick with her pheromones it almost choked me. The two *loup-garous* stared at her as if she was a page of unholy writ.

'Last man standing gets to kiss me on the lips,' she said. And then, after a charged pause of about half a second, she added, 'Dealer's choice.'

The were-thing with the teeth made a clumsy lunge for her on the spot, which just left him open for a scything uppercut from his partner that almost floored him. He got his feet back under him though, and came back spitting and snarling, slamming scarface against the wall and pinning him there with his shoulder. As they wrestled, trying to get a grip with teeth and claws, I found myself stepping forward with my own fists tightly clenched. Juliet's arm came out and blocked me, without effort.

'Not you, Castor,' she said with clinical calm. 'This one is by invitation only.'

She watched as they took each other apart. I'm not normally squeamish but I looked away before the end, because the *loup-garous* couldn't stop fighting even when they were bleeding to death and their entrails were spilling out on the floor. They lost their hold on their human forms as they weakened, the fluid flesh sliding back into half-remembered configurations. Even then they snapped at each other feebly with misshapen snouts, looking like nothing that had ever lived or moved on the face of the Earth.

Juliet breathed in and then out, savouring the tang of blood on the air – or more likely some other spoor that I couldn't even detect.

'Go and look for that rope,' she suggested, her voice thick.

It was hard to walk away from her – like walking uphill with a bag of rocks on my back. The attraction she exerted was that strong: as strong as gravity.

I took my time poking around the storeroom for a suitable coil of rope. The hormonal stranglehold on my mind had loosened by this time, and I was aware that the petrified little kids had been stuck at the bottom of the pit all this time, hearing the roars and snarls and howls of agony from above them. I was aware of it, but I truly didn't want to go back too soon and catch a glimpse of Juliet feeding.

By the time I did step back into the shed, she was sitting in the open space left by the shattered trapdoor, her legs dangling over the edge, entertaining the children with her own version of Little Red Riding Hood. Of the two *loup-garous* there was no trace, whether flesh or bone or sinew or greasy stain. I dumped the rope down next to her and listened to the end of the story, resigned to sleeping with the light on for the foreseeable future.

'It was my fault,' Sue repeated, more defiantly this time – as if warning me that any criticism of Juliet was off-limits. In the one eye that was still functional, tears brimmed but didn't fall.

With more tact than I can usually muster, I closed the street door. At the same time, Sue remembered my face-saving lie about needing a drink and fled to the kitchen, mumbling that she'd bring me a glass of water. I went through into the lounge and waited for her there. I knew her well enough to be sure she wouldn't want an audience for her weeping.

As I waited, sitting on a black leather sofa that squeaked whenever I breathed, the surly assistant at the library came back into my mind. I thought I could see now why he'd been so truculent with me. Sue kept her private life to herself and presumably hadn't introduced any of her work colleagues to Juliet, so the guy had put two and two together and got the square root of one, pegging me for an abusive boyfriend.

'Water,' Sue said, coming in with a tray. 'And some biscuits. Just ginger thins – that's all we've got. I haven't . . . I didn't do my weekly shop at the weekend.'

She set the tray down and retreated to a chair opposite me, angling her body so that the damaged side of her face was mostly out of my line of sight. She'd brought a glass of water for herself too, because a good hostess doesn't let her guest drink alone. She held it in both hands but didn't raise it to her lips.

'Can you tell me what happened?' I asked. Any small talk would have sounded grotesque in these circumstances, so I just cut to the chase.

Sue's shoulders twitched, a subliminal suggestion of a shrug.

'We had an argument,' she said, her voice slightly tremulous. 'It was the usual thing, really. Jules doesn't like it that I go out to work. She'd rather I stayed here and just . . . well, just . . .' I nodded emphatically to get her over the bump. I knew exactly what she meant. It wasn't that Juliet saw Sue just as a sex object; she saw her as the provider of many pleasures and diversions, with sex at the top of the list. But there was no getting round the fact that Juliet wanted Sue to be a stay-at-home house-wife, servicing her needs uncomplainingly whenever they arose. Maybe feminism hasn't reached Hell yet, or maybe one woman subordinating another is a special case. In any event, the question of Sue having a life apart from Juliet had been a snake in their Eden before now.

But it had never come to blows. Juliet tended to treat Sue as something precious and fragile that might break if carelessly handled, which is actually true of anyone in Juliet's hands, because her strength is as the strength of ten, even if her heart is only about as pure as New York snow.

'She'd been nervy for a few days before this,' Sue went on, staring morosely into her glass. 'Not herself. Snapping at me about things that didn't really matter. Normally she's calm about almost everything. It's only a few things that make her angry. And even then, it's sort of a . . . a big, heavy disapproval. She doesn't throw tantrums. She doesn't shout, or throw things.'

'And this time she did?'

Sue shot me a sheepish, unhappy look. 'Me,' she said. 'She threw me. Does that count?'

'How long did the fight go on for?' I asked, trying my best to make this seem like a doctor's consultation so I didn't have to respond to the hurt in her face. 'And how did she . . . you know, how did she feel about it afterwards?'

'It wasn't a fight, Felix. She hit me, and I tried to get away, and she hit me some more. You know how strong she is. There was nothing I could do.' Sue paused, frowning, reconstructing the scene in her mind. 'She was sorry, afterwards. Or . . . perhaps puzzled is a better word. She couldn't understand how it had happened. She apologised lots of times, and said it would never happen again.'

Her voice was breaking, and she was obviously close to another storm of tears. When she stopped speaking, I waited in silence, giving her the chance to pull the curtains decently closed on those terrible, shaming emotions. I suppose it must always be like that for succubi: every relationship you form has to have an element of addiction to it. You're not just someone's partner; you're simultaneously the drug they crave and the pusher who supplies their craving. Then again, as far as I knew, Juliet was the first succubus ever to set up house on Earth and try to live monogamously. It was uncharted territory.

'I told her . . . it was all right,' Sue said. 'That I forgave her. But it was the last . . . the last time. It had to be. I said if it happened again, she'd have to leave.' She laughed hollowly. 'You can imagine how convincing that sounded. If she left me, I think I'd kill myself. Or else I'd just die anyway, from not having her here.'

The surface of the water in her glass became choppy and turbulent as Sue's hand shook. Distracted, she put it down on the floor beside her chair, but then had no idea what to do with her hands.

'You said she'd been keyed up,' I said. 'Was there something specific that was on her mind? Is she working a difficult case?'

Sue shook her head, shrugged. 'She doesn't talk to me about her work,' she said. 'Not unless I ask. But I don't think she's got much work on at the moment at all. Sometimes Sergeant Coldwood calls her, to read a murder scene, but that hasn't happened for a few weeks now. She was laying down wards in a hotel that's being renovated in Ealing. And there was a geist, locally – in Wembley. But it was only moving furniture, not being violent. Just business as usual really.'

'But there could be a job she took on without telling you?'

'It's possible.' Sue didn't sound convinced.

'I'll talk to her,' I said. 'If there's something on the professional side that's distracting her, maybe she'll open up to me about it. She trusts my judgement on that stuff.'

'Thank you, Felix,' said Sue humbly. She could just as easily have said, 'Distracting her? She punched me in the face hard enough to turn it particoloured. Seemed pretty focused to me.' But Sue hasn't ever been the kind to make a drama out of a crisis.

I got up. There are a lot of things you can do at a moment like that to let the other person know you feel their pain. Most of them are outside my repertoire – or at least outside the relationship I have with Sue Book.

'I'll talk to her,' I said again, the words sounding even more awkward the second time around. 'Listen, if it happens again, and you need somewhere to go, Pen has about a million rooms doing nothing. You can come and stay any time.'

Sue nodded, giving me a weak smile, but clearly didn't trust herself to speak again.

I left her there, hanging on the cross I'd wanted so much to be nailed to myself, and went on my merry way. Which, let's face it, was getting less merry by the moment, even before I went over to the Costella Café and met up with Gary Coldwood.

But the fact that I was already looking like a wet weekend just saved him the unhappy obligation of wiping the smile off my face.

Gary looked hunted. He was sitting at the back of the long, narrow dining area, as far away from the window as he could get, dissecting a slightly watery portion of scrambled eggs on toast with grim and humourless precision.

There was no table service, so I grabbed a coffee and went over to join him.

'I'm telling you this as a friend,' he said when I sat down opposite him. 'Which means, if you tell anyone else and if it comes back on me, I'll kick you face down into a ditch and stand on the back of your head until you stop moving.'

'As a friend,' I clarified.

'Exactly. As a friend. Listen, after I left you last night, I went back over to Uxbridge Road to meet this SOCA fuckalong. Name of Brake, which was what I wanted to do to his face after five minutes in his company. He'd called me in to put a marker down.'

'Which was?'

Gary shot me a scowling glance, putting his knife down as though the memory had spoiled his appetite. 'The Ditko case. It's closed.'

For a moment that statement was too incomprehensible to be alarming. I laughed, but Gary didn't join me. 'Congratulations,' I said. 'That must be the quickest collar you ever got.'

'I'm serious, Fix.'

I nodded. 'Yeah, I can see that. But what the Hell does it mean? How can the case be closed? Rafi's still out there. Asmodeus too. The job's not done because this guy decides to move the file from one drawer to another. Did you tell him that?'

'No,' said Gary, spitting the word out. A couple of toast crumbs came along with it as unwilling passengers. 'I didn't, because he outranks me, and he made it clear right at the start that mine was not to frigging reason why. He was spoiling for a fight before he walked in the door, if you want to know. We get tied up in jurisdictional pissing contests with these arseholes every day of the week, and I think he was looking forward to a rumble. So I didn't give him the excuse. I was civil and solemn and butter-wouldn't-melt-in-my-bum-crack, which was as good as giving the bastard two fingers.'

'But you did ask what the Hell he was on about?'

'Of course I did. What do you bloody take me for?' Gary was indignant. 'I pulled out all the public safety issues and waved them in his face, and I said there was a cast-iron case for parallel parking – homicide running its own investigation alongside SOCA's and sharing resources.'

'So?'

'Nothing doing. And this is the bad news, Fix.'

'There's *bad* news?'

'SOCA aren't running the show either. It's been contracted out – his words – to a privately run agency. They're better resourced for this sort of palaver, he said, and they've already got the clearances they need to deal with a killer who can't be arrested by anything short of an army division. In fact, they're not looking to arrest Ditko at all; just to make sure he doesn't kill again. Their brief doesn't say anything about ways and means or about what state they leave him in afterwards.'

The horrible truth hit me just before he said it. I gave an incredulous laugh that almost hurt my throat coming out.

'Tell me it's not—'

'It's the Anathemata, Fix. The holy-water boys. If they can figure out a way to do it, they're going to kill Ditko and Asmodeus both.'

5

I just leaned back and waited for a few moments, trying to let that digest, but it sat in my stomach like a rock. The Anathemata. The bastards had screwed up my life every time I'd had the bad luck to run across them. And Rafi's too. They were even more to blame for Asmodeus than I was: for his being here at all, and for his still being free. This was a sicker joke than the one about the nun and the gorilla.

'Who are they, Fix?' Gary demanded. 'This is only the second time I've even heard of them, and both times I've had a case taken out of my hands and my arse smacked like I'm a kid trying to raid the sweet jar. Tell me what I'm up against.'

I opened my mouth to speak, then closed it again. Truth to tell, that wasn't an easy one to answer.

When it comes to the whole faith thing, I'm caught between a rock and a hard place. Growing up in Liverpool in the 70s, I came to the same conclusion that L. Ron Hubbard did in Nebraska fifty years earlier: that anyone can make a religion out of ingredients they probably already have lying around the house. You just take equal parts bullshit, xenophobia and moral outrage, mix well and leave to curdle.

But on one level at least, religion works. Any religion, almost, although I'd probably have to draw the line at the

Church of the Flying Spaghetti Monster. It's as though the human soul is an iron filing, and religions are magnetic fields that get all our north and south poles lined up along the same axis. As a consequence, and please don't ask me why, power flows.

A jobbing exorcist sees it every day of the week, and twice on Sundays. The crucifix, the shield of David, the star and crescent, the Hindu swastika and the Gnostic sun-cross all work as specifics against the undead, as long as they've been handled – or better yet, blessed – by some-body who actually believes in them. When Juliet first rose from Hell and tried to love me to death in my own bedroom over at Pen's, my brother Matthew, who's a priest, brought me through the worst of the after-effects with prayer and holy water. And the most commonly practised exorcism ritual is still the one the Benedictine monks wrote down in the Abbey of Metten in 1415. It starts with *'Crux sancta sit mihi lux'* and becomes really hummable with *'Vade retro, Satana'*.

So in some ways, being both an exorcist and an atheist, I'm like a tightrope walker who knows the knots will hold but kind of resents it. And when I come up against religious zealots of any persuasion, I lose the cheerful, easygoing disposition that I'm widely known for and become a surly, intemperate bastard. I mean, everyone has to choose their own poison, obviously – I'm all for freedom of choice. But if you say 'Praise the Lord', I'll be the one who answers 'Pass the ammunition'.

The Anathemata Curialis, therefore, pushes all my buttons so hard they leave permanent indentations in my spine.

'They're a holy order,' I told Coldwood. 'They were founded and given their charter by Pope Paul III. The same gent who bankrolled Ignatius Loyola when he set up the Jesuits – you know, "Give me a child until he's seven, and I'll give you a brainwashed drone that thinks its name is Harvey Maria." And he was doing all this in between trying to steal the wheels off the Reformation bandwagon, so he was a busy little bee. Quotable quote: "Of course there's a God. Martin Luther just had a stroke, didn't he?"'

I was trying to be concise and factual, but the truth was that venting all this stuff made me feel marginally better. And it was pretty fresh in my memory because I had to look it up the first time Father Gwillam waved his wedding tackle in my face.

'Pope Paul seemed to feel that the Inquisition had gone soft on crime and soft on the causes of crime,' I went on. 'The Anathemata's scarily open mission statement was to deal with anything that the Church had declared anathema – abomination – and by deal with I mean stop dead. Then a much later pope excommunicated the whole outfit, right down to the factory cat, but not before he'd voted it enough funds to keep it going to the crack of doom. Pretty neat trick, that – adding plausible deniability to the list of Christian virtues.'

Coldwood grunted. 'If they were closed down,' he said, 'what are they doing working my case?'

I shook my head. 'I never said they were closed down, Gary. The Anathemata still exists. My brother reckons they've got more than a thousand people on their payroll. But they're on silent running now. They're officially disconnected from the apparatus of the Church. They can't receive communion, be given the last rites or be buried in hallowed ground. And they eat that shit up, in my opinion. Being all virtuous and irredeemable; chucking over the chance of grace to save the world. They think they're the scourge of God, fighting the last crusade against the undead.'

'And you,' Coldwood interjected.

'What?'

'And against you. You seem to get right up their noses, for some reason.'

'Yeah, well I'd love to think that. But it's not personal, Gary. Nothing ever is with fanatics. It's Rafi. It's always been Rafi.'

Father Thomas Gwillam, the current head of the Anathemata, had known about Rafi Ditko's demonic passenger right from the start; he'd probably even been tailing Rafi as one of Fanke's votaries before he ever summoned Asmodeus. He'd considered killing Rafi, but opinions among his own exorcists differed: the death of the human host might kill the demon too, or it might simply set the demon free to be resurrected elsewhere. On the balance of odds, Gwillam had decided to do nothing as long as Rafi was safely locked up at the Charles Stanger Care Home, in a cell lined with silver and with frequent visitations from yours truly to play his inner demon to sleep whenever he got too boisterous.

But once I'd moved Rafi from the Stanger to Imelda's house, all bets were off. Gwillam had let the dogs out, and eventually they'd run Asmodeus to ground in Peckham, only to fumble the ball so badly that three of their best exorcists found their insides becoming their outsides, while the demon walked out from between them onto the streets of London, and in due course back into the life of Ginny Parris.

I could see where Gwillam might feel he had some sins to atone for. But I didn't want him paying for them with Rafi's intestines if there was anything I could do to stop it. And there was the big question, complete with neon lights, fireworks and a bank of laser beams playing across its fifty-foot-tall letters. *Was* there? Was there anything I could do to head the god-botherers off at the pass?

Coldwood seemed to be brooding on the same question, which was alarming.

'Forget it, Gary,' I advised him. 'You piss these guys off and you'll spend the rest of your life as a lollipop man on the M25. They don't play games.'

'Neither do I,' Coldwood growled. But it was just something to say. He couldn't stand up for a second against Gwillam's heavies and Gwillam's twisted cunning. I used to think I could, and the mess I was in now just went to show how badly wrong I was.

I finished my cooling coffee in three swigs, put the cup down. Coldwood watched me in silence. 'So you're advising me to lie back and think of England?' he demanded. 'Is that what you're planning to do?'

'I don't know, Gary,' I lied. 'I have no idea what I'm going to do.'

But the idea had already come to me, a whole lot more bitter and harder to swallow than the last dregs of the Maxwell House. When God has abandoned you and the devil is snapping at your heels, what you really need on your side is a bigger devil.

*   *   *

Paddington. St Mary's Hospital. The Metamorphic Ontology Unit, or MOU for short. I hadn't been here since the last time Asmodeus tried to break his chains. Life had seemed simpler then, in some ways. You knew who your friends were, even if you could count them on the fingers of a mutilated hand.

Today though, none of that really mattered. Today I was coming here to cosy up to one of my worst enemies.

I lost my way at first, because the place had moved. I went to the old building – the Helen Trabitch Wing, on Praed Street – only to find that it had turned back into a genito-urinary clinic and was filled with a random cross section of Sussex Gardens prostitutes, all cheerfully comparing notes on last night's slate. A harassed young house officer with a clipboard in his hand and a look of terminal embarrassment on his face directed me around the corner and along South Wharf Road to the Paterson Building, still billed on all the signage as the Department of Psychiatry.

But it was clear as soon as I walked inside that the building had a new tenant. The steel grille across the hall, just inside the street doors, had more of the flavour of a prison than a hospital, and the guy behind the desk was a uniformed flunkey from some private security agency. He was built like a brick mausoleum, and his head seemed to get broader as your glance travelled down from crown to jaw, as though someone had jammed the open end of a tuba over his head and left it there until the bones of his skull conformed to the shape. He bared his teeth as I approached, having been told somewhere down the line to smile at the mug punters when you weren't actually applying electrodes to their extremities. His teeth were very white and even, and not in any way filed to sharp points or stained with the blood of infants. Probably I was doing the guy a disservice: probably he was kind to children and small animals and his elderly mother, as the Krays were said to be. His uniform was very dark blue, and a single word, DICKS, was printed in grey on a sewn-in label attached to his lapel.

I pointed to it. 'Is that your name?' I asked. 'Or is it a stop-me-and-buy-one kind of deal?'

The guy's brow furrowed and his mouth quirked down, as though thinking that one out caused him mild pain. 'Can I help you, sir?' he said at last, letting the feeble witticism lie where it had fallen. His voice was well down into the bass register, but it had the front-of-the-mouth vowels of South African Dutch. That and his towering build activated a number of stereotypes I carry around with me, most of them centring on bound suspects mysteriously jumping out of fourth-floor windows under police questioning.

'Felix Castor,' I said. 'I'm here to see Professor Mulbridge.'

'And is she expecting you?'

'For the last five years,' I said.

Dicks didn't press the point, but he seemed to decide that was a no. 'Can I tell her what it's regarding?' he asked, after a slightly strained pause.

'You can tell her it's regarding Rafael Ditko.'

The guy nodded and tapped some keys on the small intercom to one side of his desk. 'What is it, Dicks?' said a voice – a woman's voice, but not Jenna-Jane's. It was a young voice, very precise but with a lilt of some exotic accent to it.

'A Mister Castor,' Dicks said. His accent almost made the two words rhyme.

There was a click as the intercom channel was closed at the other end. It stayed closed for a good long time. Then the same voice came on again. 'You did say Castor? Felix Castor?'

Dicks glanced at me, and I nodded.

'Yeah. Shall I send him up?'

Another click, and another long pause. This time, when the voice came back, it had a definite edge to it. 'Absolutely not. We'll send someone down. Mister Castor gets an escort.'

The line went dead with a short burst of static. Dicks gave me unfriendly look number 23, as taught in the barracks and prison yards of the world. I don't think he appreciated the implied reprimand in that 'Absolutely not'. Children and small animals notwithstanding, I seemed to have got off on the wrong foot with Mr Dicks. 'You see?' I told him, trying to break the ice with small talk. 'I'm a VIP.' He stared at me thoughtfully. It was a look that said louder than words, 'Sooner or later, I may have to damage you.'

Two more gentlemen cut from the same cloth as Mr Dicks appeared on the other side of the steel grille; in fact they all but goose-stepped up to it, walking side by side in near-perfect synchrony. Dicks pressed a button and there was a metallic clank as the lock released. One of the two newcomers held it open and I stepped through, then the other led the way to the lifts.

The Paterson must have been an architectural treasure once. It's got really striking porthole windows about three feet wide, in a formal nod to the art deco school, and very high ceilings for a modern building. Right now though, it looked like a bomb site. There was building work going on both on the ground floor, as we stepped into the lift, and on the second floor, where we got off. A small army of men in orange overalls, interspersed with the occasional woman, were stripping panels, laying electrical cable and nailing up plasterboard. The dominant colour was a chill, neutral blue, so evidently Jenna-Jane was remaking the building in her own image.

I hate hospitals, all exorcists do. A lot of people die there, and a significant percentage of them die scared, confused, angry or in desperate pain. Ghosts in various states from new to badly eroded congregate thickly, shouting and begging and sobbing for attention. A psychiatric unit isn't as bad as, say, a general surgery wing or a terminal ward, but it's plenty bad enough. I whistled tunelessly as I followed the two uniformed heavies. The tune was a mild stay-not, pushing the ghosts back from my immediate vicinity and giving me some room to breathe.

Jenna-Jane's office was at an intersection of two corridors. It had probably been a nurses' station at one time because two adjacent walls of it were solid glass from floor to ceiling, commanding a panoramic view in both directions. Austere white vertical blinds hung over them now, but the blinds were open.

The office was sparsely furnished. There was something monastic about Jenna-Jane's dedication to her cause. Probably she and Father Gwillam would have found a lot to talk about if they'd ever met, even though her religion of science was the antithesis of his old-school apocalyptic fundamentalism. There was only an antique roll-top desk against one wall, a number of office chairs on castors, a phalanx of five four-drawer filing cabinets in battleship grey, and a bookcase filled with formularies and medical textbooks. Jenna-Jane didn't read for pleasure. Classical music was a vice she admitted to, but most of her passions were tied up in her work. In tribute to that jealous god, a statuette standing on one of the filing cabinets – a stylised human figure with its back arched, like the Oscar statue yawning and stretching – was inscribed on its wooden base with the words EXCEPTIONAL ACHIEVEMENT IN EMPIRICAL RESEARCH. Josef Mengele probably had one of those on his desk too.

Two other people were in the room, besides Jenna-Jane – a man and a woman – but I didn't know either of them, and my attention flicked over them to land on the vivid, self-contained figure behind the desk. Jenna-Jane stood, closing the lid of her laptop with an automatic gesture. 'Felix,' she said, a warm smile on her face. She held out her hand, and I took it because there was no use straining at gnats considering the camel I'd come here to chow down on. 'You're looking really well, as always. And as always, it's very, very much a pleasure. You find us at sixes and sevens, so you'll have to excuse us: the move occupies so much of my time right now.'

Jenna-Jane is like one of those trompe l'oeil paintings where you think you're looking down a long corridor and in fact it's a solid wall. That's the only way I know to describe her, because nothing else in nature is so absolutely impenetrable while seeming so entirely wide open. You look at her small frame, her grandmotherly face, her straight, dignified bearing, and you feel an instinctive swell of affection and respect. Unless you know her; in which case the more she smiles the more you find yourself thinking about what happened to the young lady of Riga. She was dressed down today, in blue jeans and a gingham shirt. That degree of homespun camouflage boded bad news for someone, and it was probably going to be me.

I took my hand back, suppressing the urge to count the fingers and make sure they were all still there.

'This is Karin Gentle, my PA,' said J-J, indicating the woman, who stood as her name was mentioned. She had a ring-bound reporter's notebook in her right hand, but she transferred it to her left so we could shake. As we did, she bobbed her head in a subliminal echo of a formal bow. She was Asian, in her mid-twenties, and handsome despite a slightly pockmarked face.

'It's a pleasure to meet you,' she said, confirming my suspicion that it was her voice I'd heard over the intercom. 'You're the man who survived the embrace of the succubus Ajulutsikael, and then tamed her. Isn't that right?'

'You think she's tame?' I asked. 'I should introduce you.'

It was just a flippant comment, but the Asian woman's eyes widened. 'Then it's true? She stayed on Earth? She went native? I could meet her?'

The eagerness in her stare was unsettling. Maybe she was younger than she looked: no exorcist should be that happy at the thought of tangling with a demon. 'Be careful what you wish for,' I advised her. She blinked, looking a little hurt.

'And I believe you know Gil,' J-J went on smoothly, indicating with a nod of her head the man sitting in the corner of the office. Unlike J-J and Gentle, he didn't bother to stand. He just looked me over, toe to head and then back down to toe, without finding anything that he liked on either leg of the journey.

I was pretty sure J-J was wrong on that one: I didn't know the guy. He looked to be a few years younger than me, which put him just over thirty, with a slightly ratty physique, watery blue eyes, and brown hair with oddly placed blond highlights. Something about those blond tufts raised echoes in my mind, but I would have needed a quieter place to hear what they were whispering.

'No,' I said. 'I don't think we've ever—'

'My name is McClennan,' the guy said. 'Gilbert McClennan. You knew my uncle.'

I nodded slowly, wondering how to respond to that one. Gabriel McClennan had been the biggest rat's arse I'd ever had the misfortune of working with. Based in Soho, he'd systematically lied and cheated and stolen his way out of the good graces of the entire ghost-breaking community. We'd never had a whole lot in common, even before I'd accidentally got him killed.

Since then I'd met a McClennan daughter, Dana, and now here was a McClennan nephew. It seemed to bear out my theory that exorcism was a hereditary trait. Too bad it couldn't have chosen a better field to sow its seeds in.

'Yeah,' I agreed. 'I knew your uncle. How's he doing?'

'He's dead,' Gil said. The words were voiced way back in his throat, and he bared his teeth on the final consonant.

'I know,' I said. 'I meant since then. Do you keep in touch?'

Gil stared at me hard for a second or two, not saying a word. But I knew the answer in any case, and it was no. Gabe McClennan had run into Juliet back when she was still going by her old name. Physically and spiritually, he'd been chewed up, swallowed down and shat out a long time ago.

'Gil is a very valued member of our in-house team,' Jenna-Jane said, gesturing me to a chair as she sat down again herself. 'Doing your old job, Felix. The job of pontifex and psychopomp. Do you miss it at all? We'd love to have you back.'

The pontifex and psychopomp thing was one of J-J's favourite lines. They were two of the pope's official titles: builder of bridges between this world and the next, and chief dispatcher of human souls to their eternal reward. An exorcist wasn't really either of those things, but pride was always J-J's besetting sin. If even her servants held the power of life and death, then what did that make her?

'I don't have the stomach for that stuff any more,' I said, knowing as I said it that it was the kind of half-truth that everyone takes to be a lie. But Jenna-Jane nodded as though I'd confirmed a suspicion she already had.

'Yes,' she said. 'It was the moral dimension that made you feel you had to leave us in the first place. Your concerns over our Rosie.'

Our Rosie. She meant Rosie Crucis, the oldest ghost in captivity. But she said it in such an affectionate tone that the horror and cruelty of Rosie's capture were momentarily occulted by the homely phraseology.

'You won on that one,' I reminded her, since I couldn't say that my feelings on the subject had changed in the years since.

'Nobody wins when friends quarrel, Felix,' Jenna-Jane chided me seriously. 'No, I think it's true that our work induces a certain . . . narrowness of vision. Inevitably, I'm afraid. Morality reveals itself on the macroscopic scale, but is invisible in the detail work.'

'I have no idea what that means,' I said.

'It means we're serving the greater good,' Gil McClennan chipped in, offering his opinion like an apple for the teacher and getting a smile and a nod in return.

'Yes,' said J-J. 'The greatest good. I have something more to say to you on that subject, Felix, but I'd like to let it sit a little while. What was it you wanted to talk to me about?'

The crunch point. Probably better to get it over with quickly, because the longer I sat here the more likely I was to do something irrevocable – possibly involving the EMPIRICAL RESEARCH statuette.

'Rafi Ditko,' I said tersely. 'I think maybe it's time we collaborated.'

J-J affected surprise, although presumably it was the mention of Rafi's name that had got me in through the door. She glanced at Gil, who made a non-committal gesture, and then at Gentle, who nodded. 'I'm familiar with the case, Professor Mulbridge,' she murmured.

'Good.' Jenna-Jane returned her attention to me, looking a little perturbed. 'If you'll forgive me for being blunt, Felix,' she said, 'Rafael Ditko is the very last subject on which I'd expect us to find common ground.'

J-J sets the bar high, but that was a miracle of understatement even by her standards. We'd been fighting an undeclared war over Rafi for the best part of a year now. I'd only taken him from the Stanger Care Home in the first place to keep him out of her eager, grasping little fingers, and I'd told her more than once that if it came to a choice between shooting Rafi in the head and letting the MOU have him, I'd probably end up having to toss a coin.

It's funny how your own words come around to drop their pants and moon you sometimes.

'Yeah,' I said flatly. 'Times change. But the common ground was always there, Jenna-Jane. We both want Rafi alive. For different reasons, admittedly, but alive is alive. So I'm prepared to work with you to bring him in, in return for a guarantee that you won't bow to any outside pressure you might get to pull the plug on him.'

J-J frowned. 'Outside pressure? You intrigue me, Felix. But tell me, have you ever known me to bow to pressure? From any source?'

I had to admit that I hadn't. The idea had kind of a whimsical sound to it, like Jack the Ripper holding a door open for a little old lady and saying, 'No, after you . . .'

Jenna-Jane clasped her hands together under her chin with just the index fingers extended, pressed to her pursed lips. She considered for a few moments in silence while – out of a lack of other viable options – I sat and waited for the wheels to turn.

'Do you know where Ditko is?' she asked at last.

'No,' I admitted, 'I don't. But I bumped into him in Brixton last night and got close enough to touch him.'

I didn't see any need to explain that it was Asmodeus who'd been doing the touching, and that I was the hunted rather than the hunter in the whole scenario.

'He's got nothing to offer us, Professor,' Gil McClennan said, his voice dripping with contempt. 'Our teams are close to finding Ditko already. We don't need Castor to close this net.'

Jenna-Jane closed her eyes momentarily. I sympathised. Just by telling me that she was already looking for Asmodeus, McClennan had weakened her bargaining position. It must be a trial to be surrounded by idiots and yes-men the whole time: it's a cross that all tyrants have to bear.

'There might, it's true, be ways in which we could be helpful to each other,' Jenna-Jane said, as though Gil hadn't spoken. 'But – you'll forgive me for this, Felix, I'm sure – I remain to be convinced that you're negotiating in good faith. When we find Mr Ditko, why would you hand him over to me instead of absconding with him yourself – as you absconded once before, when he was confined at the Stanger Care Home.'

'Nobody knows, Jenna-Jane,' I said blandly, 'who was responsible for springing Rafi from the Stanger. It seems to have been a team effort though. Two men and a woman, from what I heard. And as you know, I work alone.'

'Of course.' J-J's smile was cold and tight. 'Nonetheless, the question stands.'

'The authorities want Rafi dealt with,' I said, 'and they don't really care how it's done. They've given the Anathemata Curialis total freedom to close the case in any way they like, and that almost certainly means they'll kill Rafi in the course of destroying or banishing Asmodeus.'

Jenna-Jane considered this for a moment in silence. 'Go on,' she said at last.

'I'll work with your people. You'll make the decisions and call the shots. I'll advise and give you my skills where necessary, and leave you to choose the when and where. You'll be in control the whole time.'

'Your skills,' Gil repeated, with a derisive emphasis.

Jenna-Jane glanced at him momentarily, as though slightly pained by his bluntness. Then she delivered her verdict. 'I'll need to think about it,' she said, opening her palms as though to show how even-handedly she'd do that. 'Gil, why not give Mr Castor a little tour of our new facilities while I mull his proposal over?'

McClennan looked like he'd swallowed a wasp, but a yes-man has to stick to the script or else retrain as a yes-and-no-man. 'Very well, Professor,' he managed. 'Just the top floors or . . . ?'

'Everything,' Jenna-Jane said. 'We're publicly audited, Gil. Nothing we do here is a secret.'

Gil crossed to the door and opened it. I lingered for a moment, staring at J-J. 'I'll give you my answer when you come back,' she said.

It was the best I was going to get, obviously. But I had to wonder, as I followed McClennan out through the door, what it was that was preventing her from giving me a straight answer on the spot. As the office door closed, she was deep in murmured consultation with Gentle, who was nodding and scribbling rapidly in her notebook.

Metamorphic ontology, a phrase that's both resonant and anodyne, hiding itself coyly behind Ancient Greek polysyllables like a coquette peeping out from behind her fan. It means the study of the undead: science's sheepish and undignified scramble to catch up with recent developments in the afterlife, especially as they impact on this one. Ontology ferrets into the nature of being; metamorphosis is change. Translation: 'When they're dead, people change into some bloody scary things. Let's talk some serious Latin about it.'

Jenna-Jane was the leader in the field, and her MO unit at St Mary's had been the first to set up anywhere in the world. It had been much copied since, and J-J now ran a lucrative sideline in advising other hospitals on how to do it – what staff and resources they'd need, how many tasers, how many shackles, how many metric tons of therapeutic narcotics, and of course how thick the soundproofing would need to be.

If I sound a bit sour on the whole enterprise, it's because I was part of it once and I know what it looks like from the inside. Consequently I wasn't looking forward to this tour at all, but I was going to roll with it anyway, and keep my eyes open the whole way through. Know your enemy, as the saying goes, especially if you're planning to be friends.

'This floor is staff offices and admin,' Gil said sullenly, as we walked back down the corridor towards the lifts and the stairwell.

'How many exorcists on staff?' I asked.

'Thirty.'

I gave a low whistle. In my day it had varied between two and six. J-J had called in extra help when she needed it, but strictly on a jobbing basis. Her budget must be colossal now. I wondered whether any of the permanent staff were people I knew. I hoped not. Maybe they were all McClennans.

We passed a number of offices, all empty. Most were larger than J-J's and better furnished: it seemed like she was taking her monastic pretensions to new extremes. One of them, squeezed into a corner between the toilets and the water cooler, bore a terse white-on-black sign that read GILBERT MCCLENNAN, VOLUNTEER LIAISON & FIELD COORDINATOR.

'Liaison?' I asked, pointing.

Gil shrugged. 'Rosie,' he grunted, grimacing slightly. 'Organising the meat train.'

'Delicate choice of words.'

'What do you want me to call it, Castor? She's burning them out faster and faster. I don't even know why we keep her around.'

Because she brings in the money, I thought but didn't say. Because academics come from far and wide to see the fifteenth-century ghost you've caught and pressed between two glass slides. And that brings the headlines, and the headlines grease the baking tin. But that was only half the answer. For J-J, the money was only ever a means to an end.

Gil led the way down to the first floor. There was building work going on here too, but not so much. Massive pieces of equipment were being welded to walls and floors in labs that looked like something out of Victor Frankenstein's wet dreams. I did the sums in my head. The MOU had only had two floors at the Helen Trabitch, and it was a smaller building. This move must have more than doubled the scale of Jenna-Jane's operation.

'Analytics,' Gil said. 'Technical and lab support. This is where blood and tissue sampling gets done. X-rays. Computer imaging . . .' We'd come to a door beyond which an autopsy slab stood in the centre of a small bare room, surrounded by shelves of chemicals and porcelain drainage troughs. The tiled floor gleamed whiter than white, and the heady smell of formaldehyde hung in the air. 'And autopsies,' said Gil, 'as required.'

'Where is everyone?' I asked. 'It's a weekday morning. Shouldn't this place be humming?'

'The official move is next week. There's only a skeleton staff here right now.'

It was such an easy straight line that I didn't lower myself to touch it.

'Everything here,' Gil said, warming up a little now that he was getting the chance to show off all these shiny toys, 'is dedicated. These facilities only serve the MOU – we're hands-off to the rest of the hospital.'

'Sure,' I agreed. 'God forbid you get your CAT scanner all crowded out with sick people when you've got a new werewolf to play with.'

Gil shrugged, indifferent to my sarcasm. 'We're healing a deeper sickness, Castor,' he said. 'But by all means, you just sit up there on the moral high ground and watch the waters rise. Bring a picnic.'

I almost laughed out loud. It was J-J's rhetoric, barely changed from the arguments I'd had with her before I walked out of here for what I thought was the last time. The end days were coming. Gwillam would call it Armageddon; J-J would call it a disequilibrum event, but they meant the same thing. The dead would fight the living for the top spot in Earth's wobbly ecosystem, and it would be a fight that would leave the world we knew looking like New Orleans after Katrina. Laws are silent in times of war, Cicero said; J-J thinks they should shut up for the preliminary heats too. She can't do her job with all that human rights garbage dinning in her ears.

I turned away from the door, my breakfast churning slowly and queasily in my stomach. Gil hadn't said anything about the leg and arm restraints, or why they should be needed on an autopsy table. I didn't bother to ask because I already knew the answer.

Part of the problem was that the law was still running to catch up with the way the world had changed. Vast edifices of legislation had been carved out over centuries to protect the rights of the living. Now we had the dead and the undead to worry about too, and the courts were barely scratching the surface of what that meant. If you died and then came back, either in the flesh or as a ghost, who owned your house, your money, your CD collection? Were you still married to the wife or husband you'd had before? Did you have the right to expect them to welcome you with open arms when you didn't have a pulse any more? Could you give evidence in court? Maybe finger the guy who'd murdered you, or sue the doctor who'd botched your heart op?

The test cases were being brought, and the questions were being asked in the parliaments of the world. In a few years' time, there might be all sorts of legal restraints on what someone like Jenna-Jane could get away with. For now, a *loup-garou* enjoyed all the legal protections that a lab rat does, and a zombie had the same civil rights as roadkill.

We descended to the ground floor. 'This is mostly therapy and interview suites,' Gil said.

'Interrogation rooms,' I translated.

'If you like.'

I didn't. But as we walked along the main drag, my death-sense picked up the faint echo of a familiar tune.

'We take security pretty seriously,' Gil was saying. 'Especially here and in the basement levels. There are alarm pulls in every room and every twenty feet along the corridors. The CCTV hook-ups have a hundred-per-cent overlap, and they're monitored in real time by a team of three. Or they will be, once we're up and running. There are weapons lockers on this floor and the one above, equipped with Mace and tasers and pepper sprays.'

'Who provides the muscle?' I asked. 'Does J-J order in? They look like Nazi stormtroopers.'

'They're not regular hospital security, if that's what you mean,' Gil grunted. 'Use your sense, Castor. You know what we get coming through here. How long do you think the average retired store detective would last against a *loup-garou*?'

He had a point, but again I was aware of what he wasn't saying: that the nature of Jenna-Jane's work called for more serious and more unscrupulous muscle than a regular security firm would be likely to countenance. Judging from the look of the guys I'd seen at the front desk, they straddled the bruised and tender line that separates private cops from mercenaries.

Gil was still talking – something about the locks and the pass codes – but his words were drowned out as that elusive sense became stronger with each step. Finally I stopped in front of a heavy windowless door with a keypad lock. A sign on the door read NO UNAUTHORISED ACCESS, and another, below that, WITH ESCORT ONLY.

Gil walked on, then looked back at me impatiently. 'What?' he said.

I pointed at the door. 'I was thinking I might pop in and say hello,' I said.

'To who?'

'To Rosie Crucis. This is where you've got her stashed, isn't it?'

By way of answer, Gil walked back to join me and tapped the NO UNAUTHORISED ACCESS sign with the knuckle of his index finger.

'So authorise me,' I suggested.

'Eat me,' Gil counter-offered. That sounded like an impasse to me.

We walked on, rounded a few corners and found ourselves in a wider corridor. But the main drag ended in a huge vault-like metal door which at first glance seemed to have more hazchem warnings on it than the staff canteen at Sellafield. At second glance it was obvious that they weren't hazchem warnings at all; they were wards of the pentagram variety, stamped onto steel, painted in high-contrast colours and riveted to the metal of the door. They were all stay-nots, carrying in a dozen dead languages their many playful variations on the theme 'One more step and you're deader than you already were.'

The door had a whole lot of locks too – a keypad like Rosie's door, a card-scan lock and two high-end ASSA Abloys. Gil unlocked them one by one, then turned to me with his hand on the bare steel pull-bar that the door had by way of a handle.

'Smell anything?' he asked me, with a nasty smile on his face.

'Like what?' I asked.

'Well, you were so spot on with Rosie,' he said, 'I thought you were going to say something.' He swung the door open, and it hit me. Not a smell; that was just Gil's way of saying we were in the presence of the dead, and the undead. From the dark space beyond the door a cacophony the like of which I'd never heard before rose up to assault my death-sense.

I took an involuntary step back, and then another, raising a hand in front of my face as though to ward off a physical assault. After the second step, the corridor wall jostled me in the back and there was nowhere else to go. Swallowing hard, I tried to cope with the madness, while Gil watched me with a certain satisfaction.

'It takes you that way the first time,' he said. 'The second time too. Come and take a look.'

He walked ahead of me into the dark, not bothering to look back to see if I was following. It was a taunt, and a challenge. It cost me a real effort to walk into that space behind him, a bigger effort not to clap my hands to my ears in a futile attempt to block out the sounds that weren't coming in via my ears at all.

We stood on a metal platform, our footsteps echoing like the thudding of a drum in a space much, much larger than a normal room. It was pitch black until Gil threw a lever on the wall just beside the door, and then a couple of dozen spots came up, stabbing down from above us to illuminate a vast cement-grey bunker.

Gil crossed to a railing, leaned against it nonchalantly and looked out. I followed after a couple of seconds, my head still so full of thunderous dissonance that I could barely isolate Gil's voice — the only real sound in the psychic tumult.

'This is all new,' he said.

Below us was a space like the floor of a vast warehouse, sub-divided not by shelves or storage bins but by multi-storey structures like sturdier versions of the temporary offices that spring up on building sites. These weren't portakabins though: they were breeze-block ramparts with steel doors but no windows — and the doors were close enough together to give some sense of what the spaces behind them might look like: there'd just about be room to swing a cat, so long as you kept the arc really tight.

Steel steps and walkways connected the blocks, and the spaces in between them — broad corridors with steel-grille floors — were interrupted about every ten feet by chain-link barriers with gates inset. Nobody seemed to be manning these checkpoints, and all the gates were currently open: presumably they slammed shut automatically if one of the cell doors was compromised, to ensure that any occupant who got out of its tomb-with-a-view wouldn't be able to wander too far.

'Two hundred and forty cells,' Gil said, 'in case you were trying to count. But some of them are two and three-berth. And every single one of them is silver-lined — three hundred thousand square feet of silver sheeting in a one-to-three steel laminate mix that Professor Mulbridge designed personally. You know what that does to the undead and the Hell-kin. This space is actually as large as the entire building. And it didn't even exist until we acquired the building. That's how much we've got rolling for us now, Castor. You walked out of this operation just as it was getting big.'

The jagged power chords of the dead and undead in their cells below us were still scraping against my nervous system, and my throat dried out in the space of three abortive swallows as I surveyed the bargain-basement Alcatraz. 'Yeah,' I croaked. 'I'm kicking myself.'

Gil turned to look at me with his lip curled.

'My God,' he said, 'why are you still in this business?'

There was no sense wasting any breath answering him.

'You want to see what we've got,' he asked, 'or shall we go back upstairs so Professor Mulbridge can fan your face with a damp flannel?'

'I'm good,' I said. I turned my back on the screaming room and walked back out through the bunker door into the main corridor. But Gil didn't follow me, and with the door still open the virtual uproar didn't stop.

This is the downside of being an exorcist. Our dark-adapted senses let us see an upside-down rainbow where the doubting Thomases see undifferentiated black; but we can't turn them off. Closing your eyes and covering your ears just doesn't cut it.

Gil was enjoying my discomfort. He leaned against the doorframe, arms folded, and watched me sweat.

'The two blocks right at the far end,' he said, deciding to give me the inventory anyway, 'are just zombies. Alpha block is decay parameter experiments; Bravo is toxicology. You *can* poison the DMWs, amazingly, if you get the right mix of shit. Stuff that accelerates cellular breakdown, or attacks the muscles.

'Charlie through Echo are *loup-garous*. We run through a lot of them, because the main thrust of the research is incompatibility vectors – ways of forcing the human spirit out of the animal flesh so it reverts to being just an animal. It tends to be irreversible, so every werewolf we get is a non-renewable asset.

'Foxtrot and Golf are a real circus. We keep all the unclassifieds there. Our resident vampire – if he is a vampire. A few referrals from other departments who've got the souls of people they used to know anchored inside them somehow and come here for a ghost-ectomy. Partially transformed *loup-garous* that got jammed halfway and can't get in or out. The minor demons we've managed to raise.

'And when we get to Hotel, well fuck . . .'

I walked away, leaving him to slam the door and cycle the locks. That took a while, so I was able to walk all the way up to the second floor by myself, taking my time so that the ringing in my ears had stopped and my pulse rate had returned to normal by the time I got back to Jenna-Jane's office.

She was alone this time, and busy typing an email, but she looked up and swivelled her chair to face me as I walked in. She gave me another of those smiles. This time I could see the flames of Armageddon behind it.

'It's taken a certain amount of arranging,' she said. 'Father Gwillam was rather hoping that the MOU's resources would be at his disposal for the duration of this little skirmish. But I've had to disappoint him. My answer is yes, Felix. I'll work with you on bringing Ditko in.'

'I changed my mind,' I answered grimly. 'Do what you like as far as Gwillam is concerned. Rafi would be better off dead than here.'

'We won't keep him here, Castor.'

I blinked. I must still be disoriented from the basement and the full-frontal assault on my death-sense. 'What?'

'We'll return him to the Stanger. Your friend will be safe. We'll even help you, as far as we can, in removing the demon from him.'

I laughed a little hollowly. 'J-J, I just saw your zoo, so I know you didn't turn into Mother Teresa while I wasn't looking.'

'No,' she agreed. 'This isn't altruism. We help you, and you help us. I give you Rafael Ditko, and you give me . . .'

She paused as if this was a game of some kind, as if she wanted me to guess.

'What?' I demanded.

'Yourself, Felix. You come and work for me again.'

6

'*The Usual Suspects*,' said Nicky Heath. '*Three Days of the Condor*. And Costa Gavras's *Missing*.'

Nicky smelled of Old Spice over other, more astringent chemicals, and the dark patches within his death-white pallor were more noticeable than they usually are. He was five years dead and doing pretty well, all things considered, but the loss of Imelda Probert's professional services had hit him hard. Before Asmodeus killed her, the Ice-Maker was a faith healer for the dead: by a laying on of hands, she claimed to be able to lower a zombie's core temperature and slow the processes of decay. Sounded like bullshit to me, when I first heard about it, but Nicky used her regularly and Nicky was unliving proof that whatever she did actually worked. Now though, he'd been thrown back on his own resources.

Nicky makes sure that the Walthamstow Gaumont, the long-disused and recently renovated cinema he's made his home, is as cold as an Eskimo's sock drawer; and he flushes his system with ferociously potent chemical cocktails every few days, effectively pickling his flesh to keep it from going bad. But from the look of things, he was facing some kind of a crisis on the preservation front. I decided the tactful thing was to avoid mentioning it, and since I'd walked in on him in the middle of setting up a late-night triple bill, another subject was ready to hand.

'You're slipping, Nicky,' I said. 'I can actually see a link between those three movies.'

'So?' Nicky was even more pugnacious than usual. Something was eating him, so to speak, but if it was my complicity in Imelda's death, I wasn't feeling up to that conversation just yet. I felt – for about the twentieth time that day – an overwhelming, almost crippling desire to get rat-arse drunk. Nicky had one of the best wine cellars in London, but he limited himself to inhaling the breath of the wine: the perfect companion for a boozy voyage into oblivion, in that he stayed sober and could be the designated driver on the return journey. But it was a joyride I couldn't afford right then.

'So, normally when you go for a triple bill it's, like, they all had Filboyd Studge as key grip or something. It's nice to see you go for something as obvious as conspiracy thrillers.'

'Meta-conspiracy thrillers,' Nicky said, clipping the film reel onto the projector's massive horizontal spindle. We were up in the projection room, which was so cold that my breath wasn't just visible, it hung in the air like a thickening fog and refused to dissipate. Nicky ignored the cold. He didn't exactly enjoy it, but it didn't bother him, whereas bright sunshine made him duck and run for cover. If you're serious about the zombie lifestyle, you have to become as narcissistic as a professional bodybuilder. You're sailing into eternity in a leaky boat, so it helps to have an obsessive nature. Nicky was born and bred for the gig.

'Meta-conspiracy thrillers,' I repeated, deadpan, inviting him to hit me with the punchline.

'They're all movies where the conspiracy is part of a

bigger conspiracy,' he said. 'Where you think you've worked it out, but all you did was tear away the first layer of wallpaper. Like those dreams where you wake up sweating but, hey, you're still asleep and it's just another dream.'

'Right,' I said. 'I get it. Is that how you see the world, Nicky?'

'That's how the world *is*, Castor. You just didn't figure out yet who's dreaming you. Maybe it's Jenna-Jane Mulbridge, because the psycho-bitch-queen certainly seems to have a soft spot in her heart for you.'

I grunted non-commitally. That wound was still a little raw. But Nicky seemed happy to stick with the subject.

'So what did you tell her?' he demanded. 'Did you use adjectives? Gestures? I want a slow-motion action replay.'

'I just walked out,' I said, which was the truth. I hadn't trusted myself to answer Jenna-Jane without going for her throat, which would have brought her pet Nazis down on me in all their goose-stepping fury. So I just turned round and headed for the door, walking past Gil McClennan, whose face as he stared at me was full of contemptuous amusement. J-J let me go without a word. At least when demons try to steal your soul they snarl and slaver and make a show out of it.

Nicky was looking disappointed. He was clearly hoping for something more in the way of dramatic byplay. To forestall any further questions I held up my phone, which was displaying the chunk of grey stone I'd found in Pen's front garden, with the red pentagram flaring on its upper face. Nicky squinted at it for a second, then waved it away. 'My eyes don't resolve down that far,' he said. 'You got anything bigger?'

'I've just got this,' I said. 'Can't you scale it up?'

Nicky returned his attention to the film, which he was threading through the projector's complex series of spools and rollers. 'Probably,' he admitted grudgingly. 'Send it on to my phone. I'll see what I can do.'

While he was still working on the film, I composed a message with the photo as an attachment and forwarded it to Nicky's mobile. It took a long time, because I'm far from slick with technology, but finally his phone buzzed and he reached into his back pocket to turn it off. Then I had to wait until he threw the mains power switch and turned on the projector to let it warm up. He leaves that to the last moment for reasons already given: warm isn't good in Nicky's world.

He didn't bother to look at the display on his own phone, because the screen-size problem would still apply; he just relayed it on to one of his computers by means of some wireless skullduggery and opened it there.

'Summoning,' he said at once, seemingly without even reading the words in the ward.

'How do you know?' I demanded. I was supposed to be the practising exorcist here, so it pissed me off a little that Nicky was able to lecture me on my own craft. But then I'd never been big on the grimoire tradition, which boasts a common-sense-to-bullshit ratio somewhere in the region of one to a thousand.

'Disposition of the runes between the inner and outer circles,' Nicky rattled off absently. 'Presence of outwardly radiating fan lines in the five negative spaces defined by the five arms of the pentangle. Use of aleph sigils to stand in for candles, as in the Gottenburg ritual.'

'Okay,' I said, giving up the point. 'It's a summoning. What's being summoned?'

'Not sure,' Nicky admitted. 'Let me check.'

He tapped at the keyboard, opening up some more files. At least one was a table of Aramaic letters. Another seemed to be a set of scanned pages from a very old book – probably one of the bat-shit grimoires aforementioned. As Nicky browsed and muttered to himself, I went to the window at the front of the projection booth, leaned on its sill and stared down into the auditorium below. It was silent and empty: most of the time Nicky plays his movies for an audience of one.

Not completely empty though. A single figure sat in the exact centre of the front row, barely visible as a silhouette against the diffused light bouncing back off the screen. Someone was watching the opening credits of *The Usual Suspects*, silent and motionless.

'Tlullik,' Nicky said from behind me. 'Or maybe Tlallik. It depends whether this diacritical mark here is meant to have a curve or an angle.'

'So who's Tlullik?'

Nicky looked round at me and gave an expansive shrug. 'Never heard of him,' he said. 'Her. It. Them. Probably a demon, judging from the name, but it can't be a big one or else I'd have come across it elsewhere. The major heavies leave big footprints.'

'Nicky, this was painted on a rock shoved under Pen's rhododendrons,' I told him. 'I thought she'd put it there herself, but she doesn't mess with necromancy. You think Asmodeus could be trying to get at her in some way?'

Nicky nodded, but he didn't look convinced. 'It's

possible,' he said. 'A guy wants to drive you crazy, he can summon a minor Hell-spawn to crawl inside your head and fuck you over. It's becoming kind of a fashion statement in gangster circles – if you don't pack demon heat these days, you're nobody.

'But if Asmodeus is behind this, he's using two very different MOs. He ran Ginny Parris through with the sharp end of a broken chair leg, according to the police report. There's kind of a mismatch between that and hiding in the bushes with a permanent marker.'

He was right, of course. But if not Asmodeus, then who? If it was aimed at me rather than Pen, it could be almost anyone. There's no shortage of people sufficiently pissed off with me to traffic with Hell if it would give me some grief.

'Can you find out what this Tlullik is?' I asked Nicky.

'I can try,' he said. 'Are we done now?'

'One more thing.'

Nicky rolled his eyes, conveying how much faith he had in the number 'one' in that sentence.

'Could you find out if Rafi Ditko has any living family or friends, besides the ones I know from Oxford?'

'That's a pretty open-ended search, Castor. What's it worth?'

'At the moment,' I admitted, 'more than I can pay. But I know a man who knows a woman who knows a goatherd in the Yemen who can get me a line on a 1940s Lester Young jam session.'

Nicky feels about early jazz the way heroin addicts feel about heroin, but he did his best to look unimpressed. He huffed out air, which he had to inhale specially for the purpose. 'Jam tomorrow . . .' he said sardonically.

'The jam's seventy years old,' I pointed out. 'It's not going to spoil in a day. It's an interesting item, I heard. On lacquer, with some kind of note from Shad Collins scribbled on the sleeve.'

'I'll see what I can do, Castor.'

'All I can ask for, Nicky.'

'Is it?' Nicky examined his thumbnail, rubbing at the cuticle with the little finger of his other hand. 'You surprise me. I was sort of expecting you to say, "How do you get a demon out of a close friend?" Something of that nature.'

The slight smirk that marred his studiously casual expression made me want to walk out without asking the question. Well, that and the fact that we'd been down this road a hundred times when Rafi was at the Stanger without finding a damn thing that would stick. But even when hope doesn't triumph over experience, it can still make you go through the motions.

'Are you onto something, Nicky?' I asked him.

'Something,' he admitted. 'I'm still trying to put it together. Ask me about it next time you come over.'

I was about to leave, but I had to pass the window on the way to the door and I looked down into the auditorium again. The silhouette was still there; it didn't seem to have moved at all. There was something very familiar about it.

'Nicky,' I said. 'Your guest . . .'

I turned to look at him. He was wearing the expression of a man who had been waiting for the penny to drop for a long, long time, and was both surprised and saddened at how long it had taken.

'She's been waiting for you for three hours,' he said.

'And she's in a shit-awful mood. If I were you I wouldn't make her come up and get me.'

Juliet was staring at the screen with unblinking eyes, watching Kevin Spacey's tribulations with no sign of empathy or engagement.

At first I thought that Nicky had exaggerated. She didn't look angry or agitated; in fact she was preter-naturally still, like one of Antony Gormley's iron men who'd wandered in off the street for a breather.

But as I opened my mouth to speak her name, she turned to look at me, and her eyes shone in the dark with a red light, self-luminous like the eyes of a cat.

'Castor,' she said. Her voice was a bass chord that started sympathetic vibrations in my guts and loins.

'Hey,' I said lightly, dropping into a seat three along from her. That meant I could look at the screen instead of those eyes. It wasn't that glowing red eyes were unusual accoutrements for a demon; it was just that Juliet had never had them before, and they scared the living shit out of me. 'Rosebud was his sledge.'

Juliet didn't get the joke, and didn't bother to ask me to explain it. I felt a wash of psychosomatic heat spill across my cheek. She was still staring at me through the intervening dark, which hid me from her about as effect-ively as a throw rug hides a rhinoceros.

'You talked to Sue,' she said, in the same low, burry voice.

'Yeah.' I nodded. 'She's . . . worried about you. So am I. Is there something I should know?'

'You should know not to talk to her behind my back,' Juliet growled.

That made me turn to meet her gaze again. 'Behind your back?' I said. 'Juliet, you hurt her. You hurt her and you terrified her. You think it's wrong that she should want to talk about that?'

Juliet stood, so I did too. It wasn't that I had any more of a chance against her on my feet than I did sitting down, but that old fight or flight reflex dies hard. Looking at her grim face, I wondered if I was about to do the same.

'What's mine is mine, Castor,' Juliet said. 'You know what I can do to you, so I'm telling you to leave her alone.'

Oh man. We were really on slippery ground now. But I've never let that stop me from trying to tap-dance. 'Juliet,' I said, 'she doesn't belong to you. We talked about this way back in the day, when the two of you were . . .' I hesitated. 'Going out together' is the default phrase, but the way I remembered it, Juliet and Sue spent most of the first month of their relationship indoors, barely surfacing for long enough to put out the empty milk bottles and feed the cat. If you start a romance with a succubus, you have to be prepared to clock up some serious hours in the bedroom – and probably on the sofa, the carpet, the kitchen table and the top of the bookcase. I settled for '. . . getting to know one another,' and pressed on quickly so the pause wouldn't show. 'Sue isn't your pet or a conveniently warm and cuddly sex toy; she's a human being. I know that doesn't mean the same thing to you that it does to me, but for the love of Christ! You can't pick her up and put her down whenever you want to; you can't dictate who she does and doesn't talk to; and you can't beat the shit out of her when she doesn't come up to scratch. Understand?'

Juliet laughed. It had a chilling ring to it. 'Who tells me that I can't do these things?' she asked, her voice caressing me roughly like the tongue of a cat. She has minute control over those harmonics, and she knows what she's doing. She knew, right then, that she was bringing me to a painfully intense erection: a casual show of force intended to remind me of what else she could do to me if she had a mind to. 'You, Castor? You're giving me commands? I might be inclined to take that personally if your words were backed by anything besides insolence.' She took a step towards me, those luminous eyes flashing like beacons in the dark. Another step and she was right in front of me, her head leaning in towards my throat. 'But they're not,' she whispered in my ear. 'Are they?'

She brushed past me, allowing the curve of her breast to press briefly against my arm in passing. The small area of my skin that had felt the contact tingled as she walked away, as though an electric charge had passed through me.

On the screen above and behind me Spacey opined that the greatest trick the devil ever pulled was making people believe he didn't exist.

My heart was hammering. My nostrils were filled with her sex smell and my mind with pornographic imagery. Something inside me was still rising, still opening, ready to meet her halfway as she feasted on me and threw me away, but the crisis was over. Juliet was just making a point, not actually moving in for the kill.

I sat down again – then slithered down onto my knees – as the crash hit me: all those homeless hormones, crashing against the walls of my veins and arteries like miniature tidal waves, my mind afloat on the flood like a pathetic Noah's Ark preserving my last two functional brain cells.

When I was able to take stock of my surroundings again, I looked up and saw Juliet standing in the aisle at the end of the row, as motionless as she'd been sitting earlier. Her back was to me, her head tilted slightly down.

'I don't know what happened,' she said, her voice suddenly flat and dead.

'You mean you lost control?' I translated.

'I mean I don't know what happened. I was hitting her. Hurting her. There didn't seem to be any conscious decision involved. Or rather . . . the moment of decision was elided. The action seemed to take the place of the decision.'

I climbed to my feet again, partly to see if I could and partly because I felt a little stupid taking the moral high ground from so close to ground level. Juliet still hadn't turned to face me. 'Suppose you saw a man beating his wife or his lover,' I said, 'and he gave you that bullshit by way of an explanation?'

Juliet sighed, an odd and disconcerting sound. 'It is bullshit,' she agreed. 'But it's true all the same. I was like that when I was younger: I rode the impulse, because impulse comes faster than thought, and then afterwards I thought about what it meant.'

'When you were younger?' I repeated.

'Your race hadn't invented written language yet.'

She made a gesture, clenching her fist and then opening it again, as though she was giving up on the effort of self-analysis. 'It's strange,' she said. 'I imagine someone else hurting her, and I feel anger. A really simple, strong anger. It's arousing.'

I thought I must have misheard that last word. 'It's what?' I asked.

'Arousing,' Juliet repeated impatiently. 'It turns me on to think of hurting someone who's injured Sue. Making him pay for it, making him beg for his life, and devouring him while he's still begging. It's pleasurable to think of things like that.' She made a move that I couldn't inter-pret: a twitch of the shoulders, sudden and swift. 'If I think there's a danger I might really harm her,' she muttered, 'I'll send her away.'

'And how long do you think she'll last after that?'

Juliet half-turned to stare at me over her shoulder: a silent query.

'Come on,' I said irritably. 'You kissed me once, two years ago, and I still wake up sweating. She's shared your bed for sixteen months. If you make her go cold turkey, Juliet, she'll crash and burn faster than the fucking *Hindenburg*.'

She scowled. 'It's possible,' she agreed. 'Or else she might survive, as you did. I'm not reponsible for every man or woman who sniffs my crotch, Castor.'

She seemed to be waiting for me to disagree with her, but I thought there was a certain mileage to be got out of just letting the words hang in the air. It was kind of a resonant image, after all.

'I didn't mean that,' Juliet said, after a strained pause. 'I don't equate her with you.'

'Thanks.'

'Or with any of those I hunted. What we have is different from that. It's . . .' She seemed to grope for words, but she was trying to explain something that was inherently inexplicable – not just for her but for anyone who ever went looking for a quick shag and got more than they bargained for. 'It's not a hunt,' she finished testily.

'Tell her you're sorry,' I suggested.

'Mind your own business,' she snapped back.

She headed for the door. I was going to call her back and ask her about Tlallik, or Tlullik, but I chickened out. Juliet may be refreshingly open about sexual matters, but when it comes to her own species she closes up again real fast. Get a finger caught in that door and you could easily lose it, she'd warned me, very explicitly, a very short while ago.

I sat down heavily. Now that she was gone, there was no need for me to keep up appearances.

'So how did that go?' Nicky asked. I looked up to see him standing over me. Incongruously, he had a shotgun in his hands.

'Could have gone better,' I admitted, hearing a slight tremor in my voice and hoping he didn't hear it too.

'I did warn you she was pissed off.'

'Yeah. You did. Nicky, what is that thing you're holding?'

'A homage.'

'To . . . ?'

'Someone else's good idea. You told me the first time Juliet tried to love you to death, your landlady shot her with a air gun filled with rosary beads. I liked that a lot. And we live in a wicked world, so I keep this baby loaded day and night. Twelve ounces in each barrel.'

I shook my head to try to clear it. 'Jesus! Have you got a licence?'

'I'm a dead man, Castor. The law doesn't apply to dead men. Legally, this is a gun without an owner.'

I tried to stand, managed it with only one slight stumble. Nicky didn't put out a hand to steady me, but I didn't expect him to. Like I said, he's very chary of his own flesh, and even more so of his bones. He doesn't have any way of healing from a wound or an injury any more.

'Thanks for coming to my rescue, masked man,' I said, tilting the shotgun's barrels a little away from me so I didn't have to look them in the eye.

'Hey, for Lester Young I'll go out on a limb. You're looking a little sick, Castor. Whatever she did to you, she stuck it in deep. You should go home and sleep it off.'

I nodded, knowing that I wouldn't. 'Get onto that ward, Nicky,' I said. 'I want to know what Tlallik is, and what it does.'

'I'll call you,' Nicky said. He looked up at the screen, where Gabriel Byrne was leading his dysfunctional team to its destruction, trying to steal illusory riches for an illusory employer, conspiracy meeting meta-conspiracy. 'I guess she's only reverting to type,' he mused. 'Demons are like wolverines: they don't domesticate all that easily. But if she goes rogue, Castor . . .'

He didn't have to finish the sentence, and I didn't offer to finish it for him. My friends were already an endangered species, and going up against Juliet meant I'd have one fewer, win or lose. That was taking the optimistic view, of course, and assuming I survived.

I stayed for the rest of Nicky's triple bill. It felt like watching home movies.

It must have been getting on for midnight when I left

the Gaumont and headed for the Tube. Nicky had broken open a bottle of some Lebanese wine which he swore was as good as a French premier cru, and I'd accounted for most of it, but I felt depressingly sober as I hopped the last train back into London so I could slingshot back out to Turnpike Lane.

The Tube is a good place for me to think, usually. Very few people die on trains, and when you're moving fast you don't pick up emotional resonances from the landscape around you. Radio Death wasn't broadcasting. I was alone with my thoughts. The trouble was, my thoughts were a sea of turbulent shit.

Asmodeus was still out there, and he was hunting. Not just me, but everyone who'd ever meant anything to Rafi at any point in his life. He'd decided to celebrate his independence with a murder spree, starting (I had to *hope* it was starting) with Ginny Parris, the woman who'd played midwife when he was born again into Rafi's flesh, and with me, the one who'd welded him in good and tight once he was there.

In a way, it could work in my favour. If I had a plan, I could use myself as bait: bring the demon in close and then spring some kind of trap. But I didn't have a plan and I had no idea what form that trap might take.

It was maddening. There was a tune out there somewhere that would do the job, I knew that. I'd even heard it once, when Asmodeus himself played it for me in Imelda's parlour on the night she died. But then he'd done a number on me before I had a chance to get my whistle to my mouth. That space in my memory no longer existed. When I replayed the events of that night, there was just a hole where the tune ought to be, a wound in my mind that wouldn't heal.

But even if I found the tune, or reconstructed it, how in hell would I ever get to use it? If I summoned Asmodeus or got in close enough for him to be bound by the music, he'd tear me into sticky confetti before I got to the end of the first bar. Maybe with Juliet to run interference for me I'd have a fighting chance, but somehow this didn't seem like a good time to ask her.

That left Jenna-Jane's offer. My mind did a handbrake turn and shot off down a side street into places no less dark.

What was eating Juliet? Over the past couple of years she'd perfected her 'nobody here but us human beings' act to the point where you could almost forget what she was and mistake her for just another unfeasibly beautiful woman whose very existence impugned your manhood and left you feeling hollow and worthless. But now she was as bad as when she first came up on the express elevator from Hell, maybe worse. She'd sworn never to take another soul, but tonight I'd felt about three heartbeats away from oblivion. And those eyes . . . This wasn't the Juliet I knew. And I didn't like the glow-in-the-dark model one bit.

I was meant to be heading home, that was what I was telling myself. But somehow, without ever making an actual decision, I found myself taking the Northern Line and getting out at Archway. Whittington's Hospital is a short walk back up Highgate Hill, its new frontage looking cool and suave in white and blue.

Visiting hours must have wrapped up long ago, but nobody challenged me as I walked in off the street. Running the gauntlet of the restless dead for the second time in one day, I made my way to the coma ward. Once there though, I was faced with a locked door. Access to the ward was determined by a buzzer and intercom system – or in my case by waiting until an inattentive nurse came out and walked past me, then catching the door again before it swung closed.

Lisa Probert was in a side ward, by herself. A single bouquet of white lilies stood at the foot of the bed, in a plastic bucket serving as a makeshift vase. She looked worse than I remembered – she'd always been a big, loud-mouthed, sassy kid – unconscious, tied up with tubes and gauze, fed by drips and drained by catheters. She'd already lost enough body mass for it to show. She looked like a bird that had crashed into a kitchen window and fallen half-broken to the ground. On the dark skin below her eyes, which were only three-quarters closed, darker semicircles showed like bruises. Her lips glistened with gelatine, but the skin was dry and cracked just the same.

I sat beside her for a while, listening to her. I can do this with the living as well as the dead: open the doors of perception and catch the spoor of some immaterial essence, a soul or atman or whatever you want to call it, distilled into music. Lisa's music was a riotous polyphonic jumble. Its strength didn't depend on the strength of her body, and it didn't correlate in any direct way with what she was like as a person. It was just there, propagating outward from her at an acute angle to the world we know.

When I had the music fixed in my head, I took out my whistle and started to play it. It sounds stupid, but it's been known to work. I did it for Juliet once, when she was almost killed in a fight against the demon Moloch, and the tune had given her strength. It's the summoning, essentially: the first part of an exorcism, when you raise the spirit up and make it attend you. I was calling Lisa back into herself, or trying to. But after ten or fifteen minutes of playing she hadn't moved and there was no visible difference in her condition.

'Could you please tell me what you're doing here.' The voice yanked me out of the half-trance I sink into when I play. I looked up to see a ruddy-faced man in a white doctor's coat standing over me. The badge on his chest read DR SULLIVAN. He didn't look happy.

'The door was open,' I lied. 'I'm Felix Castor. I made the call to the emergency services the night Lisa was brought in here. I think you've got me down as next of kin.'

The doctor's expression changed, but it didn't soften. 'Oh,' he grunted. 'That's you, is it? We've tried to contact you a dozen times.'

'I know,' I said. 'I've been away.' It was as good an explanation as any – as good as I felt like giving him, anyway. 'I understand you want me to sign some permissions.'

'We did,' Doctor Sullivan corrected me. 'But we decided we couldn't wait any longer. Since Lisa has no living relatives, we were able to have her declared a ward of court. It went through yesterday, in your absence since you didn't respond to the court summons.' I remembered the large brown envelope on Pen's hall table. 'So there's nothing more we need from you now, Mr Castor, and your visiting rights are at my discretion. I'm going to have to ask you to leave.'

'I'd prefer to stay a while,' I said. 'I'll stop playing, if that will make a difference.' What I meant was that I'd hum under my breath. The tin whistle is a conduit for the power and helps to keep it focused, but it's not an essential part of the process.

'It won't,' said Doctor Sullivan. 'I'm asking you to leave right now. If you refuse, I'll call security.'

I weighed up the pros and cons, found that there weren't any pros. If I pissed this guy off, he could shut me out of here altogether. I had to be meek and mild now if I wanted to come back another time and try this stunt again.

'Visiting hours,' I said. 'When would they be?'

'Two o'clock until eight o'clock, seven days a week.' He remained in the doorway of the room, staring in at me. He obviously wasn't going to leave before I did. He didn't seem to trust me to find my own way out.

I gave it up, and let him escort me to the door. 'Is she responding at all?' I asked him on the way. 'Has there been any change in her condition?'

'None,' he said bluntly.

'And . . . the prognosis . . . ?'

'It's too early to say. There are lots of different physical and psychological mechanisms that can induce this kind of extreme fugue. Until we understand the aetiology of Lisa's condition, we can only treat the symptoms.'

'The aetiology? She saw her mother murdered . . .'

'And that was certainly a factor. Probably the dominant factor. But we can't assume it's the only one, and we're not in the habit of prescribing treatment on the basis of unsupported opinion.' He went on talking about brain chemistry and traumatic shock, but I'd stopped listening because something had begun niggling at the back of my mind. Since Lisa has no living relatives . . .

I stopped dead in my tracks. 'Who left the flowers?' I demanded.

'What?' Doctor Sullivan looked mystified.

'The lilies!' I didn't wait for an answer. I was already striding back down the corridor and into the small room where Lisa lay. 'Mr Castor!' the doctor yelled at my back. 'I'm calling security! I'm doing it right now.'

There was a note with the flowers, in a white envelope about three inches square, but since Lisa couldn't read it, nobody had bothered to open it. It was still tucked into the white ribbon that bound the stems of the flowers together. Lilies. White lilies for the dead.

The card inside the envelope bore a bloody thumbprint and ten words written in a tortured, angular hand so large that they filled the available space and in places overlapped each other.

I haven't forgotten her. All things in their place.

A

7

I remember a game we used to play as kids at school, a conceptual game which consisted of endless variations on the same question. If it was a choice between doing X or dying, which would you do? X might be buggering a dog, or killing your mum, or pissing in the communion wine. Usually the game started with stuff like that and then veered slowly but inexorably into even more fantastical waters. If it was a choice between having a third eyeball or dying, which would you do? If you were stuck on a tiny rock in the middle of outer space and it was a choice between eating a bucket of cockroaches or starving to death, which would you do? The fun part was comparing answers and picking holes in each other's code of ethics. We all knew that *some* things were so bad that dying was preferable, but we didn't always agree on what they were. You'd be amazed, for example, how many people found the cockroach diet a sticking point. I always said I'd tuck right in. I suspect that when it comes to the crunch, if I can put it that way, most people would.

But here I was, standing on the lonely heights of my own personal moral watershed. And I was frozen like a rabbit in headlights, dazzled by the appalling vista that presented itself on either hand.

Asmodeus had made it clear that he wasn't going to stop until everyone who knew Rafi was dead. The Anathemata could stop him, I was pretty sure, but they'd kill Rafi in the process – then go to confession, have their sins washed away and go out on the razzle.

Somewhere in the middle was Jenna-Jane Mulbridge. The devil at the crossroads.

The phone rang three times. The static on the line sounded like claws scratching at the bottom of a door: something scrabbling to be let in, or out.

Jenna-Jane picked up on the fourth ring. 'Hello?'

'I'm calling your bluff,' I said.

'Felix!' That same tone of simple and sincere delight that she always used whenever I was dragged kicking and thrashing back into her life. 'You left so suddenly this afternoon, I was afraid I'd offended you.'

It was a tempting phrase, just hanging there in the crackling void. But there was no point taking the cheap shots, not if I was dining from the à la carte menu. 'You've been after Asmodeus for years,' I said. 'We do it my way, and I promise you, you'll get him. Yes or no. Which is it going to be?'

'That's not something you can guarantee, Felix,' Jenna-Jane chided me, using another tone I knew well from times past – the more-in-sorrow-than-in-anger one. 'From my point of view, you're asking me to divert a lot of the resources of my department into a hunt that might not bear any fruit at all. I'm asking you, in return, to shore up those resources by offering me your own professional services – not in the longer term, but just while this operation is in progress. Just until we have Asmodeus under restraint.'

I laughed in spite of myself. 'You make that sound so reasonable!' I said. 'My professional services. Who do you want me to entrap, Jenna-Jane? Who do you want me to destroy? I mean, give it a name. Let me know exactly how much I'm going to hate myself in the morning.'

Jenna-Jane sighed a little theatrically. 'I can accommodate your scruples, Felix,' she said, like a waitress confirming that the restaurant did indeed have a vegetarian option. 'You wouldn't be required to do anything that made you feel uneasy or compromised.'

'What, you want me to sweep the floors? Make the coffee?'

'I want you to investigate a situation and then advise on it.'

'What kind of situation?' I felt like I was sniffing around the outline of a bear trap only half-hidden among the leaves on the forest floor.

'A haunting.'

'You've already got exorcists, Jenna-Jane. You've got an army of exorcists. Why not get one of them to advise you?'

'I've put several of them onto this case already. None of them has been able to account for it or eradicate it.'

'I don't do eradications any more.'

'So I've heard. But you do offer spiritual services.' She said the words with a slightly ironic emphasis. It was what the sign on my office door said: FELIX CASTOR, SPIRITUAL SERVICES. I felt it covered enough sins to give me a running start.

'Question stands,' I said. 'Why me?'

'Because we've hit a stone wall, frankly. And this is a new phenomenon, in some ways. It's something I want to have explained to me, Felix, and that's what you'd be offering me: an explanation.'

'And you'd be offering me . . . ?'

'You know the answer to that. That's why you came to me in the first place. Oh, we'd pay you, of course. Initially you'd be on a probationary contract. The term for that is usually a week or a month, but given our past history, perhaps we should review your progress after the first three days. Your stipend for those three days would be at an emergency rate of a hundred pounds a day, after tax. But that isn't the issue, is it? I have an equipment and skills base uniquely suited to finding and capturing Asmodeus. Alive. Intact. With a minimum of damage to the host body he's currently using. I can get you your friend back, in other words. I can bring Rafael Ditko back into some kind of secure and stable environment. I may even be able to excise the thing that's living in him.'

'I'll think about it,' I said.

If it was a choice between working for Jenna-Jane Mulbridge or eating a bucket of cockroaches, which would you do?

I wasn't kidding anyone but myself. I called her back about two hours later, which at least gave me the satisfaction of waking her up after she'd gone to bed, and spat out the two words that would make everything else happen, for good or bad.

'I'm in.'

'Excellent,' said Jenna-Jane briskly. 'So happy to have you back, Felix. 'It's like old times.'

I could only cross my fingers and hope that she was wrong.

* * *

Pen had already retired to bed when I let myself in, or at least all the lights were out, and there was no sound either from the basement or from her first-floor bedroom. I trudged up the remaining two flights of stairs, lay down on the bed with good intentions about getting undressed and getting under the covers, and was dragged down immediately into an exhausted sleep.

There were dreams, but they were of the kind you always get when you're so tired you're almost sick with it: fragmentary, repetitive, meaningless, anchored more in formless feelings than in comprehensible images. The dominant feeling was urgency – the sense of something important that I'd forgotten and still needed to do. I stumbled from one half-imagined scenario into another, locking and bolting doors, looking for car keys, turning off gas rings, but the feeling persisted. If anything, it got worse. Music was playing somewhere: a tune I knew and really didn't like at all. It sounded something like a waltz played backwards, the notes of the violins sucking themselves up into a dimensionless point and disappearing into themselves instead of expanding and reverberating. A waltz from Hell. I knew bad things would happen if I danced to it.

I woke an hour or maybe two hours later, in pitch dark. The music was still there, playing not in the air but in my mind. Something dead or unborn was nearby, and I knew its pattern as well as I knew my own face in the mirror.

I got out of bed, crossed to the window and looked out.

He was standing at the bottom of the drive, his gaze fixed on the front door of the house. Absolutely motionless, his arms at his sides, he was a darker stain on the fabric of the night.

'Asmodeus,' I murmured.

As though he'd heard me, he raised his head and looked up at my window. I couldn't see his eyes but I could feel his stare like a physical pressure against the surface of my skin.

I kicked off my shoes, shrugged my greatcoat on and walked back down to the front hall, taking care to make no sound as I passed Pen's room. I unlocked the street door, feeling the skin between my shoulder blades prickle even though I knew rationally that the door – as a physical barrier – made no difference to whether or not Asmodeus could enter the house. It was Pen's wards that were keeping him out, and nothing else.

Asmodeus was still standing in the same place, and he was still staring up at the window under the eaves where I'd been standing a minute before.

Mindful of what Pen had said about seeding the garden with stay-nots, I took a calculated risk and walked out onto the front step – two paces away from the house, then three. Asmodeus still didn't move, but I didn't take my eyes off him for a second. If he did attack, I wanted to be sure I could put the door – which Pen had blessed and anointed and talked to and generally strengthened with her own will every day for the past six or seven years – between us before he got in close enough to do me any damage.

'The three stars in a row,' I said, 'that's Orion's belt.'

Asmodeus turned slightly to look at the constellation, which was right above us. He nodded.

'Really?' he demanded, in a grating, metal-on-metal voice.

'Really.'

'Well you know what that means, Castor.'

'No. What does it mean?'

'That Orion wasn't considered a suicide risk.' He grinned mirthlessly at his own joke, flashing teeth that didn't look as though they'd fit inside a human mouth. Flesh is a plastic material to demons, but Asmodeus had never bothered to change Rafi's body very much. It looked as though he'd done a fair bit of redecorating since I'd seen him last, though. He was both taller and broader across the shoulders, with muscular forearms which tautened the ripped fabric of his shirt. His arms looked longer, and so did his fingers – not long enough to make him look simian, but subtly out of proportion with the rest of the body.

'Did you catch your bus okay?' I asked.

Asmodeus stopped laughing. He shook his head at me disapprovingly.

'I told you once that you were missing the big picture,' he said. 'That you don't know the right questions to ask. That you have no idea what's really happening, or how you fit into it.'

'I remember,' I agreed. 'Didn't stop me from whipping you back to kennel the last time you stuck your nose out.'

Asmodeus flexed those overlong fingers, very slowly. He seemed to be measuring the distance between us, and I tensed to run. Maybe Pen's new stay-nots would hold the demon back, and if they broke maybe they'd still slow him down enough for me to get back over the threshold of the house, where the older, many-times-inscribed wards would protect me. I didn't want to bet my life on those maybes.

But Asmodeus still didn't move. 'I'm kind of glad I didn't finish you off last night,' he grated. 'I really ought to build up to it properly. It was just the heat of the moment. Seeing you there, and feeling Ditko pull back from the thought of it. He's still seeing you as a way out, Castor. When you die, it's gonna be a real blow to him. But personally I think that ship has sailed. I'm making my own arragements now.'

'Me too,' I said.

'So I'm not here to kill you. Or Ditko's whore. You can relax. I just wheeled him over to take a look at the old place.' He snickered, making the noise a blade makes on a strop. 'Build up his morale a little. You want to say hello?'

For a moment I thought I'd misheard him. 'Say hello?' I repeated stupidly.

'To your old friend. He's right here, listening. Just like he was last night. Fuck, wake the redhead up and she can even have a conjugal visit.'

'Yeah,' I said, ignoring this last suggestion. 'I'd like to talk to him.'

The demon bowed his head and was silent for a moment. Then, still staring at the ground, he spoke in a different voice, a voice that was as faint as a day-old echo. 'Fix?'

'Rafi. I'm here.'

'I know. I know. My God, Fix, he's got me . . . staring out of the window here. I can't stop him, but I have to watch . . .' He gave a choking sob. 'Ginny!'

'Ginny got you into this mess in the first place, Rafi.'

It was meant to console him, but I realised even as I was saying it that it wouldn't have that effect. 'She was working for Anton Fanke – the grand panjandrum. She was just using you.'

'We were using each other.' Rafi's voice was barely a whisper. I took a step forward, straining to hear it. 'I knew what she was, Fix. And it's not as though I loved her. I've never loved anyone except Pen. But . . .' He gave another sob and lapsed into silence. One of the dark figure's arms twitched slightly in a vague, abortive gesture – some random nerve impulse of Rafi's getting past Asmodeus' guard – but only for a fraction of a second. 'She didn't deserve what she got.'

'I'm going to free you,' I promised him.

'Sound familiar?' The demon's voice intervening, forcing itself out of Rafi's mouth like hissing steam out of a pipe. 'He lives like fucking Nero, Ditko: he fiddles while you burn. Three years, and all he's ever done is lie to you. He's lying now. You belong to me, and there's nothing he can do to stop it. I'm so sure of that, I'm not even going to bother to kill him just yet. We'll leave him till the end.'

'I will nail him, Rafi,' I insisted, ignoring the demon's taunts. 'I'm onto it, I swear to you. The bastard won't even see me coming.'

'Fix . . .' Rafi's voice again, a gasping sigh at the lower limit of audibility. 'Tell my father . . . and Jovan . . . Tell them I'm sorry. Do that for me. Please.'

And then nothing. Slowly Asmodeus straightened until his gaze met mine again. 'I meant what I said,' he grated. 'I'll kill you last, Castor. And it won't be all at once. I'm thinking of going home for a while, when I'm free of this meat: I'll take you along as food for the journey. In the meantime . . . breast pocket, left-hand side.'

Something dropped out of his sleeve into his hand, glinting momentarily in the light from a street lamp. I ducked reflexively, but Asmodeus was so much faster than me that his arm was back at his side before I'd even registered that it had flicked up and out – long before my own lazy nervous system had carried the message down the royal road of my spine to my distant arms and legs.

I felt something like a punch in my shoulder. Dazed, I stared at the long slender handle of a knife sticking out of my own flesh. One of the buttons of the greatcoat hung in neatly severed halves on either side of it, dangling from separate lengths of the same frayed thread. The buttons were solid brass, but Asmodeus had thrown the knife with enough force to hammer straight through it, then through the thick cloth, and still embed itself an inch or so deep into the soft flesh below my collarbone.

'I only said I wouldn't kill you,' Asmodeus snickered. 'That doesn't stop me from whittling you into a more interesting shape.'

My teeth clenched on the pain, I groped inside my coat for my whistle, but I'm a southpaw, and it was my left shoulder that Asmodeus had hit, so my movements were jerky and uncoordinated. The demon watched in silent amusement.

I got the instrument out at last and fitted it to my lips. I started to play the opening notes of a tune: not a banishing but a soporific, a piece of music I'd composed for Rafi during the long months when he was stuck in his silver-lined cell at the Charles Stanger Care Home. Asmodeus just laughed and walked away, seemingly unaffected.

'Be seeing you, Castor,' he called over his shoulder. 'Eventually.'

'First of all, he's lying,' Jenna-Jane said. She said it in a didactic tone, like a maths teacher stating an axiom. 'So a logical question to ask would be why.'

We were in her office, and it was still early enough in the day for the workmen not to have clocked on. There was silence throughout the vast building, and a slightly disconcerting echo to our words.

'About what?' I demanded, probably sounding childishly truculent. 'He meant what he said about not wanting to kill me yet. I'm not dead, am I? *Ecce homo*, ergo elk.'

Reflexively, I rubbed my shoulder. It hurt like hell. The knife hadn't gone in too deep, all things considered, but it had been thrown with spectacular force. I was bruised as well as cut, and my arm had already stiffened in spite of Pen's expert ministrations.

'But his motives for not killing you are far from clear.' Jenna-Jane leaned back in her seat, one finger touched to the point of her chin. 'Certainly he needs nothing from you now. As he said, he no longer believes you can free him from Ditko's flesh.'

'What if that's the lie?' I threw in for the sake of argument,

Jenna-Jane shook her head brusquely. 'He's removed himself from your sphere of influence. If he had any faith in your abilities, or your efforts, he would have stayed where he was, in Imelda Probert's custody. Or else, when he left there, he would have come to you and made his demands clear. No, it's something else, Felix. He chose his moment. Oh, I know the Anathemata gave him the opening which he seized on to escape, but I believe he acted on a decision he'd already made. He has a project, and you are a part of it.'

'You just said he didn't need me.'

'As an exorcist,' Jenna-Jane amended, with a touch of impatience. 'He doesn't need you in a professional capacity. But he is still interested in you. He sought you out on no fewer than three occasions, first in Brixton and then at Pamela Bruckner's house. He hovers around you, and he lets you see him doing it. I don't believe for a moment that's random.'

'What is it then?' The ache in my shoulder and chest made me terse.

Jenna-Jane was silent for a moment, musing. 'Something we can exploit,' she said at last. She stood up and crossed to a filing cabinet, where she opened the second drawer and took out the file she wanted without hesitation, seeming to know exactly where it was. She brought it back to the desk.

'The problem resolves itself into two problems,' she said, as she took her seat again. 'Finding Asmodeus, and dealing with him once we have him. You, Felix, are probably the key to the first of those. At least you are our default option. If all else fails, it's reasonable to hope that the demon will come to you.

'The second part of the equation will tax us more. We need a mechanism that will bring Asmodeus into our power without permanently harming Ditko.' She was leafing through the file now, holding it so that I couldn't see its contents. 'You say you crafted a lullaby? A sedative of some kind?'

I nodded. 'I used to use it on Rafi when he was at the Stanger. And then I worked on it some more with Imelda. It seems to knock Asmodeus offline for a while. Sometimes it sends Rafi to sleep too, but other times it lets him be himself for a while.'

'May I hear it?'

Wincing, I took out my whistle. I played a few repetitions of the tune, clumsily and stiffly. When I'd finished, Jenna-Jane nodded. She had that schoolteacherly look on her face again, as if she'd been listening to a proposition in pure logic.

'I'd like you to record that for our technical team,' she said. 'Before you leave today.'

I made a negative gesture. I didn't want Jenna-Jane and her white-coated cut-throats to go chasing up any blind alleys, diverting as that might have been at any other time. 'I tried it on Asmodeus last night,' I told her. 'He just ignored it.'

'But it worked in the past.'

'It worked when I had him as a captive audience,' I said, pointing out the obvious. 'It's slow, J-J. It does the job, but it's slow. It's never going to make a difference in an ambush.'

'My people will look at it,' she said. 'Dissect it. Possibly turn it into something that works a little better.'

'How?'

She gave me an austere look, hearing the scepticism in my voice. 'Amplification,' she said. 'Distortion. Tonal variation. Peak–trough manipulation. Subsonic harmonic mapping. Instrumental translation. Modal translation. Conceptual reflection and repetition.' She didn't bother to wait for my inevitable reductionist put-down. 'The craft has developed its own specialised vocabulary here at St Mary's, Felix,' she said. 'Its own theoretical under-pinnings. Trust me. You made the right decision when you came to me. Now, I wanted to pick your brains on two other matters.'

'Go on.'

'The first is the one that Gentle raised with you yesterday. The succubus, Ajulutsikael. I have it on the very best authority that what Gentle said is correct: that the demon remained on Earth after she was raised to kill you, and that you remained on . . . shall I say, friendly terms with her.'

I waited her out. Knowing how sharp she was, I wasn't prepared to say one word on that particular subject. There was always a chance that I'd give something away without meaning to.

'She ought to be in my custody,' J-J said.

I kept up the deadpan for as long as I needed to. Finally, Jenna-Jane sighed theatrically.

'Very well,' she murmured. 'That will have to be a discussion for another day.'

She took a single sheet of paper out of the file and set it down in front of me. It was a badly photocopied pass-port photograph. Badly enough that it took me a few seconds to identify the person I was looking at.

'Trudie Pax,' I said.

'Yes,' Jenna-Jane confirmed. 'She's applied for a position

here at the MOU, as an exorcist. I've already assigned her to a team, on a probationary basis. What do you know about her?'

I paused for a couple of seconds of reflection. Was J-J really using me as a reference for Trudie, or was this some kind of loyalty test for me? Given the circumstances in which my path and Trudie's had last crossed, it could be either. But ultimately I didn't care enough about this political bullshit to lie.

'She gets the job done,' I said.

'You've worked with her?'

'Yes. Recently. When I was trying to clear up that mess at the Salisbury. You probably read about it in the papers.'

'The riots. Yes, I was aware that something interesting was happening there, and that you were involved in some way. I offered my services, but the detective in charge of the operation – Trotwood, Deadwood, something of that nature – declined. So you and Miss Pax performed an exorcism together?'

'No, a summoning. She's good.'

'But you don't like her?'

'She was part of Gwillam's bunch. You know how much I love religious fanatics.'

'But you'd have no misgivings about working with her again?'

Another pause for thought. 'No,' I grunted at last. I prefer known quantities to unknown ones. Trudie hadn't flinched when the shit started flying.

'Good,' said Jenna-Jane. 'Because she's here now. And given her background, I was very much inclined to make her part of our Asmodeus plan.' She put the sheet back in the file, scribbled something on the inside of the file folder and closed it again.

'The plan,' I echoed sardonically. 'You mean amplification, distortion, attrition and general masturbation?'

Jenna-Jane looked at her watch, a little theatrically. 'I think it's time to introduce you to the rest of the team,' she said.

I followed Jenna-Jane, about as enthusiastically as Dante followed Vergil, down a maze of branching corridors into a room labelled STAFF LOUNGE. Even as a work-in-progress it was pretty well appointed: big enough for a couple of dozen people to chill out without bumping shoulders, widescreen TV, Tchibo coffee machine. I guess if you can afford to use pure silver as wallpaper, then a few comfy chairs and a coffee machine aren't going to break the bank.

Three men – one of them Gil McClennan – and a woman were sitting in a group at the far end of the room, talking animatedly, but they stopped and turned to face us as we came in. The woman stood, seemed about to put out her hand for me to shake and then thought better of it. After the discussion in J-J's office she came as no surprise, but I still found seeing her called up enough unpleasant memories to make me grit my teeth momentarily.

'Trudie Pax,' Jenna-Jane said.

'We've met,' I answered bluntly. The tall dark-haired woman flushed slightly and looked away. I noticed that she had several dozen thicknesses of string wound round each wrist. Where I conducted my exorcisms via music, Trudie channelled hers through the children's game of cat's cradle, making visual patterns where I made auditory ones.

I also noticed that she'd cut her hair extremely short. It had been a good decision. The ponytail she used to wear made her resemble a Lara Croft strippergram, whereas now she looked as though she'd switched role models and gone for Ellen Ripley.

'The newest member of our little family,' Jenna-Jane was saying. 'And she comes with truly impressive references.' Knowing all about Trudie's references, I decided the safest bet under the circumstances was to nod and say nothing.

'I'm not counting you as new, Felix,' Jenna-Jane went on, in a teasing voice that set my teeth on edge. 'I see you more in the light of a lost sheep who's come back into the fold.' She turned her attention to the two remaining strangers, who'd also stood. Gil McClennan remained resolutely seated. 'This is Victor Etheridge,' Jenna-Jane said, and the younger of the two gave me a nod. He had sandy-coloured hair, a slightly exophthalmic stare and a physique that made a hatstand look broad in the beam. He was wearing a jet-black suit over a jet-black T-shirt, which had the effect of making him fade into the background of his own outfit.

'Felix Castor,' he said. And then he winced, his head jerking to the side as though someone had punched him in the mouth. His eyes clenched shut, then opened again and looked at me sidelong. 'I'm really . . . very . . . I'm pleased, because . . . Pleased to meet you. Because . . . Peckham . . . Peckham Steiner always spoke of you with respect.'

The kid's head swung round again so that he could look at me full on. His expression was wide-eyed, expectant, as though he'd brought out the big guns and expected to see an appropriate response; but even leaving aside his curious delivery, dropping Steiner's name didn't impress me all that much. The crazed millionaire godfather of the London ghost-breaking scene had lost his marbles long before he died, and if this Etheridge character had been his protégé, he might be more of a liability than an asset.

'You were a friend of Steiner's?' I asked, keeping my tone as neutral as I could.

Etheridge stared at me, looking slightly perplexed as though the question was a tough one that he hadn't expected. 'He was my patron,' he said at last. 'He . . . yeah . . . was going to start a school, if you . . . For exorcists. A school. To teach his own skills to a younger generation. It never really got off the ground, but there were . . . he . . . three or four of us . . .' He tailed off, looking to Jenna-Jane like an actor asking for a prompt. She said nothing.

I resorted to the dumb nod again. I'd heard of that school before, and I knew damn well why it had never happened. In the last years of his life Steiner had had a million schemes. Some of them had come to pass – like the Oriflamme, the exorcists-only club on Castlebar Hill, and the exorcists' hostel that had become known as the Thames Collective (built as a houseboat, because ghosts can't cross running water) – but most had fallen by the wayside, forgotten, as Steiner moved on to the next big thing.

What was the matter with Etheridge? Finding no comfort or support from Jenna-Jane, he ducked his head again, slight tremors shaking his shoulders. He looked like a naughty schoolboy dragged up in front of the class to explain his misdemeanours and promise never to do it again. No, more than that: he looked damaged. A sort of faint, fuzzy-edged misery came off him in waves.

'And this is Samir Devani,' Jenna-Jane said. I shook hands with the last man. He had a book in his other hand, his thumb between the pages to mark his place: Kurt Vonnegut's *Man Without a Country*. He was Asian, well built and surprisingly tall, maybe a year or so younger than me but in much better shape. And, like everyone else in the room except Jenna-Jane and Etheridge, he was dressed down – as befitted a dirty job, in a denim shirt, slate-grey chinos and well-worn DMs. He gave me a thoughtful, appraising look, his eyes narrowing slightly, as if he was trying to remember where he'd seen me before.

'Looks like you've been in the wars,' he said. 'You're favouring that left arm. It's Sam, by the way.'

'Fix.' I said it automatically, and cursed myself silently as soon as the word was out of my mouth. I didn't intend to be on first-name terms with anyone here. Unlike me, they'd presumably chosen to be in Jenna-Jane's employ. I didn't owe any one of them the air to breathe, let alone civility. 'It's just an old war wound,' I finished tersely.

'We tend to work in groups of four or five,' Jenna-Jane said, forestalling any further getting-to-know-you chit-chat. 'I make the allocations myself, balancing different techniques so that each team can deal with a broad spectrum of supernormal phenomena. Trudie performs her bindings and exorcisms via a purely physical-manipulative modality, Samir by channelling a second personality, Gil by means of spirit drawing and Victor through actual prayer.'

'Who's on drums?' I asked. Samir laughed, and Jenna-Jane looked pained.

'We all deal with the emotional stresses of our peculiar line of work in our own individual ways,' she said dryly. 'Felix chooses to do so through inappropriate levity. He is, however, a very fine exorcist, and we can all be grateful that he's been unable, thus far, to push his comedy career to the professional level.'

I took the rap on the knuckles like a man.

'Okay,' I said, getting down to brass tacks. 'I'm thinking we'll start from what we know. Asmodeus has been staking out the house where I live, in Turnpike Lane. We need someone watching the house on a rota. Two someones, ideally. The rest of us can spread out across the city and scry towards the cardinal points until we get an echo. If we do that enough times, and if he's not moving around too much, we'll be able to zero in on him a bit at a time. Then when we think we've got it narrowed down enough, Jenna-Jane can bring in the heavies. We'll use nerve gas first – OPG, assuming you've got enough to go around. Soften him up with that, because in my experience he won't sit still long enough for us to try anything fancy. If we play our cards right, nobody ends up dead.'

The silence that met my little Agincourt speech was deafening. By turns, everyone looked to Jenna-Jane, who glanced at Gil and nodded. 'Mr McClennan,' she said.

'Everyone's already briefed,' said Gil, as if I hadn't spoken. 'I'll be briefing Castor on the Strand haunting later, but there's nothing we can do there until after dark, so the order of the day is Asmodeus. Pax and Etheridge are staying here to work on the raw data from the sightings. Pax is going to apply her own techniques to the map I was setting up. I'm still working through the grimoires with Klee and Middleton, so Sam and Castor can go over to the Stanger and grab us a focus. Sam's in charge on that little outing, Castor, and you speak when you're spoken to. Dr Webb, who's in charge over there, made it clear to me when we spoke that he hates your guts, and the only reason he's letting you back into the place at all is because of the respect he's got for Professor Mulbridge. Does anyone have any questions?'

I had one, but since it was 'What the *fuck*?' I didn't ask it. I didn't have to; J-J answered it anyway.

'You don't just walk in and head a team, Felix,' she pointed out reasonably. 'You've been away from the unit for a long time, and our operating methods have changed very significantly. Gil has my complete confidence, and I'm sure you'll find him an inspirational leader.'

She turned on her heel and left, with a final nod to my new colleagues.

'Any questions?' Gil asked again, in a voice that expected the answer no. 'Okay, then get moving, people. There'll be time enough to sleep when we're dead.'

'Or possibly not,' Samir observed scrupulously as we headed for the lift.

8

Samir seemed disposed to talk on the way to the Tube, and most of his talk consisted of questions. How long had I been on the staff at the MOU? Had I really been part of the team that raised Rosie Crucis? What did I think of Peckham Steiner's books? Was the London scene any different now than it had been ten years ago?

I fielded most of these queries with grunts and monosyllables. Sam was affable enough, but I really wasn't in the mood. Since I'd gone to bed the previous night, I'd been stabbed by a demon, patronised by Jenna-Jane and broken back to the rank of poor bloody infantry. On top of all that, being civil seemed like way too much effort.

But in the absence of any input from me, Sam had no trouble keeping up the conversation all by himself. He told me about how the 'shit', as he called it, had kicked in for him: how his secondary personality, who he referred to as Turk, had shown himself first in mischievous and even destructive ways – mocking his parents, picking fights with his friends. A posse of psychiatrists had examined Sam, and after flirting briefly with Tourette's syndrome had converged steadily on a verdict of acute psychosis. Medication of increasing ferocity failed to do anything except make him as dopey as a punched-out prizefighter. 'I was heading for a rubber room until I saw my first ghost,' Sam said, laughing as though he found all this genuinely funny now. 'Then Turk started swearing and catcalling and insulting it. And it just went away. Piecemeal. As though the words blew holes in it. Exorcism by fucking verbal abuse, can you believe that, Castor?'

I said I could. The window wasn't wide enough to say anything else.

'My mum and dad wanted me to carry on with the meds, but I was up and out. I'd had enough of that bloody game. And Turk was easier to control now, somehow. It was like he'd found something to occupy himself. He didn't mouth off at the living any more now he'd found the dead.' Sam laughed again. 'So yeah, my superpower is to tell ghosts to fuck off. It's ridiculous, really. But Professor Mulbridge loves me because I proved a point for her. There were already loads of exorcists who did it with words, but it was always either spells or prayers. She argued that any words would do, because the modality only has to make sense to the person who's using it.'

The modality, another of Jenna-Jane's favourite abstract nouns. Maybe it's easier to have theories about the way it all fits together if you can't actually do it yourself. Then it occurred to me that this massive theoretical construct that Jenna-Jane had created served the same purpose for her that my tin whistle did for me: it enabled her to touch the invisible world, and bring it within her grasp. For some reason, that insight didn't make me feel the slightest sense of kinship with her.

At the Stanger Care Home, Dr Webb predictably refused to see us himself, but detailed one of the male nurses to be at our disposal and give us whatever we needed. In the first instance, that meant access to Rafi's cell.

'We're looking for something that was close to him,' Sam explained. 'Physically or emotionally, doesn't matter which – best of all would be something that was both. Some object that he kept with him and thought about a lot. That's what makes a good focus.'

But there was nothing in Rafi's cell; there never had been. It was kept as bare as Mother Hubbard's cupboard because you never could tell what Asmodeus would take it into his head to use as a weapon. Nothing was safe in his hands, so the only option was to make sure his hands were empty. They were dangerous enough even then.

Sam wasn't discouraged. 'There's always something,' he said, crawling across the floor on his hands and knees, nose to the ground. 'It doesn't have to be big.'

'What's the focus for, exactly?' I asked him.

'For Trudie,' he explained – although in fact it explained nothing. 'She's got an idea. Well, it's Gil's idea, but she picked up on it because it fits in really well with the way she does her exorcisms normally. It's all about psychic geography. Scrying by sympathies, Gil calls it. It was pretty much theoretical until now, but Pax is sure she can make it work.'

Well, it stood to reason that the two of them would get along, I thought, surprised at how pissed-off that made me feel. I tried to focus on the job in hand. Something close to Rafi. Something he thought about a lot. 'We could go to Imelda Probert's house,' I pointed out. 'Most of his stuff is there.' My stomach knotted at the thought. Vivid images strobed in red and black in front of my eyes: Imelda's torn and broken body sprawled on bare boards, her crushed head resting in the crook of her daughter's arm. If we did go there, I might not even be able to bring myself to walk inside.

'Ditko only stayed there for a few weeks, didn't he?' Sam answered over his shoulder, sounding indifferent. 'He was stuck in here for years. Got to be a better bet.' He was combing the floor inch by inch with his fingertips. Trying to get into the game, I scanned the wall before me from floor to ceiling, right to left, then did a quarter-pirouette and started in on the next wall.

The walls were pure white – or rather impure white, disfigured by a million ancient and mercifully unidentifiable stains, but they shone with a silver lustre here and there where the demon had hammered at the plaster hard enough for the undercoat of metal to show through. Asmodeus didn't like silver. Proximity to silver weakened him and made him sluggish. Enough of it could hurt him, perhaps even kill him, but probably only if you heated it to 961 degrees Celsius and poured it in through the bastard's ear – which wouldn't do Rafi a whole lot of good either.

A particularly damaged area of the wall's surface caught and held my gaze. There were rucks and gouges in the plaster, near-vertical jags where it had come away in narrow strips. Maybe my mental picture was inaccurate. Maybe Asmodeus hadn't hammered on the walls at all. Maybe he'd attacked them in a different way.

Moving in closer, I traced the line of one of the gouges down to groin level and – unbelievably – hit the jackpot first time. Something pale and slightly curved protruded from the bottom end of the furrow where it tapered slightly to a point. The something was about a quarter of an inch long and shaped like a gibbous moon.

'Is it okay to touch the focus?' I asked Sam, who was still genuflecting in the far corner.

He looked up, surprised, responding to the suppressed excitement in my tone. 'It's better not to. What have you got?'

I pointed. 'Rafi's fingernail. He was clawing at the wall, and he tore it off clean.'

Sam swore loudly, or maybe that was Turk, rejoicing that the game was afoot. He came over to examine the prize, then gave me a ringing slap on the back. 'You clever bastard, Castor,' he said. 'We're in business.'

He fished the nail out with a pair of tweezers and dropped it into a ziplock bag, both items taken from a small kit in his jacket pocket. Watching this manoeuvre closely, I noticed that he was wearing a Spiro Agnew watch: the punchline to the ancient joke *What does Mickey Mouse wear on his wrist?* and as far as I knew the only public memorial Richard Nixon's VP had ever earned.

He took out his mobile, flicked it open, and was instantly immersed in a long technical discussion with Gil McClennan. 'Fingernail. Yeah. Well there's no way of telling that, is there, but it was a fucking *part* of him. About three millimetres wide and eight long. Yeah, exactly. Well there's nothing else here. The nurse said they incinerated all his clothes after he escaped . . .'

The words washed over me, became abstract sounds as I stopped listening. I was feeling hot, light-headed and more than a little claustrophobic in the ten-by-ten-by-ten cube where my friend had spent three years of his life. I stepped out of the cell into the corridor. It wasn't much better, but right then I preferred the sour institutional stink and the yells and moans of distressed patients in the middle distance to the oppressive silence and stillness of Rafi's cell. I breathed in and then out, slowly, releasing a tension I hadn't felt building.

With immaculate timing, a young girl ran through the solid wall to my left, passed straight through me and kept on going, vanishing into the solid wall to my right. I'm not normally startled by ghosts, but the suddenness of her appearance and the fizz of psychic static as we intersected made me stiffen and shudder. Three more phantom girls streaked past, hot on the tail of the first and not even seeming to notice me as they pelted through me. My hair prickled, the neon tube above my head flickered once, and they were gone. The faintest echo of a giggle hung in the air for a moment, distorting as it faded.

I leaned against the wall, my heart beating fast and my momentary calm well and truly shattered. 'We already asked,' Sam's voice came from inside Rafi's room. 'No, they didn't keep anything . . .'

I knew those ghosts well. Three of them had died more than half a century ago, murdered by the psychopath after whom the Charles Stanger Care Home was named. The fourth – the one in the lead – had only been dead a little more than a year. Abigail Torrington. I'd been hired to find her when she went missing – already deceased – from her parents' house, but there had been a lot more to that commission than met the eye, and a lot of blood under the bridge before I had the light-bulb moment and introduced dead Abbie to her new posse. The Stanger ghosts had welcomed her with open arms, and she fitted right in here.

Why they *stayed* here was more of a mystery. I'd cut them loose with one of my better tunes, a partial exorcism that permitted them to roam as far as they liked away from this sick building with its self-and-mutually-tortured inmates. And they did roam. They were a common sight in the West End, and there were reported sightings as far afield as Greenwich and Stanmore. But for some reason they always came back. This was where they lived, in spite of everything.

An association of some kind stirred in my mind.

'Everything all right?' Sam asked, stepping out into the corridor and slamming the door behind him. The half-formed idea skittered away to the back of my mind and hid itself under a clump of childhood traumas.

'Fine,' I said. 'Are we good?'

Sam made a *tch* sound. 'Gil says we should have gone for something bigger,' he grumbled. 'Doesn't understand a bloody thing, that man. The shit's like static electricity, isn't it? It focuses to a point. I know this will do the job.'

We went back to the MOU, Sam regaling me all the way with war stories about some of the weird stuff he'd seen and dealt with while he was working for Jenna-Jane. He had a lot more respect for her than he did for Gil, it seemed. I was curious to know how he felt about the Gulag in J-J's basement, but I'd probably have to wait until I knew him better before I could ask.

Trudie received the fingernail with genuine excitement. We found her and Etheridge in one of the rooms that hadn't been redecorated yet, a builder's shell with bare plasterboard walls scrawled with measurements and instructions for the electricians. There were no wall sockets, but someone had run an extension cord from the room next door and an anglepoise lamp had been plugged into it. The lamp was on the floor, so the room had adequate lighting up to about knee level.

The two of them had laid out a colossal map on a row of trestle tables. It was a composite, made from about thirty Ordnance Survey maps taped together at the edges, and it covered most of London, from Oakwood in the north to Richmond in the south. Etheridge looked happy taping the edges of the maps together. He still twitched and flinched from time to time, but he seemed calmer than when he'd tied himself in knots trying to say hello to me. And he couldn't do enough for Trudie. He kept showing her the progress he'd made so she could thank him and he could say it was no problem, a ritual that was repeated three times while I was there.

'This is definitely Ditko's?' Trudie demanded, tipping the bag and allowing the jagged fragment of fingernail, brown with blood along one edge, to slide out onto an unused table on which a carpenter's hammer and a dozen or so six-inch nails were lying. She was looking at me, but Sam answered.

'It was stuck in the wall,' he said. 'We checked, and the cell hasn't been assigned to anyone else since Ditko left. Webb doesn't think it will be. You couldn't stick a human being in a place like that; it'd be like Guantanamo Bay!'

I started to speak, but Trudie beat me to the punch. 'Rafi Ditko *is* a human being,' she said sharply. 'He's just carrying the demon the way you carry a virus or a para-site. It's not a good idea to forget that, Sam.'

Sam put up his hands in a mean-you-no-harm gesture. 'Sorry to offend your liberal sensibilities, Pax. I didn't know you were a Breather.'

That word – that label – can be almost value-neutral in everyday use; spoken by an exorcist, it always carries an implied insult. The Breath of Life movement is the Amnesty International of the Twilight Zone, its members lobbying to extend human rights to the risen dead. If they ever manage this, exorcism as a profession will vanish overnight, so there's a lot of cordial hatred on both sides.

Trudie didn't acknowledge the slur. She was passing her hands over the broken fingernail, first the left and then the right, moving them in small circles as though she was making some kind of blessing.

'Oh yes,' she said, her voice sinking almost to a whisper. 'It's his. It's good, Sam. It's very good.'

'You're welcome,' said Sam. He looked at me over Trudie's head, rolling his eyes.

'Shall I fix up the plumb line?' Etheridge asked, looking to Trudie for another pat on the head. Possibly he was even younger than he looked. Jenna-Jane did the university milk rounds these days. She could have snatched this kid right out of the cradle. I wondered if he'd been in better nick when she acquired him.

'No.' Trudie shot him a distracted smile. 'Not yet, Victor. I need to charge up. And Gil said we weren't to start until he was here. Perhaps you could go tell him we're ready?'

Etheridge scooted off eagerly to do her bidding, while she made some more passes with her hands over the nail. 'I think this might actually work,' she murmured. 'I wasn't sure, but . . . I'm feeling it really clearly.'

She straightened and started to unwind the string from her hands. I suddenly had an inkling of how she was going to put all these bizarre ingredients together, but it was such an insane idea I thought I must be wrong.

Voices in the corridor told me that Gil and Etheridge were returning. Then Gil himself breezed in, waving his arms like a conductor. 'All right,' he said. 'I'm here. Get it moving, Pax. This isn't the only thing on the clipboard.'

Trudie didn't bother to answer. She'd unwound about three feet of string from each hand now. They were loops, but she'd untied the knot in each one to unravel them to their full extent, and now she was tying them together into a single length.

While she worked Etheridge scooped up the hammer and one of the nails, jumped up onto a chair and drove the nail deep into the bald plasterboard of the ceiling. Trudie passed him one end of the string and he made it fast around the nail with an inelegant lasso knot.

'Okay,' he said. 'It's . . . we're . . .'

'Thank you, Victor,' Pax said gently.

Since Etheridge had mentioned a plumb line, I thought Trudie might actually tie the broken fingernail to the other end of the string and make the most lightly weighted pendulum in the history of the world. What she did was even stranger than that, if anything. She tied another lasso knot in the free end of the string, looped it over her hand and lowered her arm again until the string was taut. It meant that her hand could only move in a circle defined by the length of the string.

As we watched in silence, she moved her hand to left and right, up and down over the map, keeping the string stretched out tight so there was no give in it. She started in the centre, and the arcs at first were very tight, but they got wider as she worked. Her eyes were closed, and there was a look of intense concentration on her face.

'You should probably start somewhere where he's actually been,' Sam pointed out, but Trudie winced and Etheridge raised a finger to his lips, as stern as a school librarian.

Trudie went back to the centre and started again, this time moving out in long slow loops. Etheridge had now picked up a pen from somewhere and stood expectantly by her side, but she didn't speak.

The area of the map was huge, but her hand was a good two feet above it. The circles she was describing made up the cross section of a cone that had its base on the map, so she was making relatively small movements to cover wide areas.

After a couple of minutes of this, she went back to the centre for a third time. Sam let out a long breath, like a sigh, and that seemed to break the spell. 'Are you getting anything?' Gil demanded a little irritably.

Trudie looked him straight in the eye. 'Yes,' she said. 'I am. But it's not directional yet. There's a sense of him, and it changes when I move but . . . randomly, almost. It's not like I'm getting warmer or colder.'

'Maybe you want to keep the focus in the loop,' I said.

She gave me a look, irritated or just uncomprehending. 'What?' she demanded.

I pointed to the nail, still lying on the table. 'You're relying on a second-hand contact,' I said. 'Slip the finger-nail under the string so it's pressed against your palm.

Like calls to like, right? That's the principle here. Also, you want to get your hand in closer to the map. That's the hardest part, logistically, but what's the use of getting a bite that could come from anywhere between Charing Cross Road and Dulwich? If you're in close, that sense of direction might come through a bit more strongly.'

They all stared at me for a moment, in silence.

'Do it,' Gil grunted and walked out. Then he stuck his head back in through the doorway and said, 'Castor, you're with me.'

I threw Trudie a nod and followed him out. It was a cold nod, but there was grudging respect in it. Trudie was trying to do something I'd never managed to do myself. To use Jenna-Jane's cute terminology, she was making fine adjustments to her modality.

Every exorcist has their own special way of doing the necessary: a tin whistle, a typewriter, a deck of cards, any damn thing you can think of. It's the same knack in each and every one of us, the same synapses closing somewhere and making the same things happen, but the tools we use depend on who we are and where we've been. That's a pretty good indication that the tools don't ultimately matter; they only reflect our experience, our tastes, our comfort zones. Faced with the unknowable, we hide behind the known and take potshots from cover.

I'd seen Trudie perform an exorcism, or try to. She had woven the string around her fingers in intricate and changing patterns, like kids do in the game of cat's cradle. But Trudie knew that the string was just a security blanket. The real power was inside her, and it used the string as an excuse to come out and play. So now she was making it work for her in a different way. Whether she succeeded or failed, she deserved a certain amount of credit just for trying.

On the other hand, she'd gone from Gwillam's employ straight into Jenna-Jane's – from the foam-flecked zealots to the necro-vivisectionists – so what the hell did I care? I only had to work with her.

'You're on late shift tonight,' Gil said, as we rode the lift down to the first floor. 'Midnight. Charing Cross station, Strand north-side exit. Bring your whistle. In the meantime, Professor Mulbridge wants to record you playing your tune. She thinks we can learn something from it.' There was a sardonic edge to his voice.

'You don't agree?' I asked mildly.

'I think if you knew how to deal with Asmodeus, you would have done it years ago,' Gil said. 'The fact that you're here at all means you're out of ideas.'

'And the fact that J-J took me back?' I asked. 'What does that mean? I got the distinct impression she's got some shit going on that you people can't deal with.'

The lift doors opened with a flattened *pinging* sound, like a bullet bouncing off a bum coin. Gil laughed with what sounded like real amusement. 'Yeah,' he said. 'You're her favourite ghost-breaker. But it's not because you're any good. It's just because you're the one that got away.' He pointed down the corridor. 'Lab 3,' he said. 'They're expecting you.'

I started to walk away.

'Castor.'

I turned back. Gil was holding the lift door open with his finger on the button. 'She hates you for that too,' he said.

'For leaving, I mean. So the way I see it, she's going to fuck you into roadkill sooner or later.'

'Thanks for the warning,' I said.

Gil shook his head. 'It would only be a warning if it was going to make a difference,' he said. 'You killed a good man, you bastard. A father. You wrecked a family.' The lift *pinged* again several times, and the servos in the doors groaned as they tried to close.

'Gabe raised a demon,' I pointed out. 'It killed him. All I did was get out from between them.'

'And then the demon ended up as your partner. Watch your back, Castor. Because I will be.'

He took his finger off the button, and the doors slid shut between us. The lift mechanism whined slightly as it carried him back up to the second floor.

In Lab 3 a stolid, stocky guy who looked more like a longshoreman than a medical technician was tweaking the controls of a graphic equaliser as big as a two-car garage. 'You're Castor?' he demanded. 'Great. I'm Davey Nathan. Let's do this thing. I got a shit-load of transcriptions piling up here.' He hustled me into a soundproofed booth rigged up in a space that might once have been a toilet cubicle. He had a transatlantic drawl, and when I asked him where he was from he said he was on loan from the CIA. 'Seriously,' he added, looking at me warily in case I was going to question his word.

'Langley?' I asked.

'No, not Langley exactly,' he admitted, looking sheepish. 'OSINT. Open Source Intelligence. We're just geeks, really, sieving publicly available sources for useful information. Only we don't say useful. We say *actionable*.'

'How'd you wind up here?' I asked.

Nathan shrugged morosely. 'Pissed off the wrong people, Mister C. Pissed off all the wrong people, from God on down. But fuck, you know? *A bi gezunt . . .*'

'A what?'

'Yiddish. Means "so long as you've got your health . . ." But you have to look unhappy when you say it.'

We did some run-throughs for acoustics, then he locked me in and I played my 'Etude for Hell-spawn', the tune I'd developed to give Asmodeus a sedative when I'd first discovered that I couldn't exorcise him. The recording sounded okay to me on playback, but Nathan wasn't happy with it.

'It goes way flat around 8,000 hertz,' he grumbled. 'This equaliser is a piece of shit. Go on back inside and hit me again. I'm gonna fuck with the RF bias.'

The second take sounded identical to the first, but Nathan liked it better. 'Three's the charm,' he said. 'Go on, we'll nail it. Trust me.'

Apparently we nailed it. At any rate, there wasn't a fourth take. I thanked Nathan for his efforts and asked him what the transcriptions were he was working on.

'Fifty per cent of my time,' he said, throwing his hands in the air in exasperation. 'The ghost-breakers go to some place where there's a spook – in your sense rather than the CIA sense – and they record it. Only the sound doesn't show up on tape, right? When ghosts talk, either they don't make the air vibrate at all or they got some way of hitting the human ear selectively. So that's what I'm looking for – a wiretap for the fucking spirit world. I told Professor M., if we find it, it's gonna be just white noise. A billion voices all at once. Only we won't find it unless it propagates through the air and why the hell should it? So that's what I'm wasting my life on. All because I missed some survivalists saying, "Let's all make a bomb." I didn't think they could tie their own goddamned shoelaces.'

I was about to leave Nathan with his woes, but a few things clicked together in my mind before I got to the door, and I turned on the threshold. 'Yeah?' he asked.

'The transcriptions. Fifty per cent of your time?'

He shrugged. 'Give or take.'

'Is the other fifty per cent Rosie Crucis?'

'Give the man a cigar. Yeah. She gets an hour with either the professor or that McClennan guy twice a week. I tape the conversations and index them.'

'You can keep the cigar,' I told him, 'but how about the combination for the keypad on her door? Rosie and me go back a long way. And it's been a while since we got to talk.'

Nathan shook his head theatrically, as though to snap himself out of a trance. 'Security, Castor. It's called that because it's meant to be secure.'

I took a long slow look around the cramped room. 'You worried about losing your job?' I asked.

Nathan laughed full-throatedly. 'Fuck it,' he said. 'You remember that battle you guys fought, against the French?'

'Oh man. There've been so many . . .'

'The one that mattered. The one where they kicked your asses all over the countryside and then moved into the big house.'

'Hastings.'

'Bingo. Add twenty, and that's your magic number.'

'Thanks, Nathan. You're a mensch.'

His face lit up at the Yiddishism. '*A shaynem dank dir im pupik*, Castor. You're welcome.'

I went down to street level and, after a couple of wrong turns, found Rosie's door. I tapped the keys and the lock clicked. 1086. Jenna-Jane hadn't had the Battle of Hastings in mind when she set that code; she was thinking of the Domesday Book. That was an enterprise after her own heart.

I opened the door and stepped inside. It was like walking into another world. Rosie's quarters were schizophrenic in the extreme. The bed was a hospital bed, big and ugly, mounted on a hydraulic pillar for raising and lowering and adjusting of angles. And beside the bed there was a fearsome assemblage of machines with red LED readouts and old-fashioned pressure dials on their fascias. But elsewhere there was a sofa, table and chairs, a TV, cheap prints on the walls – evidence of a general effort to make this institutional space, which in reality was a prison cell, look a little like home.

Rosie was in bed, which is where she spends most of her time these days. It's a side effect of the wards that J-J uses to keep her contained, and it's worsened steadily over the years. She spends about half of every day asleep, and it never takes very much effort or emotion to exhaust her. The weird thing is that these symptoms persist and repeat themselves in every body she occupies.

Currently her fleshly tabernacle was male. A guy of about twenty stared back at me from the bed. He blinked a couple of times, and then a smile gradually suffused his features.

'Felix!' Like the exhaustion, Rosie's deep sexy burr always sounded the same no matter whose body she had squatter's rights in. 'My darling! My sunbeam! Come and shine on me.'

'Hello, Rosie,' I said. 'How's your love life?'

'Entirely . . . theoretical.'

I ambled over and sat down on the edge of the bed. She lifted her pale hand and rested it on mine. Maybe the guy was already pale when he got here, or maybe Rosie's transformative magic was working on him, making him over subtly into her image.

The rules that govern the afterlife are unfathomable, but they seem to be pretty consistent. Whatever form you take in death, flesh or spirit, you don't stick around for all that long. Twenty or thirty years is the average, fifty is already pushing it, and a century seems to mark the upper limit. For zombies the attrition is rapid, ruinous and irrevocable; for ghosts there's a slower and more subtle disintegration as the ego – the glue that holds a human being together – atrophies and melts away.

Rosie is the anomaly. A dozen exorcists working in an insane daisy chain had raised her, pulling on the psychic threads attached to a box of Tudor artefacts that J-J had acquired from God knows where. We caught her in a web made out of our own guts and our own arrogance, and then we decanted her into a waiting body, the first of many. It was a feat that had never been repeated.

Technically what Rosie does – the way she manages to keep on going on the material plane – is spiritual possession. The bodies are those of willing volunteers – psychology and medical students, mostly, who house the old ghost for a week or a fortnight and then walk away clutching (by way of payment) the tapes and transcripts of what she's said through their lips. The quick turnover means that Rosie's sedentary lifestyle does no harm to her hosts, although some of them have claimed that they got flashbacks weeks or months later, spontaneous memories of events from Rosie's life. I suspect that's part of the draw. To a certain kind of mind, there's something attractive about the idea of a cheap holiday in the Wars of the Roses.

Rosie is a strange woman. Her name is a joke, or a mask, and she's never told anyone what name she went by back when she was alive. What I can tell you is that she's playful, coquettish, filthy-minded and full of life – impressive in a lady who's been dead for five centuries. She's also garrulous. She likes to talk about her adventures, and that occasionally includes stories about where she's been during the 500 years between her death and resurrection. She lies outrageously, contradicts herself without blushing, kids us all straight-faced and then laughs her leg off when we fall for it. And Jenna-Jane writes it all down and pores over it, looking for the needle of truth in the city-sized haystacks of Rosie's magnificent bullshit.

I left the MOU mostly because of how Rosie was treated there. Because of the way she'd gone from honoured guest to precious resource to de facto prisoner. Jenna-Jane had started to obsess quite early on about undocumented access, and had started to control the comings and goings of Rosie's visitors. Rosie was allowed out of the MOU only with an escort. The outings got more and more infrequent, until finally they stopped altogether.

I'd seen her just once since then, and that was the last

time Asmodeus had tried to break free from his moorings in Rafi's flesh. It had been more than a year ago now, but Rosie would never have been so indelicate as to tear me off a strip for not visiting – and I guess when you've clocked up more than half a millennium the odd year here or there isn't worth arguing about.

'It's so sweet that you came,' she whispered. 'Unless it means . . . you've taken that bitch's shilling again.'

'I've missed you too,' I said, dodging the question. 'How are they treating you?'

The truth was that she didn't look all that well. Again, the borrowed flesh thing makes it harder to tell, but given that the guy whose body she was borrowing was a healthy young volunteer, the listlessness and lethargy had to be coming from Rosie herself.

'They keep me occupied, Fix,' Rosie said, her lips quirking upwards very slightly. 'Like an expensive pet. They do everything they can to make sure I'm happy.'

'And are you?'

The half-smile disappeared. 'No. Not very. The company isn't as . . . select as once it was. I see . . . a great many dullards. A great many bullies. I endure. I let them come and go, and they leave no mark on me . . . or on the world, but still . . . it saddens me.'

'Well, I'm going to be able to visit you for at least the next few weeks. Is there anything I can get you? Grapes? Booze? Porn? A newspaper?'

She seemed to consider this for a moment. 'Nothing,' she said solemnly. 'Well, porn, perhaps. If it's witty. But I'd rather you just talked to me. Tell me how the world works.'

I did, for about an hour or so, concentrating on the sort of things I knew she'd be interested in: politics, but only broad strokes and colourful intrigues; fads and fashions, the more extreme the better; stuff from my own life, luridly exaggerated. After a while she began to interrupt me with the occasional question, but they were questions I couldn't answer. They bore on the big intangibles, the way London looked and felt these days. I did my best to describe the city as I saw it, but I'm no poet.

Finally Rosie gave a loud sigh, which I took to be a signal that I should shut up. 'I can't catch it,' she lamented. 'I can't catch it, Felix.'

'Can't catch what, Rosie?' I asked. Given my part in getting her into this mess, I figured the least I could do was play straight man to her.

'It's changing,' she murmured. Her eyes were closed now, and her head was tilted to one side as if she was listening for something. 'But so slowly. Like the light in a room when the sun comes up, or when it goes down. You don't notice it until it's happened.'

'Are we still talking about London?' I asked.

'About the world.' The silence that followed those three words lasted for so long I thought she'd gone to sleep, but when I stood up to leave she reached out and took my hand again. 'Don't get hurt,' she said.

'I never do,' I said. 'It all rolls off me, Rosie. You know that. It's part of my ineffable charm.'

She ignored the invitation to banter. 'It's going to get hard to breathe,' she said. 'I really believe . . . yes . . . the changes will go on and on. Like water, rising over your head. Don't drown, Fix. I'd be sad if you drowned. There's a man here who hates you . . .'

'Gil McClennan,' I said: 'It's okay, Rosie. I had his number the first moment I saw him.'

She shook her head slowly, emphatically. 'You think you . . .' she began, but for some reason she didn't finish the sentence. She shaped unspoken words with her mouth, but in the end only shook her head again. 'Never mind,' she sighed. 'It all passes. It all passes. Perhaps you'll be his . . . comeuppance, Fix. I know what a rogue you are. How hard to pin down. I hope you hurt him. I'd like to see that.'

She said it calmly enough, but I read some old pain in her face. It's hard to hide your feelings when you're relying on someone else's muscles. I made a mental note to ask one of the others, most likely Sam, whether there was any bad blood he knew of between Gil McClennan and Rosie. Gil was her main link to the outside world now, in charge of selecting and briefing her volunteers – organising the meat train, as he put it – so he was in a position to do a lot of harm if he had a mind to. And he was a McClennan. That didn't earn him the benefit of any doubts in my book.

'Rosie,' I said, 'I need to move, but like I said, I'll see you again soon. If Gil gives you any grief, you let me know.'

'Assuredly, my knight in arms.'

'Seriously. I'll break his arm. I think Jenna-Jane would let me get away with that as long as he doesn't take a sick day.'

I kissed her on the cheek, hoping the volunteer wouldn't object to the liberty when he went through the tapes, and let myself out. She didn't say goodbye; she was lying back with her eyes closed again, seemingly exhausted just by the conversation.

Walking back along the corridor, my head full of vague and unserviceable thoughts, I was hit full force by an atonal tidal wave of white noise, so suddenly and so painfully that it almost made me stagger. I hadn't realised I'd gone the wrong way and was walking past the vault-like steel door that led down to the holding cells in the basement. I retraced my steps hurriedly, the cloying atmosphere of the place pressing in on me so that I felt like I was breathing through petrol-soaked rags.

My instinct was to get the hell out, but the mapping was still going on upstairs and I had to see how far they'd got. If Trudie Pax had a line on Asmodeus, I wanted to be the first to know. I went back up and found the room again. Trudie didn't seem to have moved in the two hours I'd been gone: she was still standing at the table, the taut string linking her hand to the nail in the ceiling as she passed her hand over the map. Some things had changed though. The tables had been banked up at an angle somehow, their back legs precariously balanced on stacks of cardboard boxes, so that the centre of the composite map was only a few inches away from Trudie's hand. She was holding a steel ruler, to the nether end of which a pencil had been attached with wads of Blu-Tack. This ramshackle apparatus allowed her to stab down onto the map and mark points on it. Victor Etheridge was scuttling around with a pencil and ruler of his own, joining the points up carefully with perfectly straight lines.

Trudie had her eyes closed, but I caught Etheridge's

gaze from the doorway. He held up his hand in the universal stop sign and shook his head vigorously: don't interrupt.

I wished I could pretend I hadn't seen his high sign, because I wanted more than anything right then to breeze on in and find out where those marks were falling: where the demon might have pitched his tent. But clearly Trudie was getting into her stride now, and Etheridge was feeling protective of her. Equally clearly, from a purely logical point of view it wasn't going to be any damn use knowing where Asmodeus was hanging out until we had a weapon that would actually work on him. Trying to take comfort in that thought, I gave Etheridge a nod and a wave and retreated again.

But the logical point of view was a long bus ride from where my head was at. I was seething with restlessness, with the feeling that I had to be doing something right then and there even if it turned out later to be the wrong thing.

So I called Juliet. It seemed to make a crazy kind of sense.

9

'A hundred pounds?' Juliet repeated. She sounded suspicious.

'Yeah,' I confirmed.

'Per day?'

'Exactly.'

'Plus expenses?'

I rolled my eyes. 'Shit, no. What expenses are there likely to be, anyway? All I'm asking you to do is to watch Pen's house and make sure Asmodeus doesn't get near it. Pen's already got the place hot and jumping with stay-nots, so the chances are you won't have anything to do in any case. But if the wards go down, I want there to be another line of defence. That's you.'

Juliet sipped her coffee, which was black and thick and treacle-sweet. The waiter, who had a hangdog look and a ridiculous bandito moustache, hovered nearby with the pot, hoping she'd hold up her cup for a refill. That way he'd have an excuse to get in close enough for another lungful of essence-of-succubus.

'It sounds dull,' she said, setting the cup down and dabbing her lips with the serviette. She left a smeared imprint of vivid red lipstick on the folded edge of it, like a streak of blood.

'Oh, I think it will be a lot duller than it sounds. But it's easy money, right?' As in, 'Easy come, easy go,' I added mentally. It was everything I was getting from Jenna-Jane. I had very mixed feelings about that. On the one hand, it was kind of a relief to shunt J-J's tainted favours directly onto a third party. On the other hand, you can't eat air. If this thing didn't wrap itself up quickly, I was going to be dining in the bins behind Pizza Hut.

'I'm not interested,' Juliet said.

'What?' I was dismayed. I'd started with my best offer, knowing from experience that you can't drive a hard bargain with a woman who can smell your soul, so I had nowhere to go now but down. 'At least think it over, Juliet. Please. It won't be for very long, and you can always—'

'I'm not interested in the money,' Juliet clarified. 'Give it to her.'

'To her? Her who?'

'The one who bruises so easily. My little friend.'

She spat the words out with searing contempt.

'Susan?'

'Exactly. She's the one who needs clothes to wear and food to eat and toys to play with. Make her happy, if she's capable of being happy. I'll give you three days.'

I didn't answer. To tell the truth, I was still trying to digest 'bruises so easily', and it was sticking in my throat like a chicken bone. Juliet stared at me with an edge of challenge in her narrowed eyes.

'She's . . .' I began tentatively. 'That is . . . Sue has been a lot more to you than a friend.'

'Has she? How would you know, Castor?'

Okay, that was an easy one. 'Because you can get sex anywhere,' I pointed out bluntly. 'You can have anyone you want, on whatever terms you want, for as long as you want. So if you choose to live with one woman, and to stay faithful to her, then it has to be because—'

Juliet's coarse laugh cut across me. 'Faithful?' she repeated. 'Please. It's only your species, Castor, that makes a virtue out of not following its instincts. If I'm hungry, I eat something. If I'm angry, I kill something. And if I feel lustful, I make someone satisfy me. Where does *faithful* come into the equation? It's just a word you use to hobble someone you love. To tie them to you. It's a weapon the weak use against the strong.'

'Interesting choice of words,' I commented, looking studiously at the dregs in my own cup.

'Weapon? What would you call it?'

'Not that word,' I said. 'The other one. Love. There was a time when you would have said desire or want. Two years on Earth has changed you more than you know, Juliet. I bet Baphomet wouldn't even know his kid sister if he saw her now.'

I met her gaze again, and the silence stretched. It's a high-risk strategy, needling a succubus. Normally I'd have been pretty sure where the line lay and when to stop, but this was a Juliet I didn't recognise, and I tensed under her stare like a small rodent under a stooping buzzard.

Then she laughed, and I relaxed.

'You're right,' she said. 'I have changed.' She put down the cup and gave the waiter a tenth of a second's glance – enough to make him come scampering over and give her the refill. He was happy to be of service, happy to be in the vicinity of this amazing woman, who for the moment was filling his mind to the exclusion of his wife, his kids, his other customers, his mortgage, the entirety of his past and the entirety of his future. He filled the cup and then made to raise the pot. Juliet rested a finger lightly on his hand, and he kept on pouring. Hot coffee splashed over the edge of the cup to soak into the tablecloth in a spreading brown stain.

'Maybe I've changed too much,' Juliet said. 'Maybe I've lost something. A lot of what I'm doing right now bores me.'

The waiter made a small, helpless sound, a half-swallowed moan of dismay. Juliet wasn't pressing down on his hand; she was holding him in place with the strength of her will, not with any physical force. The coffee had saturated the tablecloth now and was spattering down onto the floor and onto the waiter's well-shined shoes.

'Then maybe you need a new challenge,' I suggested. 'I mean, as opposed to the same old same old, like making guys have wet dreams while they're awake. Too easy, surely?'

Juliet lifted her finger. The waiter took an involuntary step back as the skin-to-skin contact was broken, gasping like a landed fish.

'Everything is too easy,' Juliet said with heavy emphasis. 'As I said, I'll watch your woman for three days. If Asmodeus is really hunting her, that might be a fight – or a fuck – worth having. But three days is my limit. If he hasn't come by then, he isn't coming.'

'Pen isn't my woman,' I pointed out scrupulously.

'Then I'm even less interested. Let's make it two days.'

Juliet stood up, leaving the refilled cup untouched in the centre of the swamped table. The waiter was staring at her with huge, hapless eyes, haunted by his own unrequitable desire. A lot of other people were staring too, but Juliet's well used to that. It never bothers her.

We walked back to Sue's house in silence. Juliet stopped me with a firm push to the chest as I made to walk in through the gate.

'As you were, Castor.'

I stared at her in surprise. 'I just wanted to say hi to Susan,' I said. 'Since I'm in the neighbourhood.'

Juliet smiled mockingly. 'I'm sure you did,' she agreed. 'But she belongs to me, and I get to say who she talks to. I make sure she stays *faithful*. Go home. Tell your land-lady she's got a guardian angel. For two days, I think we said. After that, she'll have to make her own arrangements.'

She walked to the door, let herself in and slammed it behind her.

As I stood there at the gate, my death-sense unexpect-edly pricked up its metaphorical ears. I might have noticed it sooner, but Juliet's emphatic presence tends to elbow almost everything else right out of my perceptual field.

This was a tiny *ping* on my metaphysical radar, but it was very close – and I didn't see any ghosts or zombies abroad in the bright sunlight who could have been responsible for it. There was something familiar about it too, and whatever the association was, it had a nega-tive feel to it. Negative. Recent. Necromantic. Out on the street in broad daylight . . .

I had it. This was what I'd felt when I held the stone I'd found in Pen's garden: the invocation to Tlallik, whoever or whatever that sonofabitch might be.

Okay. So since I was here already and wasn't invited in to tea, I might as well give the place the once-over at least.

Hoping fervently that Juliet wasn't watching out of the window, I hopped over the low wooden fence into Sue Book's front garden – if that isn't too grandiose a term for a lawn the size of an Oyster card, a dead-and-alive privet hedge and three beds of geraniums.

I squatted down and pushed aside the lower leaves of the hedge, looking for any evidence that someone had been there before me. At first, everything seemed to be kosher, but as I cast my gaze to left and right I caught a glimpse of red. In among the flowers, half-buried in the friable soil, was a second stone: grey like the first, and once again bearing a circular ward, crudely but legibly painted in bright red. It was fresher, so this time I could tell from the smell what the red was. It was nail varnish.

I photographed it, as I had the first, and put it back in place. It was clearly different from the first one I'd seen: not in the general design, which was identical, but in the collection of Aramaic symbols at the centre. Only two symbols this time. If the stones were summonings, and I saw no reason to doubt Nicky's accuracy on that score, then they were summoning two different beings. Spirits of mischief, rage and paranoia, whistled up to drive Juliet off her head? No, that made no sense. One demon couldn't possess another demon, and Juliet would know in a second if anyone tried to pull shit like that on her. Her succubus-sense would tingle, she'd follow the magic spoor to its source, and some unhappy necromancer would be trying to put his internal organs back with one hand while he wanked with the other. And in any case, the first penta-gram I'd found had been at Pen's house: Pen was still Pen, and as far as I knew, I was still me, not afflicted by any unusual mood swings or sudden bursts of indiscriminate rage.

Something else then. But what? And why? I'd promised Sue I'd sort out Juliet's scary abreactions. My record with promises is a little patchy, but I was determined to keep this one. I couldn't let Juliet be Somebody Else's Problem, any more than I could do that with Rafi. On some things your room for manoeuvre is effectively zero.

I killed the rest of the day in various unproductive ways. I went to Bunhill Fields cemetery and sat among the old graves – old enough now to be completely ghost-free – to think about Rafi, and Asmodeus, and magic bullets. Normally I get good value for money out of that place. Something about the silence, or maybe the proximity to William Blake's hallowed bones, makes my mind work at about 150 per cent efficiency when I'm there. Not this time though. I sat and watched the darkness come on, chasing the same few thoughts around in smaller and smaller circles. It would be hard enough to bring Asmodeus down, even with the gloves off and using every low blow in the book; doing it without killing Rafi seemed impossible.

I called Nicky Heath at odd intervals, got him on about the third or fourth time. He'd been down in the main auditorium of the Gaumont, fucking around with the seating layout yet again. I refrained from asking what the point of that was, given that he was the only one who ever got to sit there. Instead, I asked him if he had any news for me.

'Yeah,' Nicky said, 'I do. On the Ditko front, quite a lot of stuff – but it's more quantity than quality, if you get my drift. Anyway, there's too much to go over on the phone. Come and pick it up whenever you're free.'

'Anything on that ward I picked up at Pen's place?'

'Not so far. I did the grimoires, came up with a big zero. Now I'm feeding Tlallik and Tlullik into some weird-arsed meta-search engines, and trailing them across my favourite necromantic noticeboards, but if anyone's ever heard of them, they sure as fuck didn't write it down anywhere.'

'I've got another one for you,' I said. 'Same pentagram, different payload.'

'Shoot it on over. The more the merrier.'

Nicky's funereal tone belied his words, but I took the invitation anyway. Then I checked my watch.

'I've got to be somewhere at midnight,' I said. 'Is it okay if I come over after that?'

'I don't sleep, Castor. Night and day's all the same to me, except at night I can take a walk round the block without going rotten.'

'Not in this weather,' I pointed out.

He snorted. 'Yeah, you got that right. Come over whenever you like. My door's always open.'

'Your door is booby-trapped, Nicky.'

'Well, that too.' I was about to hang up when he spoke again. 'Oh, wait. I won't be here. I'll be over in High Street. High Street Market.'

'In the early hours of the morning?' I demanded.

'Yeah.'

'Okay. Which end?'

'You'll find me, Castor. The crowds will have thinned out by then.'

So I was looking at a night on the town with Gil McClennan, followed by a visit to a dead man in a deserted street market. You can see why people don't go into exorcism for the glamour.

When I got to Charing Cross station it was still five minutes before the hour. Midnight isn't particularly late by West End standards, so there were a fair number of people around, even though most of the restaurants and coffee houses on the Strand had already closed their doors.

Thinking I was the first one there, I leaned against the cheap replica of the Eleanor Cross and settled in to wait for the others. Then I spotted Trudie Pax standing just inside the station entrance, nervously winding and unwinding the string on her left hand.

She saw me at the same time and headed over, saving me the trouble of deciding whether or not to join her. She was wearing a khaki army fatigue jacket, jeans and boots, but despite the urban-adventurer chic she looked tired and a little distracted.

'So how is the mapping going?' I asked.

She made a non-committal gesture. 'We've got something,' she said. 'The start of something. I'll show you tomorrow, and you can tell me what it's worth. You don't know what to say to me, do you, Castor?'

'I don't think I've got anything to say to you,' I corrected her.

'The last time we met—'

'The last time we met you set me up, Trudie. Without you, Gwillam wouldn't have got to Rafi, and we wouldn't be in this shit now.'

She scowled where I thought she might blush. 'I didn't know what he was planning to do,' she pointed out coldly. 'When I told you there'd be no bugs, I meant it. There were none on me. Gwillam managed to take you anyway, but how is that my fault? I did what I could to keep my word. But he turned me into a liar, so I quit. I left the Anathemata that same night.'

'To join the MOU,' I mused. 'That's a really principled stand. Bravo.'

Trudie sighed. 'I'm not asking for your approval, Castor,' she said.

'I'm glad to hear it.'

'I just want you to know that it was a two-way deal. If you were screwed over, I was screwed over too – and I trusted Father Gwillam, so it was probably a harder knock for me.'

'Still a good Catholic girl though, yeah?'

Trudie threw out her hands, her temper getting the better of her contrition. 'What do you want from me?' she demanded.

'Not a thing,' I growled back. But it was a fair question. I was sniping at her like a jealous husband, and she was probably right that she was more screwed against than screwing. I just couldn't unbend with her because she was a part of that night – of the blood and the horror and the guilt. My guilt, mostly, but clearly I was more than happy to spread it around.

'Look,' I said. 'We're working together, so I'll try to be civil whenever we're rubbing shoulders. Beyond that, we don't really have to talk, do we?'

Trudie stared at me unblinkingly. 'I'll leave that up to

you,' she said with an edge in her voice. 'I know something about Ditko – Asmodeus, rather – that I haven't told Professor Mulbridge. I was thinking that I'd tell you, and leave it up to you who else finds out. But maybe I'm giving you the benefit of too many doubts, Castor. Maybe you're more concerned about your own righteousness than you are about helping your friend.'

She turned to walk away and ran straight into Gil McClennan, who had somehow got up really close to us without either of us seeing him. 'Not interrupting anything, am I?' he asked, with an expression on his face that was the second cousin to a leer.

'Group prayers,' I said. 'Where are the others?'

'It's just the three of us tonight.' Gil moved his index finger round in a circle to indicate Trudie, me and himself. 'Devani and Etheridge have already seen this, and they came up blank. You two are new, so now it's your turn to look comically amazed. Whenever you're ready.'

He walked on, heading away from Trafalgar Square, up the Strand. I glanced at Trudie, who shrugged and followed him. Whatever she had to tell me, it would clearly have to wait.

We walked almost the full length of the Strand, stopping just short of Aldwych. On the side of the street opposite the Savoy, a little way past the Vaudeville theatre, Gil stopped and waited for us to catch up. He was standing in front of an inconspicuous door jammed into a narrow space between a camping shop and an Italian restaurant. To one side of the door, a glassed-in display cabinet contained nothing but a poster. SUPER-SELF GYM AND FITNESS CENTER, it proclaimed, flaunting the American spelling like a visible link to a far-off land of tans and six-packs. Underneath the gilt-edged words, a sprawl of photos showed exercise bikes, treadmills, a swimming pool, a sauna.

Gil produced a bunch of keys, put one in the lock and turned. As he opened the door, a red light flashed in the darkness beyond and a siren started a two-tone sotto voce complaint. Gil tapped numbers into a keypad just inside the door until the light and noise stopped. Then he flicked some switches and the lights came on, showing a small lobby with another door directly facing us. He crossed the lobby and held the far door open for us.

'Okay,' he said. 'Over to you.'

Pax and I moved forward in a truncated skirmish line, death-sense awake and receptive, like soldiers advancing across a minefield. The space beyond was just a corridor, but it was much wider than the lobby as well as longer. One wall was a painted frieze on the theme of physically perfect human beings running, jumping, swimming, touching their toes. The other wall was entirely of glass, with darkness beyond. Staring into that fathomless black void, I felt something like dread rising inside me, so suddenly it took me by surprise. I wasn't scared of the dark: I was scared of how little I knew about that darkness. The unlit room, separated from me by a single thickness of glass, could be as big as a cathedral or as small as a cupboard. What would it feel like to be lost in that darkness? To have no idea how far away from you the walls were?

Beside me, Trudie drew a shuddering breath. Her hand sought mine for a moment, then she seemed to realise what she was doing and lowered it again with a visible effort.

'Yeah,' Gil agreed dryly. 'You're starting to feel it, aren't you?' He hadn't moved from the threshold; in fact he was standing a little way back from it, which meant that he'd propped the inner door open somehow. The street door too, I noticed. Over his shoulder I saw a night bus roll by, heard the distant hoot of a garbage boat on the Thames.

'Feel what?' I demanded.

Gil smirked, or tried to. He had his hands in his pockets, trying for a casual pose, but I could see from their outline that both fists were clenched. 'Well, you tell me, Castor,' he said. 'What are you feeling? The joys of fucking spring?'

Not bothering to answer, I waited him out. After a few moments he gave an impatient toss of the head as if he despaired of me.

'What have you got here?' I demanded.

'I wouldn't want to prejudice your professional objectivity,' Gil said, deadpan. 'Here. Go take a look for yourself.' He took his right hand out of his pocket and threw something through the air to me. It smacked into my palm with a metal-on-metal clank. The bunch of keys. Gil pointed towards the far end of the corridor. 'Check out basement level one. The swimming pool area. Pax, you and me will make a circuit of the outside of the building. Then we'll meet back here and compare notes.'

Well, it was what we'd come here for. But before I moved, I found another bank of light switches and flicked them all on. Neon strips flash-bang-flickered into life in the room beyond the windows. It was an exercise area, reassuring in its complete banality, full of nothing more menacing than ski machines and rowing benches.

Feeling a little stupid, I walked on down the corridor and started to descend the stairs. When I got to the first bend I heard Gil yell something, followed by the sound of footsteps. I looked back as Trudie rounded the turn behind me. She passed me and kept on going, ignoring my questioning glance.

'I thought you were meant to be doing the outside,' I said.

'I told Gil I wanted to get the full picture,' she muttered. 'He tried to pull rank and I left him to it. What's the outside of the building going to tell us?' I could see from the grim set of her jaw that this place had her as rattled as it had me, but that seemed to make her all the more determined not to show any fear.

Basement one was bigger than the street level – or at least the part of the street level that we'd seen. This was the gym's reception area, with a counter in the centre of an open space, a quarry-tiled floor, a set of signs pointing away towards AEROBICS, WEIGHT TRAINING, PILATES STUDIO. With the lights blazing and the whole room deserted, it looked more like a stage set than a place in the real world – and thinking of it like that made me wonder whether someone or something was about to make an entrance. The irrational feeling of unease, even of fear, that had stolen over me upstairs came back even more strongly now. I had to fight the urge to look over my shoulder. The sense of threat was palpable. Something brushed faintly against the edges of my awareness, on the wavelength reserved for the dead.

'There,' said Trudie, pointing to a sign that read OLYMPIC POOL. Her voice trembled a little. Clearly I wasn't the only one having a bad time of it down here.

We followed the sign to a double door, where there was a pause while I found the right key. Opening the door released a rush of chlorinated air. We stepped through into a smaller anteroom, with doors on either side bearing the male and female symbols and an open archway straight ahead, darkness beyond. We looked around for light switches but couldn't find any. Somehow that seemed sinister. Why hide the light switches? What didn't they want us to see?

Whatever it was, I had the sense that it was directly ahead of us, that what we'd come here to find was only a few steps away, on the other side of the arch. As if to confirm that, I was suddenly aware of the rhythmic slap of water against stone very close by. We'd found the pool.

'Let's go back,' Trudie whispered from just behind me. I shook my head, as much to clear it as to disagree with her. This was absurd. The place was empty, and there was nothing down here to be afraid of. True, it might be haunted, but we were both exorcists. We were well placed to deal with anything that might be waiting beyond that archway.

'We'll just . . . take a look,' I said with an effort. 'And then we'll come away.'

'We won't see anything,' Trudie pointed out queru- lously. 'It's too dark.'

I put an end to the discussion by taking ten steps forward, passing under the arch and into the larger space beyond. I was walking on tiles again, hollow echoes rising with each step. A faint phosphorescence in the water showed me the edge of the pool now as my eyes began to adjust to the darkness.

In fact, it wasn't completely dark. Even though we were below ground level, there was a light well in the centre of the room that must lead up through the centre of the building to the sky far above. Muddy radiance filtered down; seemed to hang in the air in granulated drifts.

But the light from the pool was unconnected to the light that came from above. It was stronger now, more defined, and there were eddies of movement within it. I was aware of two things: the first was that Trudie was standing at my side; the second was that my death-sense, which had been registering faint scrapes and whispers ever since we first came down the stairs, flared up now into a thousand-throated shriek like an air-raid siren.

It froze me in place for a second, and in that second Trudie walked past me to the edge of the pool. Silhouetted against that faint unsteady glow, she stared down into the depths. A strangled cry escaped her mouth. Her knees gave way and she almost fell. Lunging forward to catch her, I saw what she was seeing.

It was only incomprehension that saved me from falling myself. It took a couple of seconds for the movement below me to resolve itself into coherent shapes, and a couple of seconds more for my mind to process those shapes into meaning.

There were people moving around at the bottom of the pool, lots of them. They were visible by their own faint light, like so many Chinese lanterns burning under the water. Some wore armour. Others wore long, pale gowns that left their arms bare. All had sandals on their feet. One carried a short staff like a badge of office, which he brandished emphatically as he talked. And he was talking a lot: to the armoured soldiers, to another man dressed almost identically, to a woman whose long black hair was held back by a comb. They listened respectfully, all eyes on him as he gestured, turned, gestured again.

It was a convocation of ghosts – a caucus, a parliament of the dead – and it was impossible on a great many levels. But why did the sight of it fill me with such dread? Why was it suddenly impossible to draw a breath?

Trudie struggled free from my grip and backed away from the water's edge, throwing up her hands as though to protect herself against some physical attack. I would have been happy to do the same thing, but I couldn't move. Darkness was seeping in again from the edges of my vision, bringing with it an incandescent panic that swept away thought, deactivated muscles.

It was coming from above, I realised suddenly. It was hanging in the air over my head, and it was descending: falling around and over me like sand pouring into the lower half of an hourglass, burying me a grain at a time.

I tried to think through the fear, and then I tried to listen through it, which was even harder. This thing, whatever it might be, was dead, and it had an imprint, an essence that I could hear with my death-sense. It was almost drowned out by the screaming of my nerves, but it was there: the suggestion of pattern, of coherent form. If I had my whistle in my hands, I could start to play it. I'd have the beginnings of an exorcism.

Forcing my hands to move, I groped inside my coat,

found my whistle on the third try and hauled it out. It slipped from my half-paralysed fingers, but I groped, flailed, caught it again before it fell. I pressed it to my lips and blew a note — a random, forlorn, pointless note, but it was something just to have made a sound. My fingers moved on the stops, and the next note crept a little closer to a place that meant something. I elided it into a phrase, unlovely and shrill.

Out of the corner of my eye I saw Trudie's hands move. Then she raised them in front of her face and the spider's web of lines stretched out between them was dimly visible in the faint light from the pool. A cat's cradle. She was working with me, bolstering my patterning with her own. It gave me strength, and the strength became music, still ham-fisted and painful to hear, but elbowing at the fear and pushing it away on one side and then the other. It became possible to think.

'Castor!' Trudie panted.

'I'm with you,' I snapped, taking my mouth away from the whistle as briefly as I could. 'Move!'

We backed towards the arch, like two unwary picnickers who'd blundered into a minefield. Trudie wove her hands through forms that looked as though they had names like the two-headed cow and how to sever your thumb, and I supplied the music. I got one last glimpse of the ghosts at the bottom of the pool. Ignoring us, ignoring the pall of dread, they continued their lofty and animated discussion.

With each step we took, the fear lifted a little more. When we reached the archway, the feeling had diluted to the point where it was only a knot in my bowels where previously the knot had taken in my entire body. Trudie shuddered – an involuntary shrug of her whole body, like a dog shaking itself dry after climbing out of a river – then she turned and fled for the stairs. I was a negligible fraction of a second behind her.

But some wordless communication passed between us in the reception area, and we forced ourselves to slow down to walking pace. When we reached the turn of the stairs and ascended back into Gil McClennan's field of vision, we were walking at something like normal strolling speed. Gil's face fell. He was obviously hoping for something a lot more dramatic and demeaning. It was a real pleasure to disappoint him.

'So,' Gil said. 'That was Super-Self.'

Perhaps because we hadn't come screaming back up the stairs with our nerve broken and our trousers fouled, he seemed to feel the need to play it as cool as he possibly could. Leaning against one of the arches at the westernmost end of Covent Garden Market, which was where we'd retreated to, he rolled a cigarette one-handed, stuck it into the corner of his mouth and carried on talking around it as he lit up.

'It's a new operation. Just opened last year. The building was offices, previously. And before that it was a haberdasher's or something, back to when it was first built in around 1901. Nothing out of the ordinary. No ghost stories or unsolved crimes. Nobody died on the premises, as far as we know.'

He exhaled smoke that smelled of menthol and wet socks. Trudie leaned a little back, away from the primary impact area.

'Some time around the end of May,' Gil went on, not deigning to notice, 'the current owners contacted Professor Mulbridge, looking to get the building disinfected. They'd opened six months before that and hit the wall pretty fast. Reasonable volume of sign-ups, but everybody cancelled as soon as they could. No returns, almost no new business. The atmosphere, people said. The place had a really bad vibe.'

'So?' Trudie demanded. Our close encounter with the thing in the swimming pool had left her somewhat short on patience.

'So the professor sent one of her ghost-breakers over. David Franklin. She had better people available, but this didn't seem like anything particularly difficult or dangerous. The only odd thing about it was that nobody had seen an actual ghost. They just didn't like the place. It made them feel uneasy.'

'There are ghosts,' I pointed out. 'And uneasy doesn't come close to describing what we felt down there.'

'Yeah,' Gil agreed in a detached tone. 'It's getting stronger. Franklin didn't see any ghosts either, but he felt something, so he did a standard exorcism. Old school *retro-me-Sathanas* stuff with a bell, a book and a stub of candle. The next thing he knew, he was out on the street, bouncing off the bonnet of a Ford Mondeo. The thing hit back when it was poked – gave him the screaming shits – so he just cut and ran. Didn't even know what he was doing. He wouldn't go back after that. When Professor Mulbridge gave him a straight order, he quit: just gave his notice in and walked.'

'The ghosts,' I said. 'When did they turn up?'

Gil scratched his chin. 'Couple of weeks later. We'd

made two more attempts to exorcise it, and they'd both been fiascos. The third man up was Etheridge, and he had to be carried out on a stretcher. You've seen what he's like, right? Well, that's all new. Before he went down into that basement, he was pretty solid.'

'Why didn't you warn us?' Trudie demanded grimly.

Gil looked away, shrugged, then met Trudie's gaze again with cool indifference. 'I was interested in your first impressions,' he said. 'If I'd briefed you, then you'd have seen what I told you to see. This way . . . you saw it cold. With your own eyes. Got a lot more out of it.'

Trudie's shoulders were tensed and her eyes were narrowed to slits. She still hadn't come down from the terror-rush, and Gil's bullshit was rubbing her up all the wrong ways. 'You lying sonofabitch,' she snarled. 'If you were interested in our impressions, you would have fucking asked.'

Gil dropped his half-smoked cigarette and stubbed it out with his heel. 'So,' he said, 'Ms Pax, what were your impressions?'

She actually looked as though she was going to take a swing at him. Fun though that would have been to see, I stepped in to take the heat. For better or worse, I still needed the help that Jenna-Jane's team could offer me. If they were at each other's throats, they'd be able to offer me a whole lot less.

'My impression is that we're dealing with two separate phenomena,' I said, steamrollering over whatever Trudie was starting to say. 'The big scary one, which is invisible, and the ghosts.'

'Crap,' said Gil simply. 'They're two aspects of the same thing.'

'Then why weren't the ghosts in the mix to start with?'

'Obviously they were. But there are no rules about this stuff. A lot of people can walk right through a ghost without seeing it. We're dealing with imperfect observers who may or may not be sensitive across the full range.'

'Yeah, but also we're dealing with at least three exorcists. You're telling me an exorcist could walk into a roomful of ghosts and miss them?'

The corner of Gil's mouth twitched. 'When they're on Etheridge's level? Yeah. I could believe that.'

'You're missing the point,' Trudie said, still glaring at Gil as if she was hoping to gore him to death with her eyeballs. 'Both of you. You're saying ghosts as though you know what those things are. But they're not what they look like. They can't be.'

That was bothering me too. Something here was way out of whack, in fact, a lot of somethings. Apart from Rosie, nobody had ever seen or raised a ghost from more than a century ago, and the older a ghost was, the less likely it was to manifest as anything that looked remotely human. They lost their shape and their coherence as their memory of themselves, or else the residual energy left over from being alive, slowly and inexorably faded. Again, Rosie was the exception, but her resurrection had taken the sweating, straining best efforts of a dozen exorcists, and she was barely 500 years old. The spirits in the swimming pool were dressed as Roman centurions, Roman legionaries, Roman civilians in togas and sandals. I wasn't sure exactly when the Roman empire had sold its UK holdings, but on the face of it the ghosts we'd seen had to be getting on for 2,000 years old. That was flat-out impossible.

But Trudie took that as read and went for the other impossibility. 'Ghosts don't team up,' she said between gritted teeth. 'They can haunt the same place, but they almost never acknowledge each other, even if they died at the same time. Those spirits were talking, interacting: they were replaying something they'd all been involved in. And there are at least a dozen of them. When has that ever happened before?'

'I've never heard of it,' I agreed. I was thinking of the Stanger ghosts. The three little girls who'd been Charles Stanger's victims, and Abbie Torrington, whose death had come five decades later. They managed to interact okay, were the best of friends and seemed (allowing for the fact that that they were dead) to be having the time of their lives. But I'd had to intervene to cut them free from their past, from their place, with the help of my tin whistle. And they were young ghosts, in both senses, not beaten down and partially erased by the passage of time, whether pre- or post-mortem.

'Something about the place,' I mused. 'About the history of the place. Maybe it's got unusual properties. Has anyone researched that angle?'

'I already told you we pulled the records,' Gil pointed out with exaggerated patience. 'All the way back to when the block was built. It was part of a big land-clearance project some time in the 1890s, when they built Aldwych. There used to be a road cutting through from the Strand to the market back then – Wych Street – right around here. But it was a shithole and they knocked it down. So yeah, before it was a building it was a street. A street with kind of a bad rep, but not in any way that would matter to us. It was just thieves' rookeries, gin dives, that kind of thing.'

'Do we know what it was like during the Roman occupation?' I pondered.

'Probably harder to get a smoke,' Gil said. 'Listen, my brief was to bring you here and show you that thing. I've done it. The professor wants to hear your thoughts tomorrow morning at eight. Me, I couldn't care less. I'm not expecting you to see anything I've missed. So unless you want to tell me you've cracked this thing, and pour forth your enlightenment on the grateful masses, I'm out of here.'

He gave me a sardonic look. I shrugged, and he nodded, satisfied. He held out his hand.

'Keys,' he demanded.

'I'd like to hold on to them,' I countered. 'I think it might be useful to get some measurements. Maybe take another look into that swimming pool.'

Gil's eyes boggled. I was bullshitting him about going back down to the pool: there was no way I was up for that just yet. But I was serious about wanting to take another look at Super-Self. Probably in daylight though, and probably not alone.

'I keep the keys,' Gil said.

'I'll give you them back first thing in the morning.'

'I keep the keys.'

'It would be really helpful to—'

'Castor, give me the fucking keys!'

I shrugged and handed them over. 'Thanks, Gil,' I said. 'Don't let us keep you.'

Still bristling, giving us both a bare nod of acknowledgement, he walked away. I gave him a cheery wave.

Trudie looked at me with scorn and exasperation then laughed incredulously as she saw what was sitting between my index and forefinger. It was the key to Super-Self's front door, which I'd slipped off the ring and palmed, one-handed, as soon as it was clear Gil was going to be awkward.

'Smooth,' Trudie said.

'My middle name.'

We looked at each other. 'What was this thing you had to tell me?' I asked.

She gave me an appraising stare. 'Buy me a drink?'

'At this hour? Where?'

'I know a place.'

'I'm skint.'

'I'll spot you a tenner.'

'Then yeah,' I allowed. 'I'll buy you a drink.'

The place that Trudie had in mind was the Bridge that Fell, on Victoria Embankment directly behind the Savoy. It was a hot and cold bar: in other words, an establishment where the living and the dead were equally welcome. Like I said, zombies really shouldn't eat or drink at all, because they don't have functioning digestive systems any more and the stuff just sits in their stomachs and rots, hastening the final collapse of their bootstrapped bodies. But some go ahead and do it anyway, and others like Nicky Heath like the smell of booze even when they don't actually drink it. Bars that take that kind of custom tend to stay open way past midnight, because their daytime trade is virtually non-existent.

We sat in the first-floor bar with a view over the river, in a room that smelled of cheap incense, embalming chemicals and organic decay. Most of the other patrons were zombies, and they were keeping themselves to themselves, nursing half-pints of beer through the watches of the night and dreaming of long-gone glories in the days when their hearts still pumped blood. I wondered as I got the drinks in how the place kept going. DMWs aren't big spenders, after all. It's hard for them to hold down a job, and since they can't legally own property they mostly don't succeed in taking any of their wealth with them when they die.

I realised the answer as a large party came in – three men and four women – talking in hushed, excited voices and taking photographs of anything that moved. Yeah, of course. The tourist dollar must subsidise a lot of places like this, the same way it did the London theatre.

That thought glanced off something else in my recent memory, something that seemed important but refused to come clear. I left it alone, knowing that chasing it wouldn't work.

Trudie took her whisky and water out of my hand before I'd even sat down, and emptied a good half of it in a single, prolonged swig. She shuddered as the alcohol went down, shaking her head as if to clear it. 'Cheers,' she said belatedly, clinking glasses.

'Cheers,' I agreed. 'Super-Self still in your system?'

'Yeah. Yours too?'

'More than somewhat.'

The tourists ambled past our table, saw that we were alive and kept on going. They didn't bother to take any photos of us.

'How did you first get into this business?' Trudie asked.

'By not being any good at anything else,' I said. 'How about you?'

She thought about it for a second before answering. 'The redemption train,' she said at last.

'Which is what, exactly?'

Trudie swirled the liquid in her glass, staring down into it like my mum reading tea leaves. 'What it sounds like. You try to make up for something bad you've done. Balance the books. That's how a lot of people get into the order. It makes a lot of sense, at first, even though it's never that easy. Atonement's got its own built-in logic. But you, Castor . . . you're a mystery to me.'

'Yeah?' I asked. 'In what way?'

Trudie shook her head. 'You've been through all this shit – Ditko's possession, the White City Riot, the insanity at the Salisbury – but you never seem to put two and two and two and two together.'

'Meaning . . . ?'

'Meaning that it's not just isolated incidents. So why do you pretend it is? "Nothing is at stake." Do you remember saying that to me? I remember it. It was the night when the Salisbury burned and Asmodeus got free.'

'The night when you and Gwillam carved me up,' I reminded her – not to pick a fight, just to keep things clear.

She rolled her eyes. 'If you like. But my point is that you said it, even when the world was coming to pieces all around us. You're like some anti-Chicken Licken, running around telling everyone the sky isn't falling, when you ought to be able to see that it damn well is.'

Some of the things that had happened since that night

flashed through my mind like a slide show, things that weren't on Trudie's list but made her point, if anything, even stronger.

'I may have been wrong about the sky,' I conceded. 'But if I admit that it might be falling, will you at least consider the possibility that fanatics like Gwillam and Jenna-Jane aren't doing anything to hold it up?'

Trudie tapped the side of her glass, watched the ripples chase each other from edge to centre and back again. Then she looked up and met my gaze. 'Doing something is better than doing nothing,' she said flatly.

'Is it? So if your bed's on fire and you've got no water, you might as well douse it in petrol?'

'You know what I mean, Castor.'

'Yeah, I do. Have you seen what J-J keeps in the cellar yet? If not, take a look. Then we'll talk some more.'

An uncomfortable silence descended. Trudie finished her drink and I made some serious inroads into mine.

'You said you had something to tell me about Asmodeus,' I reminded her. I just wanted to hear her out and get away now. The sense of camaraderie that comes from any shared ordeal had dissipated quickly, and I was feeling the distance that separated us more keenly than ever. I'd been wrong to think there could be any common ground between us.

'After I left the order . . .' Trudie began hesitantly. Then she lapsed into silence again. After a moment she stood up. 'I think maybe I need another drink,' she muttered and headed for the bar.

It took her a while to get served. Another bunch of guys with flashy cameras had rolled in and there was a logjam at the bar. Two in the morning seemed to be happy hour in this place. When she came back, bringing me another pint of London Pride and herself what looked like a triple whisky, she tried again.

'I told Father Gwillam that same night – the night when we met – that I was out of the game,' she said. 'I was angry at the way I'd been set up. I told him I couldn't be a part of the order because I couldn't trust him any more.'

'How did he take that?'

She laughed ruefully. 'It didn't seem to bother him all that much. He certainly didn't beg me to stay, anyway. And he didn't apologise. He just said I should think carefully about my decision, because it would be irreversible. Once I left, I couldn't come back. The Anathemata would strike me from their list retroactively, so I wouldn't ever have been a part of their operations. I'd be forbidden from contacting anyone in the order or talking about our work, with the implied threat that if I didn't keep quiet, they could turn my volume down permanently.

'So . . . I walked. And I thought that would be the end of it. But it wasn't.'

'Harder to make the break than you thought?'

Trudie was grim. 'No, Castor. I said I was through, and I was through. But despite what Father Gwillam said, they weren't quite through with me. About three weeks later I went back to the hostel where I'd been living. It was more of a barracks, really, for the members of the order, but it looked like an ordinary church hall from the outside. I needed to clear out the last of my stuff, and I'd emailed one of the deacons to say I was coming.'

She scowled into her drink, her hand gripping the stem of the glass tightly enough for the knuckles to show white. 'I walked into the aftermath of a battle. They'd turned the dormitory into a field hospital. Every bed was occupied, and there were people running around with bandages, tourniquets, buckets. Doctors stitching up wounds. Members of the order – people I knew – screaming or sobbing or shrieking out swear-words. Some of the bodies on the beds weren't moving. They were dead. And the wounds . . .' She stared at me. 'They looked as though they'd been clawed by wild animals or . . . or been dragged along behind a truck, or something.

'I just stood there in the doorway, staring. I didn't know what to do. I couldn't move. The . . . the smell was worse than anything. Blood, and shit, and sweat, all mixed together.

'Then someone shoved a bucket and a sponge into my hands, and at least I had something to do. Mopping up the blood, so nobody would slip in it and break their neck. I got stuck in. It was a way of shutting my mind down, so I didn't have to think about it.

'I worked for hours. Not just with the bucket. I stitched up a wound too, which is the first time I've used a needle and thread since I left seminary school. It was Speight. I think you met him. Something had gashed his arm really badly, from the shoulder down to the elbow. I stitched it up the best way I knew how, while someone else – a man I didn't know – held his arm still and stopped him from struggling.'

'Why do this there?' I demanded. 'Why not take them to a proper hospital?'

Trudie had a hard time focusing on the question. She

was back in that room, in her own vivid memories, breathing in the stink of other people's pain and terror. 'I think . . . operational secrecy, mainly,' she said at last. 'We're legal in some ways, but we're vulnerable in others. It's a difficult balance to keep, and if . . . if our people had left other people dead . . .' I nodded and waved her on. I got it. When you're an excommunicated secret sect fighting an undeclared guerrilla war, sometimes it's best not to invite too much scrutiny. At the Salisbury the Anathemata had moved openly, but then at the Salisbury there were tower blocks burning and dead people falling out of the sky. The cops had been grateful for all the help they could get. Evidently this operation was different. More like the Abbie Torrington business, in fact, when Gwillam's lunatics were shooting it out with another secret army in a west London church. That was an unwelcome memory. A prickle of presentiment made the hairs on the back of my neck stand up.

'Speight was raving,' Trudie went on. 'Feverish. I think his wound was poisoned in some way. They'd shot him full of antibiotics but he was burning up. I wasn't listening; I was too busy trying to sew up all these loose shreds of flesh into the shape of an arm. But I heard him anyway. Enough to put it together. There's a group called the Satanist Church of the Americas . . .'

'I've met them,' I said. 'Twice.'

Trudie nodded. She knew that, of course. The Anathemata had a file somewhere with Rafi's name on it, and she'd presumably read it from cover to cover before she ever met me in the flesh. Most of the last three years of my life would be in there.

'We thought they were defunct,' she said, sombrely. 'The man in charge – Anton Fanke – died, and after that there was a schism. They spent a lot of last year fighting among themselves. But from what Speight said, there was a clear winner in that contest. And then the order got word that SCA people were filtering into the UK, in ones and twos. Some of them were travelling on false passports, but we had people in place, watching them. We were able to track them as they started to come together.'

My throat was dry by this time. It wasn't just the vividness of Trudie's description, it was the growing certainty that I knew where she was going. 'How long ago was this?' I asked tersely.

'Last weekend. Six days ago. But Father Gwillam was tracking these arrivals for two weeks before that, so the Satanists started to gather in London about a week after Asmodeus broke free.

'They didn't come here to see the sights, Castor. They came to perform an invocation of some kind. They'd brought a girl with them: a sacrifice-child, like Abbie Torrington, born and bred to be ritually murdered. But the order was right on top of them, every step of the way. Father Gwillam called down an attack before they could finish the ritual.'

'The girl,' I said. 'Did you—?'

'Not me,' Trudie corrected, deadpan. 'I wasn't there, remember? But yeah, the order got her out in one piece.'

Remembering Abbie, I bared my teeth. 'How long is that likely to last?' I demanded. 'Gwillam is all about the greater good, isn't he? He'd kill this kid in a heartbeat if he thought there was any risk the satanists would try again.'

'That's just it.' Trudie tapped the back of my hand with her index finger. It was the first time we'd touched, and the tiny, subtle gesture of intimacy made me start slightly. 'There isn't a risk. Not any more. The order took casualties, but we wiped them out: not one of the satanists got out of that room alive. And they put everything into this. Our agents in America raided all their known chapter houses and found nothing. Even the sacrifice farm in Iowa was deserted.'

I tried to get my head round this. So either Asmodeus had contacted his acolytes as soon as he was free, or else they'd known by some other means that he was back in circulation. They'd tried to mount an operation that was a carbon copy of the one they'd pulled off two years ago when Fanke was still alive: to summon the demon out of Rafi's body by means of an esoterically prepared human sacrifice. And they'd failed.

After that, Asmodeus had murdered Ginny Parris, attacked me, started to stalk Pen. Why? Just out of rage that plan A hadn't worked? Or was he already working on plan B? I had to ask myself what I was missing, because there was bound to be something. Following the demon's terrifying corkscrew logic was like trying to figure-skate on the pitching deck of an icebreaker.

Trudie was staring at me as though she was waiting for me to speak. 'Thanks,' I said awkwardly. 'I did need to know about that stuff, and I appreciate you telling me.'

That seemed to exasperate her. 'Oh you're very fucking welcome,' she said, throwing out her hands. The tourists looked across at us from their table, startled at her loud imprecation. When you're having a cheap holiday in someone else's death, you don't expect to hear bad language. 'Castor,' she said, shaking her head, 'whatever you think of me – of my opinions – you have to see that we're on the same side in this one thing. We were both there. We both helped to set Asmodeus free because somebody else lied to us and tricked us.'

She leaned in closer to me, not for intimacy's sake this time but because she'd realised she needed to lower her voice. 'So you feel dirty? Compromised? Played? Well, snap. That's why I'm here. That's why I went straight from the Anathemata to the MOU – because there wasn't anywhere else I could go, if I still wanted to be in this fight. I'm going to do what I came for, which is to put that monster back in its cage. And I'm doing that whether you help me or hinder me or blank me or sabotage me, or whatever the hell you choose to do. But I think if we trust each other we might get further.'

She didn't wait for an answer this time: she was too angry and too full of the restless energy the memories had stirred up. She downed her second whisky in a single swallow, grabbed her bag and walked, leaving me to it.

She was right, of course. We were both enemy agents, in effect, in the monolithic structure of the MOU, and we'd be a lot more effective if we were prepared to at least watch each other's backs.

It was a big if, though. It was a very big if.

10

Walthamstow High Street hosts the longest street market in Europe. It's a proud boast, but it's also one that's worded with legalistic precision: it's not the biggest market, just the longest. It's a market shaped like a bootlace, in other words, stretching from Hoe Street in the east practically all the way down to Coppermill Lane in the west. By day it's an ever-running river of people moving to the fractal music of a thousand shouted conversations.

At this time of night though, it was just me and the ghosts.

I'd had to take another cab – no choice, so long after the last train – but I'd asked the cabbie to drop me at Blackhorse Road Tube station so I could walk the last mile or so on foot and clear my head a little. It was a good idea in principle, but it didn't work out all that well. The air was muggy, and heavy with a pre-thunderous load of unshed rain. There was a faint luminosity in the air, like the glow of a false dawn, although that was still a good few hours away. Around the railway bridge at the top of Vernon Street the ghosts of suicides clustered, a voiceless choir waiting for a cue that would never come. I felt like I was walking in the bulb at the bottom of a barometer: all those hundreds of miles of atmosphere, pressing down on me with a precisely calibrated intensity. One life, one load, one size fits all.

My bed was calling me, but Nicky – like rust – never sleeps, and we had a lot to talk about. This was a good time; I wasn't going to let it slip just because I was tired. You can come out through the far end of tired into a productive if slightly dangerous place. I knew how that felt and I was consciously searching for it, even though it seldom comes when it's looked for.

The street was twice as wide at night as it is by day, because none of the pitches are permanent. All the stall-holders pack their goods and their booths back up into a million white vans and depart with the setting sun, an east London caravanserai wending its way across the border into Essex, which for most of these wide boys is both physical and spiritual home.

But as I passed Manze's pie and mash shop, I saw there was one stall still out, probably in violation of a hundred local by-laws. A few steps closer, and I recognised the stall-holder as Nicky. Only it was Nicky dressed as Del-Boy, in a herringbone jacket and a black shirt with a white yoke and collar.

He had a good pitch, as far as that went. Close to Sainsbury's, which guarantees more passing trade than you can handle, and on a corner, which is always an advantage in terms of display space. What he didn't have was any stock, or – this being four in the morning – any customers. He was showing off his bare trestle tables to me and the man in the moon.

'Hey, Nicky,' I said, as I drew level with him.

'Hey, Castor.' He didn't look up from what he was doing, which was measuring the interior space of the stall and the dimensions of the three display tables with a tape measure.

'So, may I politely enquire what the fuck?' I asked him.

'Give me a minute,' Nicky said distractedly.

I waited while he paced up and down, applying the tape measure to every straight line available. He wasn't writing anything down, but I knew he didn't need to. Death hadn't done anything to impair Nicky's scarily efficient memory; if anything it had cleared his mind of a lot of distractions.

Finally he wound the tape measure around his hand – making me think momentarily of Trudie and her cat's cradles – and slid it into his pocket. 'Okay,' he said, 'I'm done here. You want to help me pack all this stuff up?' He pointed to a large, battered Bedford van standing with its doors open on the other side of the road.

'You don't think it's worth hanging on for a few more minutes?' I asked. 'Trade's bound to pick up once the word-of-mouth starts working.'

Nicky gave me a tired look. 'Trial run,' he said. 'I wanted to see how much space these things give you.'

'Why?'

'Why the hell do you think, Castor?' He started to fold up the tables as he spoke. 'I'm going into business.'

I stared at him blankly. It was actually about the least likely explanation I could think of for this nocturnal ramble. 'Selling what?' I demanded.

'DVDs. VHS tapes. Videodiscs. Actual film prints. Hard-to-get stuff in a variety of formats. In fact that's probably going to be the name of the stall: Hard-to-Get.'

He was starting to fold down the stall's marquee, which is a two-man job. Mechanically I stepped in to help. 'But Nicky,' I pointed out as tactfully as I could, 'the market's only open during the day.'

'I know that.'

'Whereas you're kind of a nocturnal life form, give or take. Plus you just flat-out hate people. You think two's a crowd.'

'Thanks, Castor. Believe it or not, these things had not slipped my mind.'

'Fine. Just checking.'

Nicky laid a bundle of scaffolding legs in a canvas bag, one at a time, where a living man might just have thrown them all in at once and taken a chance on the odd ricochet. You didn't last long as a zombie if you were cavalier with your mortal remains – and when it came to longevity, Nicky intended to break all known records. 'I'm buying a lot of stuff,' he said, 'and sometimes to get the stuff I want I have to buy a lot of shit I can't use.'

'So wouldn't A Lot of Shit I Can't Use be a more accurate name for the stall?'

He didn't rise to the bait. 'Maybe. We'll see how it pans out. Anyway, the point is, selling this stuff helps me finance my own hobby. It cost a lot to get the Gaumont up and running again. Defraying the expense seemed like a good idea.'

'Seriously, Nicky, how are you going to get around the going bad and stinking problem? You keep yourself chilled for a reason.'

He stuffed some canvas in on top of the ironmongery. He'd folded it quickly and expertly to the dimensions of the bag, which zipped shut with military precision. I had the sudden suspicion that he'd practised erecting and dismantling the stall in the auditorium at the Gaumont before bringing it out onto the street. 'I thought about it,' he said. 'A lot. The truth is, Castor, unless I can find someone who can do for me what the Ice-Maker was doing, I'm gonna start falling apart sooner rather than later.'

'You said there's a guy in the Midlands somewhere . . .'

'Yeah. There was, when I said it. Now there's a pile of ashes in the garden of rest at Walsall Crematorium. He got cancer. Died last month. And he seems to have decided against bodily resurrection as an option for his own future.'

I hefted one of the bags. 'So?' I prompted. 'Doesn't that mean it's even more of a bad idea for you to spend any time at room temperature?'

Nicky gave me a stony look. 'Actually, what it means is that I'm just prolonging the inevitable. Which is probably what I was doing anyway, with or without the Ice-Maker. This just brought it home to me. Yeah, I can stay in the deep freeze the whole time, last another six months, maybe a year. Then take my chances when I hit the wall.

'Or alternatively I can try coming at the problem from a different angle. Like I said, I've been thinking about it. The way I look at it, life is like matter and energy: it can't be destroyed, it can only be transformed. So my working plan right now is that I'm going to see this body out and then maybe rethink my options.'

That proposition stopped me in my tracks. Nicky hadn't got to be the longest-lived zombie in the known world by taking unnecessary risks; he'd done it by clinging stubbornly to what he had and what he knew, and advancing into the void one tentative, begrudged step at a time. This sort of thinking was way out of character for him.

'What options, exactly?' I demanded.

Nicky fiddled with the zip fastener on one of the bags,

his expression turning a little shifty. 'I've been out,' he said.

'Out?' I echoed, but I already knew what he meant.

'Out of the flesh. I tried it a few times right after I died, and got nowhere. Now . . . it isn't even hard. I decide to do it, and it's done. Suddenly I'm looking at the back of my own head or more usually looking down from on top like my body's an actor in a show and the real me is up in the dress circle, watching. I guess it's a skill you just pick up as you go along.'

Or else, I thought, this was another piece of evidence that the world's coefficients were shifting, tumbling us all – whether we liked it or not – out of our comfort zones into the infinite.

'So yeah,' Nicky summarised. 'I know the ejector seat's working, after all. That makes me feel a little bit more relaxed about letting the bodywork get all messed up. I'm gonna survive, Castor. Whatever the Hell happens to this meat. Knowing that changes the way you look at things.'

I didn't answer because I couldn't think of anything to say that wouldn't sound either banal or apocalyptic. We carried the dismantled stall over to the van. Such was Nicky's precision that it only took two trips. 'Thanks,' he said. 'Okay, I got some stuff for you. You want it here or back at the movie house?'

Neither alternative seemed all that attractive. The night was a curdled bowl, but the Gaumont would be as frigid as a tomb. I went for the bird-in-the-hand option. 'I'll take it now,' I said, 'unless you need help unpacking at the other end.'

'It can stay in the van. Okay, you asked me whether

Ditko had any living relatives. The answer is one, and counting.'

He fished in the pocket of his jacket and handed me a folded sheet of paper. I took it and opened it up, but the light from the street lamps wasn't good enough to read Nicky's crabbed handwriting.

'A brother,' he summarised. 'Name of Jovan.'

Tell my father . . . and Jovan . . . tell them I'm sorry. Do that for me. Please.

'So where is he?' I asked.

'In FYROM.'

'In what?'

'The Former Yugoslav Republic of Macedonia. It's a place. In Europe. You've just got the address there, no phone number or email. That's all she wrote. Apart from Rafael, this is the last Ditko in the known universe. And if you want to talk to him, I suggest you move fast.'

'Why's that, Nicky?'

He flicked a corner of the paper with his thumbnail. 'Because the address is death row, Irdrizovo Prison. He killed a guy, the cops caught him, and now he's all out of appeals. Near as I can tell, the execution is going to be the day after tomorrow unless there's a last-minute pardon.'

I carried on looking at him expectantly. He shrugged, deadpan. 'What?'

'It's just a little barebones for you,' I said. 'It's not that I'm not grateful. It just seems like . . . maybe . . . you left a stone unturned for once in your life.'

'Yeah? Like what, for instance?'

'Like "He killed a guy"?'

'Well there's more, but it's ugly and would it help you

to know? Irdrizovo is one fucking big oubliette. They're not gonna let you see him. And they're not gonna pardon him. That's not the way the system works. But if you insist on wading in, there's another name on there, and a telephone number. Jovan's defence lawyer. Maybe you could get some questions to him somehow. Have to be fast, though.'

I slipped the paper into my pocket. 'Thanks, Nicky. What else?'

Nicky feigned surprise. 'That isn't enough? Too bad. On the magic circle front, things are not going so well. The other one you sent me – you found it close to the first?'

'Nowhere near,' I said. 'The first was at Pen's place, the second was at Juliet's.'

Nicky grimaced. 'Would it surprise you to know that there was a third?' he asked. Without waiting for an answer, he delved into his pocket, came up with a flat stone very like the two I'd already found. He flicked it into the air and I caught it at the height of its arc.

I opened my fist and examined it. It looked identical to the others, except that once more there was a different set of symbols at the heart of the pentagram. Four again, as with the stone I'd found at Pen's.

'Where'd you get it?' I demanded.

'Where do you think?' Nicky countered. It was a fair question: it wasn't as though he had a jet-setting lifestyle.

'At your place.'

'Up on the roof. So what's the common denominator?'

I didn't bother to ask him what he was doing up on the roof. Nicky is the kind of paranoiac who other paranoiacs feel should lighten up a little. I didn't bother to answer his question, either, because it was clearly meant to be rhetorical.

'They're all in London,' I mused.

Nicky rolled his eyes. 'Yeah, right. Well done. What are you waiting for? Until you find one shoved up your arse? They're aimed at you, Castor.'

'Maybe,' I allowed. 'Maybe not. But yeah, so far I'm the common denominator.'

'The first one was in Pen's drive?' Nicky demanded.

'Yeah,' I confirmed. And what was it that was scratching at the back door of my mind as I said that, begging to be let in? Whatever it was, it was playing games with me, because when I opened the door there was nothing there.

'Second?'

'Sue Book's garden.'

'And the third was tucked in behind my satellite dish. So whoever it was didn't come inside any at any point. Suggesting maybe they couldn't, because they're dead or undead and don't like to get tangled up in whatever wards are on the buildings. Anyway, they're all summonings, and they're all done in the same style. I was right about that much.'

'All petitioning the same entity? This Tlallik?'

'No. As I'm sure you noticed, all three of them carry different names. So now, in addition to Tlallik we've got demons named Ket and Jetaniul. And I can't find word one about any of them.'

'Nothing?' I was both amazed and disconcerted.

'Almost nothing,' Nicky qualified. 'There's a passage in

Foivel Grazimir's *Enaxeteleuton* that includes Tlallik, but the context makes it completely useless. Crazy Foivel is talking about demons that are worth dealing with as opposed to demons that aren't. I could do it from memory, but here.'

He'd taken a second, much larger sheet of paper from the same pocket, which he unfolded now before handing it to me with a ceremonial flourish.

'Nicky,' I said, 'if this is from one of the Russian hermetics it's in fucking old Cyrillic.'

'You can transliterate though, right? Look.' He ran his finger down the right-hand side of the page. 'Agathonou. Dyspex. Idionel. Tlallik.'

'Yeah, but what is that? Grazimir's Christmas card list?'

'Probably not, Castor. He was Jewish. I can give you the rough sense of it. He's been saying "bespeak this name for wealth" and "this demon can set you up with some female company for the weekend". Then he goes "but you must know from lore, or else learn it by hard experiment, that some names thought to be potent don't do Jack shit" – I'm paraphrasing, you understand – "so call not on these, for though they be of great renown and great power, they don't pick up when you call".'

I pondered this, looking down the list for some other names I recognised. There weren't any.

'Grazimir is writing when?' I asked.

'Thirteenth century. About the same time as Honorius and Ghayat al-Hakim.'

'So, way early?'

'Yeah.'

'And he's got Tlallik pegged as a has-been.'

'Exactly. And as far as I can tell, none of the high medievals mention him at all. Whoever drew those circles, Castor, they're either dipping into some very old magic or else they're so far behind the curve they're staring up their own arseholes.'

I breathed out heavily – almost a sigh – and tucked the list into my pocket along with Jovan Ditko's contact details. 'Thanks again,' I said. 'Feel like adding another chore to the list?'

'Not so much.'

'It's an easy one.'

'Then try me. But don't be surprised if I tell you to go fuck yourself. I've got a new line of business now; I don't have to worry so much about pissing you off.'

'Like you ever did. I need some information about a place. An area of London.' I told him about Super-Self, and what I'd seen there. He listened in silence until I got to the part with the ghosts in the swimming pool.

'No fucking way,' he said then.

'I'm telling you what I saw, Nicky.'

'Then you were stoned. Roman ghosts? In togas? Please! Were there any ghost-cavemen there, throwing spears at ghost-mammoths?'

'The Aldwych end of the Strand,' I repeated doggedly. 'Close to what used to be Wych Street. Apparently there was some work done there around the turn of the century. The twentieth century, I mean.'

'Some work done?' Nicky snorted. 'They levelled the whole area to build Aldwych. Which is Anglo-Saxon, by the way – it means "old settlement". From a logistical point of view, you could take that as a hint that there might have been buildings of some sort there when the Romans came through. But it's still ridiculous.'

'Why?'

'Why what?'

'Why is it ridiculous? Give me the reasons.'

He didn't even have to pause for thought. 'First off, ghosts don't last that long. You know that as well as I do. Second, ghosts don't interact with other ghosts. I know you've got that weird little dead-girl posse, but I never heard of anything like that anywhere else. Ghosts interact with the living, or else they're locked in on themselves and they just replay their death. What they don't do is have kaffee-klatches with other ghosts. And third, the ground level would have been a good thirty feet lower back then. I know you were in the basement, so that's a few feet below the street, but it still wouldn't have been low enough.'

'Suppose their anchor isn't a physical place. It could be something that was used in the building. Some of the stonework behind the tiles of the swimming pool, say. Maybe they moved because their anchor was moved.'

'And they end up twenty feet closer to God, still playing out whole conversations like scenes from a silent movie? Why doesn't that explanation convince me? Face it, Castor, the behaviour you're describing doesn't fit with anything you've ever seen before.'

'That's precisely the point,' I said. 'It doesn't. So whatever the explanation turns out to be, it's going to be new. I don't want to rule anything out just because it sounds weird.'

'Or insane,' Nicky added. 'Yeah, I hear you. But even Sherlock Holmes liked to eliminate the impossible before he got moving. Otherwise he would've fingered a lot more leprechauns and unicorns than he did.'

I was too tired to argue. 'Just check the site out,' I asked him. 'Tell me if anything weird has happened there before now.'

Nicky shrugged irritably. 'Castor, that's what libraries are for. Seriously. Don't use me to research stuff that's in the public domain. It's fucking insulting.'

'Why do you care, if I'm paying?' I asked, exasperated in my turn. 'What, you have to have job satisfaction too?'

He gave me a sour look. 'Yeah,' he said. 'I do. Because what you pay me, frankly, it's symbolic. It's stuff I like to get, but I can get it elsewhere. I work with you because it's interesting. You start treating me like Wikipedia, we're done.'

He was serious, so I backed off. I knew damn well how many favours I owed him, and how much more I needed his digging skills than he needed the old sounds and rare reds I trawled for him. But since our relationship is based on a foundation of solid bullshit, I backed off bullshitting all the way.

'Sorry to injure your professional pride, Nicky,' I said. 'I'll make sure only to use you for big, philosophical stuff in future. And since the payment's symbolic, I'll switch to IOUs.'

'Try it,' he suggested, his voice dripping with sarcasm. He slammed the van's doors shut and then turned to face me again. 'I'm still working on the Tlallik thing,' he said. 'I've got a couple more avenues I haven't tried yet. Far-Eastern mystical texts, and some African stuff. Different demons seem to work different territories, or at least to go by different names when they travel. I'll be in touch.'

He headed round to the front of the van, then stopped halfway. 'Oh, one other thing. On the subject of demons, and how to survive them . . .'

'Yeah?' My interest quickened. 'Is this the thing you were so cagey about last time?'

'I wasn't cagey; I just don't like coming out with half of the answer to a question. But I'm stretched on other fronts, so I figured you'd rather hear this now. Maybe get the bitch queen to put some of her people on it, because I'm not making much headway. You ever hear of a guy name of Martin Moulson?'

'No. Should I have?'

'Maybe not. This was a while back, and he was never in with the in crowd, as far as black magic is concerned. But the word I'm getting is that he had a passenger – a big bastard too. Not as big as Asmodeus, probably, but who is? But he got out from under, somehow. Fixed himself a spiritual enema, and came up demon-free. That, at least, is how the story goes. Unfortunately, it's a story that ends with a whimper, because the guy seems to have vanished off the face of the Earth. If you can track him down, I figure you and him might have a few things to talk about.'

'Yeah, I'd say so,' I agreed, falling in with his understated tone. 'Any leads at all?'

Nicky blew out his cheek. 'Urban legends, mostly. It's kind of like an Elvis deal: everyone's got a story.'

'Well if all else fails, you can look him up in Wikipedia.'

'Drop dead, Castor.'

'Working on it, Nicky,' I said as I walked away. 'One day at a time.'

*   *   *

'My Lord, Felix, you look exhausted!' Jenna-Jane's face was the picture of concern. Maybe someone had hung the picture a little crooked; the effect was subtle enough that you had to look twice to see it.

'Long night,' I said, stating the obvious.

'And productive, I hope.' J-J was standing, I was sitting, which gave the meeting the flavour of an interrogation, even though she hadn't asked me any questions yet. Slowly and deliberately, she pulled the cords that angled the slatted blinds to their closed position. She had to lean over Gil McClennan to do it, because the cords were in the corner where he was sitting. She treated him as part of the furniture, which to be fair was probably nothing personal. I was sure it was how she thought of all of us deep down.

'You don't mind if Gil sits in, do you?' she asked me belatedly. 'His experiences of the Super-Self entity will make a useful double check against yours, assuming' – a momentary hesitation – 'you're able to take us beyond what we know already.'

It was the next morning, although for me it was continuous with the night before. I was contending not just with physical tiredness but also with a lingering feeling of disconnectedness which had hung over me ever since I walked into the pool area at Super-Self. At some point during the day I was going to have to find or make the time to crash, if only for half an hour. I'd probably wake up more exhausted than ever, but I'd be back in the real world, not floating a few feet above it.

'What do you know already?' I asked Jenna-Jane. The best defence is sometimes a pre-emptive strike, but it was her game and her rules. There was no way she'd ever play with an open hand. She didn't even bother to answer; McClennan did it for her.

'Everyone on my team has already filed a report on this. We're here to listen to yours.'

I shrugged, giving it up. 'All right,' I said. 'Start with the obvious. It's not what it looks like.'

Gil sneered nastily, and Jenna-Jane favoured me with an austere frown. 'It's an apparition, Felix, with no physical substance. It can be perceived by the naked eye but fails to register on any recording medium and is opaque to every other human sense. Surely by its very nature, it is *exactly* what it looks like.'

'So a layman might think, Professor Mulbridge,' I said solemnly. 'But a woman of science and erudition like yourself knows the difference between phenomenon and epi-phenomenon – between the causal and the merely collateral.'

Jenna-Jane actually smiled, but only for a second, acknowledging both the distinction and the fact that I was slapping her in the face with her own overblown technical register. 'Go on,' she said.

'The ghosts in the pool,' I said. 'They're so weird and inexplicable, everyone looks at them first and assumes that they're what needs to be explained. I did that myself. But then I went away and thought about it, and on second thoughts they're pretty much beside the point.' Nobody interrupted me, so I went on. 'The bigger mystery – and certainly the bigger danger – is the one you can't see. There's something in that room that makes everyone who goes in there experience sudden, blind terror. You' – I flicked a glance at Gil, who I was ignoring for the most part – 'said that some of the other exorcists who've been into Super-Self have actually had mental breakdowns as a result of contact with that thing. You took them into the pool and made them stay long enough to attempt an exorcism. They failed, and they were fucked over. It broke them. Am I right?'

There was a moment's silence. 'You put the situation very dramatically,' Jenna-Jane chided me, 'but yes, we have had casualties. Poor Victor Etheridge, to name but one. And it's true that this is a peculiarly tenacious haunting.'

'No,' I said, 'it isn't. Call it that, and you're never going to get anywhere – because you'll be charging off to battle in the wrong direction.'

'Meaning . . . ?' Jenna-Jane asked.

'What I said. It's not a haunting at all. It's something else that has a haunting as part of its furniture. The ghosts aren't the thing we need to be looking at. Whatever lives in that room, and makes grown men and women want to piss themselves and run under moving cars – that's what we need to be looking at.'

Gil had been having trouble sitting still through this sermon. 'I disagree,' he said now, emphatically. 'Both with the reasoning and with the conclusion. What we know, Castor – the only thing we know – is that those ghosts break all the rules we thought couldn't be broken. They're more than a thousand years older than any other ghost we've found, and yet they show no signs of morpho-logical decay; and they acknowledge each other's presence, talk to each other, even seem to hand each other objects. Physical objects.'

He tapped the corner of Jenna-Jane's desk as if to remind

me what 'physical objects' meant. 'I think whatever explains the ghosts will explain the fear too,' he said. 'If you're right that we're talking about cause and effect, the ghosts are the cause. Why shouldn't ghosts that old generate a psychic-emotional field?'

'Why shouldn't ghosts that old ride in Cadillacs and smoke fine Cuban cigars?' I countered. 'McClennan, we're not even arguing about how many angels can dance on the head of a pin, here; we're trying to guess what colour their underpants will be.'

Gil started to say something, but Jenna-Jane spoke over him and he let her run with the ball. 'Does it make any practical difference,' she asked, 'whether we make the ghosts or the room's emotional resonance the centre of our investigation? We're assuming, either way, that there's a single agency at work here. We're aiming to understand – and then to eradicate – both manifestations.'

I didn't bother to challenge the mission statement. I've been skittish about casual eradication for a while now, but if J-J wanted to believe that I was toeing the company line and strumming the company banjo, I was happy to let her. 'It makes a big difference,' I said, 'because it ties in with some other stuff that's happening, and if I'm right, it opens up a new line of attack.'

I'd finally reached the point, but I hesitated to put it into words. It would have been hard, even with a more sympathetic audience. I was thinking of a lot of things: of Nicky, a few scant hours ago, talking about the new options that had opened up for him; of the ghost on the Salisbury estate, the spirit of a teenage boy that had meta- morphosed into a newly born demon; of the time, even more recently, when I found myself sitting in the gutter in a drunken stupor with my whistle in my hands, trying to hit a note that had crept into the world while I wasn't even looking; of the story of Chicken Licken; of the sad, wrecked old zombie in Somers Town saying, 'World's changing. It don't want us no more'; and of Rosie, repeating the same sentiment almost word for word. *Like the light in a room when the sun comes up, or when it goes down. You don't notice it until it's happened.*

'I think we're starting to see some stuff that's totally new,' I said, taking refuge in the jargon. 'Things that won't be in the grimoires, because nobody's ever encountered them before. I think we might be coming to a point where the rulebook won't help us all that much.'

Jenna-Jane was staring at me intently. She hadn't sat down all this time; she'd been standing over me, like a teacher over an unruly pupil who'll stop working as soon as he knows he's not being watched. 'And why do you think this is happening?' she demanded.

'I have no idea,' I said, and it was the truth. 'Maybe a balance shifted somewhere. Some big cosmic constant wasn't quite as constant as we thought, and now it's tilting. Maybe the sewers are blocked in Hell, and all the shit is backing up. I don't know, Jenna-Jane. I'm just throwing it out there. But if I'm right, then I think you'll probably already know what I'm talking about – either because you've had this conversation with some of your own people, or because you've found some way of measuring it for yourself.'

She was staring at me with an air of cool, detached appraisal that didn't quite ring true. I met her gaze stolidly, until after a few moments she looked away.

'Interesting,' she said. 'This is why I missed you, Felix. Because you work through the evidence without preconceptions.'

'With respect,' Gil said, his voice sounding a little thick, 'he's told us nothing at all about the Super-Self ghosts. He's only justifying his own failure to reach any solid conclusions.'

Jenna-Jane smiled indulgently. 'He's told us his conclusions, Gilbert – although it's true they don't amount to a solution as yet. In that regard, Castor, do you *have* a solution? It would be an excellent way to round off your first twenty-four hours on my staff.'

'No,' I admitted. 'I don't. Teamwork helps, I can tell you that much. Pax and I got out in one piece because we ran interference for each other. But we didn't even get close to attempting an exorcism. You just can't keep your head together enough for that. Maybe you need a sort of Normandy landing approach, with exorcists advancing in waves. But even then . . .'

'I like that,' Jenna-Jane mused. 'A brute-force approach. It has the merit of simplicity.'

'And the drawback that we'll be throwing all our people into a blind alley,' Gil objected. 'If it goes wrong, they could all end up like Etheridge.'

Actually, that was a fair point. If Etheridge had become the jumpy little bag of nerves he now was by getting too close to the Super-Self entity, that made a strong case for staying away from it at least until we knew what it was. It suddenly occurred to me that we should have asked Juliet that question. Erratic as her recent behaviour had been, she was still the acknowledged expert when it came to matters demoniacal: our inside man. And since I was already paying her to babysit Pen, it might not be too much of an ask to have her come down to the Strand for a consultation.

Jenna-Jane put on her Solomon-come-to-judgement face. 'I understand your concerns, Gilbert,' she said. 'Still, a combined attack did pay very definite dividends in the summoning of Rosie Crucis. It's possible that a number of simultaneous exorcisms might work where individual attempts have failed. You can organise your people into teams of two, with one leading partner in each team. The second man watches the first from further back, and pulls him out if he starts to show signs of strain.'

Gil was getting exasperated, persumably at the prospect of my plan being adopted after he'd given it the thumbs down. 'What if the trailing man gets hit first?' he demanded, throwing out his arms in an indignant shrug. 'We know the pool is ground zero, but you can feel the effects of this thing from a long way away. It would be stupid to just go in there thinking that we're attacking the pool, or what's in it. It would be like . . . like going after a wasps' nest with a baseball bat and thinking you can't get stung as long as you kill the queen.'

'Nice analogy,' I conceded. 'Look, I'm not saying that going in mob-handed is a good idea. I was just thinking aloud.'

Jenna-Jane made a dismissive gesture, as if this was all just a matter of fine detail.

'Still,' she said, 'I see no harm in trying. Make a list, Gilbert. Ten lead exorcists, with ten in support. Castor will be one of the leads, as will you.'

She stared at Gil for so long it was impossible to miss the point that he was being dismissed. He stood up but didn't leave, fighting a visible psychomachia against his strong instinct to roll over and die for the queen.

'If it doesn't work,' he said, 'that's twenty of us in the shit.'

'The larger number spreads the risk,' said Jenna-Jane, her tone cold and deliberate.

Gil stood his ground for a moment longer. Then he nodded curtly and headed for the door.

When it closed behind him, Jenna-Jane turned back to me with a look on her face that was almost arch. 'Gilbert doesn't like you very much, Felix,' she said. 'I've tried hard to bring him round to my way of thinking, but I'm afraid it's an uphill struggle.'

'I killed his favourite uncle,' I pointed out. 'Makes it a little hard for us to bond.'

'Oh, it's not that,' Jenna-Jane assured me, sounding surprised at the very idea. 'It's much more personal, and much more straightforward. He's afraid that you might be a better exorcist than him. That thought niggles at him. It throws him off his stride.'

'Really?' I demanded. 'Why me, particularly? Everyone on the team is probably a better exorcist than him.'

Jenna-Jane shook her head admonishingly. 'You're wrong,' she said. 'He has a lot of raw power. More than anyone else in the family. I tested his cousin Dana, and she was impressive. She worked here for a year, and did a lot of good work for us. She left in the end for personal reasons, after a quarrel with another woman on the team turned into something more ugly. Gilbert is better than

Dana, but he's still not what you might call emotionally stable. In order to manage him, I've bonded with him on a very personal level. Now he sees you as a threat to that . . . closeness.'

I stared at her in silence, a smart answer dying on my lips. The thought of being part of a love triangle that had Jenna-Jane as one of its other two vertices made my stomach go through some complicated and unpleasant revolutions.

'Now,' she said, moving briskly along, 'the Ditko situation . . .'

Right, I thought. And the Rafi situation too, while we're on the subject. I squared my shoulders involuntarily, because I was about to tell J-J some bare-faced lies and I wanted to do it with an upright posture and a lot of eye contact.

'I think you should send me to Macedonia,' I said.

Jenna-Jane tilted her head to one side, looking faintly puzzled.

'Really?' she said. 'Why?'

'Because Rafi Ditko has a brother. Jovan.' J-J didn't exclaim in surprise or ask any further questions. She just stared at me, knowing there had to be more. 'He's on death row,' I went on, 'convicted of murder. If we want to talk to him, we've got precisely two days to do it in.'

'But why should we want to talk to him?' J-J asked, sounding genuinely puzzled. 'Ditko only became possessed after he arrived in England. It's not likely that his brother would know anything that could help us.'

'I copy you on that, as far as it goes,' I agreed. 'I started looking for Rafi's family in the first place so I could warn them that Asmodeus might be dropping into their lives.

But now I'm thinking that it might be worth a trip to meet this guy. Did you know that Asmodeus can't walk through wards drawn by Pamela Bruckner?'

J-J frowned. 'No, I didn't. Bruckner is the vile-tempered little redhead, correct? Ditko's former girlfriend, as well as yours.'

'Pen was never my girlfriend,' I corrected her scrupulously. I let the 'vile-tempered' stand, since Pen wouldn't have taken it as an insult in any case. 'She's my landlady. Sometimes. The point is, I've seen Asmodeus ignore wards drawn by strangers. They hurt him, but they don't slow him down all that much. The personal connection seems to make a difference.'

'So you believe Ditko's brother might have a similar power over the demon? But if he's in prison . . .'

'I just want to talk to him,' I repeated. 'Mostly about Rafi's childhood. It may come to nothing. Probably will. But at the very least, deepening our understanding of Rafi may help us to bring his consciousness and his re-actions to the fore when we meet Asmodeus again. At the moment the bastard seems to have things all his own way. Rafi can't get any purchase, so he's led around like a dog.'

I'd said my piece. It was all garbage, of course, and I felt pretty uneasy about that. Not about lying to Jenna-Jane, of course, but about going AWOL at a time when the hunt for the demon might finally be starting to get somewhere. But Rafi had begged me to deliver his message to his father and his brother. I'd already missed the boat as far as Mr Ditko senior was concerned, and this was my last chance to talk to Jovan. I really didn't have any other option, unless it was to write Jovan a letter, send it first class and hope it beat the hangman.

Jenna-Jane appeared to consider. 'If you think this could actually be of some value . . .' she said.

'I don't think we can afford to pass up the opportunity,' I said.

She nodded. 'I'd need you to fly there and back today,' she said. 'You're wanted here.'

'It should be a short flight,' I said. 'I don't see there'd be a problem getting a day return.'

Jenna-Jane picked up the phone and dialled, still without sitting down. 'Hello, Edward,' she said. 'Could you please book a flight to Macedonia in the name of Felix Castor. Flying out and returning today. No, I have no idea. If there's more than one airport, we need the one that's closest to the capital city. Get him some currency too. And ground transport. Soonest would be best. Thank you.'

She put the phone down. 'Anything else?' she asked me.

'Get your research team looking for a man named Martin Moulson.'

'Who is he?'

'I don't have the slightest idea. But he was possessed by a major demon, and he survived. It was a long time ago, and the name's pretty much all I've got.'

Jenna-Jane wrote down the name and looked at me expectantly. I shrugged. 'I'm done,' I said. 'For now.'

'In that case, you should go and talk to Ms Pax. Her mapping experiment has borne some fruit.'

As I stood, she favoured me with a warm smile. 'I value your expertise, Felix. I know we've had our differences in the past, but I believe that this time we'll make the part-nership work.'

'It's a point of view,' I said as non-committally as I could manage. As an answer, it was better than sticking two fingers down my throat and hurling on her carpet tiles.

The first thing I saw when I walked out into the corridor was Gil McClennan standing at the far end of it, staring out of the window. He turned as I walked towards him and stared at me hard until I came level with him. I stopped, because he looked as though he wanted to say something, but he just kept on staring.

'If it pisses you off so much that she thinks this was my idea, then leave me out,' I suggested. 'You think I give a fuck? I didn't come here to upstage you, McClennan. I only want one thing and then I'm out of here.'

'I don't want another Etheridge on my conscience,' he muttered, his voice a little thick. 'You hate the unit so much, you think everyone here is expendable.'

I couldn't keep the surprise off my face. Maybe I didn't try. 'You thought me and Pax were expendable last night,' I reminded him. 'You sent us down those stairs hoping the thing in the pool would fuck us up.'

'Would fuck *you* up,' he corrected me angrily. 'I tried to keep her out of it.'

That was true, as far as it went. 'A McClennan with a conscience,' I grunted, shaking my head. 'Must be a reces-sive gene or something.'

He telegraphed the punch, so I was able to knock it aside before it connected with my face. He followed up fast though, and my own uppercut glanced off his chin as he closed with me and locked both of his hands around my throat. It wasn't a smart move, because it didn't leave him any limbs free for defence, but he held onto me with the strength of blind rage. Two punches to the side of the head didn't loosen him, and his thumbs were compressing my windpipe agonisingly. Reflexively, I tried to draw breath, and felt my heart race on an adrenalin flood as I failed.

Improvising desperately, I hooked my foot behind his leg and threw my weight forward. We sprawled on the floor of the corridor, with me on top, and then I rolled to the side, finally breaking his grip.

We came up together, more or less, but I'd had more than enough of this bullshit. I feinted with my right hand and threw a roundhouse punch with my left almost at the same time. It smacked against Gil's cheek with a meaty sound. A jolt of pain shot from my fist to my elbow, but it did the job: Gil folded and went down again heavily.

I leaned against the corridor wall, getting my breath back. That was painful in itself, because my throat felt as though I'd swallowed a cricket ball. My left hand throbbed painfully, the index finger in particular refusing to bend when I tested it. It was already starting to swell up around the bottom joint.

Gil pulled himself together slowly, levering himself into a sitting position with his back against the corridor wall. The building work had evidently drowned out the sound of our fight, so nobody came out to see what was happening.

'You . . . bastard,' Gil panted, his voice slurred. 'Get out of my . . . fucking . . . life!'

'I told you,' I panted back. 'I'm here for one thing. If you want to see the back of me . . . give me Ditko.' I lurched away before he could answer. I needed to plunge my hand into some cold water before it swelled up any further. I'd be fuck-all use to anybody if I couldn't play.

Trudie showed me her map with a proprietary and slightly nervous air. It had changed a lot since the last time I'd seen it: it was marked now by hundreds of short black dashes, clustered together and aligned to form longer lines. The lines swept and swirled across the face of the city like the tracks left by primordial particles in a bubble chamber, the spoor of something both ephemeral and eternal, struck from violence the way sparks are struck from stone.

'This is where he's been,' I said, tracing the nearest lines with my finger.

'Yes.'

'But where is he now?'

Trudie's expression went from anxious midwife to grieving parent. 'I have no idea. There's a faint sense when I'm tracing the lines that some are fresher than others. They're the ones that are easiest to find, the ones that have the strongest attraction. But there's no . . .' She hesitated, searching for a word.

'Gradient?' I suggested.

'Exactly. No real gradient, so no way of telling which way he walked along each line or how long he spent in any of these places. It's just a map of his movements.'

'Which means it will get less and less useful as he goes to more and more places. Eventually the map would be solid black.'

Trudie eyed me grimly. 'Thanks, Castor. I only spent

twelve hours on this. Don't spare my feelings.' Behind her, Etheridge glared at me fiercely, outraged on her behalf.

'I didn't say it wasn't useful now,' I pointed out. 'It's amazing. I never expected you to get this far.'

Trudie seemed as unhappy with praise as she was with criticism. 'Well, it's only the first stage,' she said defensively. 'We've still got to go over the map again and try to figure out where he's actually spending his time.'

I pointed to one of the densest tangles on the map, and then to another: two places where a great many lines came together, merging into areas of pure shiny black. At the heart of those areas the paper had rucked into hard wrinkles, swollen and saturated with ink. It was like looking at one of Trudie's cat's cradles translated onto a flat, static medium – because, of course, that's what it was.

'Here,' I said, 'and here.'

'Yeah,' said Trudie. He's been to those two places a lot. Both in north London, about seven miles apart. Do you have any idea what's there?'

'This one – that's a couple of miles north of King's Cross – is where I live. No surprises there – I knew he was staking out Pen's house. This one over to the west though, that's more worrying.'

'Why?' Trudie stared at me hard, hard enough to let me know that my face was showing too much of what I felt.

'This is Royal Oak,' I said. 'I've got a friend who lives out there.'

The penny dropped. 'Oh my God,' Trudie murmured.

'About as far from your God as it's possible to get, strictly speaking,' I said grimly.

'The succubus. The fallen creature you used to work with.'

'Exactly.'

I weighed my options for a few moments. I'd already said too much in front of Etheridge. Damaged as he was, he still owed his allegiance to Jenna-Jane, and I had to assume he was going to report back to her. I wasn't ready to trust Trudie either, come to that – at least, not all the way – but probably I needed to tell her at least something about what was going down on the Juliet front. 'Let's take the air,' I suggested, looking pointedly at her alone.

Trudie hesitated, then nodded. Turning to Etheridge, she gave him a notepad and a pen. 'Start writing down the names of the streets, Victor,' she told him. 'When I come back we'll start checking them out with Google maps.'

We went to Paddington Basin, which runs right behind St Mary's. Part of the basin had been drained a few months back, and the council had erected a sculpture of a giant plug and plughole to raise the morale of local residents while their picturesque canal was a plain of stinking mud. This was where we fetched up, sitting out in front of a pavement café that hadn't opened for lunch yet.

After extorting a promise from Trudie not to pass any of what I was about to say on to Jenna-Jane, I told her about the bizarre glitches in Juliet's behaviour, including the beating she'd administered to Susan and the threat she'd made to me. I mentioned the ward I'd found in Juliet's garden, too, but only in passing because it was part of a wider pattern whose meaning seemed to lie elsewhere. Trudie heard me out in silence, then as soon as I'd finished she started in with the questions.

'Isn't this creature savage by her very nature?' she demanded. 'Why is any of this a surprise?'

'It's a surprise because it goes against everything that Juliet has done since she decided to stay on Earth,' I explained patiently. 'She knows damn well that she can only live here as long as she manages to stay on the wagon. If she starts to eat people, even just on special occasions, every exorcist in London is going to come looking for her. And good as she is, sooner or later someone is bound to sneak up on her blind side and finish the job.'

Trudie didn't look convinced. 'But what would that do?' she asked with a shrug. 'It might just send her back to Hell. She'd be free to rise again whenever she wanted.'

I stared her down. 'Is that what you think exorcism is?'

'I don't know, Castor. And neither do you.'

'But we know that demons avoid it strenuously. Desperately, even. It's got to be more than a cab ride home.'

There was a silence. A waiter unlocked the front door of the café, obviously thinking we were his first customers of the day. Not being in the mood for coffee, tea, or any other drink that wasn't at least 30 per cent proof, I got up and moved on. Trudie followed.

'Can I see the wards you found?' she asked.

'I've got a photo of it on my phone,' I said. 'I'll send it on to you.'

'What about you, Castor? What's your next move?'

'I'm going to Macedonia to meet what's left of Rafi's family. How about you?'

'I'll work over the map with Victor. See if it gives us any clues to where Asmodeus is hiding.'

'And then when I come back we're going to make a second raid on Super-Self.'

Trudie rolled her eyes. 'That'll be fun.'

'Working for Jenna-Jane is like being in the army,' I said. 'Every day is a holiday.'

'Send me those pictures before you go,' Trudie said.

'Sure.' I turned to face her. Might as well have this out now as later. 'But these are the standard terms and conditions,' I told her. 'We don't share any of this with either your former or your current employer unless I say we do.'

After the barest moment of hesitation, Trudie nodded. 'Agreed.'

'And anything new you come up with, you run it by me before you go to Jenna-Jane.'

Another pause. 'If you agree to do the same thing,' Trudie said. 'Share whatever you find in Macedonia with me. And pass me anything you get from Nicholas Heath.'

That came as something of a shock. 'How did you know I'd seen Nicky?' I demanded, tensing involuntarily.

Trudie smiled, a little smugly. 'I researched you very thoroughly when I worked for the Anathemata,' she said. 'You're too set in your ways, Castor. Got your habits. Your superstitions and foibles. Your prime directives. Heath is one of them.'

'I'm still alive,' I reminded her.

'Yeah,' she agreed. 'That's another.'

II

From Alexander the Great International Airport I went straight to downtown Skopje. The airport was a strip of tarmac and a Coke machine, but the city itself was pretty impressive. Sprawling along both sides of the Vardar River, and standing on the main drag from Belgrade to Athens, it's always seen a fair bit of passing trade. Admittedly it's also had its fair share – maybe slightly more – of wars, pogroms, earthquakes, corruption, industrial collapse and apocalyptic mismanagement, but it's always managed to pick itself up, dust itself off and start all over again. Today it looks like any other medium-sized metropolis, with old and new buildings jostling each other for position on most streets, and a pall of smog closing down the middle distance.

From my hotel – a Holiday Inn on Pijade Street – I called Jovan Ditko's lawyer, a guy named Anastasiadis, and left a message. I'd already called twice from London, had the receptionist take down my contact details with agonising thoroughness, then got no reply. If he didn't call back this time, I'd grab a cab out to the prison by myself and take pot luck. They could only say no. Well, that and beat me with rubber truncheons; but with EU membership still pending, I was gambling they'd be wanting to keep their noses clean.

As it turned out, though, the phone rang less than ten minutes after I'd hung up.

'Mr Castor?' The man's voice was rich and resonant, and held barely a trace of accent.

'Yes,' I confirmed.

'Dragan Anastasiadis. I believe you wanted to see a client of mine.'

'That's right. Jovan Ditko.'

'And you are interested in Jovan Ditko because . . . ?'

'I'm a friend of his brother, Rafael.'

A sound like soughing wind came down the line. 'Ordinarily,' Mr Anastasiadis said, 'this would be a difficult thing to arrange. Since you are a foreigner, I would have to submit your name to the prison authorities and wait for approval. But today it is relatively easy. If you take a cab to the prison gates, I will meet you there.'

'Thanks,' I said. 'Thanks a lot.' And then, before he could hang up, 'Mr Anastasiadis?'

'Dragan.'

'Dragan. Why is today easier?'

'Because Jovan's last appeal failed this morning, Mr Castor. Tomorrow he will hang.'

All prisons I've ever been in have felt pretty much the same to me. They may be more or less grim, more or less grey, more or less tolerant of torture and the meticulous demolition of the human spirit, but the same pall of despair and abnegation hangs over them all, a psychic fog sublimed out of shipwrecked lives. For an exorcist, the *genius loci* is always a very real presence: after my first few minutes in Irdrizovo Prison – an innocuous cluster of low whitewashed buildings behind an endless chain-link fence, vaguely reminiscent of a high-security Butlins – there was a taste in my mouth like rancid tin and a throbbing pain behind my eyes.

Dragan Anastasiadis seemed oblivious to this miasmic atmosphere. A tall fat man dressed immaculately in a light blue linen suit and a cream shoestring tie, he had met me at the gates as promised, shaken my hand and offered heart-felt commiserations that I didn't really need – I'd never even met Jovan Ditko – and shepherded me past the various guard posts with dispatch.

He kept up a courteous, consultative manner in front of the guards, talking about the mechanics of the appeals process and the hopes he'd entertained that the president might be persuaded to intercede with a stay of execution at the last moment. But when we were briefly alone, waiting in a bare anteroom for someone to escort us through to the maximum-security wing, he let the mask slip.

'The truth, Mr Castor,' he said, 'is that this entire legal process was a farce. The death penalty in Macedonia is available only for treason and the most atrocious war crimes. The man Jovan killed was a colonel in the army, but the motive had nothing to do with war. It was about a woman. The prosecution did not even contest this. But to kill a colonel, apparently, is a war crime – even if you kill him because he is having sex with your fiancée. And even if there is no war.'

He shrugged lugubriously.

'What about The Hague?' I asked. 'I know you're not part of the EU structure yet, but even a theoretical ruling . . .'

I broke off because Anastasiadis was already shaking his head. 'For that very reason,' he said, 'they turned us down. They can't afford to prejudice future relations with the Macedonian state by interfering in their sovereign affairs before they have any legal right to. No, my route ran along well-worn channels, and it became clear quite early in the process that the verdict would always be guilty. And to be fair, Jovan *is* guilty, as far as that goes. It was a horrible murder, marked by extreme and shocking brutality. But the death sentence offends me in my soul. And for a man I have defended, the offence is double. It is a guilt I have to carry now – that I could not stop this. It is a dyspepsia of the soul that will not go away.'

The expression on his face made the comparison seem like a valid one: he looked like a man who'd eaten a big lunch very quickly, and was now finding to his dismay that it didn't want to sit still where it had been put. I've got enough guilt of my own without going looking for extra helpings, but I felt sorry for Anastasiadis. The law is a poor fit for a man with a tender conscience.

The sound of keys turning in locks and of bolts slamming back brought us both to our feet. Our escort had arrived, in the form of two prison guards as heavily armoured as riot police. They talked to Dragan, ignoring me. Their language was quick-fire, full of Greek-sounding liquid labials. Dragan answered in the same language. He pointed to me, and one of the men nodded. Then they led the way back through the door by which they'd just entered, locking it again behind us, across a small bare cinder yard where a solitary ghost loitered, almost invisible in the sun of noonday, and into a concrete bunker only two storeys high.

The yard was pleasantly warm, but a wall of heat hit us as we entered the maximum-security wing. The guards must have felt it even more than we did inside their elaborate body armour, but they gave no sign of discomfort.

Anastasiadis fanned himself gently with the back of his hand. The air smelled of sweat, urine, disinfectant and something greasy and insinuating that might have been pomade.

The space inside was open-plan: ground floor and first-floor gallery all of a piece, both with cells leading off a bare, bleak central space. The cells we passed were open-plan too, with bars for walls. Each held two men: two pallets, side by side rather than bunked one above the other, two chairs, a table, a slop bucket. Men played cards in monastic silence or lay on their pallets and read. A uniformed guard sat at one end of the structure on a plastic chair, lethargic and disengaged. He looked as though he wouldn't have stirred himself for anything less than a full-scale riot.

We went up to the first floor via a circular staircase, blocked off at the bottom by a lockable grille. There was a second grille at the top, which another guard had to open before we could step out onto the landing. Up here, close to the ceiling of the low building, the smell of piss was pervasive, hanging heavy in the still, overheated air. The prisoners in these second-storey cells lay to a man on their pallet beds, as still as the dead, arguably more so. A suicide net was slung over the open space in the centre of the gallery; more bizarrely, so were a few clothes lines on which socks and T-shirts in subtly varied shades of institutional grey hung limply.

Anastasiadis led the way to the furthest cell on the right, then waited while one of the two guards unlocked the door. Both guards remained in place while we entered, locking us in and then standing to either side of the door like unlovely bookends.

Jovan Ditko was sitting on the floor of the cell, dressed

only in vest and pants. His head was bowed, the slop bucket cradled between his spread legs. He'd vomited into it, and he looked as though he might be about to do so again. Anastasiadis looked back through the bars at the guards, pointed to the bucket and spoke to them again. They shook their heads, only very slightly out of synch. Anastasiadis shouted, his face flushing suddenly red. One of the guards shouted back, while the other turned his face aside as though the controversy embarrassed or upset him.

'They will not empty the bucket,' the lawyer said to me apologetically. 'I reminded them that this is Jovan Ditko's last night on Earth, but they say the buckets are only emptied on the morning shift.'

'It doesn't matter,' I said, although the stench in the room was close to stomach-churning. I tuned it out with an effort of will. My preferred sense is hearing, so I focused on the sounds of the place: the sounds and the meta-sounds – the spirit music that plays in the background for me wherever I happen to be. Irdrizovo was a symphony in a minor key, bleak and formless and unresolved.

'Jovan,' I said gently.

He looked up at me and nodded, then ducked over the bucket again. It wasn't really a greeting, just an acknowledgement that I was there. He had Rafi's face but harder and heavier, a lot less handsome. A three-day growth of stubble darkened his chin, and his face glistened with sweat.

'Do you speak English?' I asked him.

He muttered something that I didn't catch. Mister Anastasiadis translated at once. 'He understands English, but he doesn't speak it very well. He'll answer you in Macedonian.'

'Okay.' I turned back to Jovan. 'Thank you for seeing me. I know it's the worst possible time, in a lot of ways, but I thought you might like some news of your brother, Rafael.' I thought of my cover story and decided it might be useful to have something to show for this trip besides one less notch on my conscience. 'And I'd like to talk to you about your memories of him,' I added.

This time Jovan didn't even look up. He just rattled off a quick response to Anastasiadis, who replied to him rather than to me. For a while they batted something around between the two of them. I suspected the three-way communication system was going to be a real pain in the arse.

'He says it's been years since he even saw Rafael,' Anastasiadis said to me at last. 'They argued, a long time ago. When their father died, Rafael did not even come to the funeral. There is nothing between them now.'

'How long ago was that?' I asked. 'When their father died?'

Another quick exchange yielded the answer. 'Three years ago.'

That was after Rafi's botched necromancy and my botched exorcism had landed him with his demonic passenger. He was already locked up in the Stanger by then.

'He didn't know,' I explained. 'He was in a hospital and . . . not really in touch with the outside world.' Not in touch with anything, I thought. Rafi's life had become pretty surreal at that point. His time perception, his awareness of self, his ability to lay down new memories and to make sense of the world, all had to be compromised.

I tried to explain this to Jovan, but it was a tricky concept to get across and I hit the rocks almost immediately. 'Rafi has a demon inside him,' I said, and Jovan was off on a tirade, glaring up at me from the floor.

'Yes,' Anastasiadis said. 'He has a demon. I have a demon. Everybody has a demon. It doesn't change who you are. It doesn't change your obligations. You have to be a man, don't you? Whatever else you are.'

'Yeah, but I'm not trying to be poetic,' I said. 'Rafi tried to do some magic, and he messed it up. There's a demon stuck inside him like a . . .' Having no clue what sort of referents Jovan would feel comfortable with, I groped for a non-technical simile. '. . . like a toad in a well. He's been like that for years now. And for most of that time, he's been locked up in a lunatic asylum. The demon controls his body, his actions. He's not free to do what he wants to do.'

The lawyer was staring at me with an almost comically surprised expression, but Jovan emitted a snort that needed no translation. Clearly he didn't think demonic possession was a good enough reason to miss your dad's funeral.

'Rafi wanted to tell you that he was sorry,' I persisted. 'Not specifically for that. For losing touch with you, I guess, and for any other bad blood there was between you. That's why I came. To deliver that message. It seemed to be very important to him.'

In Jovan's terse reply, Rafi's name appeared twice.

'The only thing that was ever important to Rafael,' Anastasiadis translated, 'was Rafael.' Jovan was speaking again, with more animation, and the lawyer slipped into simultaneous translation. 'He was always selfish. He cared nothing about the family, or anyone else besides himself. He always wanted to get out of here, and when he did he never looked back. Once or twice he's written to me, but only to ask me to send his things on to him. His photos and his journals especially. I didn't reply. If he wants those things so badly, he can come back – pardon me, he can *fucking* come back – and get them himself. Now, no more, please. No more of this. I have too little time left to make myself angry by thinking about Rafael.'

A silence followed this speech. Jovan seemed drained by it. His head lolled lower than ever over the foul, stinking bucket.

'Is there anything I can get you while I'm here?' I asked lamely. If nothing else it would be a way of keeping the dialogue open, but Jovan made a slashing gesture with his right hand.

'Nothing,' he muttered in English. 'Give me nothing. And give him nothing, from me. No word.'

He lapsed into Macedonian again, and Anastasiadis laid a hand on my arm. 'He wants us to leave,' he said apologetically. 'He says he won't answer any more of your questions.'

'The journals,' I persisted. 'Rafi's journals. Do they still exist?' I felt ashamed to ask, but I was thinking again about having something to show Jenna-Jane. More than that though, there was an outside chance – a tenuous thread of possibility – that the journals might throw up something we could actually use. I was a good salesman, obviously. I'd talked myself into believing there was some point in having come here.

'*Sepidye*,' Jovan growled. 'They were burnt,' Anastasiadis said. 'Please, Mr Castor. We have to respect my client's wishes.'

I offered my hand, but Jovan didn't take it. No exchange

of hostages, no using the last few hours of the present to ransom back some little piece of time past. Jovan Ditko was beyond that now. He was preparing himself for a drop much longer than the precisely measured fall from the gibbet.

I left him to it.

Back in the city I found a café – walking past three bars with increasing difficulty – and knocked back three tiny, deadly espressos. They were way too sweet, but so stiff with caffeine they made my nerves vibrate like a million tiny tuning forks. Then I trudged back to the hotel to collect my things.

But as I was packing – which consisted of throwing my washbag and my phone back into the rucksack I'd brought – there was a knock on the open door of my hotel room. I turned to see Anastasiadis standing on the threshold, looking slightly awkward and apologetic.

We'd parted company at the prison, after I'd thanked him for his help and offered him a translator's fee (from the bountiful coffers of the MOU), which he'd refused. My first thought was that he'd changed his mind, and I reached into my pocket. He reached into his at the same time and produced a Yale key.

'There is a house,' he said without preamble. 'It belonged to the parents, then to Jovan. Now, presumably, it belongs to Rafael. But I have no address for Rafael, and I under-stand that he is not to be found. Perhaps, Mr Castor, you will take the key and give it to Rafael the next time your paths cross.'

I hesitated. It seemed unlikely that anything of Rafi's would still be in the house after all this time, or that it could be of any use to me if I found it. It might be worth the trip if his journals had survived, but Jovan had closed that avenue.

Anastasiadis was still holding out the key, and – in his other hand – a small rectangle of card. 'The address,' he said, as though I'd already agreed. 'It would be worth your while, perhaps, to visit the place before you leave. If there are any valuables or keepsakes, they should be taken away now. The neighbourhood is not of the best, and empty houses in Skopje seldom escape the notice of squatters for long.'

He wore me down just by keeping his hands held out towards me. Or maybe I felt that this was one more duty I owed to Rafi, one more small expiation for the big fuck-up that had taken his life away from him. I had just enough time, if I left at once, and if the house wasn't too far from the airport.

I looked at the card. It was one of Mr Anastasiadis's own business cards with the address of the Ditko house jotted down in a small, neat hand on the back. While I was still looking at it, a sheet of paper covered in closely typed paragraphs was thrust under my nose. The writing was presumably Macedonian, but it was all Greek to me.

'You will sign?' Anastasiadis asked hopefully.

'What am I signing?'

'For the key. A receipt. You understand, Mr Castor, with this my duties are finished. I have waited a long time for them to be finished. This would be a kindness to me.'

Despite what my dad had drummed into me about signing papers without reading them, or indeed signing anything presented to you by a man in a suit, I gave the lawyer my scribbled name. He smiled in what looked like genuine relief, folded the sheet again and tucked it into his shirt pocket.

'I will take you to the house,' he offered in a burst of warm fuzzy feeling. 'And to the airport afterwards.'

'Deal,' I said.

As we drove through the narrow streets in Anastasiadis's shiny silver Lexus, he filled me in on recent Macedonian history – recent meaning everything since the Byzantine empire went down the Swannee. The main theme was how Macedonia kept getting dragged into other people's wars despite a national predisposition towards dancing, strong liquor and healthy pragmatism. First it was the Greeks who wouldn't leave them alone, then the Ottomans. More recently, they'd managed to keep their heads down through the regional rough and tumbles of the early 1990s, only to get badly screwed by the Kosovan conflict. Even then, Anastasiadis said, they did their best to stay out of the scrum. They were victims of drive-by ethnic cleansing at one or two removes when a quarter of a million Albanian refugees fled across the border from Kosovo and stirred up the nationalist aspirations of Macedonia's own Albanian minority. What ensued was nothing as vulgar as a civil war, the lawyer assured me. There were skirmishes, minor engagements, manoeuvring on both sides, and then instead of falling on each other like wolves the government and the Albanians signed an agreement not to be so hard-arsed in future. Anastasiadis seemed very proud of this outcome, seeing it as a mark of how civilised his people were. The Macedonian compromise: let's not have a war, and say we did.

As the recitation went on, we were driving through

narrower and narrower streets, until we reached a point where the rough-cast walls on either side almost clipped the Lexus' wing mirrors. Now, as Mr Anastasiadis reached his low-key but impassioned conclusion, we turned – with about as much room for manoeuvre as an elephant has in a tanning bed – into an overgrown yard with high walls painted lemon yellow. Three of the walls were free-standing, while the fourth was the frontage of the Ditko house.

It was built on the same scale as the yard, which was one degree up from Lilliputian, and despite the paint, which made a bold and optimistic statement, it had clearly been allowed to fall almost into ruin in recent years. The pitched roof was sway-backed, like a spavined horse, and there were great pockmarks in the limed rough-cast, showing bare single-skin brickwork beneath. Weeds grew up between the slate-grey flagstones of the yard, almost to the height of a man, and one of the windows had a perfectly circular hole through it, starred all around with fracture lines, the hallmark of a local kid with a catapult and a relaxed attitude to other people's property.

The place made a bleak enough impression, but when Mr Anastasiadis wound down the car window, between one breath and the next a sweet smell of honeysuckle flooded in on us. It was growing wild up the outer walls and the house's frontage, annealing the decay by immersing it in its own opposite.

'I will wait for you here,' Anastasiadis informed me. 'In this neighboorhood, it is best not to leave the car unattended.'

It was hard to argue with that. In front of this tumble-down cottage, the Lexus looked like news from nowhere

– something not just from another world but from another age of humankind.

I got out and crossed to the door. It was painted black, the paint now blistered and flaking where the slo-mo blowtorch of entropy had played across it. At first glance there was no keyhole, but actually it was only the lock plate that was missing. A small, neat circle had been drilled into the wood, close enough to the jamb to be in shadow and not immediately noticeable. I had to jiggle the key around in the blind hole until it found its berth, but then as soon as the key was turned the door sprung open of its own accord, the warped wood pushing it away from the frame with a dry *twang* like the sound of an arrow hitting a target.

The door gave directly onto a small living room. It was filled with an immense profusion of things. There were six ill-assorted chairs, beautifully carved but from two different tribes, the ladder-backs facing the wheelbacks across a farmhouse table piled high with old newspapers. Newspapers served as curtains too, taped across the two narrow windows. Out in the centre of the room, beyond the table, stood an ancient iron mangle. Boxes lined the walls, two and three and four high. A tall dresser held not plates and cups but more papers along with a meerschaum sculpture of a tram and a radio with a red plastic casing that had to be 1960s vintage. From the ceiling (why waste a surface just because it's upside down?) a massive drying rack hung on four pulleys. Yet more sheets of newspaper had been folded neatly over its wooden runners to shield any clothes that might be hung there from dust or splinters. There were no clothes, but a great many electrical flexes had been slung over the rack in long, neat rows, all ending in the two-pronged European plug. They looked like dead snakes hung up to cure, lolling their forked tongues.

The room smelled of dust and lavender. A slender blade of sunlight bisected it neatly where one of the sheets of newsprint had been poorly fitted into the window frame. Thick motes swirled in its glow on sluggish thermoclines, showing the air to be as heavily freighted as the solid ground.

I picked up a pile of papers at random from the dresser: old letters, old bills, old articles laboriously cut out with short-bladed scissors from defunct periodicals. The Ditkos had bought a lot of newspapers and had put them to a lot of uses, but clearly they had read the news in them too, and set aside the items that seemed worthy of being remembered.

The boxes seemed mostly full of crockery and cutlery, although one that I opened contained books. Crabbed writing on the lid of each presumably recorded its contents. It looked as though the family had moved from a bigger place and had never finished unpacking, maybe because there just wasn't enough room here to hold their things. Or maybe some of these boxes held the things that Rafi had asked his brother to send on to England after him. In any case, there was nothing that corresponded to Mr Anastasiadis's phrase 'valuables or keepsakes'.

A single door led to a back room, off which a narrow staircase opened. It was much darker here. I groped for a light switch, found one at last to the right of the doorway and flicked it on.

A bare hundred-watt bulb flared into life over my head. From all around the room, a hundred Rafis stared back at me.

'Sonofabitch!' I muttered involuntarily.

'His photos and his journals,' Jovan had said – and he'd sneered at Rafi's obsessive self-regard. Judging from this evidence, he hadn't been exaggerating.

Some of the photos were five by three or six by four, snapshots taken with an ordinary thirty-five-millimetre camera, but many of them had been blown up – the largest, poster size with the grainy stippling that comes from trying to squeeze too much detail out of a poorly resolved original.

They were all portrait shots, not family groups nor even whole-body studies. A relentless gallery of head-and-shoulders close-ups, the blurred backgrounds merging into one, the only variety coming from Rafi's facial expressions and from the vagaries of the lighting.

It was unsettling to meet my friend's gaze so many times at once in this sad, abandoned place.

I took a few steps further into the room, and something shattered under my foot. I looked down, startled: more photos, in glass-fronted frames. No, I realised, as I knelt to examine them more closely. These were actually photographs printed on glass rather than paper, in black and white, but backed with coloured card so that the lighter areas became islands of intense red or green or gold.

The one I'd shattered had a silver backing. The memory of Rafi's silver-lined cell at the Stanger Care Home came forcefully into my mind, and then, although silver isn't gold, the tune of that old vaudeville favourite 'I'm only a Bird in a Gilded Cage'. Rafi had gone a long way from this cramped room to find an even smaller cage in London, but both rooms were spacious compared with the vaulted oubliette of his own skull, which was where he was really trapped.

I pulled myself out of this pointless reverie with an effort. I still had a plane to catch, and even to appease Mr Anastasiadis there was nothing here I wanted to take with me.

I went upstairs briefly. I found two tiny bedrooms, a double bed in one, two small singles in the other. There was no room for any other furniture. The double bed still had blankets strewn across it, so it looked as though it had been vacated only recently, but no sheets covered the bare, stained mattress.

I went into the other room, glanced perfunctorily around. Through the dust-smeared window – no curtains here, not even of newspaper – I could see the yard below and the laywer's big, imposing car. Half a dozen or so of the neighboorhood children were watching it from the yard entrance, their faces mostly sullen and disapproving as though the vulgar display of wealth offended them on principle.

Turning from the window, I noticed a small fleck of bright red colour against the bleached grey of the floorboards. There was something under the left-hand bed. I squatted down to look a little closer.

The something turned out to be the top-most of a pile of four or five small fat notebooks. I picked it up, flicked through the pages. Lines of tight Slavonic script in faded blue ink met my gaze.

Rafi's journals? Jovan said he'd burned them, but perhaps he'd only wanted to. At the front, where the writer of a diary might be expected to write his name, there was indeed a short string of characters. Rafael Ditko? Maybe. I picked up the little stash of books, slipped them into my greatcoat's capacious outer pockets and headed for the stairs.

If they were Rafi's journals they might be worth having. The better I knew Rafi, the deeper and stronger my sense of him became, the more likely it was that I could separate him from his demonic bunk-buddy – assuming I could get a translation done before Asmodeus cornered me in a dark alley and strangled me with my own intestines. It was still a long shot, but it was something. At least I could tell myself – and Jenna-Jane – that I wasn't coming away completely empty-handed.

I retraced my steps, down the stairs and back through the room of photos. One I hadn't seen before caught my attention, one of those where the image had been printed on glass. In this picture, Rafi seemed to be about twelve years old. He was standing on the broad stone steps of a large old building, and whatever he was wearing must have been of a very light colour, because the pale gold backing shone through most of it. Perhaps it stood out from the rest because Rafi was so young in it, while in most of the others he was either in his late teens or early twenties – a period at which his self-love seemed to have reached its pinnacle – or perhaps it was just that his smile was so radiant, his satisfaction with the world and his place in it so transcendantly perfect.

Whatever it was, I took the damn thing with me.

Mr Anastasiadis was very pleased to see me emerge from the house. The feral kids had doubled in number now, and they were eyeing the Lexus with a malevolent hunger. 'The airport,' the lawyer said without preamble. Then he said a whole lot more, loudly, in Macedonian, looking at me but obviously playing to the wider audience.

'What was that?' I asked, when we were both in the car and backing out of the yard. The kids parted reluctantly to let us through. One or two of them took a kick at the body-work *en passant*. Anastasiadis winced at each dull clunk, as though he was feeling the blows himself.

'I called you chief inspector,' he said a little disgruntledly. 'And I asked you how your investigation was coming along. I thought this might deter those little thugs from hurting my car. But sadly, Mr Castor, such a deterrent is still beyond the grasp of human science.'

His gaze fell on the photo, which I was holding in my lap. 'This is all you took?' he said. 'Well, it is a nice moment to commemorate, I suppose.'

'What moment?' I asked him.

'The first communion. This is Jovan or Rafael?'

'Rafael,' I said. 'How do you know when it was taken?'

The lawyer shrugged. 'The white robe,' he said. 'And the steps of Hagia Katerina. Every house in Skopje has a photo like this.'

It was funny and painful at the same time to think of Rafi taking communion. The wine and wafer would stick in his throat now, and make the demon bellow like a bull under the gelding knife. Was there a possibility there? I wondered briefly. Trick Asmodeus into swallowing the host or drinking communion wine? The answer was no, of course. I could hurt him easily enough, but tricks like that wouldn't pull or push or blast him out of his human vessel, and he'd recuperate with terrifying speed. If there was a magic bullet, that wasn't it.

We stopped at a red light, which didn't seem to be in any hurry to change. I was a little worried about catching my flight now, but I took advantage of the delay to fish one of the books out of my pocket and show it to Anastasiadis.

'I took these too,' I told him. 'I think they may be Rafi's journals.'

He took it from me and flicked through it curiously.

'His name is inside the cover,' he acknowledged. 'Rafael Cyril Ditko. Yes. This is a diary of some kind. Or at least each entry has a date attached to it.'

'Do you know of any way I could get them translated?' I asked.

Anastasiadis handed the book back to me, returning his attention to the road as we started moving again. 'Of course,' he said. 'I use translators myself all the time, for deeds and contracts. If you were willing to leave the books with me, I could arrange to have it done.'

'I need it done quickly.'

'Then it will not be cheap. But still I can arrange it.'

I chewed on that one for a moment. Expense was no object for Jenna-Jane, but if I took her money to get the journals translated, I'd have to share the contents with her. Actually, that was an optimistic projection. More likely, Jenna-Jane would get first dibs and I'd be copied in on a need-to-know basis.

'How much is it likely to be?' I asked.

Anastasiadis made a one-handed but expansive gesture, suggesting very concisely how painful it was for him to have to ask for cash down for what was really a favour to a friend, and how distasteful he found monetary transactions in general. 'Five hundred pounds sterling,' he suggested. 'One hundred for each book.'

Not an easy sum for me to scrape together right then. I considered. The diaries were still a long shot. Most likely they were full of the same sort of stuff that fills all adolescent boys' diaries – wet dreams, football scores and cod philosophy. All the same, I decided to keep it in the family.

'Do one of the books to start with,' I said. 'I'll wire the hundred quid when I get back to England.'

'Thank you. All the necessary details are on my card.'

We got to the airport with about twenty minutes left before check-in closed. Rolling to a halt in a no-stopping lane and cheerfully ignoring the soldiers on security duty at the kerbside, Anastasiadis got out of the car to say goodbye to me. I shook his hand and thanked him for all his help.

'It was my very great pleasure,' he assured me solemnly. 'I did little enough for Jovan, when all is said and done. If I can help his brother, at no additional cost to myself because I am not after all a charity, this will please me. You will send that money, Mr Castor, yes?'

'Consider it sent,' I assured him.

'Then in the expectation of its arrival, I will make a start on the translation.'

Since I had a few minutes' leeway before I had to sprint for the gate, I decided to check in with the Führer-bunker and see how things were going there. I tried my mobile first, but it couldn't find a service, so I had to use a payphone. That meant changing bills into coins – coins which were impossibly small and thin, as though metal was in short supply locally and they were making a little go a long way. Dropping a couple of dozen little silver wafers at random into the slot got me a dialling tone, and that got me the MOU switchboard. It didn't get me Trudie Pax though, even though I asked for her. Instead – I suppose predictably – I was put directly through to Jenna-Jane.

'Felix,' she said brightly. 'You've been much on my mind. Was the journey worth your while?'

'Afraid not,' I said bluntly. 'Jovan and Rafi haven't talked in years. He couldn't tell me anything we don't already know. Or maybe he just didn't feel like talking, since he's going to be executed tomorrow. I had a chance to visit the family house and go through some old stuff of Rafi's, but I came up empty there too.'

'Things that belonged to Ditko? Might there be a stronger focus than the fingernail for Pax to use in her divination?'

I thought of the photo. 'Potentially,' I said. 'I've got something she can throw into the mix, anyway.'

'So the time wasn't totally wasted.' J-J sounded irked all the same, as though she realised she'd been taken for a ride for once in her life and wasn't enjoying the novelty. Abruptly, she switched tack. 'When do you arrive back in London?' she asked.

I glanced up at the departures board. It was easy to locate my flight, because there were only another three heading out that evening. 'About midnight,' I estimated.

'Get a good night's sleep. Gilbert has assembled his team for the Super-Self exorcism. He claims he has a full complement without your participation. I'd still like you to be there though. If things don't go to plan, an additional exorcist might make a great deal of difference. Especially one of your experience. I've delayed the operation until tomorrow night for that reason.'

'I'll be there,' I said.

'Excellent. Before that though, I think another early meeting is in order. I've been unable to locate your Mr Moulson, despite having tracked down his previous three addresses. But we've been reviewing Pax's maps, and we have a few insights to offer.'

'With regard to what, Jenna-Jane?'

'With regard to the issue of where Asmodeus might be found.'

The hairs on my neck pricked up like good little dogs at their master's voice. 'You've found him?' I asked, trying to keep my tone neutral.

'Not yet. But I may be able to direct your search. Tomorrow, Felix. Eight o'clock. Sleep tight.'

She hung up, leaving my mouth open on a question. I checked my watch. Time was really tight now, but it was a small airport and the gate was probably fairly close to the check-in. I hung up, fed the machine some more coins and dialled again.

The ringtone sounded half a dozen times, and I was about to give it up as a bad job when someone finally picked up.

'Hello?' Juliet said.

'No rest for the wicked, babe,' I told her.

12

Jenna-Jane was right about the value of an early night. Standing outside Super-Self at half past one in the morning, asleep on my feet, I asked myself for the hundredth time what the hell I was doing here when my bed was five miles north and two east.

But then the answer came stalking down the street towards me, the cynosure of all eyes – I counted six, including mine, the other sets belonging to a homeless guy and a roosting pigeon on a window ledge. All the same, she walked like a queen in procession, the night unrolling its monochrome carpet before her.

I detached myself from the doorway and waved, but Juliet had seen me already. Of course she had: her eyes were adapted for much darker places than this. They had the same faint glow to them that I'd noticed back at the Gaumont. More unsettlingly, the proportions of her body looked subtly different. She was taller, leaner, longer-limbed, without being any less beautiful, any less perfect. She was dressed in red rather than her usual black, and it was shocking to look at, the leather jacket shining with a liquid gloss, as vivid as an open wound, the pleated skirt infolded like labia.

'Thanks for coming,' I said when she was in earshot.

'You piqued my curiosity,' she answered. 'Show me this thing. But you'd better not let me down, Castor. I don't like men who make promises and can't deliver.' The shape of her face had changed too. It had elongated and thinned, the cheekbones becoming higher and sharper. The overall effect was to make her look less human, or rather to make her humanity seem like more of a conscious affectation. Her body had become an ironic quote.

'I'm as good as my word,' I promised her, trying to make my voice resonate with a confidence I really didn't feel. 'I said I'd show you something new, and I'm going to. But anyway, you're still on my payroll, right? Still on demon watch. I was hoping you could give me an update on that.'

Juliet tilted her head back very slightly, her red eyes fixed on me like rangefinders. 'You want to make sure you're getting your money's worth?' she translated, with a dangerous edge of anger in her voice.

'I want to make sure nothing happened to Pen while I was away,' I said. 'Or to you. That's all.'

'I haven't seen Asmodeus, or felt him. If he's watching your house, or the woman, he's doing it from a distance. Circumspectly. Patiently. Does that sound like Asmodeus to you?'

It didn't, I had to admit. On the other hand, he's the kind of devious bastard who gives devious bastards a bad name. 'You know what they say about barn owls?' I asked her.

Juliet stared at me as though I was something she'd found crawling in her armpit. 'No, Castor. I don't know what they say about barn owls.'

'They call twice when they're hunting – the first time loud, the second time soft. It puts the prey off its guard. Makes it sound like they're heading away from you when they're about to drop out of the sky and put their claws through your eye sockets.'

'The "you" in this sentence being a mouse or a rabbit,' Juliet observed with cold amusement. 'I don't find it easy to identify with prey, Castor. It's interesting that you do. Now, given that you could have asked me these questions by phone and not disturbed my sleep, why am I here?'

There was a pause – barely perceptible – before the word 'sleep'. It made me hope that relations between Juliet and Sue might have improved somewhat, but since I've got a well-developed sense of self-preservation I didn't ask. 'Come and see,' I said.

The invitation had an unintentionally biblical ring. Wasn't that what the angel said to John when the Book of Revelation was opened? Thinking of apocalypses, I unlocked Super-Self's front door and stood aside for Juliet to enter.

Super-Self felt different tonight. Juliet stepped inside, casting her gaze to right and left. She opened her mouth and stuck out her tongue to taste the air.

'Nothing,' she said at last, her vivid red eyes narrowing slightly.

'We're not there yet,' I said.

I walked past her to the stairs, expecting to hear after a moment or two the *clack* of her heels as she fell in behind me. Nothing. Despite the stiletto heels of her blood-red shoes, she walked as silently as a cat. I knew she was there, because she was a radarblip in my awakened death-sense, and the back of my neck prickled from the near-physical pressure of her stare. Otherwise I would have felt like Orpheus. Orpheus on the downward leg of the journey, heading into Hades on a busker's prayer.

The reception area was silent and pitch black. I went to

turn on the lights, but Juliet's hand blocked mine. 'Hurts my eyes,' she murmured absently.

'I can't see in the dark,' I pointed out.

'You'll adjust.'

She was right. There was a little light filtering down the stairs – the street lamps shining in through Super-Self's open doors. It wasn't much, but it was enough to show me the outlines of objects. Paradoxically, despite the vivid scarlet tones of her outfit, now Juliet was darker than the darkness, a silhouette against solid black. Even her eyes had stopped glowing, as though their light had shifted into a part of the spectrum I couldn't see.

'Show me this thing,' she said again. The playfulness in her tone was the most terrifying thing I'd ever heard.

Moving slowly to avoid falling over any low-lying items of furniture, I crossed the dark space to the far door, which opened not onto the pool but onto its anteroom.

I put my hand to the door, bracing myself for what was on the other side. I was a little surprised that I hadn't felt it already, but perhaps this was how it worked: sitting like a spider in a web, dormant, almost asleep, until something touched one of the threads and woke it.

Juliet pushed me aside impatiently and walked into the anteroom ahead of me. There was more light here: the phosphorescence from the pool beyond cast shifting blue highlights onto the walls. Juliet tilted her head back, seeming to listen, but there was no sound except the arrhythmic lapping of the water against the tiles.

'If we go a little closer—' I began. Juliet made a brusque gesture, silencing me.

'Yes,' she murmured at last, her voice husky. Her lips

peeled back from her teeth in a feral grin. 'That's what it wants. Go on, Castor. Move in closer.'

I hesitated. Juliet's mood was hard to read, but those bared teeth were unsettling. I was suddenly more afraid of her than I was of the thing in the swimming pool beyond.

'Closer,' she said again. 'It won't show itself until you do. It's hidden itself, used the souls of the dead to break up its outline. I won't see it clearly until it moves, and it won't move unless we throw out some bait. I'll be right behind you.'

Yeah, that was very reassuring.

I went on through the arch to the water's edge. The moving lights below me resolved themselves again into human shapes – became men and women in the depths of the water, circling and gesturing in an endless dumb show. At that moment I felt an aching solidarity with them. They'd lived and breathed once, been fully human, unlike either the thing that crouched invisible in the darkness above me or the siren at my back.

I leaned forward to see better. There were fewer figures in the pool than I remembered from the night before – seven or eight, where my confused memories had conjured up a crowd of several dozen. The two men in togas were arguing – one calmly, the other with a lot of emphatic gestures and striding back and forth. Another, older man watched them, majestically detached, while two women stood off to one side with their faces averted, looking sad and afraid. Two Roman soldiers with breastplates and helmets stared straight ahead, patient and impassive.

One of the women put her hand to her face. Something clutched in her fist caught my eye, and I leaned forward to see it more clearly. That was when the fear-thing fell on me like the giant foot in a Monty Python sketch. The last time I was here the process had been more gradual: an inexplicable sense of unease in the hall above, creeping paranoia on the stairs, pure, pants-wetting terror at the poolside. This was different. It was like having my brain ripped out of my skull and dropped into liquid nitrogen while it was still bleeding and pulsating.

Thought was impossible. So was movement. Fuck, so was breathing. My chest locked up as though all my ribs had twanged free and got tangled up together like one of Trudie's cat's cradles.

Poleaxed, and already off balance, I toppled forward into the water. I didn't hear the splash even, but my eyes were open and I could still see as I sank down among the ghosts. They ignored me completely, playing out their pantomime around and through me in the blue-white spotlight created by their own phosphorescence.

For a moment I was staring into the face of the woman I'd been watching from above. It was a tragic face, eyes pleading and haunted, mouth tensed in a just-about-to-lose-it grimace. But I kept on sinking down and down. Now I was level with her shoulders, her chest, her arms. Her hand clutched tight around the flimsy thing she'd drawn out from the voluminous folds of her gown. It was a lace handkerchief, embroidered with the letters EC in elegant – if slightly over-elaborate – needlepoint.

Water was starting to trickle into my mouth, down my throat. Since I wasn't breathing, it hadn't found my airway yet, but it wouldn't be long.

In the meantime, as my shoulder bumped against the

bottom of the pool, I'd noticed that the woman's shoes were wrong too: they were low boots made of leather, with scrimshaw buttons up the side. God damn it, she was even wearing socks.

Still unable to move a voluntary muscle, I turned slowly in the water, rolling over onto my back. The trickle of water became a torrent, and I cursed my luck silently as I prepared to say goodbye to the world.

Then something locked hard onto my ankle and hauled me upward like a hooked fish. I exploded out of the water into the cool night air, and the shock of the cold and the sudden movement started me breathing again. Okay, I was breathing water: a small detail, easily adjusted once I'd coughed and hacked and vomited myself back into equilibrium.

Juliet dumped me on the tiles without ceremony and left me to it. When I was in a state to take notice of her again, she was staring up into the light well above the pool, her knees slightly bent as though she was ready to spring. But the fear had gone – gone completely, in an instant, just as it had arrived. I was about to listen in through my death-sense to confirm my conviction that we were alone, but I stopped myself just in time. That was how the damn thing worked. That was what it responded to.

Yesterday, when I'd come here with Trudie, the pair of us had come through the door on a hair trigger, knowing – because we'd been told – that this was a woodshed with something nasty in it. We were tuned into the psychic wavelengths, using the sensitivities that made us exorcists, and the fear-thing had woken up instantly. We'd started to feel it as soon as we crossed the threshold.

Tonight, I'd let Juliet take the lead and make the running, wanting her to see for herself. My death-sense hadn't stirred until I looked down into the pool and focused on the ghosts and what they were doing. That was when the fear-thing had pounced.

And that was why the bad shit just kept on escalating. The more exorcists Jenna-Jane sent in here, the harder she poked this thing, the harder it hit back.

I came up on one knee, groggy and hurting. Juliet hadn't put me down any too gently, and there was an ache all the way up my right forearm and shoulder, but it felt great just to be able to think straight.

'Did you see it?' I asked her.

She looked down at me, seeming slightly surprised that I was still there. 'Of course I saw it.'

'So tell me what it is,' I persisted.

'Tartharuch,' Juliet growled, her mouth twisting around the gutturals. 'From Tartarus. Tartharuch Gader'el.' She was still staring at me, her eyes hot coals in the darkness.

'So it's a demon.'

'Yes. It's a demon.'

'And how do we kill it?'

'Kill it?' Juliet's flawless brow furrowed. 'Why would I want to kill it? It smells of home.'

Something in the set of her mouth rang alarm bells in my mind. They were still vibrating anyway from my second round with the fear-thing, the Gader'el, so it didn't take much to set them off. I started to climb to my feet.

I didn't even see Juliet move. Something – her fist or her foot, I couldn't be sure – hit me in the middle of my chest and knocked me sprawling. Then she was on top of me, her face about an inch from mine. She licked her lips and my heart surged, clamouring like a monkey in a cage. Her sex scent filled me in a second to bursting point, the way a water balloon held against a running tap is filled, distends and then explodes.

I tried to speak. 'This . . . this is . . .' Her parted lips, impossibly full and dark, were descending towards mine. It seemed like a waste of time talking when I could just give myself up to those lips and the terrible release they promised. But I'd been here once before, on Juliet's event horizon, and survived. Clawing for purchase on that memory, some part of me was able to grab a microscopic distance from the agonising, all-consuming lust and remind me that I was about to die. 'Bad idea,' I forced out. 'Sue . . .'

Juliet hesitated. A wave of some very human emotion – irritation, impatience, something like that – passed across her face, displacing for a moment the wanton mask she wore when she was hunting. I have no idea what had risen in her mind: the echo of an old argument maybe, a domestic quarrel between her and her human lover in the early, honeymoon days, about the ethics of devouring the odd guy on the side when you're in a monogamous relationship.

Whatever it was, it gave me a window. I whistled into it: whistled Juliet. It was desperate improvisation. I couldn't think around her, couldn't pull myself out of her orbit, but as an exorcist I could put what I was feeling to good use. It was the summoning, the first phase of an exorcism, when you make the spirit you're binding stand to attention and pay heed to you. I called Juliet back into herself, as I'd done for her once before after she fought

Moloch at the Mount Grace Crematorium, and as I'd tried and failed to do for Lisa Probert.

Dumb luck counts for a lot in my business. Doing that gave me my second big insight of the night, the first one being when I looked at the lace handkerchief in the Roman matron's hand and realised she wasn't Roman at all. What I realised now was that Juliet was all wrong. There was a mismatch, a discord, between what I was playing and what I was feeling – between the Juliet I knew, whose soul-music I'd memorised by heart, and the Juliet who was crouched above me now preparing to devour me. They weren't the same being. They overlapped, but they weren't the same.

If I'd had time to think about the implications of that, I might have got the answer there and then, and everything that happened later might have played out differently. But the moment wasn't really conducive to calm reflection. Juliet's pheromones still saturated the air, my heart was still trying to start up a new career as a road drill, and it took all my effort, all my concentration, just to keep forcing that tune out between my pursed lips.

We must have stayed like that for the best part of a minute, a tableau from a Benny Hill sketch. Then Juliet leaned back, shifting her weight, and made a gesture with her right hand: stop. Seeing her hand from so close up, I noticed again that it was too long, the fingers impossibly tapered. Physically as well as psychically, Juliet was in a state of flux.

She climbed off me. It hurt to be released from that weight, to feel her attention pass over me and shift away. I'd survived her attack again, and just like the first time it was agonising. My maddened hormones threshed in my innards like waves against a breakwater, and a fevered tremor went through me, leaving me breathless and weak. My teeth chattered out a crazy, Morse code lament. It was like the alcohol craving all over again, but worse.

Juliet hauled me to my feet without apparent effort even though I wasn't able to contribute much to the process. She propped me against the side of the arch, looking me up and down with an abstracted frown, inspecting me for damage maybe.

'Told you . . . a long time ago . . .' I panted, 'I wasn't that kind of boy.'

'Shut up, Castor.' Juliet seemed to be her old self again, or something close to her old self, but it hadn't improved her mood. Still, it shortened the odds on a meaningful dialogue.

'Tell me what happened,' I threw at her. 'Explain to me what just happened.'

She took her hand away from my shoulder to see if I'd fall down again. I didn't. Satisfied, she walked back to the edge of the pool and stared up into the grey void of the light well.

'I lost control,' she said at last.

'You seem to have been doing that a lot lately.'

'Yes.'

'Any idea why?'

She took on that attentive stance again, shoulders rigid, head tilted slightly back. She was feeling for the presence of the fear-thing. Bearing in mind what had happened when she made contact a few minutes ago, I wasn't thrilled with the idea of sitting around and letting the two of them cuddle up some more.

'Juliet,' I called.

With visible reluctance, she turned and faced me.

'Did this thing – this Tartarus whatever-it-is – do something to your mind?'

She gave a brief, harsh laugh. 'The Gader'el? No, Castor. It's just an animal.'

'An animal?'

'An animal from Hell. It's dangerous, to the unwary, and hard to eradicate, but it can't think. Its repertoire is just what you see here: it hides itself, and it strikes while your back is turned. It feeds on fear, in the same way that I feed on lust or the Shedim feed on the souls of murderers.'

I rubbed my bruised shoulder. 'Then what?' I said. 'What the fuck is happening to you?'

She stared at me in silence. She was just a silhouette now, because the ghosts in the pool had gone and the blue light had died, but the red fires in Juliet's eyes told me I had her attention and that she wasn't entirely the Juliet I knew and sexually obsessed about, even now.

'I don't know,' she admitted. She seemed to pull herself together. 'We should leave. I startled the Gader'el, and interrupted its feeding. If it comes back again, it will be bolder.'

'Why should it come back?' I asked.

Juliet smiled a bleak, humourless smile. 'Because you're scared of me, Castor. Why else?'

On the pavement outside she made to walk away, but I reached out and caught her shoulder. It was a symbolic thing: light and slender as she was, she was as strong as ever, and she could have broken my grip without trying. She half-turned, waiting for me to speak.

'Go home,' I said. 'Promise me you'll go home.'

Silence.

'Juliet, you can't hunt tonight. I can't let you.'

'You can't stop me,' she said with dead finality.

'I know,' I acknowledged. 'So give me a break, and don't make me die trying. Go home to Sue. Have a quiet night in. Remind yourself what you've got to lose.'

'Fuck you, Castor.'

'Again?' I made my tone astonished and outraged. 'Are you insatiable, woman?'

In spite of herself, she laughed. But the feeble joke was a challenge too, and the word 'woman' gave her the benefit of the doubt.

'I'll go home,' she agreed. 'But tomorrow . . .'

'Tomorrow we'll figure something out.'

She nodded without conviction. Then she turned her back and walked away from me down the Strand. A staggering cluster of drunks on the opposite side of the street shouted out some sort of sleazy invitation to her, and I tensed, ready to intervene if necessary. But Juliet didn't even seem to see them. Head down and shoulders squared, she marched on into the hot, breathless night.

Back in Turnpike Lane, paranoia still sitting like a monkey on my back, I reconnoitred thoroughly before approaching Pen's door. Asmodeus had promised to leave me until last, but I knew exactly how much his word was worth.

I didn't see or sense any sign of the demon's presence, or any clue that he'd been there while I was away. In another way though, I felt myself surrounded and crowded by him. What he was doing wasn't random – I knew that much. Behind the casual malevolence there was something much more calculating and purposeful, and much more threatening.

I let myself in quietly. I heard voices from downstairs, Pen's basement sanctum, which surprised me, but only until I heard the laugh track. She'd fallen asleep in front of a repeat of some ancient sitcom, snoring away on the sofa while Reg Varney and Michael Robbins traded accusations of sexual dysfunction without ever using the word 'penis'. I sat down next to her and stared at the screen while the flaccid shenanigans played themselves out. In a way it helped me to think, if only because thinking distracted me from *On the Buses*.

There was a way through this maze. It just meant figuring out where Asmodeus was going so I could get there first. Of course, I also had to get myself a secret weapon to use when I got there, because a tin whistle wasn't going to do the job. It hadn't even been enough to beat the Gader'el, which Juliet had dismissed as an animal.

The trouble was that you couldn't get close enough to the Gader'el to perform an exorcism. I had its pattern clear in my mind now, but I knew damn well that as soon as I started to play, it would be on me hard enough and fast enough to knock the tune right out of my head. Close enough to play meant close enough to be attacked.

Inspiration came out of nowhere. No, it came out of thinking about Trudie, and the way she'd bootstrapped her own MO to create the meta-map of Asmodeus' movements. The trick was seeing through the metaphor to the thing itself: distinguishing how your power actually worked from the interface you'd developed for it. It could be done. It could be done without risk even.

That solved Jenna-Jane's problem. Now what about mine?

'Fix.' Pen stirred on the sofa beside me, rubbing her eyes. 'What time is it?'

I didn't bother to check my watch. 'Later than you think,' I said. 'Like always. How was your day?'

She blinked and shook her head, restoring some shape to the incendiary mop of her hair. 'Wonderful,' she said, her voice husky and slurred with sleep. 'Like one of your days. Alcohol, self-hatred, more alcohol and daytime TV.'

'I don't watch that much TV,' I pointed out. 'What do you hate yourself for?'

'Just the obvious.' She sat up, still groggy but gradually coming awake. 'I can't do this, Fix. I can't sit here and wait for you to sort it out. I'm going to start looking for Rafi again tomorrow.'

'You won't find Rafi,' I reminded her, my voice hard, 'you'll find Asmodeus.'

'I don't care. This isn't any way to live.'

She was right. We were under siege, and it was affecting both of us in our different ways. The sense of pressure – the feeling of being stalked – was throwing me off my stride, so that I just kept running from one thing to the next instead of stopping to think about where I was going. Worse, I was letting Jenna-Jane set the agenda, when I should have been using her as she was using me: bouncing off her thick, impervious hide in the direction I most needed to go.

That was going to change.

Right now I was going to get some sleep. And in the morning, which was only two and a half hours away . . .

In the morning I was taking back the initiative.

13

'Felix! Welcome back. Come and give us the benefit of
your expertise.'

Jenna-Jane's voice was courtesy itself: no snide cracks
about broken alarm clocks, no sarcastic sallies of the 'So
good of you to join us' variety. Then again, Gil McClennan,
at her elbow, radiated enough resentment and disapproval
to make anything she felt like doing in that line redundant.

I'd knocked on J-J's door, found the office empty, then
followed the sound of voices to the map room. Everyone
was there, sitting or standing at the edges of the room,
around the circumference of the sprawling map-sheets:
Jenna-Jane and Gil, obviously, Trudie, with Etheridge
hovering at her shoulder like Tinkerbell to her Peter Pan,
Samir Devani, looking like he might have gone to bed even
later than me, and a man and two women I hadn't seen
before – presumably exorcists on loan from other work
teams.

'Sorry I'm late,' I said insincerely. 'Keep talking. I'll get
up to speed.'

There was an awkward silence. 'Actually,' Trudie said,
after glancing briefly but curiously at the flat brown-
paper-wrapped package I held under my left arm, 'I think
we'd better recap, because this is important. Gil, would
you mind telling Castor what you found?'

McClennan gave a show of impatience, but Jenna-Jane

made an open-handed gesture, giving him the floor. He couldn't very well say no after that.

'I started off by looking at the clusters,' he said, pointing to the map. 'The points with the densest concentration of lines. One right where you live, Castor, in Turnpike Lane. One over here in Wembley – Pax says that's Juliet Salazar, who helped you break up Asmodeus' game last time he tried to get free, so maybe he's out to settle old scores there too. Another cluster down here in south London. Peckham Rye.'

'The Ice-Maker's,' I confirmed. 'That's where he was until he escaped.'

'Right. And then a few more in the centre of the city, here, here and here.' He pointed to King's Cross, Holborn, Waterloo. 'Maybe these are just hubs – not places he's visiting, but places he has to go through to get to where he's going. You'd expect to find some stuff like that.' Gil paused, staring across at me. 'You with me so far?'

I nodded wordlessly.

'Okay, then look at this.' He tapped the map, at a point where Trudie's ink lines were so densely overlaid on each other it was almost impossible to see the streets beneath. Gil's finger traced a line away from Turnpike Lane to the south, which was where most of the lines seemed to bleed off, Asmodeus either coming or going by the same route each time.

The lines weren't exactly straight: they veered to left and right, while still heading broadly south into the centre of London. Some of them diverged at this point, heading west; others kept right on going.

'Why the zigzags?' Gil demanded in the tone of a man who already knew the answer.

I took a closer look, but it seemed like an easy one. 'Because the streets don't head exactly where he wants to go.'

'Yeah.' Gil nodded. 'Exactly. He turns into Tollington Park here, and Stroud Green Road there. No straight lines. You can't walk through London and go in straight lines, right? Maybe New York, but not London.'

Trudie made an impatient tutting sound, obviously wanting Gil to cut to the chase, but he was going to do this his way. 'Now look here,' he said, moving his finger down into the centre of the map – the centre of London.

The difference was obvious, but only because he'd told me what to look for.

'Straight lines,' I said.

'Straight lines. Mostly around Holborn, which is one of our secondary clusters. See, he's going either north or south here, but he doesn't cut to the left to go into – whatever that is, Old Gloucester Street. He keeps right on going. Walking through walls. Making like the street grid doesn't matter to him. Which it doesn't.'

'Because he's underground,' I finished.

Gil looked annoyed that I'd got to the punchline ahead of him, but all I was doing was joining the dots. It was still his insight, and I was impressed. Jenna-Jane was right: he was a good exorcist and nobody's fuckwit.

'Or flying,' Trudie added scrupulously. 'We didn't want to rule out the possibility that he might be able to transform himself somehow.'

'But in that case,' Gil broke in again, 'we'd be seeing straight lines all over. We don't. They're just in the centre. So he's got an underground route that takes him through just this stretch here.' He indicated with a broad sweep of his hand an area that extended from the river up almost as far as Russell Square. 'The next question is why does he use it? I mean maybe it's quicker, but not by much. And he's not afraid of bumping into people. If he's got to go overground for most of the time, why use this one little stretch of tunnel that he's found? And why keep going back to it?'

'He's got a base there,' I said, playing straight man again. 'This is where he hangs his hat.'

'And that,' said Jenna-Jane, taking charge of the proceedings again, 'is the conclusion we'd reached just before you arrived. The puzzle that remains is to determine what tunnels he's using. The London Underground network seemed the likeliest option, given the density and depth of the tunnels in the centre of the city, but there's no obvious candidate.'

'We got hold of some maps from the city engineers department,' Samir said. 'They give a pretty exact mapping of the tunnels onto the streets above. The Piccadilly Line goes up here, about a hundred yards east of this nexus of main roads. The demon's path veers west, if anything, so it's not that. Central Line's too far down . . .'

'He wouldn't be likely to use tunnels that are actually in use in any case,' I pointed out. 'Too risky and too inconvenient. Do the inspection tunnels follow the same plan?'

'Not exactly,' said Trudie, 'but they run parallel with the main line and they're still too far out.' She showed me some red lines traced on the map a long way from the black flecks that marked the demon's comings and goings. 'We thought of disused stations too,' she added, forestalling my next question. 'No joy. There was a lot of old digging around King's Cross and the Angel, and some of those tunnels extended quite a long way to the south and west, but he's not following the line of any of them that we can see.'

'So now we're working on sewers and sealed-off water-ways,' Gil grunted. 'Which could take us days, because there are literally hundreds of miles of them to cover, and the maps don't always correlate to street level except at known access points.'

'Any insights, Felix?' Jenna-Jane coaxed.

I stared hard at the map: at the way the black flecks siphoned into High Holborn and Kingsway and then splurged outwards again at Waterloo Bridge. I tried to imagine myself walking that route, as I'd done a thousand times. Down Woburn Place, past Russell Square Gardens, into Southampton Row . . .

'No?' J-J seemed disappointed. 'Well, then I suspect you work on two fronts, Gilbert. Keep someone here, adding the sewer and waterway information to the map grid, while the rest of your people go out and walk the ground. Assuming the demon has gone to ground for the day, we might get a current time fix on him just by being there.'

McClennan became brisk. 'Teams of two,' he said. 'Cartwright and Powell. Greaves and Etheridge. Devani, you can come with me. That leaves you and Castor on the map, Pax. Let's move.'

He probably thought that grounding me would piss me off. It probably would have too, if I intended to do as I was told. I wasn't done with Gil yet though, and I stepped into his path as he headed for the door.

'We need to talk about Super-Self before you go anywhere,' I said.

He stared at me, deadpan. 'That's all in hand,' he said.

'If you're looking to clock up some overtime, Castor, you can forget it. I don't want you, and more to the point I don't need you.'

'You might want to know what you're facing, all the same,' I said. 'And you might need this.' I held up the key to the gym's front door. McClennan recognised it at once, or maybe just guessed what it was. He took it out of my hand, looked at it thoughtfully for a moment, then nodded.

'You've got your assignments,' he said to the other exorcists in the room. 'Get moving. Samir, wait for me downstairs.'

'I'd rather make a start,' said Samir.

Gil didn't even look round; his eyes were locked on mine. 'Make a start then,' he said. 'I'll call you when I get over there.'

The room gradually emptied until it was just the four of us: Trudie, Jenna-Jane, McClennan and me. Gil looked at Trudie and motioned with his head towards the door. She didn't move. 'If it's about Super-Self,' she said, 'I'd like to hear this. I'm part of that team too.'

'If you need to hear it,' Gil said with heavy emphasis, 'I'll brief you later, at the same time as everyone else. Right now this is private. Go make yourself a cup of coffee, Pax. Make me one too.'

Reluctantly, Trudie headed for the door. As soon as it closed behind her, McClennan turned to Jenna-Jane, holding the key up in his hand. 'He stole this from a secure cupboard,' he said. 'That's where the rest are. I signed them back in yesterday morning, as soon as I got here. You think he stopped at the keys? He's probably raided med cabinets, equipment, case files . . .'

'I took it off the ring while I was talking to you, Gil,' I told him. 'Sleight of hand, not breaking and entering. Not that I've got anything against petty larceny, you understand; it's just more effort.'

'I want him off my team,' McClennan said to J-J as if I hadn't spoken.

'Gilbert . . .' she said, sounding as though this rift between her little lambs distressed her beyond bearing.

'It's not as if he brings us anything. It's not as if we need him.'

Jenna-Jane turned to me. 'What do you bring us, Felix?' she asked in a colder and more businesslike tone.

'The rickety twins,' I told her.

She made an open-handed gesture. 'Go on.'

'Between the Strand and Wych Street,' I said, 'from the middle of the nineteenth century right up until they levelled the whole area to build the Aldwych in 1901, there were two theatres: the Opera Comique and the Globe. They were mostly underground. In fact the Opera Comique was reached through tunnels; it didn't even have a street-level entrance.'

'I've heard of the Opera Comique,' Jenna-Jane said musingly. 'Some of the early Gilbert and Sullivan operettas were performed there – before D'Oyly Carte built the Savoy.'

I shrugged. 'If you say so, Jenna-Jane. I'm not big on Victorian theatre. I can tell you though, courtesy of the London Metropolitan Archive, that there was a really nasty incident there in 1879. The theatre had fallen into debt, and some bailiffs tried to repossess the sets and props. They got into a stand-up fight with the cast in the middle of a performance. Then someone knocked over a lantern and the set caught fire. Four hundred people in the audience, all trying to get out of a burning basement through the same three tunnels. Mostly in the dark . . .'

'Why is this relevant?' Gil demanded angrily. 'What has the fucking nineteenth century got to do with—?'

'Hasn't the penny dropped yet?' I yelled back at him. 'The ghosts in the swimming pool are actors. They're not from Roman Britain; they're from the cast of some crappy play. I saw one of them last night blowing her nose on a lace fucking handkerchief. And she was wearing button-up boots!'

That shut him up for a moment, so I pressed on, determined to get to the point that really mattered.

'So the ghosts are about a century old,' I said, addressing myself to Jenna-Jane. 'That's still unusual, but it's not impossible. It's just right at the end of the bell-shaped curve. What is unusual is the thing that's in there with them.'

McClennan opened his mouth to bandy some more words with me, but J-J held up an imperious hand for silence. 'What thing?' she asked.

'My source calls it a Gader'el,' I said. 'It's demonic, but it's something we haven't met before. It feeds on fear. Probably the fear still attaching to that site was what brought it there in the first place. It's like an angler fish, J-J. It sits down there in the dark, dangling those old ghosts like a lure. When living people come in close to look, it gets its hooks into them. It amplifies any fear they're already feeling, turns it into blind terror, and somehow it takes nourishment from that.'

I turned to look at Gil now, seeing only resentment and suspicion on his face. 'The point is,' I told him, 'you can't destroy it with a frontal attack. It's not like the demons we've met before; it's . . . I don't know, a lower life form.

More primitive. More instinctive. Trying to exorcise it just makes it hit out harder. That's why Etheridge got damaged the way he did, and why your other man – Franklin – ran under a car.'

McClennan shook his head, but slowly and without much conviction. He was thinking, and thinking was taking some of the momentum out of his anger. It was hard for him to listen to the message when he wanted so badly to kill the messenger, but I could see that I was getting through to him.

'So what are you saying, Felix?' Jenna-Jane asked.

'I'm saying you need to wait,' I said. 'There's probably a way to drive this thing out without facing it head on. I had an idea last night: sort of a time bomb. A way of giving this thing some grief from a safe distance. I don't know if it will work, but I want to try it. It will take a while to set up, that's all. A day or two. Maybe longer.'

'From a safe distance?' McClennan echoed me. 'How would that work?'

But Jenna-Jane was already shaking her head, very firmly. 'We go ahead with the plan as agreed,' she said.

'Why?' I demanded. 'Why take the risk?'

'Because we're scientists,' she said simply. 'We gather data and then we reach conclusions based on that data. We don't prejudge, however tempting a particular prefabricated theory may be. By all means proceed with your own plans too. If Gilbert's team doesn't succeed tonight, you can try your alternative method. I see no harm in that – in having two strings to our bow.'

'The harm is that your first string might snap and put

someone's eye out,' I said caustically. 'You're sending your people into a dangerous situation when there's no need.'

I looked to McClennan for support, but J-J's rationalist call to arms had stiffened his sinews. 'I think the team I've put together will be up to the job,' he said, toeing the company line. 'You can tell me what your back-up plan is, if you want to. If I think it's got any merit, I'll put someone on it.'

There was a dead silence. Both of them looked at me expectantly. All I could think of was to quote Gil's own words back at him, like a snot-nosed schoolkid doing dumb insolence.

'Well maybe I'll brief you later,' I said. 'If you need to hear it.'

Nobody was going to give me any exit music, so I just left. Jenna-Jane called out something to me, but I was already halfway down the corridor and I didn't hear it.

Trudie Pax was loitering by the lifts, leaning against the wall with her arms folded and a grim look on her face. She straightened as I approached. 'I have to get out of here,' she said.

'I thought you were on map duty,' I reminded her.

'I'll come back later. Right now I need the air.'

'When you go back,' I said, 'take this with you.' I handed her the package and she hefted it, feeling its weight.

'What is it?' she asked.

'A photo of Rafi. Take a look.'

She tore away the paper from one corner and examined the contents of the package without enthusiasm.

'I've seen this technique before,' she said. 'The photo was developed right onto the glass, right?'

'Printed onto the glass,' I corrected her. 'Right. It was

all the rage back in the Victorian era. But apparently
Macedonia gets the fashions late.'

'So is the picture significant in some way?'

I see-sawed my hand. 'Maybe. Maybe not. It was Rafi's
first communion. Big day for most Catholic kids, right? A
lot of emotion invested, a lot of vivid memories laid down.
I thought it might give you another focus, if you need one.'

Trudie didn't seem impressed. 'It's a lot older than the
fingernail.'

'I know. Look, try it if you think you need it. Otherwise
don't. And either way give it back to me when you're done.
I'll give it to Pen for a keepsake.'

I shied away from the implications of that statement:
that whether Asmodeus won or lost, keeping Rafi alive
might turn out to be a trick outside our collective skills;
that the photo might turn out to be the last thing Pen had
to remember her former lover by.

'I'll try it,' Trudie promised. 'I'll put it back in the map
room now and feed it into the loop later on.'

'Later on? Why not now?'

'Because if you're going to go down to Holborn and look
for Asmodeus' rabbit hole, I'd like to join you.'

I tried the idea on for size, and found I hated it less than
I would have expected. 'I've got something else I need to
do first,' I warned her.

Pax seemed nonplussed. 'Something more important than
Asmodeus?'

'No, less important. A lot less. It's just . . .' I threw up
my hands in a shrug, found that I had to unclench them
in order to do it. I hadn't realised how angry and frustrated I was until that moment. I almost punched the wall,

but my left hand was still stiff and sore from punching Gil McClennan's jaw exactly twenty-four hours before. 'Super-Self,' I exploded. 'Fucking Super-Self. Jenna-Jane is determined to send in the troops, even though they don't have a blind clue what it is they're facing. She thinks blitzkrieg is the right answer no matter what the question is. No, actually it's worse than that: she thinks the data you get from a wipe-out are as good as any other kind. If some of Gil's people die in the process, or get their brains fried like Etheridge, well, what the fuck? Science marches on.'

Pax was giving me a curious look. I threw it right back at her. 'What?' I demanded.

She shook her head. 'Nothing. It's just . . . do you think it will help?'

'Help what? What are you talking about?'

Trudie looked as though she was picking her words with care. 'The MOU exorcists aren't your favourite people in the world, are they? They're as bad as the Anathemata, in your book.'

'So?'

'So why does any of this matter to you? If you save some bunch of people you don't really know and don't really care about, is that going to make you feel any better about letting Asmodeus get free and kill somebody you *did* care about? Because that's what this is about, isn't it? The redemption train. You're standing on the footplate and sounding the whistle, Castor.'

'The whistle's all I've got,' I muttered sourly as I punched the button for the lift. 'Don't knock it.'

*   *   *

I never did like being psychoanalysed, even before I grew up, read the literature and realised that Freud only got into that game to pick up girls. Maybe that was why I asked Trudie to cover for me on the Holborn beat while I went across town to see a woman about a tune. Or maybe I was still reluctant to trust her further than I had to, even though we were de facto partners now. She was still Anathemata on some level: still fighting the same war against the same enemies. It felt like all there could ever be between us was a truce. I arranged to meet her in an hour's time, at Seven Dials, and headed west.

On one level I was close to screaming in frustration. Asmodeus had fallen off the map after his second visit to Pen's house, the night before last, when he'd left me a knife and a neatly bisected button to remember him by. He was still out there somewhere, still working, and I didn't even know what it was he was working towards. Just that it involved the deaths of everyone Rafi had ever known, that I couldn't possibly stop that from happening, and – hardest to take of all – that those deaths would turn out to be some sort of horrendous fringe benefit. They weren't the point. They arose out of some bigger scheme that Asmodeus had cooking.

Maybe his priorities were the same as they'd always been. *'I'm thinking of going home for a while,'* the demon had told me, *'when I'm free of this meat.'* He wanted to scrape Rafi off his shoe and rise in all his splendour, one hundred per cent guaranteed Hell-spawn: that had been on his mind ever since I'd inadvertently trapped him. So was that the big plan now?

He'd gone to the satanists first, but they'd let him down. The Anathemata had broken up the party before the mages of the SCA could complete their rituals and tear the man and the demon from their non-consensual embrace. Plan B had to be under way by now. Asmodeus wouldn't stop because he'd been put down once; he'd just come back again harder than ever.

And now, when we were finally closing in on the brimstone-arsed bastard, I was trudging halfway across London on a different job entirely, working to an agenda set by Jenna-Jane Mulbridge. That zombie in Somers Town had been right, and so had old Rosie: the world had changed all right. It had shaken itself inside out and all of us who thought we had the high ground were living in the valley of the shadow. What goes around, comes around, and it turns out to be a chainsaw blade.

In Kensington Church Street, I gave Evelyn Caldessa the schematics I'd sketched out on the train, and asked her if what I wanted could even be done. Caldessa is an antique dealer, and a good friend of mine ever since she helped me out on the Abbie Torrington case. She's imperturbable normally, having seen so much crazy shit in her seventy-four years that nothing surprises her any more. This commission made her raise an eyebrow though.

'Well there's no reason why not, in theory,' she said, after scanning the sheets several times over, tracing the lines with her stick-like finger as she puzzled out the sequence. But despite that hopeful start, she shook her head dubiously.

'In practice?' I prompted.

Caldessa glanced across at her only other customer, a middle-aged man in a three-quarter-length fawn coat who was ogling a case full of porcelain shepherdesses with the furtive air of a punter in a porn shop. She clearly had some hopes that he was going to make a purchase; either that or she thought he might have sticky fingers.

'None of the standard designs would work,' she said. 'They have a very tiny range, because the mechanism is very small and very crude. So you want something bespoke . . .'

'I'm prepared to pay,' I said, four words that have a magical effect in a lot of situations.

'. . . but you want it done quickly. Bespoke and quick turnaround don't sit well in the same sentence, dear heart. The people who I could ask to do this would enjoy the challenge, but they'd want to take weeks over it and charge you thousands.'

'Okay,' I said, rubbing my chin ruefully. 'I thought I was prepared to pay, but it turns out I'm not. I can't raise that kind of money, Evelyn. And the time won't shift. If I can't have it today, there's no point having it at all. Tell me if there's another way.'

'Those items,' Caldessa said, not to me but to the well-dressed shepherdess-fancier, 'are part of a collection. I'm afraid I can't split them up.'

Turning back to me, she winked conspiratorially. 'Never make it too easy for them,' she murmured. 'Obsession thrives on surmountable obstacles. Yes, Felix, there is another way. Several movements set side by side in one casing would do the job. Each mechanism would still be in the standard range, but together they'd be able to do what you need them to do. What a job though! Not making the individual cylinders – that's no effort at all. But making them work in time with each other . . .'

'If you could do it,' I said, 'how much would it cost?'

She gave me a slightly surprised look. 'Oh, more than you could afford, my lamb. A lot more than you could afford. But I assume there's a story attached?'

'Yeah, there is. Very much so.'

'And I'd very much like to hear it.'

'Done.'

'I'd very much like to hear it at Claridge's. Gastronomy Domine says Gordon Ramsay is back on form this year. A coarse and odious little man, but he knows how to cook.'

'Cheap at the price, Evelyn.'

'Then I'll see what I can do. Keep your mobile phone on vibrate, Felix, and in your back pocket. When I goose you, you'll know it's time to come see me again.'

From Kensington I grabbed a number 14 bus back into town: not as quick as a cab but cheaper. Now that I was committed to dinner for two at Claridge's, I was already counting the pennies.

Having Caldessa on the case gave me a sense of having made some progress, maybe spurious, but when your own wheels are spinning in the air it helps to know that other people are moving. In that regard, I called Nicky and asked him about the three stooges known as Tlallik, Ket and Jetaniul.

'A couple more bites,' he said. 'One on Jetaniul this time, and one more on Tlallik. The references are really fucking old, like with the Grazimir citation. Again, just lists of names from a couple of early grimoires: translations of translations of translations, so far from the original context that it's not worth chasing up. Nothing to indicate who they are, or what they are, or what they do. Judging by the company they keep though, they were pretty big players at one time.

Which makes me wonder how come none of them stayed in the hit parade after the thirteenth century.'

'And no known aliases?'

'Not yet. I tell you what though: Juliet could ask her brother.'

'Say again?'

'She comes from Baphomet's lineage, doesn't she? *She is of Baphomet the sister, and the youngest of her line*, et cetera. His name turns up on one of these lists too, so maybe him and Tlallik ran in the same crew.'

'I don't think she phones home all that often,' I said. It was an automatic response, dating back to when Juliet was trying to keep her nose clean. After last night's performance, maybe I'd need to revise that estimate.

'Doesn't hurt to ask, anyway,' Nicky said. 'I'm still on it, but I'm thinking this is a waste of time. These guys all closed up shop a long time ago.'

'Do demons retire, Nicky?'

'You can run that one past her too.'

I got off the bus at Trafalgar Square, then walked up St Martin's Lane, where I found a bank and wired a ton, in pounds sterling, to the personal account of D. Anastasiadis. A hundred quid a book, he'd said, so now he could make a start on Rafi's journals if he hadn't done so already. If you'd asked me what I hoped to find in there, and what I thought I could do with it, I'd have had to admit I had no idea. Again, it was the illusion of moving forward that was comforting, even though forward doesn't really mean anything if you have no clue where it is you're going.

As I carried on towards Seven Dials and my rendezvous with Trudie Pax, I made one final call, to Juliet – or as it turned out, to Sue Book. She sounded scared and hunted, as though picking up the phone was an act that was fraught with danger. I asked her if Juliet had seemed okay when she got home last night.

'Last night?' Sue echoed, sounding uncertain. 'She wasn't here. She didn't . . . I thought . . .' There was a pause, and then the sound of another voice in the background. Sue answered the other person, but her voice was muffled now – a hand over the receiver, most probably.

'Sue?' I prompted.

There was a spate of rattles and clicks.

'Who is this?' It wasn't Sue's voice. It wasn't Juliet's either – or rather, not quite. It was close, but it had a ragged edge to it with oddly placed peaks and troughs, as though it was being played back on the wrong device and in the wrong format.

'It's me,' I said. 'Castor.'

'She called you?'

The threat in the tone was palpable. 'Uh . . . no. I called her. I just wanted to see how you were feeling. If you're managing to . . .' I groped for a circumlocution that avoided words like devour and soul. 'If you're keeping it together,' I finished cravenly.

There was a long silence, long enough to make me think that the connection had broken, but Juliet spoke again just before I did.

'Tell me where you are,' she said.

From behind her, I could dimly hear a squeal of dismay from Sue. 'Jules, no. He's just a friend. He's your friend too. It's not—'

The crash that obliterated the end of the sentence was

loud enough to make me flinch away from the phone. 'Juliet,' I shouted. 'Don't hurt her. Fuck it, don't hurt her. I'm in town. On Seven Dials. What do you want?'

At that moment Trudie rounded the corner of Shorts Gardens, about fifty yards away. She waved to me, then registered my expression and lowered her hand. Only silence now on the other end of the line.

'Juliet?' I yelled again.

There's a weird experience I get every now and then, where I look at my watch and I think it's stopped, because the second hand doesn't seem to be moving. It just sits there, seemingly for a whole lot longer than a second hand should, until finally it wakes up and jumps to the next notch. It's just a second, but it's a second you're glancing at sideways somehow, and from that angle it looks longer. That's probably what happened here. It felt like I was waiting for a night and a day, but since nothing else happened in that time, it's a fair bet that it was no time at all.

'She's fine, Castor,' said Juliet in her normal voice.

'What do you mean, she's fine?' I snarled. 'I heard you tearing the whole place apart.'

Her voice was eerily calm, and the dislocation from what had just happened was so complete it was terrifying. 'I swung a chair against the wall, and it broke. Sue wasn't hurt. But now she won't let me touch her or come near her. Can I ask a favour?'

Trudie had come up to join me now, and was waiting silently at my side, trying to piece together what the hell this was about from my side of the conversation. 'A favour?' I repeated blankly.

'I told you I'd send her away if I thought I might hurt her again.' A pause. 'She can't stay here.'

'I'll be right there,' I said. 'Don't either of you move.' Inspiration struck, and I added, 'Give Sue the phone.' I looked around for a cab, but there were none in sight. I started walking rapidly along Mercer Street with Trudie in tow. I'd reached the end of the street before Sue's voice sounded down the line again, breaking even on the single word 'Hello?'

Plenty of cabs on Shaftesbury Avenue. I flagged one down with my right hand, holding the phone in my left.

'I'm going to put a friend on,' I said to Sue as we climbed into the cab. 'Keep talking to her. Let her know if anything happens.' I passed the phone to Trudie, adding 'Royal Oak' for the cabbie's benefit, and we were away.

Thanks to Mr Livingstone and his wondrous congestion charge, we made good headway through the centre, but then got hopelessly snarled up as we headed up Edgware Road toward the Westway. Trudie was keeping up a non-stop stream of meaningless conversation with Sue Book the whole way, which was what I was hoping she'd do: taking Sue's mind off the terror and at the same time letting me know that she was still alive. I sat with my eyes closed, thinking about Juliet, or rather thinking about the tune that corresponded to Juliet. If I had to fight her, I needed to have that music clear in my mind, and at the moment it was rubbing shoulders with other tunes, to their mutual detriment. I had to unremember the harsh skirls of the fear-thing in the Super-Self swimming pool and the insidious discontinuities of Asmodeus, had to put them way to the back of my mind where they couldn't be heard.

I was kidding myself, of course. The tin whistle is a great specific against ghosts, but when you're fighting demons it has the disadvantage of a crossbow against an AK-47: you get off one shot, and then you're dead before you can ratchet up for the second. But this was yet another fine mess I'd invited an innocent bystander into, so there was no walking away from it. No, as usual, I had to walk right into it whistling a jaunty refrain.

Bourne Terrace was quiet and deserted, and from the outside Sue's house looked similarly untroubled.

'We'll be right back,' I told the cabbie. 'Don't move.'

Trudie kept up her running commentary all the way to the door. 'We're coming up the driveway now. We're right outside . . .' But it was Juliet who opened up, and stood aside to let us in. I stared at her questioningly. Her gaze flicked to the tin whistle I still had clutched in my hand, and she quirked an eyebrow.

'You won't need that,' she said. 'Luckily for you.'

'Maybe I won't,' I conceded. 'Do you?'

'Need you to play me back into my right mind?' Juliet asked with sardonic emphasis. 'No. I don't. Not for the moment, anyway. But get her out of here quickly. She won't look at me, and she cries when I come near her. It makes me . . . agitated. I can feel myself slipping.'

'You're sure there's no other way?' I asked lamely. 'You don't have any clue why this might be happening? You can't get any kind of a handle on it?' I remembered the painted stones. 'I found some summonings around your house and in a few other places. You think maybe someone could have . . . ?'

Juliet scowled. 'Could have raised one of the other

powers against me? No, Castor. Not without me noticing. I think . . .' She gave a sudden shrug. It looked almost involuntary, as though she was shaking off some unwelcome touch. 'It's my nature,' she said, her tone tight. 'There are limits to how far you can change yourself. I've come to the end of an arc, Castor, and I'm swinging back.'

She was staring at me, and I realised suddenly that her eyes were back to their usual black on black. The red fires had died for the time being. But there was no mistaking the rigid tension in her posture: she was fighting her own instincts, guarding the borders of rationality from one second to the next.

'Go wait in the kitchen,' I suggested. 'Shut the door. Turn the radio on. Make yourself a coffee.'

Juliet considered this, nodded and retreated. 'Decaf!' I shouted, as the door closed on her.

Sue was sitting on the living-room sofa, the wreckage of the chair scattered across the carpet a few feet away from her like debris from an explosion. The TV set had had its screen staved in too, and was lying on its side in the corner of the room. A ragged hole in the plaster above it showed how it had got there, and roughly how fast it had been travelling.

Sue rose to greet us as we entered, saying hello to me and then shifting her gaze enquiringly to Trudie in a way that invited me to make introductions. I'd been afraid we might find her in shock, but there was a desolate calm about her. She looked like someone who's finally let go of the last shred of hope, and is just beginning to discover the terrible relief that despair brings.

'You should pack some things,' I said. 'Clothes. Toiletries. Anything you can't do without. We don't know how long it will take to sort this.'

'Sort it?' Sue gave me a pitying look. 'You can't, Felix. You can't sort it. Whatever she felt for me . . . it's gone. I don't even know her.'

'Me neither,' I agreed. 'But it's happened so suddenly, Sue. Maybe it's a sickness. Or something that just happens to demons when they get to a certain age. What we're doing now . . . it's not forever. It's damage limitation until we can work out something better.'

Sue wasn't convinced or consoled, but Trudie stepped in at this point and took her away upstairs to help her through the process of packing. I was left alone in the living room, surveying the destruction. Sue had lived here all her life: with her mother, until her mother died, then alone, and finally with her demon lover. Maybe I should have suggested that Juliet be the one to go, but then when her self-control evaporated again she'd probably head straight back here and reclaim the things that were hers – including Sue. This way was better.

The room stank of her anger, and Sue's fear. Having a death-sense makes me sensitive to emotional resonances too, and when they're strong and recent they can be over-powering. My own heart rate started to climb, riding a second-hand adrenalin rush.

I retreated into the hall just as Sue and Trudie came down the stairs. Trudie was carrying a suitcase, Sue a small flight bag.

'Everything?' I asked.

Sue nodded, her face expressionless.

'Go ahead and wait in the cab,' I said to Trudie. 'I'll be right there.'

I watched them down the drive, then tapped lightly on the door of the kitchen. Juliet opened it instantly. I suspected she'd just been standing there, on the other side of the door, waiting for the coast to clear, waiting for the woman she'd lived with for more than a year to depart.

'She's gone,' I said.

Juliet nodded. She already knew that.

'Would you rather not know where she is?' I asked her. 'I was going to take her to Pen's, but I could find a hotel, if . . .' I let the sentence hang. *If you're so afraid of losing control that she'd be safer in hiding*, was the implication.

'Let her be among friends,' Juliet said, her voice a throaty murmur. 'I won't . . . I don't believe I'll seek her out. The wards at your house are strong. And you're there, which is some protection – not because of the whistle but because you're such a slippery little bastard.'

'Okay,' I said. On another occasion I would have thanked her for the compliment, but right then didn't feel like the time. 'I'm still tied up with this other stuff. With Asmodeus. He's cooking something up, and I really need to find him before it comes to the boil. You're sure you won't . . . ?'

She shook her head emphatically. 'You don't need me at your back right now. Half the time I'd be at your throat instead.'

'And parts south,' I acknowledged. 'Yeah. You're probably right. But when it's done . . . we'll talk.'

'Castor.'

I'd got to the door. I paused with my hand on the latch

and turned back. She was holding something out to me. By reflex, I took it. A small sheaf of fifty-pound notes, the four I'd given to her two days ago, when I'd paid her to keep watch over Pen.

'You're right,' Juliet said. 'She's more than a friend. I don't want her to be hurt. I need you – I'm employing you – to make sure that doesn't happen.'

'I'll do that without the money,' I said.

'Do it with the money. Friendship is hard for me to understand or to believe in right now. Bargains I understand. Say yes.'

'Yes.'

'Bind yourself to it.'

'I bind myself to it. I won't let her get hurt.'

'Good then. Go away.'

I hesitated. 'What will you do?' I asked.

She made another of those abrupt movements, like a shrug that was close to getting out of control. 'I don't know,' she said. Her voice was cold and flat, with none of its usual thrilling harmonics. 'I might give up on this experiment. Go home.'

I felt an unnerving shifting in my stomach. It wasn't pleasant hearing Asmodeus' words echoed so closely by Juliet.

'Don't do that without talking to me first,' I said.

She shot me a bleak hard stare. 'Be careful what you wish for,' she growled.

14

Despite what she'd said the night before about going hunting on her own account, Pen was home when we arrived, and once I'd explained the situation, she rolled with the punch of having a new tenant landed on her.

'We've got lots of empty rooms,' she said to Sue, taking the little sheaf of fifties from me without comment. 'Come and find one you like, and we'll open the windows and air it out a bit.'

She spirited Sue away into the remote fastnesses of the house – the no-man's-land between her basement and my attic, where she scarcely ever ventured. Like Sue, she was living on in the house where her mother had lived. In fact, she could boast three generations of Bruckners who'd all lived and (with one exception) died on this soil. Maybe that would give the two of them something to talk about.

Judging by the look on Trudie's face, we had something to talk about too, and I knew what it was before she spoke.

'That thing is dangerous,' she said. 'Probably too dangerous for you to handle yourself. The fact that it's been playing house with a human being doesn't change what it is underneath. You should tell Professor Mulbridge about what's happening here.'

'Juliet isn't a thing,' I said. I helped myself to a large brandy from a bottle on Pen's sideboard, then realised what I was doing when the glass was halfway to my lips. Tense and frustrated, I set it down again untasted. 'I count her as a friend.'

Trudie shook her head grimly. 'Then you're an idiot,' she said. 'Castor, didn't you learn anything from what happened with Ditko?'

I fought down a surge of anger. Trudie had been a tower of strength out at Royal Oak, but every time I got close to lowering my guard around her her she pulled something like this.

'Rafi is an old friend who got ram-raided by a demon,' I said, deadpan. 'Juliet is a demon I happen to like. I don't see the analogy.'

Trudie saw the warning in my look, but she had no intention of backing down. 'Yes,' she said, 'you do. You just don't want to. If you anthropomorphise these things, you blind-side yourself. You start expecting them to behave like people.'

'Well, I haven't given up on *you* yet,' I pointed out.

Surprisingly, the sucker punch seemed to hurt her. She affected a laugh but blinked a few times quickly and looked away. I'd been seeing her as Joan of Arc up until then: armoured in righteousness, no time for losers. It was a surprise to find that the armour had weak points.

'They're our enemies,' she said, automatically adjusting the strings around her hands. 'They torture and they kill and they poison everything they touch. I don't understand why you don't see that.'

'And I don't understand why you think you already know all the answers,' I said, but with a lot less heat. 'Look, the point about Juliet is that she doesn't always kill when she can, or when she wants to. She didn't kill me, two years ago. That was what broke the ice between us.'

I could see she wasn't the slightest bit convinced, and for some reason, now, I wanted to plant the seed of a doubt. 'Trudie,' I said, 'think about this. There's a difference between Mount Ararat and Noah's Ark. Have you ever been to Ararat? It's in Turkey. You can go up there on a day trip, take a picnic. But does that prove that Noah washed up there when the flood waters fell?'

Trudie was giving me a blank stare. 'You think I'm a literalist?' she asked incredulously. 'You think I believe every word of the Bible is infallible truth?'

'No. I just want you to see the difference. Ararat exists, but it doesn't prove Noah, or the flood. Now we know that Hell exists too. But it doesn't necessarily follow that you, or Gwillam, or any other Christian soldier, knows what Hell is. Gossip isn't fact, and when it comes to Hell, the Bible is just the *Hello!* magazine of the ancient world.'

This was too much for Trudie. She gave a wordless yell of exasperation. 'Castor, you don't have to believe the Bible; you just have to believe the evidence of your own eyes. Ajulutsikael may wear a dress and have a nice arse but it was never a baby or a child or a teenage tearaway or anything you'd see as female. It's nobody's daughter, nobody's mother. It's a woman the way a stick insect is a stick. No, in the way a praying mantis is a leaf. The moment you forget that—'

She stopped dead in the middle of the sentence, looking past me towards the door of the room. I turned involuntarily, following her gaze. Pen was framed in the doorway. Sue had already taken a few steps into the room, but had then stopped dead, brought up short by Trudie's wall of words. Now she came forward again.

The colour had drained out of her face; even her lips were white. For a moment she had the ivory pallor of Juliet herself. Her fists were clenched at her sides, her body so rigid it looked like it would ring out with an A sharp if you touched it.

'I'm sorry,' Trudie faltered. 'I didn't mean . . .'

'A stick insect.' Sue's voice was an ugly, grating thing. 'A praying mantis. What have you . . . What did you ever touch? Who have you . . . loved and cared for and, and, and lain with, you twisted bitch? How dare you stand there and pass . . . pass judgement on my . . . *wife*?'

On the last word she launched herself at Trudie in a flying leap. Trudie had six inches on her, and had been trained by the excommunicate sergeant majors of the Anathemata to hold her own against men and demons, but she didn't fight back as Sue went for her, punching and clawing; she just raised her arms to protect her face.

It was a tricky job to disentangle Sue from Trudie without hurting her, but Pen and I managed, taking an arm each and half-lifting her off the floor to take away her leverage. Trudie took a hurried step back, lowering her *en garde*.

'I'll wait outside,' she said, and then to Sue, 'I'm sorry. I'm really sorry.'

She fled out of the room and up the stairs. When the street door slammed behind her, we carefully let go of Sue and stepped away from her. Anger and indignation had done her a power of good. She looked more like herself than she had at any time since I'd found her nursing her black eye three days before.

'I'm fine,' she said. 'I'm calm.' A second later she

exploded with another 'Bitch!' – which showed us exactly
how calm she was, and probably brought her lifetime tally
with that word up to two. Pen took her into a consoling
embrace.

'I've got to get back out there,' I said to Pen. I thought
of explaining why, but 'Asmodeus is underground' wasn't
a revelation that could help her very much. She couldn't
join the hunt, and the thought of Jenna-Jane's exorcists
combing the streets for Rafi would just make her miser-
able. 'Back on the case,' I finished lamely. 'I'll come by
again later, if I can. Will you be okay here?'

Pen nodded to me over Sue's head, and I cravenly left
them to it.

'Call Leonidas!' Pen shouted to me as I was on my way
up the stairs to ground level. I turned around and went
back down.

'That's the guy from *300*,' I pointed out. 'Gerard Butler.'

'Something like that, anyway.'

'Anastasiadis?'

'Exactly.'

Progress on the journals? Some good news would have
been pretty welcome right then. I joined Trudie out on the
street and asked her if she'd give me a minute or two to
make the call. She still seemed a little shaken up by the
storm she'd provoked from Sue.

'Take as long as you need,' she said, and walked off to
the end of the drive, out of earshot.

Anastasiadis's secretary spoke only Macedonian, so all I
could do was repeat my name until she gave up and put
me through.

'Mr Castor.' The lawyer sounded tired and dispirited.

But then given what day it was, that was hardly surprising. I looked at my watch. Allowing for the time difference, it must have been about three hours since Jovan walked the last mile.

'Feeling rough?' I commiserated. 'You did everything you could, man. Like you said, Jovan's cards were marked in advance. They probably put the execution on the docket before they fixed up a trial date.'

'That is why I called you, Mr Castor.' Anastasiadis's tone was grim. 'There was no execution.'

I blinked. 'What? You mean the pardon came through, after all?'

'That is not what I mean. Jovan Ditko was murdered last night. Someone broke into Irdrizovo Prison, tearing a gate off its hinges, and killed him in his cell. It was not quick, and it was not clean. There was . . . mutilation. His eyes, in particular . . .'

I didn't hear the next few sentences, because the moment-ary paralysis of shock had allowed the phone to slip through my fingers. I had to flail and lunge to retrieve it before it hit the ground. When I got it back to my ear, the lawyer was still describing what had been done to his client before – or perhaps, to take an optimistic view, after – he died. I cut him off in full flow. I could fill in the details without any help from him.

'Did they catch anyone?' I demanded. But he'd already answered that: you don't say *someone* broke in if you know who the someone is. 'See anyone?' I amended.

'Neither,' Anastasiadis said. 'The other prisoners in the block heard – it would have been impossible not to hear – and they screamed for the guards. But the guards feared a riot, which is a very common thing on the night before an execution, so they did not come. He was found when they came in the morning to take him.'

Asmodeus. Asmodeus had travelled a thousand miles to murder Rafi's last living relative hours before he was due to die in any case. How? How had he done it? When Juliet had flown with me to the United States, the experience had almost destroyed her: it had left her weak and sick and at half-strength for weeks afterwards. Demons are chthonic powers, and too much distance from the ground hits them like a bad dose of flu. For that very reason Juliet had refused to take the flight back to Heathrow. She told me she had other ways of travelling that wouldn't involve leaving the ground.

'Mr Castor? You are still there?'

'Yeah. I'm still here.'

'I apologise. I had not meant to burden you with the unpleasant details. But they weigh on my mind. It is hard for me to stop thinking about them. And I wondered – inevitably I wondered, given the things you said to Jovan yesterday – whether this demon you spoke of might have been involved in his death.'

'We don't have any way of knowing for sure,' I said bleakly.

'But in your own estimation?'

'Yes. It was Asmodeus.'

The lawyer sighed – a drawn-out sound with a slight tremor in it. 'I have a translator working on the books,' he said. 'You have an email address?'

I gave him Nicky's and Pen's, and asked him to send the translation on to both accounts.

'You are still looking for this thing?' he asked me.

I didn't quibble about the choice of words this time. 'Yeah, I'm still looking for him.'

'Be careful, Mr Castor. And be lucky. I do not believe that any god holds me in his good graces, but still I will pray for you.'

'Thanks. I'll take all the help I can get.'

I slipped the phone into my pocket and rejoined Trudie. She didn't look any happier. For a moment I considered keeping what I'd just learned to myself, but a deal is a deal. I filled her in as we walked to the Tube station.

'Macedonia!' She seemed more amazed at the logistics than disturbed by what Asmodeus had done, but then she'd never met Jovan Ditko, or Rafi for that matter: a lot of this was still theoretical for her.

'Macedonia,' I agreed. 'Some time in the middle of last night. God knows how long it took him to get there, or whether he's back now.'

'Maybe that's why nobody has got a hit yet,' Trudie mused sombrely. 'Even if he has got a tunnel under Holborn, we might not get a fix on him if he hasn't been there recently. We're probably wasting our time.'

She filled me in on the morning's activities. Most of the area between Holborn and the river had been searched pretty thoroughly, and McClennan had told his teams to fan out to the east and west. Trudie herself had criss-crossed the backstreets around Kingsway for most of the morning, but the only things that had impinged on her death-sense were the local ghosts and zombies.

'Maybe what you said,' I mused. 'The trail's not fresh enough. Or maybe he's just too deep. There could be

Victorian sewers down there, fifty feet below the regular ones. Or Tube tunnels that were never documented, for that matter. We only know what someone decided to write down.'

Trudie didn't answer. Since the argument at Pen's she seemed to have drawn in on herself. She kept up the silence all the way into town, and while we were retreading the beat she'd walked for most of the morning. We ran into Etheridge and his partner – the woman Gil McClennan had referred to as Greaves – coming towards us along Kemble Street. Etheridge was his usual nervy, tic-ridden self, no better and no worse than when I'd seen him last, but Greaves was tired and disgruntled.

'Nobody's got a trace of anything,' she said. 'And we've walked every square foot of this area ten times over by now. If there was anything to find, we'd have found it. But Gil says we have to keep on going until the light fails.'

'He's very keen,' I commented neutrally.

Greaves snorted derisively. 'He's shit-scared,' she retorted. 'This keeps his mind off it, doesn't it?'

'Off what?' Trudie asked.

'Off Super-Self. He's got to go in tonight, and he doesn't know how it's going to pan out. Keeping himself busy is his way of dealing with it.'

I thought about the fight I'd had with McClennan the day before. Greaves might be right, but if Gil was scared, I suspected it wasn't just for his own safety. He'd thrown that punch at me because he saw my off-the-cuff battle plan as putting his exorcists in danger. But then this morning he'd rejected my suggestion, which would have given him an easy out. He must be wondering now what he'd let himself and his team in for, and whether he was going to end the evening with blood – someone else's blood, I mean – on his hands. He might be the first McClennan ever to fret on that score.

We kept on going to the end of the street, then did one more long trek up and down Kingsway. At that point Trudie announced she was going back to the MOU – back to her map. Maybe the fact that Asmodeus had been out of town would make a difference. There'd be new lines to draw now, with a jump discontinuity from the old ones because Asmodeus had nipped over to eastern Europe on his murderous little day trip. That time lapse might be enough to allow her to distinguish his present movements from older ones.

I was going to offer to go with her, but my phone rang and a glance at the display told me it was Caldessa. 'I have to take this,' I apologised to Trudie. She shrugged and backed off a few steps.

'Hello?' I said, turning my back on her.

'Hello, dear heart,' Caldessa said. 'Good news. My friend Burgerman was able to help me with the internal workings of your dread device. It transpires that the drilling and pinning process is done by means of a computer these days – *quelle surprise*. Burgerman knows a man who makes them up in batches for the tourist dollar, from old chocolate boxes and jewel cases. He boggled a little at your specifications, but he was able to run off the cylinders in no time, and the combs are standard.'

'So it's all done?' I demanded.

'Not quite, but it will be by the time you get here. I'm just fitting everything into the case now.'

'You're the eighth wonder of the modern world, Caldessa,' I said fervently.

'Of the ancient world,' she sighed, 'unfortunately.'

I hung up and looked around for Trudie, but she was nowhere in sight. She must have got tired of waiting for me, or maybe she felt being on her own for a while would be an improvement on my company. I couldn't fault her logic on that one.

I looked at the time and weighed up my options. I wanted to go back to Pen's and make sure both she and Sue were still there and still safe. I wanted to check in with Nicky and see if he'd managed to get the dirt on Tlallik and Ket and Jetaniul. More than anything, I wanted to sleep, but you can do that when you're dead, at least if your luck is in.

Before doing any of those things, I took the Tube out to Kensington and collected my order. Caldessa demonstrated its workings to me with pardonable pride.

'Three keys,' she said, rotating the drab little wooden box in her hands. It hadn't been painted or varnished, and unlike Burgerman's enterprising friend, Caldessa hadn't used a Victorian chocolate box or jewel case as her starting point; she'd just nailed six roughly sanded pieces of MDF together into a cube, cutting slatted holes into one of them to allow the thing to function. 'But once they're all wound up, you can turn it on and off with this toggle switch here. It doesn't open, of course. And it doesn't look like anything very much. But I assume function is more important than form, and it's a lot sturdier than the regular kind.'

'It's perfect, Caldessa.' I kissed her on the cheek, and

she yelped because my stubble was more than usually obtrusive. 'I'll be in touch about that date, as soon as I'm done with this. I'll even shave.'

'You needn't bother as far as that goes,' Caldessa allowed. 'Your louche charm is a selling point, Felix. A shave and a manicure would just make you look like a used-car salesman.'

She had a point. I never did scrub up more than halfway decent. I thanked her again and retired with some of my dignity still intact.

No answer from Pen's house, or from Nicky either at the Gaumont or on his mobile. Fatigue was catching up on me with a vengeance now, and my eyes were doing that thing where they only stay open while you're actually making them, and close by infinitesimal degrees whenever your attention slips.

It was only six thirty or so, more than five hours yet before I had to be at Super-Self to head Gil McClennan off from his Little Big Horn. I bowed to the inevitable, caught a Circle Line train running widdershins through South Ken, and put my head down for half an hour.

Well, half an hour was the plan. When sleep opened its black throat at my feet I lost my balance and pitched in head first, like a drugged honey cake into the gullet of Cerberus, and lulled by the motion of the train we both went rocking into the dark together.

It was a sleep that was almost deep enough to be dreamless: or at least the things that populated it were too primitive and unformed to resolve themselves into actual images or sounds. They were just inchoate feelings, made up of unease and familiarity in equal amounts. It was as though I was sliding down an endless helter skelter of déjà vus.

What woke me was the sound of the PA system at Moorgate reporting a good service on all lines. It's like they say: there are lies, damned lies and London Underground service announcements.

I was groggy and crumpled and slumped into a corner of the seat. The first thing I realised was that I'd slept with my tin whistle jammed against my third rib, so that I winced in discomfort every time I breathed in. The second was that the man in the snow-white mac sitting opposite me, staring at me with an expression of distant, contemplative calm, was Father Thomas Gwillam.

'Good evening, Castor,' he said solemnly.

Evening? I looked at my watch. Half past nine. I'd slept for three hours. Still no need to panic, but this had to be my last turn on the merry-go-round.

'Evening, Father,' I muttered. 'It's been sixteen years or so since my last confession.'

Gwillam's thin lips pursed slightly: he doesn't like it when people make light of grave matters. His pale eyes blinked and then opened again slowly, like a cat's. 'I've been excommunicated,' he reminded me. 'I'm therefore no longer qualified to take confession. Your sins will have to remain on your conscience a while longer.'

I looked around me as I came awake properly, belatedly taking in the fact that Gwillam wasn't alone. Two of his team – a very young woman and a man built even more solidly than Mr Dicks – stood to either side of me, close enough to intercept if I tried anything that smacked of lèse-majesté.

'You're playing a very dangerous game,' Gwillam told me.

I laughed out loud. I couldn't help myself; it was just so obviously something he'd heard someone say in a Bond movie.

'What do you suggest?' I asked him. 'Twister's no good. I'm just not as supple as I used to be.'

'You set this thing free in the first place, Castor. All the deaths that have resulted from that act are on your hands. And it's your responsibility more than anyone's to see that it's destroyed before it can do any further harm.'

Anger crawled up my throat like bile. In spite of his two bodyguards – and I was under no illusions that the girl was at least as dangerous as the bruiser – I was tempted to lunge across the aisle and take a poke at him. One good whack on his self-satisfied snout: that would almost make up for being beaten into lumpy porridge immediately afterwards.

But I still had promises to keep.

'It was your people who set him free, you fuckwit,' I snarled instead. 'I got him out of the Stanger, but your hit men opened his fucking door and let him walk right out. It's on you as well as me.'

To my surprise, he nodded. 'Yes,' he agreed. 'It's on me too. I don't deny that. It's the reason I've allowed you to operate as a free agent. I know what you're trying to do. I don't hold out any great hope that you'll succeed, but the smallest chance that you might outweighs the risk that you'll sabotage our own operation.'

He paused for a second, frowning at me. He tilted his head to one side to get a better angle on the only slightly faded bruises on my face, the ones left over from my first encounter with Asmodeus down in Brixton.

'But we suspect that the demon has plans of his own in train,' he said. 'Plans that are already far advanced. So I'm swallowing my pride, Castor. I'm here to suggest that we work together to bring him down.'

'No thanks,' I said.

Gwillam didn't seem surprised, but his eyes narrowed into a severe frown.

'You're making no progress alone. You're flailing in the dark.'

I laughed again. 'Gwillam, do you think I'm an idiot?' I demanded. 'You're here because you've fired every shot in your locker and you didn't hit a blind thing. You're coming up empty. This is no-stone-unturned time, and I'm probably the last stone you got to. But you think offering to share will play better than asking if you can pick my brains for free.'

Gwillam's expression didn't change. 'You're wrong,' he said. 'Your cynicism demeans you, but it's understandable, to some extent. It's true that we haven't run Asmodeus to ground, any more than you have, but we've succeeded in closing down his support system.'

'The American satanists,' I translated, and I took a certain pleasure in seeing in his face the surprise he tried to hide.

'Exactly,' Gwillam confirmed. 'The remnants of Anton Fanke's organisation, now completely eradicated. Whatever Asmodeus is doing, he's been thrown back on his own resources. We have a window, and if we use it wisely – if we cooperate and pool our intelligence – we can bring him down.'

I shook my head firmly. 'No,' I said, 'we can't. Because

that – bringing him down, I mean – is exactly where we part company. You want him dead; I just want him caught.'

'I want the demon dead,' Gwillam corrected me.

'And you don't care who else gets left in the dirt – or under it – along the way. I've seen you work, Gwillam. I chose Jenna-Jane Mulbridge as a partner over you – that ought to tell you a lot.'

'Suppose I swore – on the book that I love – not to kill Ditko unless it's absolutely unavoidable?'

'You're excommunicated. You've got nothing to lose now, have you?'

The train pulled into the next station, and Gwillam stood. The young woman turned her head to stare at him, but he moved his hand in an almost imperceptible horizontal gesture: *No*.

You can call me,' he said. 'A message left at the house in St Albans – where you tracked me down last time – will still reach me. Don't let false pride lead you astray, Castor. You're right that my word on this thing, even my sworn word, is worth nothing. I'll break any promise and betray any trust, to cauterise this evil. But if your methods were a little more like mine, fewer people would have died. Consider. And when you reach the end of your own pathetic Calvary, let me know. My offer will still be open.'

He stepped down, followed by his two asymmetrical minders. Four stops to go before Paddington. I used the intervening time to get my head together and to try to shake off the lingering atmosphere of that fucking dream.

The estimable Mr Dicks was on duty at the front desk again, and his flatulent grunt as he pressed the gate release said louder than words that seeing me had made his day.

I walked on by, whistling a slightly out-of-tune 'Nkosi Sikelel' iAfrica'.

The place was dark and all but deserted. Another guard was checking windows in a desultory way, but I didn't see anybody else around until I got up onto the second floor and noticed the faint glow coming from between the slatted blinds of Jenna-Jane's office. I went by on tippy-toe, very keen not to alert her to my presence.

The map room was in darkness, but when I turned on the light I found that Trudie was there all the same. She'd been sitting in the dark, up to her knees in shredded paper. That at least explained where the map had gone, although not why.

She looked up and gave me a hollow-eyed stare. She looked as though she'd been crying, but she wasn't crying now. Her fists were clenched, but the cat's cradles normally wound round her knuckles trailed across the floor now like Pierrot's sleeves, giving her a tragic air.

'You okay?' I asked her.

'No,' she said. 'Not really.' Her tone was hard, but brittle too – a catch at the back of it warning me to tread carefully.

'I was going to ask you how it went,' I said, indicating the torn fragments of map, 'but I guess I've got my answer.'

'He's not back yet. Not in London, anyway. No new lines. Nothing to go on. Waste of time.'

I waited. If she wanted to tell me what had happened, she'd tell me. If she didn't, asking about it might bring on a crisis we probably didn't have time for. For something to do, I started to clear up some of the mess. Where the black lines had been too thickly overlaid on each other, becoming a single indecipherable mass, Trudie had at some point resorted to a silver Sharpie marker. The silver lines, their lustre deadened by the thick black tracery underneath, looked like day-old snail slime.

'I took your advice,' Trudie said in that same dangerous tone.

Down on one knee, my fists full of scraps like the guy who lays the trail on a paperchase, I looked up at her. Her red-rimmed eyes blinked once, twice, three times.

'What advice was that?'

'You said I should look in the basement here. If I wanted to know who I was working for.'

Okay. That explained a lot.

'Those cell blocks are a logical extrapolation from a certain position,' I said carefully. 'I just wanted you to think about the implications of—'

'I know what you *wanted*, Castor,' Trudie growled. 'I told you I've been down there. Tonight. About an hour ago. I'd have to be pretty fucking dense not to get it, wouldn't I?'

A pause.

'Look. Look at this,' Trudie said. She held out her hand, which was shaking visibly. 'An hour. It just won't stop.' She took a deep breath and stood. Her hand fell to her side again, the fingers flexing and clenching. 'Principled resignations,' she said, shaking her head sombrely. 'They look really bad on your CV, don't they? Nobody likes a quitter. Especially a holier-than-thou quitter.'

I took a step towards her, but the hand came up again like a shot, warding me off. She didn't want any consolation that I could offer, even though it looked as though the tears were starting again.

'You're still wrong,' she said, 'and Mulbridge is still right. That's the horror of it, Castor – that we have to turn ourselves into what she is if we want to survive. Hell is coming to Earth, one piece at a time. Not the sky falling, but the ground opening up under our feet. There's nowhere that's safe to stand any more. If I walk out on this, it will just be because I'm a coward, like you.'

I didn't argue. It wasn't just her hands that were shaking, it was her whole body. She looked down at the trailing strings that dangled from her wrists, made a half-hearted gesture towards rewinding them, but then gave it up after the first two or three turns.

'Will you?' I asked her. 'Walk out?'

Trudie shook her head slowly. 'I don't know,' she admitted. 'Not yet. Not until we've found Asmodeus and got him locked away again. After that . . . I'll see how I feel.'

'Then can I ask for your help with one other thing?' I asked, keeping my tone studiously neutral.

'What's that?'

'The Super-Self entity. Gil is scheduled to start his demolition run at midnight. I want to get in there first and see if I can take it down myself.'

Trudie stared at me, mystification rousing her for the first time from her own tortured thoughts. 'Take it down?' she repeated. 'Last time it chewed us up and spat us out. Why should tonight be any different?'

'Because tonight I've got a secret weapon,' I said. 'Inspired by you, actually. I liked what you did with the map – the way you pushed yourself out past your comfort zone and did the necessary. I think maybe I can do the same thing here. But I want an anchor in case things go Pete Tong on me. The two of us working together damped that thing down just enough so that we could walk out of Super-Self on our own four feet. That's what I want you to do tonight: be my back-up, and give me some room to manoeuvre if it drops on me before I make my play.'

Trudie hesitated for a second, then shrugged. 'Okay. Why not?'

'Thanks. Is there anything else you need to do here?'

She surveyed the devastation she'd wrought and shook her head again. 'No. I think I'm done.'

We were both pretty near stony, as it turned out – I should have kept one of those fifties back for emergencies – so my first idea of grabbing a cab down to the Strand foundered on an absence of hard cash. We used our travel-cards from earlier in the day instead, taking the Circle back round to King's Cross and then changing to the Piccadilly Line. But Holborn was closed because of a suspect package, so we were booted off at Russell Square and had to walk the rest of the way.

That didn't feel like much of a hardship. The day had been another scorcher, and even this late in the evening, with the rush-hour crowds long gone, the train had smelled like one titanic armpit. It was a relief to walk in the cooling air, and to feel the city poised on that luminous knife-edge where day becomes night. There was still light in the sky, but the buildings were black masses on either side of us, the occa-sional still-open shop looking like a cave in a cliff face.

Another dark mass rose ahead of us, and it took me a moment to realise what it was. When I did, I stopped dead and stared at it in blank-faced wonder.

Trudie looked at me curiously, then followed my gaze. The same penny dropped a moment later.

'Mary, mother of us!' she whispered.

London hasn't had a tram system since before the Second World War, but some of the infrastructure is still kicking around. You can see stretches of track in a hundred places where old street surfaces haven't been asphalted over, or have been restored, and in my west London stamping ground the Acton tram depot, which looks like a Victorian siding shed with white-brick walls and a massive fan-vaulted ceiling, was still used for buses right up until last year.

What we were looking at was the north end of the Kingsway underpass – an underground tramway closed down in the 1940s. Later on, the council converted part of it into a tunnel for cars and buses coming from Aldwych by the simple expedient of building a new steel-and-cement corridor within the tiled and brick-built passage that already existed. The rest had been closed off and left to rot.

'How did we miss it?' Trudie demanded, amazed.

I was asking myself the same question. The answer – beyond 'We're thick as bricks and we can't find our own arses without a map' – was that the tunnel had no opening between Holborn and the river. This end was on Southampton Row, a couple of hundred yards up from Holborn station, and the other end was somewhere on the Embankment west of Waterloo Bridge. Both ends were closed off now, and apart from this short stretch of black stone parapet wall there was nothing to show on the surface that the tunnel was there.

We looked at each other, probably thinking in tandem.

If this was where Asmodeus was hiding, then going inside with the light failing and no torch was probably insane. On the other hand, with the demon still out of town, this might be the best chance we were ever going to get.

'Do you feel anything?' I asked Trudie.

She raised her hands in front of her face, fingers flicking back and forth, weaving complex traceries out of her looped strings. 'Nothing,' she said tersely. 'How about you?'

'Nothing,' I admitted. 'You think we should call J-J?'

'I think we should go in,' Trudie said without a moment's hesitation. 'We don't know when Asmodeus will be back. If we wait for the MOU people to get here, he might arrive first and get a whiff of us somehow. The best thing would be to find out exactly where he's been hiding, then back off. When he goes in, we seal the exits and pump OPG or Tabun in – incapacitate him at a distance.'

It sounded good to me. I looked at my watch. Almost eleven. If the timing worked out, we could even kill two birds with one stone. When we called Gil in to lay an ambush for Asmodeus, he'd have to call off the Super-Self raid. Then I could come back tomorrow and try out my secret weapon in daylight, with the wind at my back.

'Let's do it,' I said.

15

The tramway tunnel slopes down from the regular road surface at an angle of about twenty degrees. For the first fifty yards or so, it's not a tunnel at all because it's open to the sky; it's just a cobblestoned ramp, bordered on either side by black stone walls, with wrought-iron gates closing it off from the street.

We didn't bother checking to see whether the gates were locked. The walls were low enough to climb, and Trudie was way ahead of me, already vaulting up one-handed onto the parapet and then dropping silently on the further side. A couple of passers-by gave us a curious look as I clambered after her, but they didn't challenge us and I thought it was unlikely they'd dial 999. More likely than not, they'd think we were looking for a private spot to do some dogging.

Trudie walked on down the ramp, but stopped when she came to the tunnel opening. The gates here looked a lot more solid, and since they reached to within an inch or so of the tunnel roof, they couldn't be climbed.

Trudie rattled them experimentally, then turned to me as I came up beside her. 'Did you bring your lock picks?' she asked.

I shook my head. Picking locks was a hobby of mine, dating back to a doomed attempt in my early twenties to make my name as a stage magician. I always appreciated a chance to keep my hand in, but I tended not to carry my burglary kit with me unless I knew I was going to use it. I'd had too many painful brushes with the long arm and short temper of the law to court any more of them when I didn't have to.

It was impossible to see anything beyond the gates. We were entirely below the level of the street now, and almost no light filtered this far down. Perhaps that was why it took me a few seconds to see what was staring me in the face. The big padlock on the lower gates had been twisted with immense force, until the hasp had snapped off clean at one end, and then hung loosely in place again on the chain so that it looked as though the gates were still secured.

I slipped it off and let it fall to the ground, then took the chain and pulled it through the gates' central uprights. I pushed the gate open, wincing a little at the loud squealing of the hinges even though I knew there was nobody inside. I bowed and threw out my free hand, inviting Trudie to go through first.

'We're not going to be able to see much,' she pointed out as she crossed the threshold.

'That depends,' I muttered. I slipped through the gates behind her and pulled them to. 'They connected all the lights back up for an art installation a few years back – something to do with the twentieth anniversary of 1984. Pen covered it for the Art Attacks webzine. If we're lucky, there'll be a switch somewhere.'

There wasn't, or at least not at first. We advanced into the gloom, skirting huge grey bags full of builders' rubble and canted stacks of MEN AT WORK signs. Dead leaves from seasons past didn't so much crunch as sigh under our feet, crumbling instantly into dust like vampires caught out at dawn. There was no obvious sign that anyone had been here recently before us, but I put my trust in the broken padlock and kept on going.

For the first ten feet or so, the walls were whitewashed particle board; beyond that, the tiles of the original tunnel appeared. At the point where they joined, I found the switch at ground level and threw it. For a long moment, nothing happened. Then the lights woke slowly, dithering in spastic strobe before finally settling for on.

The tunnel gaped open in front of us like the gullet of Leviathan. It was unnerving, a trompe l'oeil in reverse, opening up a third dimension where the wall of darkness had seemed flat and solid and close to. Half a mile or more to the river, and the underpass went all the way there. This would be a bad place to get caught with the demon between us and the outside world.

I turned to Trudie. 'Stay here,' I told her. 'Keep lookout for me.'

She met my gaze squarely.

'No,' she said.

'This is a dead end.'

'I don't care, Castor. If he comes back, the two of us together have got a better chance of staying alive.'

I was going to argue the toss because she was flat-out wrong on that one, but she forestalled me by walking ahead into the tunnel. I had no choice but to follow.

Without discussion, Trudie took one side of the tunnel and I took the other. We moved fast, scanning walls and floor for any obvious breaks, openings or trapdoors. The dust underfoot deadened the echoes of our footfalls, but the sound of our breathing came back to us, amplified and distorted, from the tunnel's further end, adding to the illusion that we were being swallowed alive.

We kept moving, roughly in sync. I was setting a good pace, but Trudie's long stride easily matched mine. There was no sign of any opening off the tunnel ahead of us; it seemed to extend into unfathomable distance.

Then I spotted the mouth of a cross-way. It was invisible from a distance because the white-tiled tunnel wall stood proud at that point, concealing the actual opening until we were very close to it.

We quickened our pace until we reached the intersection. The right-hand tunnel was blocked after about ten feet by a concrete wall that looked fairly new. Road signs and traffic cones were stacked in this shallow space in great profusion. On our left the side tunnel went on for about twenty feet and then angled sharply, again to the left.

It made sense to cover this side branch first, rather than leave it to be explored on on the return leg. We walked quickly to the corner, skirting it widely to avoid being surprised.

Ahead of us there were only a further ten feet of corridor, ending in another wall of grey concrete. Set into it was a door, over which a sign – hanging slightly askew – read THAMES FLOOD CONTROL CENTRE.

'That's just surreal,' I muttered.

'It's obsolete,' Trudie answered, her voice pitched as low as mine. 'Before they built the Thames Barrier, every borough had its own flood warning centre. This must have been where Camden's was based.'

We tried the door, found it locked, and went back to the

main corridor. As we advanced now, I became aware that there was something wrong with the endless perspective of the tunnel ahead of us. The proportions were subtly – and then not so subtly – off true. A few moments later, Trudie muttered a profanity.

'The ceiling is closing in on us,' she said.

She was right. It had been high above our heads when we started, but now it was almost close enough to touch. As I stared up at it, I heard a distant basso rumble.

'The road tunnel,' I said. 'They built it inside the shell of the underpass. The road is right over our heads here.'

This stretch of the tunnel was more untidy, with piles of bricks, steel buckets and even the occasional hammer or trowel stacked against the wall or casually dropped on the floor. Dead leaves had drifted in ragged heaps against all of these objects, giving each of them its own dull brown comet tail.

We kept on moving, and the distance between floor and ceiling kept on narrowing, so that after another couple of minutes we were having to stoop. It was hard to fight off a feeling of claustrophobia. Trudie reached up and touched the underside of a manhole cover, gave it a tentative push, but it was rusted into place. It was obvious it hadn't been opened in decades.

Up to now the air had smelled only of dust and damp stonework, but in this stretch of the tunnel it had curdled into something much more unpleasant: a sweet-sour tang like rotting vegetables, overlaid with something hard-edged and chemical. It was subtle at first, but it intensified as we went forward.

Up ahead it now looked as though the converging

perspective lines met within a few hundred yards, rather than at some distant horizon. I was about to make some remark about running out of road and suggest we turn back, when I realised that I'd been tricked again by the flat light and the ubiquitous white tiles.

The floor and the ceiling didn't actually meet at all. At the point where we would have had to go down on all fours and crawl to keep moving forward, the corridor ended at a letterbox-shaped opening about two feet high but stretching across the full width of the underpass. Just in front of it, on Trudie's side of the corridor, a dark irregular mass resolved itself as we approached into a human body.

This was where the rotting-vegetable smell was coming from, and Trudie covered her mouth with her hand as she knelt to examine it. I crossed the tunnel to look over her shoulder.

The raincoat, piebald Doc Martens and grubby workmen's trousers with pockets on the knees gave the overall impression that the body was that of a man; otherwise it would have been hard to say. He'd been dead a long time, which meant that rats and flies and the elements and the chemicals inside his own body had had their way with him. What flesh was left looked dry and mummified: one side of his face was staved in almost flat; from the other side, where most of the flesh had fallen or been picked away, the empty orb of his eye socket stared up at us with an expression of innocent surprise. He'd left no ghost to warn our death-sense that he was there, and mercifully he hadn't risen in the flesh. There was nothing left of him except this sad ruin, and the smell.

'Homeless guy,' Trudie surmised, probably on the evidence of the boots. 'How do you think he died?'

'I think we can rule out natural causes,' I said grimly.

I pointed to the tunnel wall above the man's head. A dark stain on the tiles there had dried black, but with dark red highlights still visible here and there. It was shaped like an exploding firework, rising up on a slender column to blossom out in all directions. But the column had come last, of course. That was where the tramp had slithered down the wall after Asmodeus had slammed his head into it hard enough to shatter his skull.

It *was* Asmodeus; there was no reason to doubt that any more. The dead man might have left no echo of himself in this place, but the demon's sickly essence hung around us now like a pall, and I knew it beyond all possibility of mistake. He hadn't just passed through here; he'd lingered, and made himself at home. Trudie's face showed that she felt it too. We'd struck the mother lode.

Without a word, we ducked and clambered through the narrow opening into a much larger space beyond. This was where the corridor ended, in a concrete wall about twenty feet ahead of us, but it came out beyond the road tunnel here, so it resumed its full height for this last stretch. What we were in was like a room whose only doorway was the one we'd just entered through.

It was even furnished, after a fashion. There was a grubby mattress on the floor, a sleeping bag on top of it, both of which must once have belonged to the poor bastard outside. In the near corner a dozen or so overstuffed carrier bags clustered like chubby little children cowering from an ogre: the dead man's worldly goods.

But these melancholy, mundane details were pushed to the edges of my attention by the sight of the far wall, at which Trudie was staring open-mouthed. The chemical stench was stronger here. It was coming from a sprawl of pots and cans at the base of the wall, and from the wall itself, where Asmodeus had made himself busy.

From floor to ceiling, the space was covered with symbols, with words and with wards. The words were in Aramaic, so I couldn't make them out, but the design was instantly familiar. A downward-pointing pentagram, with aleph sigils at the point of each arm and radiating lines fanning out across the negative spaces between the arms. Even if Nicky hadn't listed those features for me, I would have known it. Whoever had drawn these designs had also left the unidentified wards in Pen's drive, under Juliet's hedge and on the roof of the Gaumont.

'Tsukelit,' Trudie spelled out. 'Ket. Ilalliel. Jetaniul. Tlallik. Aketsulitur. Castor, do you know any of these names?'

For a moment I didn't; they were just sounds. But then the thing that all the sounds had in common drove itself into my brain like a railroad spike. I'd been way, way off, and so had Nicky. The common denominator had never been me. 'I know *all* of those names,' I said, my mouth suddenly dry. 'Or at least I know who they belong to. Jesus Christ, this is—'

The lights went out before I could finish the sentence, plunging us into absolute blackness. A whole second later, snaking down the corridor like a whiplash, came the chunking sound of the switch being thrown.

'Fuck!' Trudie gasped.

We were in the dark, half a mile away from the light switch, and we both knew who was out there, standing between us and the light, even before we heard the chilling boom of his laughter.

'Run,' I said tightly.

'Run where?' Trudie snarled. 'We can't see to run. Get out your whistle, Castor. Let's give the bastard a fight at least.'

I found her arm in the dark, gripped it tightly and hauled her back towards the opening. 'Not here,' I said. 'Not on his terms. He can see in the dark, Pax. If we stay here, we're dead. Come on.'

She pulled back against me for a second, then gave in. We crawled on hands and knees back over the demon's threshold into the corridor beyond. Trudie gave a sobbing cry of protest, which I took to mean that her hand had made contact with the corpse. I dragged her to her feet, though we still had to crouch, and set off at a stumbling jogtrot back up the tunnel.

It was hard to make myself move. I knew that Asmodeus was sprinting through the darkness towards us, fast and sure, homing on the smell of our souls. He could probably see us already, the way an eagle stooping over a meadow can find and focus on a fieldmouse in a square mile of tall grass.

'Where are we going?' Trudie demanded. 'Castor, we're going to run right into him!'

'No we're not,' I muttered. I was still holding her wrist, but my other hand was running across the ceiling, fingers spread wide. When I couldn't reach up high enough to touch it any more, I knew we'd gone too far. Quickly I retraced my steps, again yanking hard on Trudie's arm. There! There it was!

'What are you—?' she demanded.

'Here,' I said, cutting across her. 'Help me.'

It was the manhole we'd found earlier, the only way back up to the surface that didn't involve getting past Asmodeus. Groping blindly in the dark, I'd finally found the outline of it, and now I put her hands on it too. 'Push,' I commanded.

'It's rusted shut!'

'Try again!'

We braced ourselves against the tunnel floor, straightened our backs and strained against the unyielding cast-iron cover. The tunnel walls channelled a soft rhythmic sound to our unwilling ears: the sound of Asmodeus's feet slapping the cobbles as he ran. It sounded like a barber stropping a razor.

My spine felt like it was breaking already, but I poured on the effort. Beside me, Pax growled low in her throat. The manhole cover didn't budge by a fraction of an inch.

Pax moved away from me, and I heard her scrabbling around on the floor. Then I felt the vibration through the palms of my hands as she came upright again and drove something – one of the loose bricks that had been lying against the tunnel wall – repeatedly against the edge of the manhole cover. She was trying to dislodge the rust that had welded it into place, and it seemed to be working. It gave slightly, shifting against the pressure of my hands.

'Push again!' I grunted.

Trudie added her efforts to mine. With a squeal like a stuck pig, the manhole cover started to move. The light that rushed in was pale and washed out, but it was still startling. It showed the demon closing on us soundlessly in the dark, as fast as a torpedo.

With a booming clang, the manhole cover fell out onto the street. I grabbed Trudie before she even knew what I was doing, lifting her by her lower legs so that she had no choice but to grasp the rim of the hole and haul herself up. It was that or go over backwards into the dark.

Then I gathered myself and jumped, getting a grip on the edge and trying to pull myself up by my hands. My head cleared the rim of the hole, and I had a momentary, skewed vision of the road tunnel above: strip lights high overhead canted at a crazy angle, a soot-streaked crash barrier only a foot or so away, a car swerving around us and almost hitting the kerb. Trudie gripped my forearm and leaned back, using her weight to land me the way an angler lands a big fish. But something gripped my ankle hard and dragged me back into the dark. I clung desperately to Trudie's arm, kicking out with my free foot but making contact with nothing more substantial than air. I went down heavily on my back, with a jarring impact that knocked the breath out of my body.

Asmodeus stood over me, grinning like the wicked landlord in a melodrama. 'It's a mess down here,' he said, conversationally. 'You should have told me you were coming. I'd have made a bit of an effort.'

I scrabbled backwards, agonisingly aware that I was retreating not just from the demon but from the only exit. 'You said . . . you'd save me for last,' I reminded him, groping in the dark for something – anything – I could use as a weapon.

Asmodeus shook his head. 'But you will keep putting yourself in harm's way,' he chided me gently. 'What am I to do, Castor? I love our little talks, but I've got things to do and you keep tugging at my coat-tails like a kid who wants a lollipop. Anyway, I'm pretty much done here. Got all the ducks in a row. So I think I may go ahead and give you a spanking, just so you remember your place.'

His face went from light into shadow as he walked past the open manhole and out of the narrow, wan little spotlight it was casting down into the tunnel.

'You know why the lion limps?' he asked me, his voice a low, exultant growl.

I braced myself to rise as he bent forward and hit him with as much force as I could manage. He didn't even seem to feel it.

At that moment, Trudie appeared in the hole behind and above him, head down. Dangling over the abyss, she flung her right arm out to its full extent, and there was a smacking sound as something hit the back of Asmodeus' head. He grunted in surprise and faltered in his step. Then he raised a tentative hand to his head, which had sprouted – as if by magic – a vertical appendage. He turned his head slightly, and I saw that it was the shaft of a claw hammer, the business end of which was embedded several inches into his skull. So that was what Trudie had picked up in the dark: not a mere brick but a handy multi-purpose assault weapon.

I rolled to the side and jumped up. Asmodeus turned to keep me in his sights, but there was a drunken list to his body and a jerkiness to his movements. Still, he was between me and the manhole and there was no way I was getting up to ground level without going through him first.

I headed straight for him, then as he moved in to close me down I stopped suddenly and jabbed out with my left hand. Ordinarily the punch wouldn't have had a chance of getting past the demon's guard, but now it connected with his face, Asmodeus' momentum adding to mine to give it some real heft.

Asmodeus stopped in his tracks, his knees buckling slightly, and I did what felt natural and inevitable at that moment. I reached past him, grabbed the handle of the hammer and wrenched it down and to the side, turning the bifurcated claw inside his skull like a spoon inside the shell of a coconut. The hammer came free in my hand with a liquescent crunching sound, and Asmodeus crashed down onto his knees, then onto his knees and elbows.

He was trying to rise, but for the moment Rafi's nervous system wasn't cooperating. The switchboard was down, and there was no way of routing messages past the crimson ruin at the back of his skull to the still functioning limbs and torso.

I dropped the hammer – reluctantly, but I needed both hands – stepped onto the demon's back and launched myself from it towards the manhole in a graceless lunge. Trudie got out of my way just in time to avoid being headbutted, then helped me to clamber up as I got my arms and then my upper body through the gap.

'We did it!' she gasped, her voice hoarse with disbelief.

'Yeah,' I agreed, 'we did. Now run like fuck!'

Trudie looked towards the open manhole. Judging by her face, she thought the fight was over. A groping hand thrust over the rim made my point for me. We took off down the road tunnel like two sprinters vying for gold.

We were running against the traffic. Car after car braked and slewed to avoid hitting us, then accelerated past us with a blast on the horn or a bellowed curse from the driver-side window.

We put enough distance between ourselves and the demon for me to think we were free and clear. Younger and fitter than me, Trudie got an early lead and kept it, but then as she reached the steeper ramp at the tunnel entrance she turned like Orpheus at the doorsill of the Underworld to see if I was coming. Something whipped past me, something perfectly round, flashing a startling silver-grey with reflected light so that it looked for a moment like a lightning bolt caught in a bubble. It flashed past Trudie too, missing her head by a few lazy inches but bumping her shoulder and spinning her on her axis like a skater doing a sudden unplanned bracket turn. Her eyes widened in shock and she made a sound like a gasp broken in two.

I was level with her in a second and caught her before she could fall. There was a splintering crash from somewhere up ahead of us, where the manhole cover had ricocheted off the concrete wall of the tunnel and struck the wing of an articulated truck a glancing blow. The truck jackknifed, its trailer swinging round to form a wall-to-wall roadblock. For a moment it looked as though it was going to keel over on top of us, but it rocked back on its wheel base at the last moment and settled.

Trudie's mouth was working, but no sound was coming out. A dark stain spread out and down from her shoulder across the front of her shirt. The manhole cover had barely seemed to tap her, but it must have weighed close on a hundred pounds, and it had whipped through the air like a discus. The damage was obviously a lot worse than I'd thought. She sagged in my arms, but I took the weight and kept her more or less on her feet.

'Not yet, Pax,' I yelled. 'Not yet. Stay with me!'

I manhandled her on towards the truck, whose driver was now climbing down out of his cab with a look of anger and confusion on his face. He shouted something at me but I ignored him, heading for the narrow gap between the back of the trailer and the tunnel wall. There was just room for us to squeeze through.

Trudie was taking some of her own weight by this time, but her breathing was ragged and shallow as we stumbled up the ramp. Even in the baleful light of the street lamps I could see her face was pale and glistening with sweat.

'Can't . . . move my arm,' she muttered. Then she stopped dead in the road and was violently sick.

I looked back towards the mouth of the tunnel. A dozen or so cars were stopped there, and the trucker was having a loud argument with some of their drivers. At any moment I expected to see them flung aside as Asmodeus came storming through, but there was no sign of the demon. For some reason he'd given up the pursuit, maybe because flinging the manhole cover had taxed Rafi's damaged body too far, and he'd had to stop and recuperate.

We still had to get out of there though, Pax to an A & E department and me to— Shit, what time was it? I looked at my watch, which showed 11.59. The Super-Self raid was about to start.

Trudie's gaze met mine. 'Go on,' she said, teeth clenched on the pain. 'I'll flag down a car.'

'I can't leave you lying in the street,' I protested.

She pushed away from me, stood swaying but un-supported. The whole of the front of her shirt was soaked in red so dark it looked black under the street lights. 'I'm not lying anywhere,' she snarled. 'Go, Castor. I'm not dying; I've just got a broken arm. If you think your little toy will do the job, you have to get it over there before Gil sends the troops in and somebody dies.'

A car was coming towards us, slowing down as its driver saw the snarl-up ahead and realised that the tunnel entrance was blocked. Trudie finessed the argument by stepping into its path and forcing it to a sudden halt. The driver was a young guy in a Kings of Leon T-shirt, his windows wound down and his stereo banging out some Jamaican dance-hall number. He stared at Trudie's blood-soaked shirt in almost comical horror.

'I have to get to a hospital,' she said.

'Y-yeah,' he stammered. 'Okay. Jesus!' He opened the car door and got out to let her into the back seat, although he cast a woeful glance at his light-tan upholstery. He looked almost as pale as Trudie did.

'Go, Castor,' Pax said again. 'I'll be fine.'

'I've memorised your number plate,' I muttered to the dance-hall fan as I passed him. 'Get her to where she needs to go. Don't leave her.' Then I accelerated into a run as I headed on down Kingsway to the junction with Aldwych.

The Strand was close by, but I was winded and sore from my tussle with Asmodeus and from the earlier hundred-metre freestyle fleeing. I couldn't keep up the pace, and by the time I got to the bottom of Exeter Street I was limping along in a slo-mo parody of a run.

The pavement outside Super-Self was deserted and the door wide open. Turning in off the street, I almost went sprawling as I tripped over a body lying right across the threshold.

It was a man, tall and well built, lying on his stomach. He was breathing like a bellows: quick and shuddering gulps of air that made his upper body rise and fall as though he was trying to do push-ups.

The Spiro Agnew wristwatch on his right hand told me who I was dealing with.

'Samir,' I said, and then when he didn't answer, 'Turk? What's happening?'

There was a sound like the stuttering *pop-gurgle-pop* of a blocked pipe, but he didn't answer. When I rolled him onto his back, I saw why.

The lower half of his face was a mask of blood. His mouth gaped open, and the stump of his tongue writhed like a snake as he tried to speak.

16

I could feel it long before I reached the stairs. The fear-thing was awake and feasting. It was almost like a taste in the air, a hot metal tang that stung the back of my throat and made my eyes start to water. More to the point, it made me want to run and hide. I had to force myself to keep walking into that solid wall of terror. Every step was like the moment when you launch yourself off a diving board for the first time as a kid – when you come to the edge and almost can't make your body do something that stupid and hazardous.

I gripped the smooth-sided box in my pocket, reminding myself that I was armed and dangerous. I wasn't the hunted here, I was the hunter, and this bloated spider, sitting in the dark in its invisible web, was going to learn that not all flies are created equal.

But all that macho talk flew out of my head when I got to the top of the stairs and saw two more of Gil McClennan's exorcists trying to crawl up them to safety. The fly analogy came back into my head full force, because that was what they looked like: dying flies, crawling blindly, trying to escape the poison that was killing them and failing because it was already inside them.

I don't know where the idea came from. I had slowed almost to a halt, fighting so hard against the instinct to

turn on my heel and flee that my muscles were starting
to lock. Walking down those stairs one at a time was
going to be like climbing Everest without oxygen. So I
just let my legs stop dead, which was what they wanted
more than anything else to do, and leaned far out over
that gulf of poisoned air.

There's an art to falling without being hurt: you have
to tuck your head and arms in, concentrate your weight,
and lean into the fall so that it turns into a controlled roll.
I didn't do any of those things, because my mind was
screaming and squalling inside my skull like a cat in a
box as it got closer and closer to the epicentre of this
psychic storm front.

At the bottom of the stairs, I climbed doggedly to my
feet again. There were more bodies here, some of them
moving, some of them not. I took one step forward, then
another. Close enough. It would have to be close enough
because a third step was beyond me.

My arms jerking and twitching like the detached legs
of one of Signor Galvani's frogs, I fought to get the box
out of my pocket. This was my sheet anchor, my ace in
the hole, my grail. This would show the thing in the darkness who was boss.

I pressed the tiny toggle switch, and threw the box end
over end towards the gaping doors that led to the changing
rooms and the swimming pool beyond. It rolled, clattered,
came to a halt.

And nothing happened.

Caldessa hadn't wound the keys.

I made a mewling sound in the back of my throat. I'd
thrown the box a good ten feet. To get it back, I'd have

to walk ten feet toward the pool, ten feet into that storm of terror.

But looking on the bright side, my trip-hammering heart would probably explode before I'd covered half that distance.

I tried the falling down thing again, but this time it didn't work. I just sank to my knees without moving an inch further forward. I couldn't even throw myself flat on the ground. My body was rebelling one joint at a time, closing shop.

Ironically, it was Juliet who gave me the strength to move. The image of her rose suddenly in my mind, as she'd looked when we'd stood here the night before. Perhaps it was because this overmastering, hectoring, screaming fear was like the equally devastating, hectoring lust that she inspired. I used the one as a bulwark against the other, raising my libido as a battered sleazy shield against the slings and arrows of outrageous, pants-wetting, heart-stopping dread.

On hands and knees I shuffled inch by inch towards the box, across the no-man's-land of my own fractured personality. When my fingers closed on it, it felt like the climax to a lifetime's questing. And then the closing of the switch was like another lifetime, and the winding of the keys an etiolated eternity of running in a lonely place.

The last, tiny, desolate nub of Felix Castor thought, *Now eat this, you little fucker*, as I threw the switch again.

The mechanism inside the box whirred and clicked into action, and a tinny, hollow tune filled the room. Actually, to call it a tune was far too generous; it was a wayward sequence of notes that bounced and bucked and sprawled gracelessly out onto the tainted air. But, my God, what a dying fall it had. And how perfectly, how suddenly, the fear-thing stopped its own game to listen to mine.

The summoning is only the first part of an exorcism, but it's the most important. *Shut up and listen to me*, it says. *Heel, Fido, and don't move another fucking inch until I tell you to.* It was the part I'd never managed to get right for Asmodeus, despite all the years of trying. For this monster, by contrast, it had come almost at once. The trick was getting the tune out there when my own frozen heart was faltering in my chest and the lights were going out all over Europe.

Like all music boxes, this one mangled the tune, turning it into a stylised, flattened parody of itself. That didn't seem to matter though. Like Noël Coward said, it's amazing how potent cheap music can be. The pressure in the air lifted, and my heart came down from DEFCON 2 to something more sustainable. I drew in a tremulous breath, feeling as though vast curtains of rotting muslin were being hauled up on all sides of me.

The fear-thing was in trouble, which was gratifying to know. What's harder to explain is *how* I knew it. There was nothing to see, and less and less to feel. The sense of it – the way the invisible monstrosity impinged on the radar of my death-sense – turned on some notional ecto-plasmic axis, and diminished as it turned.

It turned to face the music box. As the notes of the summoning tumbled out into the dark, the fear-thing's own attack faltered and died. It obeyed the summons. Overlaid and gathered in on itself in pleats and rucks of dimensionless emotion, it was pulled into the box like the endless scarves and ribbons that a conjuror folds into the palm of his hand before spreading his fingers to show that the hand is empty.

After a minute or so, I found I was able to stand. I closed the switch on the music box, killing the tune in the middle of a phrase. I waited, tense, for a moment or two, in case the fear-thing broke free again now that the music had stopped. What I'd played hadn't been a full exorcism, only a summoning. But the orders seemed to stand. As in the game of musical chairs, the entity was staying where it had been when the music stopped, its focus swapped from the swimming pool to the box. More importantly, cut off from the ghosts in the pool and the skein of old emotions it had woven there, it seemed to be quiescent now – dormant, at least for the time being.

I turned on all the lights and checked out the three people closest to hand, making sure they were all still breathing. One of them had blood trickling down her face from a deep gash in her forehead, but none of them had suffered in the way Devani had. Post-traumatic stress aside, they'd all recover from this.

Once I went through into the pool though – taking the music box with me – I could see that not everyone was going to be so lucky. Two of McClennan's exorcists were lying face down in the pool, and a third was sprawled at the edge of it with his head at a crazy angle that suggested a broken neck. The remaining stalwarts of the Jenna-Jane Irregulars – more than a dozen of them – were scattered around the room twitching and moaning and writhing. I remembered news footage I'd seen of the aftermath of a suicide bombing. There were no detached limbs here, but in other ways it was pretty close.

Gil McClennan had led from the front, I'll say that much for him. He was in the pool too: not one of the floaters, but up to his chest at the far end, holding onto another man who had obviously collapsed against him. He was keeping the guy's head out of the water with a loose armlock around his neck, although his own eyes were so wide I could see white all around the pupils. He was shouting incoherent phrases – exhortations to his team, maybe, or fragments of prayer. Whatever they were, they'd kept him alive and upright through the maelstrom. Now he was starting to retreat towards the pool's edge.

I walked around to join him, and helped him manhandle the other man – who was profoundly unconscious – up out of the water. After a moment's hesitation I gave Gil a hand up too. It seemed petty to keep up old enmities when we'd just survived death by blind panic.

McClennan got slowly to his feet, using the wall for support and then turning to lean his back against it when he was fully upright. His chest was working hard, but he was getting his breath back and starting to come down from the fear-high. He threw me a look, curious and slightly bitter.

'What did you do?' he demanded.

I'd stowed the music box back in my pocket by this time. As far as I was concerned, Gil was one end of an open mike that led straight back to Jenna-Jane, and there was no way I wanted her to know about this before I'd had time to think through the implications.

'Why do you care?' I asked him. 'It's gone. And the credit's all yours. I was never here.'

'The credit?' He laughed incredulously. 'The credit? Look at what's left of my team!' He came away from the wall. 'I've got to get some ambulances over here,' he muttered. He walked past me down the side of the pool but turned before he was out of earshot. 'You think I wanted this?' he demanded, his voice trembling slightly.

I shrugged. 'You could have said no,' I pointed out.

'She doesn't let you say no.'

'That's down to you.'

McClennan laughed again. It sounded even harsher than the first time. He seemed about to say something else, but whatever it was he locked it down and turned away.

I put my hand in my pocket, checking that the box was still there and unchanged. It was an involuntary reflex. A box full of Gader'el demon seemed to be identical in every way that mattered to a box full of nothing. It didn't hum or rattle or throb with ectoplasmic energy. It didn't even weigh any more than it had.

I'd pushed my modality to the limit, and a little bit over. I'd made the music play for me when I couldn't play it myself, and somehow the link had held. Whatever power I tapped when I put the whistle to my lips still allowed itself to be accessed in this clumsy, second-hand and mechanical way.

What did that mean? What else could I do if I set my mind to it? I had to think about this, and soon.

But before that I had to call Trudie and make sure she was okay.

And I had to do something about Asmodeus. I had

some inkling of what he was doing now, but not why he was doing it. I either had to figure it out for myself or get someone else on the case, fast. 'I'm pretty much done here now,' he'd said. 'Got all the ducks in a row.' I had a suspicion bordering on certainty that his plans were in their final phase, and I knew now who they revolved around.

I followed McClennan back through the anteroom to the reception area. He was checking his people, trying to make one of them sit up and talk to him, and I left him to it. Battlefield triage isn't my strong suit.

Upstairs, the ambulances had already arrived, far too quickly for them to have responded to any call from Gil. Samir Devani was being loaded into one of them by two paramedics, an oxygen mask over his bloodied face. A third man was walking alongside, holding a saline drip that had already been attached to Samir's arm.

In the midst of the ambulances, incongruous, a storm crow among doves, stood a black limousine. Its rear door was open, and Jenna-Jane Mulbridge stood beside it in a light raincoat, overseeing operations with a calm and slightly distant expression.

She turned and saw me as I approached, acknowledging me with a nod. 'I'm glad you were able to lend a hand after all, Felix,' she said. 'Gilbert appears to have over-stretched his own resources rather badly.'

'That's one way of putting it,' I answered. 'Another would be to say that he led the lambs to the slaughter exactly like you told him.'

Jenna-Jane shrugged. 'All's well that ends well.'

'How do you know it's even over?' I demanded.

She glanced towards the limo behind her. It had other occupants, who I could just about make out through the open door: the security man Dicks, now acting as chauffeur, and in the back seat, Gentle, who Jenna-Jane had introduced as her PA.

'I didn't commit my whole strength to this one exercise,' Jenna-Jane said. 'That would be very poor strategy, Felix, even if we didn't know that Asmodeus was still out there. Gentle tells me that the haunting here has now entirely ceased.'

'Yeah,' I agreed. 'We won.' I looked past her to where more of the injured from downstairs were being loaded into the waiting ambulances. 'Let's see if any of these poor sods want to join us in a cheer.'

Jenna-Jane was in a good mood and refused to take offence, or maybe she just realised that letting my sarcasm wash over her would be the best way of winding me up. 'You've been missing for most of the day,' she said, 'and not answering your phone. I gather the search for Asmodeus' underground route was unsuccessful.'

'It was until an hour ago,' I corrected her. 'The Holborn underpass – the part that was never reopened. He's got a little hideaway tucked in at the south end that you should probably take a look at. But don't go in half-cocked, because it's a dead end. He almost killed me and Pax when he cornered us there.'

Jenna-Jane raised her eyebrows. 'You should have called me before you went in,' she said.

'Before I went in, it was only a hunch. And then when we found the place, things kind of got away from us.'

'Things?'

'Asmodeus cornering us in the dark,' I elaborated. 'And then having to pull McClennan's irons out of the fire over here. I told you to wait, J-J.'

'Do you know what comes to him who waits, Felix?' Jenna-Jane asked. 'Other people's leavings.'

'Then you agree I was right to go in without you.'

She chuckled and wagged a finger at me, as though slapping her in the face with her own logic was just my little joke. 'Well,' she said, 'I'll be very careful. Thank you for all your hard work on this, Felix. And for sharing intelligence, as we agreed. I'll go and look at this place, if you think it's worthwhile, although I assume we'll be unlikely to succeed in setting an ambush there now. Where is Pax? Downstairs? Perhaps she can be my guide.'

'She was hurt when we fought the demon,' I said, 'and I got a passing civilian to drive her to a hospital. I'm going to go see how she's doing.'

'Then leave a message for me at the unit. Let the switchboard know where you are, and I'll join you when I can.' She cast a sombre look at the open doorway of Super-Self, from which another pair of stretcher bearers was just emerging. 'Poor Gilbert. I think he'll take this hard.'

I called Sue Book's house, and got the answerphone: Sue Book's voice, sweetly inviting me to leave a message. I explained what we'd found, tersely and probably inadequately, and asked her to call me as soon as she could. Trudie didn't pick up when I rang either, which was a lot less surprising: I called Nicky and got him to hack into the hospital databases. A patient listed as T. Pax had been admitted to the A & E unit at University College Hospital on Grafton Way, which was only a mile and a half away.

And since I already had Nicky's ear, I dropped the bomb-shell about what we'd found in the underpass. 'You can add some names to your list,' I said. 'Alongside Tlallik, Ket and Jetaniul.'

'Yeah? Shoot.' Nicky tried to keep his tone neutral but couldn't quite manage it. It niggled him that he hadn't managed to solve this one yet; it was going to piss him off royally when he found out I'd got to the answer first.

'Tsukelit,' I said. 'Ilalliel. Aketsulitur. Notice a pattern?'

'Not so much.'

'Think about Juliet, Nicky.'

'You think these names all belong to succubi?'

'No, I think they all belong to her.'

There was dead silence at the other end of the line.

'I would've seen it sooner,' I went on, 'except that I'm an arrogant sod, and the first ward I found was at Pen's place, not at Juliet's. I'd forgotten about Juliet bringing me home after one of my drunks. Asmodeus probably put them everywhere he thought she might turn up, including your place. I'll bet there are a couple taped to the under-side of her car. A few more spread around Willesden Green Library. In her sock drawer, maybe. I don't know. There could be hundreds of the fucking things.'

Still no answer from Nicky's end of the line, which probably meant he was thinking.

'You remember the passage you showed me back when Gabriel first raised her up?' I reminded him. '"*She is of Baphomet the sister, and the youngest of her line, though puissant still and not easily to be taken with words or symbols of art. But with silver will you bind her and with her name, anagrammatised, appease her.*" You explained that to me. Every name she takes on Earth – including Juliet Salazar – is a subset of the sounds or symbols that make up her real name. I think Asmodeus has been invoking Juliet by all her old, cast-off names. That's why Foivel Grazimir had Tlallik down as a dead number. It was a name she wasn't using any more, even way back then.'

'Holy mother of fuck,' Nicky intoned, his voice dropping to the limit of audibility as he forgot to breathe.

'So what I'm asking you now is why anyone would want to do that? What's he planning? Can one demon bind another demon? Get me some answers, Nicky, before this blows up in my face even worse than it already has. And get a message through to Juliet, somehow. I've dialled her a couple of times, but nobody's picking up. She needs to know about all this shit.'

'I'm onto it.' For once Nicky didn't carp or haggle about terms. His pride was on the line here, and he was only too keen to make a start. He hung up on me without another word.

When I got to the hospital, they stonewalled me. A nurse explained that Trudie was already under anaesthetic and about to go into theatre. The damage not just to the bone but to the muscle of her shoulder was spectacular. They were going to try to sew her back together before any of the tissue started to necrotise.

I called the MOU, as Jenna-Jane had suggested, to tell them where I was. Then I sat and waited for news. I called Pen too, but there was still no answer from her house – or her mobile. Both she and Sue were probably asleep by now. I left a message on her voicemail, asking her to call me, but I thought it was likely I'd get home before she got the message.

I dozed intermittently while I waited, recharging my batteries slightly. They seemed to need it. The last three days felt like a waking dream, shot through with hallucinatory moments. My three encounters with Asmodeus ran together in my mind, so that they seemed like just the one conversation, interspersed with pregnant pauses while the two of us played a prolonged game of hide-and-seek across the face of the city. I'd found him, but that didn't feel like much of a victory, not now I knew he'd been working on Juliet the whole time, driving her crazy for reasons I couldn't even begin to guess.

At 4.00 a.m. I was woken up by my own phone ringing. It was Jenna-Jane.

'Felix, this is remarkable,' she said. 'You saw the sigils in the demon's lair?'

'I couldn't take my eyes off them, J-J,' I said, rubbing the sleep out of my eyes.

'Are you aware of what they represent?'

'Yeah. Are you?'

'They're steganographic homonyms. They all denote the same entity. It appears to be the succubus who is referred to in late-medieval grimoires as Ajulutsikael.'

'Yeah. That was my conclusion too.'

'Which means that Asmodeus is trying to summon her simultaneously in multiple aspects or incarnations.' She paused as if she expected me to say something. When I didn't, she went on with sardonic emphasis. 'Despite the fast that she's already been definitively summoned.'

I'd never been sure exactly how much Jenna-Jane knew about Juliet. She'd sounded me out on a few occasions in a way that made me think she was fishing for more information based on guesswork or rumour. I sure as Hell wasn't going to play join-the-dots for her now.

'Multiple aspects?' I mused.

'Each name would correspond to a stage of the demon's life cycle,' Jenna-Jane went on, her tone heavy and resigned, as though she was letting me off the hook for now. 'One theory is that they change their names in much the same way that insects moult: sloughing off old traits and aspects, redefining and reshaping themselves through the morphic power of a new name. That's why necromancers use the demon's name to summon and command it. Castor, if you know anything more than you've told me about this, now would be a very good time to put your cards on the table.'

'I don't know anything,' I lied.

'About a succubus passing for human?'

'There's always talk,' I admitted. 'Mostly you stop believing in that stuff after you hit puberty.'

A pause on the other end of the line, then Jenna-Jane's voice again. 'Where are you now?'

'I'm still in town, but I'm probably not going to be here much longer. I'm just waiting to hear how Pax is.'

'Very well. Another early meeting, I think.'

I responded to that with a profanity. I'd had enough of turning out of bed at dawn to present myself at J-J's door. 'I'll call you in the morning,' I offered by way of compromise and hung up.

I took a stroll around the hospital's ground floor, found

a coffee machine that actually worked and – more surprisingly – enough coins in my greatcoat's many pockets to make it work. Sipping the rat's piss that passed for black unsweetened, I made my way back to the A & E waiting room. The nurse I'd met earlier was waiting for me there.

Trudie was out of surgery and awake, she told me. The surgery had seemed to go well, but it was too early to tell whether or not there'd be any lasting loss of function in the right arm and hand. I could talk to Trudie if I wanted, but only for a few minutes and only if I promised to keep it low key. I agreed docilely and was led to a ward, where Trudie lay on one of a dozen beds, her upper body propped up nearly vertical. She was shockingly pale, and her expression slack and drained. She roused when she saw me though, and twitched her left hand in a feeble wave. Her right arm was swathed in thick bandages, and her neck was in a cast.

'How's it hanging, Pax?' I asked, trying for a tone of brusque camaraderie.

'By a thread,' she murmured. 'Can't feel my fucking fingers, Castor. They're still there, right?'

I looked down. 'They look to be,' I reported. 'You want me to count?'

She shook her head weakly, her eyes bright with unshed tears. 'Can't do it one-handed,' she said in the same low monotone. 'I'm useless if I don't get it back.'

The fingers of her left hand flickered, manipulating a loop of string that wasn't there. Of course, she meant the the cat's cradles: the way she touched the spirit world and worked her will on it. If she didn't get the full use of her right arm and hand back, she'd be crippled in more ways than one.

'You'll be fine as soon as the anaesthetic wears off,' I promised – a guarantee with nothing to back it except my overdrawn account at the bank of optimism. I only said it to offer her a crumb of comfort, and I could see from her face that she took no comfort from it at all.

'What happened at Super-Self?' she asked me.

By way of answer, I took the music box out of my pocket and held it out to her. She took it in her good hand and stared at it for a few seconds, at first without seeming to realise what it was. Then she got the feel of the thing in her death-sense and swore softly.

'You caught it,' she said, awed even through the drug haze. 'In a fucking box.'

'Yeah. I did. I was thinking of tossing it in the Thames, but I may not even have to. Being separated from the Super-Self ghosts seems to have made it switch itself off. There hasn't been a peep out of it.'

'Throw it away anyway,' Trudie advised me. 'You don't want to be around it when it wakes up.'

I took it back and returned it to my pocket. 'What I want even less than that is for Jenna-Jane to get wind of it,' I said. 'It's a neat trick, but for the time being I want it to be our little secret. Deal?'

Trudie shrugged, and then winced because her wrecked shoulder made shrugging a hazardous proposition. 'If you say so, Castor,' she grunted. 'I suppose I'm lucky you confided in me. You seem to see all other exorcists as the enemy.'

'No,' I said. 'It's just that I don't see the dead as the enemy. If the MOU find out you can trap ghosts in boxes, that's going to be a bad day for ghosts.'

'But you're alive, so what do you care?'

'I'm alive,' I agreed, 'but I'm planning to be dead one day. You think I want to spend eternity in an afterlife made out of plywood and screws?'

'Castor, you're a hopeless case!' Trudie was getting exasperated, and her raised voice brought the nurse at a run to remove the source of the irritation. 'You know how many dead people there are to every one living person? And how many people die in any given day? If this does come to a fight, we're going to need all the help we can get.'

'If it comes to a fight, Trudie, we've lost.'

The nurse manhandled me unceremoniously toward the door.

'You can't believe that, Castor,' Trudie implored me, her face twisted in almost visceral dismay. 'You can't.'

'It's just a matter of time,' I said. 'Living versus dead? Sooner or later, we all defect to the other side.'

The door slammed in my face.

I walked home, just as I had on the night of Ginny Parris's murder, mulling all this stuff over in my mind. Maybe Trudie was right about me. I did seem to be pretty comfortable in the company of the dead, and the undead, and the never born. Was I a traitor to the living? A fifth columnist in an undeclared war? Could I really be the only one who saw how self-defeating that concept was?

I was still kicking those thoughts around in my head when I turned into Pen's road and saw a deeply unwelcome sight. Parked in front of her door, a hundred yards away, was the same black limousine I'd seen outside Super-Self.

Jenna-Jane had decided not to wait for that early-morning conference call.

With a sinking heart, I trudged toward that mortal rendezvous. But when I was close enough to see the house itself, that dejection was washed away in an instant by a rush of pure panic.

The ground-floor window was smashed, and the upright piano that had once belonged to Pen's grandmother was lying at a crazy angle on the lawn, with a gaping rent in its polished wooden frame and its peg-and-string intestines spilled out onto the grass.

I ran up the path to the door. Dicks was standing in the hall. He made to block me, which could have had unfortunate consequences for both of us, but as I clenched my fists and lowered my head a voice from inside the house called, 'Let him come, Dicks!' He stood aside with bad grace, at the last moment, and glared at me as I passed.

Jenna-Jane was at the head of the stairs that led down into the basement. She gave me a look of profound commiseration.

'Where are they?' I demanded, my mouth so dry I could hardly get the words out. 'Where are they?'

'Felix,' she said gently, 'if you'd only listened to me at the outset—'

Without waiting to hear how that one finished, I ran on down the stairs. Pen's basement looked as though a pack of hyenas had come through in a steam train, stopped to party a little, and then moved on. Every piece of furniture had been smashed to matchwood. Broken glass crunched underfoot, and the rich, bitter-sweet reek of spilled brandy was everywhere. The computer had been driven into the TV – an ancient behemoth – hard enough to leave the two buckled plastic casings inextricably crushed together, each partially embedded in the other so they looked like lovers in the midst of a French kiss that had got way out of hand.

Amidst the wreckage of the desk lay something like a shot-silk scarf, its glittering black flecked and crossed with deep red. It was Edgar the raven, twisted and broken and casually thrown aside. There was no sign of Arthur.

Jenna-Jane's assistant, Gentle, was rummaging through the debris with an intent frown on her face. 'The question I'm asking myself,' she remarked without looking up, 'is why the wards kept him out for so long.'

'Are you seriously that stupid?' I spat out, harshly enough to make her look up in surprise. 'They didn't. They didn't keep him out for one blind fucking second.'

You know why the lion limps?

So gormless gazelles will think they're safe, and come on down to the waterhole.

Then you can pick the luckless little fuckers off whenever you've a mind to.

17

'The names build,' said Gentle. 'One syllable at a time.'

She had rough-and-ready photo printouts of the wards we'd found underground, laid out on the table in front of her. Her hand went from one photo to the next, and she pronounced each name as she pointed to it, slowly, like a primary school teacher mouthing kuh-ah-tuh.

'Ket. Tlallik. Tsukelit. Illaliel. Jetaniul. Aketsulitur. Ajulutsikael.'

'Illaliel and Jetaniul are the same length,' Jenna-Jane pointed out.

Gentle shrugged. 'The same length to us, but if you elide the medial "i" in either word there could be a difference that our ears don't register.'

It was an hour and a half later, and we hadn't moved. Well, that wasn't strictly true: we'd relocated to the first floor, where there was a room that was still more or less intact. The furniture was under dust covers, the ornaments wrapped in plastic bags hailing from defunct supermarket chains like Gateway and Victor Value. Nobody had set foot in this room since Pen's mother died.

My first instinct had been to go back to Asmodeus' underground lair and storm the place, but Jenna-Jane said her people had it staked out and he hadn't shown there. There was no way of knowing where he was. We couldn't even use Trudie's map. She'd torn it to pieces before she left the MOU, and in any case she was out of action for now, maybe for good.

So we sat, and we talked, and we went nowhere. Jenna-Jane restated her moult theory, that demons start out as simpler organisms, and change their names as they develop. I didn't care, and I barely listened. Asmodeus had Pen and Sue, and that was all I could think about. Obviously it would help to understand what the fuck he was up to with Juliet, but I didn't think insight was going to come from looking at pretty pictures. It was something to do with what Juliet was and what she did – and it had to fit in with all the other shit he'd been doing since he escaped.

Unless I was wrong. Unless he was just rabid and tearing at the world, and in the end he'd kill us all just for the immediate sense of relief it would bring.

I got up from the table. 'I have to make a call,' I said. Jenna-Jane and Gentle continued to pore over the print-outs, and made no answer.

I crossed to the window, far enough away that I wouldn't be overheard, and dialled Sue Book's number yet again. Just the same answerphone message, and this time I found I couldn't muster a reply. How do you say to an answer-phone 'a monster has stolen the woman you love'? I just said 'Call me, Juliet. Please, for fuck's sake, just call me.' Then I hung up.

I stared down at the lawn. The piano still lay dead in the long grass, and the stolid Mr Dicks still stood by the gatepost, arms folded, glaring at the pre-dawn rubber-neckers. He looked up at the window, and when he saw me watching him his eyes narrowed. I had too much on my mind right then even to flash him a wave.

Behind me, Jenna-Jane was rummaging in her pockets – an incongruously human thing for her to do, making her seem for a moment like a forgetful grandma, looking in vain for her front door keys.

'Is the succubus his ally?' Gentle was asking. 'Could summoning all her aspects make her stronger? A sort of ontological layering . . .'

'It was driving her insane,' I muttered.

There was a momentary silence from behind me. Then I distinctly heard the dry click of Jenna-Jane's tongue against her palate, an involuntary but very discreet expression of surprise and enlightenment.

'Not a benign effect at all,' she mused. 'A form of torture.'

'Or just an uncontrolled regression,' Gentle chipped in.

A sequence of seven tinny and discordant notes sounded suddenly from somewhere nearby. J-J took her phone from her pocket and put it to her ear.

'Mulbridge,' she said, with a simplicity more arrogant than any degree of ostentation could ever be. Honorifics were for mere mortals.

She listened intently for a few seconds, then started to interject questions and comments. 'Where? How far, exactly? Good. Good. What's the address? Thank you.'

When she slapped the phone closed, less than a minute had elapsed.

'Your Mr Moulson, Felix,' she said. 'The man who was possessed, and allegedly found a way to free himself. We've finally run him to ground. Appleton House, Godalming Lane, Eashing, in Surrey. It's straight down the A3. Only twenty miles, apparently.'

I headed for the door, but I went from giant strides to dead stop again in the space of three steps.

'Shit!' I exploded. 'Pen's car. He fucking totalled her car!'

'You can take my car,' Jenna-Jane said without hesitation. 'Gentle, give Mr Castor your radio. I'll go and tell Dicks he's to take you directly there.'

She hurried out of the room. Gentle took a somewhat bulky walkie-talkie out of her pocket and held it out to me.

'What do I need this for?' I demanded, nonplussed. 'I've got my mobile.'

Gentle shrugged. 'This uses police freaks,' she said. 'Some areas you don't get good coverage from the mobile network. Radios always work – at least top-end kit like this does. You use band one unless there's local interference, fall back to two, then three, and so on. Soon as the switchboard at the MOU picks you up, you'll be patched through to Professor Mulbridge wherever she is.'

'Wonderful,' I muttered. 'A hotline to God.' I took the radio and shoved it into my pocket. I went downstairs with Gentle at my back, still explaining the finer points of the radio's operation, but I couldn't make myself listen any more. My mind was seething with questions and doubts. Why had Asmodeus taken Pen and Sue, instead of killing them here? *How* had he taken them, for that matter? In the back of a white van? Rolled up in a carpet? How did kidnapping fit in with the other things he'd done since he got free? Why did he need them alive, when he'd killed Ginny Parris and Jovan Ditko without a second thought?

Out on the lawn, Jenna-Jane was talking animatedly to Dicks. The big man shot me a glare as I approached, then nodded curtly – to Jenna-Jane, not to me.

'It's imperative,' Jenna-Jane said. 'This is the most important lead we've had so far, and we have to be free to pursue it wherever it leads.' She looked round and seemed to notice me for the first time. 'Castor. Good. Get into the car.'

'Can't I just drive myself?' I asked. The last thing I wanted was a sulky South African security guard on my case all the way from here to Surrey, when I needed to get my thoughts in order and try to figure out a plan of campaign.

'The car cost the hospital forty-eight thousand pounds,' Jenna-Jane pointed out to me in a schoolmarmish tone. 'And you're exhausted, Felix. I simply wouldn't trust you behind a wheel right now. In any case, you'll need to be in touch with me at all times.' She pointed to the radio, which I was still holding in my hand. 'I'm going to leave Gentle here, in case we've missed something in our search. Some clue as to what the demon means to do. Assuming that Miss Bruckner and the other woman have been taken alive, he may have demands. You yourself may figure in his plans in some way that we don't yet understand. Keep the radio on, and keep thinking about what we now know. About the names, and the summonings. If anything occurs to you – anything we can do that we're not already doing – call me and I'll do my best to see that it happens. When you return, come back directly to the MOU. I'll debrief you there, unless we've located Asmodeus and we're already in pursuit of him. If that happens, I'll radio you and let you know where to find us.'

This entire speech was delivered without a pause. When it was over, Jenna-Jane stared at me in a way that said more loudly than words 'Why are you still standing there?' It was a good question. I got into the car, and Dicks slammed the door shut behind me with a muttered obscenity. As soon as he'd done so, Jenna-Jane tapped on the window. No manual wind. I opened the door a crack and she held out her hand.

'Your phone,' she demanded.

'My what?' I queried, mystified.

'You've got Gentle's radio,' Jenna-Jane pointed out impatiently. 'And the land line has been comprehensively destroyed. I can't have her completely incommunicado. You'll have to leave her your phone.'

'Give her yours,' I suggested.

Jenna-Jane bristled. 'Castor, we're in a situation where every second counts. Please don't waste time arguing with me.'

I hesitated. I could see the point of the radio. If I found something that could work against Asmodeus without killing Rafi, and if Jenna-Jane's people caught up with him while I was on the road, I had to get the information back to them immediately. It could be life or death at that point, and anything that could shorten the odds had to be a good idea. Giving up my phone struck me as a really bad idea, but my mind was full of urgency and emotional static. I took it out and tossed it into Jenna-Jane's hand.

'Stay in touch,' she instructed me tersely as I shut the door again.

We headed south, and then west. Dicks drove quickly

but with skill and control, taking advantage of the pre-rush-hour quiet to push the pedal wherever there was a clear stretch of road. He didn't speak, and I had nothing to say to him, so I did as Jenna-Jane had suggested and thought about what Asmodeus had done.

By summoning Juliet's cast-off aspects, he seemed to have regressed her to an earlier stage of her own history. Either that or he'd just driven her half-mad by reminding her of her past selves – surrounding her with names she thought she'd sloughed off forever. It was one of those two things or maybe a little of both, the names themselves having power over Juliet, power to define and shape her, or the overlaying of the names tormenting and confusing her, so that the restraints she'd built up around her demonic nature had begun to fall away.

Was all of this just a more elaborate form of payback? A quick death for Ginny Parris, torture and mutilation for Jovan Ditko, slow disintegration for Juliet. But in that case, why had he been prepared to kill me twice, in Brixton and then again in the Kingsway tunnel? Surely he had to blame me more than he did her for the half-life he'd endured these last few years.

The rule of names. Something to do with names, and how they worked. Something he knew and I didn't, and because I hadn't figured it out in time, he'd taken Pen and Sue.

The sun came up behind us as we drove, and I had to turn my face away from the rear-view mirror to keep from being blinded. I'd been sunk in thought for twenty minutes or more, and so I hadn't given much thought to the route until we suddenly slowed down and I recognised the lower reaches of the Edgware Road. The traffic was getting heavier now, but we weren't in a jam and I couldn't see any reason for Dicks to hit the brakes.

Then he pulled into the kerb and came to a stop. Another burly-looking guy in the same black uniform climbed into the front passenger seat beside him. Of course, I thought. We were only a short walk from the MOU here: base camp for Jenna-Jane's grunts.

'Reinforcements,' Dicks said. 'In case we have to *insist* on seeing this gent of yours.' The newcomer – whose sewn-on name badge identified him as DeJong – shot me a look, nodded to Dicks, and then we were moving again.

We picked up speed now, rounding Hyde Park and threading our way through Victoria without hitting any real snarl-ups. Thank you again, Mr Livingstone. We crossed the Thames by Chelsea Bridge and picked up the A3 at Clapham Common. After that, Dicks really put his foot down.

Eashing is the same kind of mundanely schizophrenic market town you'll find off any A road in south-east England. It consisted of one quaint little main street with a half-timbered pub, a few old cottages that would look great on a postcard, and an ungainly sprawl of red-brick closes and steel-and-glass low-rises built in the last fifty years to the same rigorous structural and aesthetic stand-ards as your average latrine pit.

I was sort of assuming that Moulson might have retired to some dignified rustic seat, with a trellised archway over his garden gate, but Appleton House turned out to be an old folks' home, a cheerless barn built in washed-out yellow brick with a one-storey flat-roofed annexe. Dicks and his friend waited in the car while I walked to the front door and pressed the buzzer.

'Yes?' A female voice, although you could only just tell over the *fuzz* and *blat* and *crackle* of the intercom.

'I'm here to see Mr Moulson,' I said.

Crackle. Hiss. Blat. 'Are you a relative?'

I might as well be. Anything that would get the job done was fine with me. 'He's my great-uncle,' I said.

The random static was replaced by a sustained metallic chainsaw sound as the receptionist buzzed me in. I stepped through into a reception area that looked like a doctor's waiting room, except that it was deserted.

The formidable-looking woman at the reception desk took her thumb off the buzzer and instructed me to sign the visitors' book, which I did. I even used my own name.

'He's in his room,' she said, sounding apologetic. Her accent was Australian. 'We try to get him to come out from time to time, but he prefers his own company.'

'He always did,' I bluffed automatically.

She nodded, looking at me a little curiously. 'And to be honest,' she added, 'it's a bit of a relief. That's an awful thing to say, I know, but he scares a lot of the other residents when he does come out. Do you have any ID, Mr Castor?'

I showed her my driving licence, and she added a tick to the visitors' book. 'Can't be too careful,' she commented. 'After that journalist tried to get in to see him. I'll tell him you're here.'

Shit. That wouldn't do at all. 'I'd rather surprise him,'

I said hastily, but the receptionist was already lifting the receiver on her switchboard phone and tapping the keys. She kept the receiver to her ear as she looked up at me. 'Sorry,' she said. 'Trust rules. Won't take a moment.'

There was a long pause. I could just about hear the phone at the other end of the line ring three, four, five times. I was already thinking out my next avenue of attack: Great-Uncle Martin didn't know about our branch of the family, because my mother's pregnancy had been kept secret, but now I needed to see him because Grandma was dead and he was the only heir to her vast fortune. For half a heartbeat or so I considered just cutting loose while the receptionist was busy and trying to find Moulson by myself, but I had no idea what room he was in, or what he looked like besides scary, or what sort of on-site security this place might have.

'Hello, Mr Moulson,' the receptionist said. 'I've got a visitor for you here. Mr Felix Castor. Your great-nephew. Can I send him up?'

A brief silence.

'Your great-nephew. Yes.'

Another pause. I tensed, opening my mouth to get my explanation in as soon as she hit the panic button.

She put the phone down and gave me a polite smile.

'I'll show you the way,' she said.

With a slight feeling of unreality, I followed her as she left her post and led the way down a short corridor to a flight of stairs. 'Room 17,' she said, pointing. 'First floor. It's not locked. Can I bring you up a cup of tea, Mr Castor?'

'No,' I said. 'No thanks. I'll be fine.'

I went on up, passing a very old woman who was also

climbing the stairs, at a more deliberate pace. She did it by assembling both feet on each step before launching an attempt on the next one. I was going to offer her a hand, but she was muttering under her breath, and when I got close enough to hear the words, I realised she was swearing to herself. 'Fuck. Shit. Bastard. Cunt. Fuck . . .' I didn't want to break her concentration, which was scarily intense, so I squeezed round her and kept going. When I got to the top, she was still swearing and still climbing.

I knocked on the door of room 17, then opened it and went on in. The door opened onto a hall the size of a toilet cubicle, with a mirrored wall on the left and a row of three coat hooks on the right. The only door was facing me. It was half-open, but I couldn't see anything beyond it because the room was completely dark. The institutional smell of boiled cabbage and floral disinfectant was strong, but something that was sharper, nastier and not so easy to identify lay under it, half-submerged like an alligator in a mud wallow.

'Mr Moulson?' I said in a conversational tone. The space was so confined, there didn't seem to be any need to raise my voice.

'Tell me why you're here, you snot-nosed little fuck,' someone said in the darkened room. The voice was slow and quavering, with a brittle click behind the words, a harmless-little-old-man voice that conjured up an image of the ageing, amiably bumbling Albert Einstein. The dislocation between the voice and the words – or for that matter between the voice and the grim, deadpan threat of the tone – was absolute. 'And you'd better not bullshit me. I've got my hand on the emergency cord, but that's the least of your worries. The first time you lie to me, you'll be crying blood, you understand?'

'My name is Castor,' I said. 'I'm—'

'I already know your fucking name. Think I'm senile? She told me your name on the phone, didn't she? London boy. Did some good work six or seven years back, but from what I heard you were never as good as you thought you were. Why can't you people leave me alone? What, you get yourself in over your head or something? Figure you'll pick my brains? Fuck off back to Babylon, baby boy.'

My brain wasn't firing on all cylinders right then, but at that point the starter motor caught and the engine at least turned over. 'You're an exorcist,' I said.

'You're telling me you didn't know that?' Moulson snarled. 'So what, you're just out here on a frigging day trip or something? Talk sense. I mean, right now. Talk some fucking sense, or else close the door behind you.'

I drew a deep breath. 'I heard about what happened to you,' I said slowly. The truth seemed to be the only option, because I didn't know what Moulson's agenda was, what would tickle his fancy, and what would be like a flicked towel to his wrinkled arse. 'The same thing happened to my friend Rafael Ditko. He picked up a passenger. I want to know how you got yourself clean, because I'm hoping maybe the same trick will work with him.'

There was a long, pregnant silence from the darkness beyond the door.

'Tell me its name,' Moulson said at last, his voice barely a whisper. 'Who's he got?'

'Asmodeus,' I said.

Moulson laughed – a harsh, unlovely sound. 'He doesn't

have a chance,' he said. 'Go on home, ghost-breaker. You came here on a fool's errand.'

'So what you did,' I persisted, 'it can't be applied to a major demon? It only works with small fry?' I put a mocking edge in my voice. If I couldn't reason with the old bastard, maybe I could at least goad him into giving something away. 'Here I thought you'd done something unique, and it turns out you just swatted a fly. Okay. Maybe I am wasting my time at that.'

There was another dry laugh, like twigs breaking underfoot, then Moulson's voice came out of the shadows again. 'That's what I said, isn't it? I've got nothing to give you. But . . . a fly? I was possessed by *Zohruen*, son. Look him up when you leave here.' A new tone had entered the voice now, a note of anger, or defiance. 'His element is earth. I was rotting, breaking down into mulch. You think I had it easy? What I did, I did with fingers that were peeling away to the bone. I did with my teeth falling out of my jaw. So don't you fucking tell me I had it easy.'

'Then why won't you let someone else get the benefit of your expertise?' I demanded. 'You want to sit there in the dark congratulating yourself because you got away clean, while someone else goes through what you went through, and maybe goes down under it? You made a living out of this, Moulson. Are you angling for me to pay you, is that it? You looking to get a consultancy fee?'

'I don't want your money.' I hadn't realised I was shouting until he yelled back at me. The effort cost him. He broke into a spasm of dry coughing that lasted for the best part of a minute. 'Fuck you . . . and your money . . .' he spluttered out when he could speak again. 'I want to be left in peace, that's all. I want all of you people to just tear my name out of your fucking books and stay away from me. I've got nothing to give you. What I did wasn't even worth the fucking effort. I should have died back there, and got it over with. Turn on the light, you smug little prick. It won't even cost you a penny to see this freak show.'

The skin on the back of my neck prickled, but I stepped forward over the threshold. My hand groped for the light switch at the left of the door, found a cord dangling there instead. I tugged it and the light came on: a single bare bulb, painfully bright, hanging without a shade in the centre of the room.

With the heavy curtains closed, the room seemed claustrophobically small, just a cubicle really, with a bed and a table and a single chair. I thought of Jovan Ditko's cell back at Irdrizovo. Moulson at least had a carpet, although its red and orange exploding-sun pattern recalled the worst excesses of the 1970s.

The chair had a wing back and was upholstered in brick-red leatherette, darkened here and there by the sweat-and-scuff smear marks of a couple of difficult decades. Moulson was sitting in the chair, his head slumped sideways against one of the wings, his hands resting limply on its arms. He was in shirt and trousers, his feet bare. The shirt hung open all the way down, I guess because it was a little early in the day to worry about that level of fine detail.

He was in the same colour range as the chair, more or less, his skin flushed an unhealthy red that darkened locally to brown and even black. His face was like a Maori mask that had been tossed off quickly for the tourist trade, with no real feel for what a face ought to look like. Gnarled little bosses stood out from his flesh like rivets on a cast-iron bucket, stretching in two lines from his temples to the bridge of his nose, then flaring out again across his cheeks and down under his chin. There were similar bumps on the backs of his hands where they gripped the chair arm — straight lines of them radiating from wrist to knuckles. His chest, sunken in on his ribs like the sails of a becalmed ship, bore a horizontal line of swellings across the collar bone and two diagonals sweeping in towards the nipples on either side. There was also a little cluster of them to the left of his chest, where his heart would be.

Every one of the swollen bumps rose out of a nest of old scar tissue, which was what gave his skin its piebald look. There was scarcely an inch of his body that didn't bear the asymmetrical spoor of old, unimaginable excavations.

'Like it?' Moulson creaked. He raised his hand in a vague, tremulous gesture, inviting me to feast my eyes. 'It's something to see, isn't it? All done with my own fair hand.'

'Why?' was the only thing I could think to ask.

'Inoculation,' Moulson said. He said nothing more for a moment or two. Then his right hand, still raised, unfolded and flexed as he pointed towards the bed.

'In the drawer,' he said. 'A shoebox. Take it out.'

I didn't see what he meant at first. Then I saw that the bed was a drawer divan, the drawers mostly hidden by the unmade sheets hanging down to the floor. I pushed them aside and opened the left-hand drawer, where his hand pointed.

The shoebox sat at the front, ready to hand, nestling in a substrate of socks and underwear. I lifted it out and set it on the floor next to the bed.

'Open it,' Moulson commanded.

I did. It was full of tiny copper discs — halfpennies, I thought at first, but since the halfpenny hasn't been lawful currency in Britain for two decades or more, I lifted one out and gave it a closer look.

It was a little thicker than a halfpenny, and it had never been legal tender anywhere in the world. Two words had been stamped on it, slightly off centre, in letters so small I could barely read them. The spidery diagonals of a pentagram enfolded them.

Martin Moulson.

I grabbed a handful of the things and sifted them between my fingers. Every one of them bore the same imprint, on one side only. The verso was blank.

I stared at Moulson in amazement. The magnitude of what he had done was dawning on me. It was like glancing over a garden wall and finding an abyss, unsuspected, on the further side.

'How many?' I managed to ask. 'How many of them?'

Moulson grinned, his lips peeling back from regular but blackened teeth. In the virtual absence of gums, they filled his mouth from top to bottom, like the bars of a cage. 'That's the question, all right,' he agreed. 'How many? How small a hole can one of these filthy bastards crawl into?'

His hand wove across and down through the air, sketching a process I couldn't begin to imagine, and fervently didn't want to.

'The first ones were the hardest, because he was fighting me. Look at this mess here.' The old man turned his hand and tugged his loose shirt-cuff up over his skinny wrist so that I could see the inner surface of his forearm. The seamed and rutted skin was like the surface of the moon, and the bosses that stood out there were in no real order: just five ragged bumps, clustered together. 'I made the holes with a penknife, jab jab jab.' He mimed doing it. 'Then just shoved the sigils in one after another. He didn't know what I was doing at first. Probably thought I was just trying to slit my wrist, which would have been a real fucking hoot as far as he was concerned.

'Once he realised, he started to fight me. But I knew damn well it was the only chance I had, and he couldn't take my right hand back from me, and I was still holding the knife.' Moulson opened his eyes wide and stared. The light from the bare bulb was stark and eye-hurting, but he was looking into the dark of his own recollections. 'It took hours. Most of a day, I think, but it wasn't that easy to tell because he was messing with my head. You've prob-ably heard that expression about having a tiger by the tail. Well imagine how it fucking feels if you've swallowed the tiger and it's fighting you from the inside.'

I lifted the box in my hands so I could gauge its weight. Twenty, thirty pounds of metal? Madness. Madness born out of complete and utter desperation. The grudging respect I'd started to feel for Moulson shifted slightly, became something like awe.

'Did you come up with this idea by yourself?' I asked him.

His gaze flicked across to me, as though he'd almost

forgotten I was there and had to remind himself who I was. He nodded slowly, distractedly. 'It was the rule of names,' he said. 'I remembered my mother telling me that story when I was maybe four or five years old. How God brought all the animals to Adam to be named. "And whatsoever he called them, that they became." As though they hadn't been anything up until then, and the names pinned them down.'

A violent shudder went through him, but I couldn't tell whether it was something that came from the memories he was reliving, or a purely physical thing. 'We bring them by using their names,' he said. 'And we send them away by using their names. The names have got all the power in them, even now. So I drove that evil fucker out of me by driving in my own name, every few inches, until he had no place to hide, no place he could go that wasn't marked as mine.'

'Brilliant,' I said, meaning it. 'Fucking brilliant.'

Moulson showed his prison-house teeth again. 'Brilliant? If I'd had the brains I was fucking born with, I would have used stainless steel. Or gold, if I could have afforded it. Copper's poisonous. Did you know that? I didn't. Came as a real shock to the system. Started to get the shakes, first, a few months after I did it. Then the shakes turned into falling-down fits. I knew what it was, but I didn't go to a doctor because I didn't see any point. It wasn't as though I had a choice.

'Then my liver started to give out, and when they took me in for the transplant they X-rayed me. As soon as they found out I was walking around with all this metal in me, they tried to get me to agree to take it out. I told them to go fuck themselves. It was touch and go for a while whether or not they'd give me the transplant, since any new liver would go the same way as the first. In the end they did it, and gave me ovalbumin injections to keep the copper salts under control. Whole load more shit too, pills and needles and all of it. I still get the fits from time to time, but I can ride them out, mostly. Been a while now since I broke a bone or anything.'

Moulson fixed me with a grim, defiant stare. 'So that's me,' he said. 'Doing well. Doing really well. And believe me, this is the best your friend can look forward to. Except that a big player like Asmodeus won't let you get away with a move like this. He'll see you coming and melt the metal out of your fucking hands. Make you drink it hot, most likely.'

I didn't answer. For a moment or two I'd forgotten why I'd come, lost in the old man's crazy, sickening narrative. His words jolted me back to the present with deadening finality. He was right. The trick with the coins was balls-out genius, but it wouldn't work. It wouldn't help Rafi. I was still looking for salvation in all the wrong places.

'Seen enough?' Moulson demanded. 'Then turn the light out.' He pulled his shirt closed a little, pathetically trying to reclaim a little of his dignity.

'Can I . . . ?' I asked, awkwardly 'Is there anything you need? Anything I can get you?'

He stared at me bleakly. 'You can get the fuck out, ghost-breaker,' he said. 'You and all your friends. That's what you can do for me.'

The two security men were leaning against the bonnet of the sleek black limo, looking like ugly and unlikely tumours that had grown out of its smooth lines. DeJong levered his arse off the metal and opened the door for me with ironic civility. I got in without looking at him, and he slammed it shut.

We did a tight little U-turn on the drive, rejoined the road and threaded our way back through the village. I thought we'd get back up to cruising speed as soon as we were on the open road, but Dicks held the car to a leisurely thirty-five miles an hour. 'You want to pick up the pace a little?' I suggested.

Dicks ignored the suggestion. 'Learn anything?' he asked over his shoulder as he drove.

I glanced up. He was staring at me via the medium of the rear-view mirror, his piggy eyes narrowed.

'I learned it's a good idea to watch the road,' I said, deadpan. 'But that was a while back.'

DeJong chuckled softly, and Dicks scowled. 'Good idea to watch the road,' DeJong repeated, savouring the joke a second time. 'Oh, he got you, Linus. He got you there.'

Linus Dicks? What kind of a name was that to saddle a kid with? No wonder he'd become an over-muscled rent-a-cop; he'd started life with so much to prove.

'I'm serious,' Dicks pursued, his voice lowering to a growl. 'Did you get anything worth having from that old fart? I'm supposed to ask you.'

'Says who?' I asked.

'Says the professor.'

'Well she told me to tell you to face front and shut up. Let's wait till we see her, and then she can sort out the mix-up herself.'

The big man looked as though he had some further

opinions to offer on the subject, but he was forestalled by a high-pitched *beep-beep-beep* like the sound a microwave oven uses to tell you that your food is ready. It was coming from me. I groped in my pocket and fished out the radio I'd taken from Gentle.

'How does this thing work again?' I asked DeJong. He made to take it from me and demonstrate, but I remembered what Gentle had told me and tapped the SEND button. 'Castor,' I said, and flicked over to RECEIVE.

The radios were good kit, worth every penny of what Jenna-Jane had spent on them. Without as much as a whisper of static, Gil McClennan's voice came through loud and clear. Or rather soft and clear, because he seemed to be talking under his breath. 'Don't say a word just yet, Castor,' he said. 'Think of someone plausible I might be, and pretend that's who you're talking to. Do it now, before they get suspicious.'

'How'd you get this frequency, Nicky?' I improvised.

'Good,' McClennan said. 'Is it just you and Dicks there, or did he bring some back-up? Say . . . I don't know, say single if he's alone.'

'Double that,' I said.

'Shit. Okay, listen to me. They're not bringing you home.'

'What?' I tried to keep my tone neutral, but it wasn't easy. 'What are you talking about?'

'They're not bringing you home. The professor wants you far away from what she's doing here. She's told them to hold you down there until—'

I missed the rest of the sentence because the car pulled off the road into a small lay-by at the same time as DeJong shoved the short, unlovely barrel of a handgun into my face.

'Tell him you'll get back to him later,' he suggested, giving me a playful wink.

'Sorry, Nicky,' I said. 'It's hard for me to talk right now.'

'The Mad Bishop and Bear, in Paddington station,' McClennan said quickly. 'I'll wait for you. If you manage to get away from them, meet me here.'

He said something else, but Dicks pulled the radio from my grasp, tapped the OFF switch and stowed it away in the glove compartment. 'Let's go for a little walk,' he suggested.

'Fuck that,' I counter-offered.

The pressure of the gun against my cheekbone increased perceptibly. 'You get no penetrating power at all with nine-millimetre MagSafe,' DeJong observed conversationally. 'There'd be a lot of blood to clean up, but the bullet would stay inside your head. Spread out and make itself comfortable.'

'You're going to kill me after you've both been seen with me?' I demanded. 'No offence, but you boys are something special in the way of stupid.'

'Let's go for a little walk,' Dicks repeated, and DeJong thumbed off the safety on the gun. At least I assume that's what he did: I'm far from an expert in these things. He moved his thumb, in any case, and the gun made a ratcheting sound that I didn't like one bit.

I slid slowly over to the near-side door and opened it. DeJong kept me covered while Dicks got out of the driver's door and came around to join me. He hauled me out of the car and pushed me away from it towards a small stand of trees. I glanced back at the road. We were still in plain sight, and if anything had happened to come rolling by just then I would have chanced my arm and made a break for it. But nothing did. That left total surrender or trying to overpower Dicks. There was a moment or two in which I could have tackled him, but he outweighed me by a good sixty pounds or so and it was all muscle. I was still weighing up my chances and coming up short when DeJong got out and joined us, making the point moot in any case.

I let myself be pushed and poked across the narrow strip of asphalt and in under the trees. The ground sloped away sharply here towards a drainage ditch about eight feet below us. Dicks looked back, decided we were still too visible and gave me another push in the direction of the ditch.

'Down there,' he said.

'Nah,' I said. 'This will do for me. Dicks, whatever Jenna-Jane told you, this is a really bad—'

The big man planted his hand against my chest, fingers spread, and pushed. I lost my footing and fell over backwards, rolling a few feet, but I managed to put the brakes on before I slid into the ditch. Dicks and DeJong fanned out slightly, blocking me to right and left in case I decided to run. They wanted me in the ditch, and they weren't going to take no for an answer.

I stayed down, because another push like that would send me rolling down the slope arse over tip. In any case, I'd met my share of thugs and bully boys and knew this game of old. The ground was the only location from which they couldn't knock you down again.

Dicks stared down at me with unmistakable satisfaction. 'A stop-me-and-buy-one deal,' he rumbled.

'Very funny line. A bit smug though. I don't like people getting smug with me. Now what the professor actually said was that I should let you meet the old fart, use up as much time as you wanted to, then drop you off in the middle of nowhere and leave you to find your own way home. But as I understand it, the longer it takes you to do that, the better. How far are we from the village back there, DeJong?'

The other man tapped his chin with the butt of the handgun – way too casually, in my opinion, considering I hadn't heard him put the safety back on. 'Maybe three miles,' he hazarded. 'Maybe a bit more.'

'How long at a fast walk, would you say?'

'Probably about an hour.'

Dicks showed his teeth. 'And how long at a slow crawl?'

I saw the kick coming, and jackknifed at the waist to get some distance from it, but Dicks had a lot of weight to put into the manoeuvre. His foot slammed into my stomach like a freight train coming through, knocking all the breath out of me in an explosive bolus as it actually lifted me momentarily off the ground. I came down at the very lip of the ditch, staring down into it, my diaphragm spasming agonisingly as I tried without much success to suck in more air.

Dicks turned me over with his foot, then leaned down and dragged me to my feet, without apparent effort. I was still too busy with the quest for oxygen to offer any resistance. I hung from his fist, my heels scrabbling at the loose earth.

'Oh, well, crawling, that's different,' DeJong allowed.

'It is different,' Dicks agreed. 'I don't think he's going to make it.'

He punched me in the mouth. I spun like a top and hit the ground rolling. My own momentum tumbled me down the slope into the ditch, where I came to rest against the curve of a concrete culvert at its very bottom. Levering my face and upper chest off the ground, I spat out some of the blood that was welling into my mouth. A throbbing note like the buzz of a Black & Decker power drill on low speed filled my head, giving me the momentary hallucination that I was thirteen again and at the dentist's, having a bad tooth hollowed out with just a gulp or two of gas by way of anaesthetic.

Dicks and DeJong strolled down to join me, in no particular hurry. DeJong circled round towards my head, but it was clear by now that this was Dicks's show. He stood over me, a frown of concentration on his face. The ditch was his crucible, and I was an experiment he'd set aside the whole morning for. The sun was coming up behind him, giving him a halo he'd done nothing to deserve.

I tried one last time.

'Drop it,' I warned him, my voice slurred. 'Drop it, you stupid lager-lout fuckwit, or I'll make you wish you'd never left the SAP.'

Dicks drew back his foot for another kick. There was no way of avoiding this one and, truth to tell, I didn't even want to. I just put my hands out in front of my chest, where I could see he was aiming.

I might have been able to break open the cheap plywood music box by myself, but this was economy of effort. Dicks's size-12 boot smashed it into matchwood, but unfortunately spent very little of its velocity in doing so. It thudded into my ribs, and my world dissolved into abstract, incendiary gouts of agony.

It was a lot worse than I was expecting. I may even have passed out, but if I did it was only for a second or two. When the first wave of pain had finished ripping and ricocheting its way through me, I became suddenly aware of three things. The ground pressing against my hands and face, the pervasive smell of rotten leaf mould, and a continuous scream like the whooping note of a London fire engine.

I tried to sit up, found that my body had no interest in that idea. Something rose in my gut and I tried to be sick, lying there on my side, but I couldn't even do that. My muscles weren't in the right alignment to heave, and their abortive efforts just made me twitch and shudder like a half-landed fish.

That was when the terror kicked in. But the intense pain I was in acted like a kind of neural Kevlar, protecting me from the worst of the impact. I was able to hold the nauseating dread at one remove; watch it writhing in the air like a clutch of tapeworms. Dicks and DeJong weren't so lucky. The fear-thing had been rudely awakened, and it was pissed off. The two men were down, Dicks on his back and DeJong on his knees, both of them flailing and swatting at the air. It was DeJong who was screaming, although it had turned into a sort of high-pitched mewling sound now, like the protest of a hungry kitten.

Things might have gone pretty badly for me, because right then I was too far gone to move, but the fear-thing didn't seem inclined to stick around. Perhaps it was because it didn't have an anchor here. It had made itself a nice nest at Super-Self but it had been evicted, and the peaceful Surrey countryside didn't have the same appeal. Or maybe it was scared itself, because it had been taken once before and didn't know whether or not I had another shot left in my locker.

For whatever reason, the sense of panic lifted by slow degrees as the entity took to its metaphysical heels. After a couple of minutes, I was able to get back up on my feet, despite the stiffness in my chest and the fierce pain in my bruised guts.

Dicks and DeJong were slower coming out of it, but then this was their first time on the merry-go-round. I had all the time in the world to pick up DeJong's gun from where it had fallen. Not knowing how to put the safety back on, I just fired the damn thing into the air until it stopped going *bang* and started going *click*. Then I gave each man a couple of hard whacks on the back of the head, sending them into dreamland before they could get control of their limbs again. Those are my kind of odds.

Dicks had the car keys in his pocket. He also had a wallet with a clutch of credit cards and two hundred and some quid in cash. Christmas in July.

I pocketed the cash, threw the cards into the culvert. Since they brought in chip and pin, plastic has never been worth the trouble.

Dicks was already stirring again, and trying to talk as he stared myopically up at me. He must have one hell of a hard head.

I climbed up the bank, wincing with every step. There were two bands of pain, one around my chest and one around my stomach. Moving without setting them off was like keeping two hula hoops on the go in very, very slow motion. The jagged fuzz filling my head didn't help a bit.

By the time I got to the car, Dicks was at the lip of the ditch and crawling towards me, dragging one leg in a way that didn't look good at all. I got inside the car and locked the doors.

Automatic. Deadlock on the key fob. No trouble.

Dicks was fumbling with the door handle, bellowing at me through the glass. His eyes were rolling in his head and there was foam or saliva on his lips.

I pulled round in a tight arc and fed him some dust.

18

Jenna-Jane is good at a whole lot of things. One of them is logical deduction; another is thinking on her feet.

She'd already decided from things I'd said earlier that the rumours were all true: that the succubus Ajulutsikael was living on Earth and passing for a human woman. When I took out my mobile and tried to call her, with that one move I put Juliet within her reach – and from then on she was working towards that one goal. It wasn't that she forgot about Asmodeus; it was just that she rearranged her priorities and relegated him to number two.

This was the story I heard from Gil McClennan in the inelegantly named Mad Bishop and Bear pub on the main concourse at Paddington. We were so hemmed in by other people's luggage, I felt like a First World War Tommy sitting in a trench between bombardments. The comparison held in other ways too. My ribs felt like broken splints, lacerating my internal organs whenever I moved; my split upper lip had swollen to the size of a ruby grapefruit segment; and half the dirt and unnameable shit from the bottom of that Surrey ditch had come with me when I left it.

'I don't get it,' I told Gil, shifting my weight to see if I could find a position that didn't hurt so much. 'I mean, with Asmodeus there's a clear and present danger. Juliet's not – fuck! – not going anywhere, is she?'

'You know that proverb?' Gil said by way of answer.

'Give a man a fish, and you feed him for a day. Teach him to fish—'

'Yeah,' I said. 'I know it. How does it apply?'

'The circles – the ones with Ajulutsikael's old names on them – they're something totally new. A weapon that one demon used to attack another. It's got applications that go way outside this one situation. That was the first thing she saw – that if you got a handle on this, you could have something that would spike any demon, anywhere. Better than silver, better than holy water. She couldn't pass it up, Castor. And she couldn't let you get in the way of it.'

Over two untasted pints of London Pride, he filled me in on how the whole thing had gone down.

As soon as I hung up after trying to call Juliet from Pen's house, Jenna-Jane put her own plans – freshly minted – into action. Transferring her mobile from her handbag to her pocket, she waited a minute or two and then made it ring by thumbing through the menus until she got to the one where you set the ringtone. She did that blind, from memory, which tells you something about the way her mind works.

Then she took the non-existent call and pretended to get all excited about finally turning up a lead on Martin Moulson. In fact, she'd already run Moulson to ground two days earlier, while I was in Macedonia, and sent Gil down to talk to him. Gil had got nothing worth having because Moulson hadn't let him through the door, but that explained the old man's references to 'you people' and the receptionist's story of a journalist trying to get an interview.

The next priority was to get my phone away from me, because my phone had Juliet's number on it. Jenna-Jane had done that with insolent ease by means of the 'Will you trade your worn-out mobile for this state-of-the-art radio?' gag, and then while Gentle – who probably wasn't in on any of this – stalled me with an instant tutorial, she went outside to give Dicks his instructions.

As soon as she waved me off she called the switchboard at the MOU, both to tell DeJong he was needed for back-up and to start the ball rolling for the real order of business, which was trapping Juliet.

This was the most dangerous part of the exercise, and McClennan said she approached it with a meticulous eye for detail. In the weapons lockers at the unit she had plentiful supplies of the semi-legal neurotoxin OPG and a lot of other anti-demon specifics that could be relied on to take Juliet down if she came on them unawares. But Jenna-Jane was canny enough to realise that any demon who'd been in my circle of acquaintance would know better than to walk into the MOU in the first place.

So she laid her trap somewhere else and moved her people in. Then she called Juliet, and kept on calling until she got an answer. She told her the truth, at least for starters, knowing that the truth would do the job better than any lie: Asmodeus has your girlfriend and God only knows what he means to do with her.

Where? Juliet had demanded. Where is he? Where is the monster now?

The last place anyone would think of looking for him, Jenna-Jane told her. He's gone to ground in his old cell at the Charles Stanger. The staff have evacuated the place. The police have been called, but what can the police do? Castor said I should tell you, because you're the only one who might stand a chance . . .

Juliet bought it straight out. If she'd been in her right mind, she would have smelled a whole nest of rats, but she wasn't. For whatever reason, Asmodeus had maddened and confused her and raised the ghosts of her young, reckless self inside her over a period of days or weeks. By this time she didn't know which way was up. She was acting like a green kid with only a couple of centuries under her belt.

The Stanger had been cleared, as per Jenna-Jane's orders. Juliet brought her wasp-yellow Maserati Spyder to a screaming, skidding halt in the car park, leaving twin teardrops of burned rubber on the asphalt, and sprinted for the door. It was wide open.

Nobody in the foyer or at the reception desk. Nobody to challenge or question her as she strode along the broad main corridor and through into the annexe where Rafi's purpose-built cell had been installed. Probably just as well. She was in no mood to listen to reason, and anyone who'd got in her way long enough to ask her who she was visiting would probably have fallen under her stiletto heels a second later.

The cell door was closed but not locked. She turned the handle and wrenched it open. Doing that set off three canisters of OPG that Jenna-Jane's suspiciously experienced munitions team had set immediately inside the door, all of them more or less at head height. Juliet got a lungful of the stuff before she even knew what it was.

OPG is a leaner, meaner version of the Tabun nerve gas invented by Gerhard Schrader back in the 1930s — the first of the ever-popular cyanophosphides. There's a UN resolution specifically outlawing its use, but only in a battlefield context. Used therapeutically, in minuscule doses, it reverses some of the effects of senile dementia. That loophole allows institutions like the Charles Stanger and the MOU to stock it in industrial quantities and call it medicine.

Juliet suddenly found that her arms and legs didn't want to do what they were told. Spastic tremors tore through her when she tried to move, and the muscles of her throat constricted as suddenly as a door slamming closed.

Demons are built differently from people though, for all that we come from the same stock. Juliet was fighting to bring her limbs back under her conscious control when the cell door immediately behind her also opened, and three men wearing masks and full hazmat suits cut loose at her with specially adapted automatic rifles firing silver-plated hollow-point ammunition.

The white metal ripped through Juliet like fistfuls of oblivion. She was probably already finished at that point, but she leaned into the impacts and managed to fall forward rather than back, her arms thrown out in a blind, flailing sweep. She barely connected, but then again she barely had to. Two of Jenna-Jane's three sharpshooters died suddenly and messily as Juliet's razor-sharp fingernails punctured the wire-weave plastic of their decontamination suits and the airborne poison touched their skin.

But the silver had done its work, finishing what the gas had started. Juliet was down, and she wasn't moving. A second squad – including Gil himself – came up the corridor, no doubt with huge reluctance given what they'd just seen happen to their comrades, but once they ascertained that Juliet was out for the count, they bound her hands and feet with steel and silver bands, lifted her onto a stretcher trolley and wheeled her out. By the time they got her into the unmarked MOU acquisitions vehicle – a Bedford van fitted with soundproofing and top-of-the-rage restraint gear – the air filters were already being turned on inside the Stanger, kick-starting the laborious process of putting the neuro-toxic genie back in its bottle.

They took Juliet back to the MOU, and down into the basement. The door had closed in Gil's face. He'd done his job, and Jenna-Jane was keen to oversee the rest of the operation by herself. This was, after all, where she excelled: at the porous interface between scientific inquiry and legalised torture. It seems to be a happening place these days.

I sat and digested these facts in silence after Gil had finished speaking. Something in his face told me there was still some bad shit to come, but this was bad enough to be going on with. And in the meantime it was probably a good idea to clear the air by asking the obvious question.

'Why are you doing this, McClennan?' I demanded. 'You hate my guts. It doesn't make sense that you'd come riding to my rescue – or that you'd stab Jenna-Jane in the back, which would put you way out of position for kissing her arse.'

Gil's mouth set in a tight line. 'You're right, Castor,' he said. 'I do hate your guts. But you saved my people down in that swimming pool, and you probably saved me too. I felt like I owed you something. And I also felt like maybe I'd enlisted in the wrong war. We've got two women out there, in the hands of that thing, and we're not doing one damn thing about it.'

'Nothing we can do,' I pointed out, 'until he shows his hand.'

Gil shook his head grimly. 'Well, that was kind of the clinching argument,' he muttered. 'He already has, Castor. He left a note.'

The words didn't sink in for a second. When they did, I still thought I must have misunderstood. 'He what?' I echoed stupidly.

'He left a note, at your landlady's house. It was addressed to you, but Gentle found it. She gave it to the professor, and the professor opened it and read it. Then she put it back in the envelope and stuck it in her pocket. Nobody has any idea what it says, but we've been forbidden to talk to the police or anyone else outside the MOU until this is all resolved. By that time we could have two more corpses on our hands.'

I was staring down at my fists, which I suddenly realised were clenched – so tightly that the knuckles showed white.

'Fuck,' I said hollowly.

'The place is a fortress,' Gil warned me. 'Dicks and DeJong haven't reported back yet, but she's called the agency she uses and ordered a top-up. The building is swarming with them.'

'Doesn't matter,' I said. 'I've got to see that note. And I've got to get Juliet out of there.'

'I'm not interested in saving the demon,' Gil said, 'but I'll help you get your hands on the note if you feel like trusting me. At the very least, I can get you in through the door. And I still see bringing Asmodeus down as job number one, so if you're aiming to do that, I'm in.'

I met his gaze. 'I'd appreciate the help,' I said. 'McClennan, we got off on the wrong foot . . .'

'Yeah, we did. Because you killed my uncle and ruined the lives of some people I really care about.'

'Actually, I more or less stood out of the way and let him kill himself. If we both come out of this alive, maybe we should have another pint and I can tell you all about it.'

Gil thought about this. 'I'd sooner you told me how you pulled that shit off at Super-Self.'

'All yours. With diagrams.'

'You're on, Castor.' He grinned faintly, but sobered again immediately. 'It's a fuck of a big if, though, isn't it?'

At the MOU, the street doors had been locked. Gil pressed the buzzer and then hammered on the glass for attention, while I waited a few feet away, pressed flat against the wall in what I hoped was the security camera's blind spot. If the lens was a fish-eye, whoever was on the front desk was looking straight at me now and wondering what the fuck I thought I was up to.

Our luck seemed to be holding though – at least for now. The guard on the front desk, standing in for Mr Dicks, left his post and came to the door, where Gil pressed his ID against the glass for his inspection. There was a rattle and a click as the door was unlocked from inside, and Gil walked on past the guy. He was carrying a plastic carrier bag, which the security guard didn't bother to inspect.

I came out of hiding and jammed the door open with my foot as he swung it to again. He stared at me in amazement, too surprised even to be alarmed. He was just starting to reach for his baton when Gil clocked him on the back of the head with a champagne bottle, the only thing his carrier bag contained. We hadn't ordered the Moët, but the nice young stockbrokers at the next table hadn't objected to us taking away the empty.

The bottle turned out to be a one-shot weapon, snapping clean at the neck, but it did the job. The guard staggered and fell forward into my arms. I dragged him out through the door, dumped him up against the wall, then went back inside and locked him out.

So far so good.

The inner door was locked against us too, but the security window, now unguarded, was our way in. Gil clambered across the counter and buzzed me through, then joined me on the other side.

He hooked a thumb back towards the guard post. 'There's a weapons locker in there,' he said.

'Guns?' I gave him a pained stare.

'Sidewinders. Tasers, maybe. Doesn't hurt to take a look.'

'Does if the locker's fitted with an alarm,' I pointed out. 'I've got something better in mind, but I'll need a minute or two to set it up. Come on.'

He hesitated a second longer, then shrugged and followed me. I led the way around to the right, towards the steel door and Jenna-Jane's basement Gulag. But I stopped before we got there, at the door with the keypad lock. Rosie Crucis's door.

'Keep your eyes peeled,' I told Gil, and I tapped in the code that Nathan had given me: 1086. I tried the door, but it didn't give.

'What the fuck?' I growled.

'Let me try,' Gil said. He tapped in the same code, then a few more with less and less conviction. 'No good,' he muttered. 'They've done a security reset. It was probably when they kitted out the lab for your succubus this morning. If you want to go to ground, I can get the new code from Nathan.'

'No time,' I said. 'And the longer we hang around here, the more likely I am to be spotted. Looks like that weapons locker may be the lesser of two evils.'

We jog-trotted back to the security post, and I was looking around for something to prise open the door of the locker when I spotted something even better: a fire axe in a glass-fronted cabinet high up on the wall next to the door.

I looked at Gil. 'Ready?' I asked.

'Go for it,' he said.

I smashed the front of the cabinet with my elbow, and the shrieking jangle of the fire alarm broke the silence like an auditory smack in the face.

We ran with that clamour in our ears. Halfway down the corridor, Gil stopped dead and held out his hand for the axe. I handed it over before I even saw what he was looking at. There was a fuse box on the wall. It was locked, but only with a piddling little Ajax padlock. The first blow of the axe snapped the hasp clean off, and it was the work of a moment to flick the main switch off, plunging the corridor into darkness. Maybe this was over-finessing slightly, but when I took the axe back I used the blunt end to hammer the switch flat. Anyone trying to turn the lights back on was going to have a mountain to climb.

The darkness wasn't absolute. Dull red emergency lights low down on the walls had come on when we triggered the fire alarm, but had only become visible now that the main lights had been extinguished. With their help we found our way back to Rosie's door.

I hefted the axe and swung it at the lock again and again, smashing the jamb around it into jagged splinters until the door finally sagged open.

Rosie was already on her feet as I went in, and backing away from the door, but she seemed to know me even in the dark. She relaxed and came towards me, then just as suddenly tensed again and stopped dead as Gil entered behind me. She was wearing a female body today – blonde and petite and barely out of her teens – so there must have been at least one changing of the guard since I'd last seen her.

'It's all right, Rosie,' I said, half-shouting to be heard over the siren. 'He's with me.'

'Felix!' she exclaimed, 'What's happening?'

'We are, sweetheart,' I told her. 'Listen, how would you like to see the back of this place?'

Her eyes widened. 'More than anything,' she said. 'More than anything I've wanted since I died.'

'How tired are you feeling?'

Rosie smiled wickedly. 'Less than you'd ever imagine, my sweeting. And a lot less than I've been seeming.'

I nodded. I'd always half-suspected that she was piling on the agony for her own nefarious reasons, but I'd never asked because any answer she gave would be bound to be picked up by Jenna-Jane's ubiquitous spy-mikes. 'I'm going to set you free, but I need you to stick around and watch my back for a few minutes,' I told her. 'Just until this racket dies down. Deal?'

Rosie gave a single, forceful nod. I turned to Gil. 'Take out the wards,' I said. 'You know where they are.'

They were everywhere, of course, just as they had been in Rosie's old quarters. Jenna-Jane had wanted to make absolutely certain that the errant spirit stayed in this room, no matter how many of her flesh-and-blood vehicles came and went through the door. The frame of the door itself was stiff with pass-nots of every shape, size and variety, but there were more of them painted on the walls, mixed into the plaster, set into the tiles of the false ceiling, and probably set in the cement floor. The aim of the exercise was to block every exit.

Gil didn't waste time with niceties. The sound of the fire alarm covered all sins, so he just took the top hinge off the door with a few more strokes of the axe, dodging it as its own weight tore it free from the bottom hinge and it toppled sideways into the room. Then he started in on the wood of the jamb.

'There's a demon in the building,' I said. 'A succubus. I'm going to find her and set her free. Be my angel, Rosie. Ride shotgun for me.'

'Thank you, Felix,' Rosie said. 'I'm yours until you're done, I promise. And I won't leave without saying goodbye.'

She leaned forward suddenly, the tips of her fingers caressing my cheeks, and kissed me lightly on the lips. Then she went limp, slumping against me. I lowered the insensate body gently to the ground. Rosie had left the room, though not, I fervently hoped, the building.

'Good enough?' McClennan demanded, standing back from his work and lowering the axe. I just pointed to the unconscious student on the floor: she was all the answer that was necessary. Gil frowned. 'Is she going to be all right in here? She's an innocent bystander.'

'There isn't really a fire, McClennan,' I reminded him. 'She'll be fine.'

'Then let's go get them.'

In the dark, with the shrilling of the alarm in our ears, the MOU had turned into a daunting assault course. It was almost like meeting the fear-beast again. As we threaded the maze of corridors, I had to fight down a sense of urgency that was threatening to ramp its way all the way up to pure panic. The dim floor-level lighting meant that the only thing I could see clearly were my own feet. At head height, slabs and wedges and sheets of shadow slid over each other, disguising intersections and turning blank walls into doorways.

Gil knew his way better than I did, and I let him take the lead. It felt like we were heading in the right direction, and then I knew we were, because my death-sense woke and stirred at the prickly feel of the things ahead of us and below us. For me it was a noise that rode under and over and through the alarm's cacophony, untouched by it, the sound of an orchestra tuning up in a key that didn't have a name. It was good news, in a way. The massive steel door had to be open, otherwise the wards imprinted onto it would have acted like psychic soundproofing, and I wouldn't be getting such a clear fix.

But we met the first of Jenna's rent-a-cops before we got to the door. There were three of them, and we just turned a corner and came face-to-face with them. They had their sidewinder batons ready in their hands, and they were big in the same way that Dicks and adult male silverback gorillas are big. Gil flashed his ID again, but they didn't as much as glance at it. They grabbed us and slammed us against the wall of the corridor, two of the three holding their truncheons across our throats.

'Call it in,' rasped the man holding onto me. He was an ugly bastard, with squared-off hair in a US Marine Corps style which probably conferred high status in the circles in which he moved. To me it had haunting echoes of Kryten from *Red Dwarf*.

The third man – the one who had his hands free – took out his radio and put it to his ear. 'We've got two men,' he shouted. 'Ground floor. Yeah, exactly. West side. They're the ones we saw on the cameras.'

He ducked his head, covering his ear as he listened to the reply. Then without warning he dropped the radio and staggered slightly as though he he'd been about to lose his footing and had to shift his balance to stay upright.

'What did she say?' the square-headed guy demanded.

The third man bent, very deliberately, and picked up the fallen radio. He straightened, still without saying a word, and brought his hand round in a sweeping arc. The radio impacted on the left temple of Gil's captor with enough force to break the casing wide open. The guy dropped like a stone.

'What the fuck are you . . . ?' Squarehead spluttered.

The radio man went for his throat, massive hands clamping to his windpipe, and he forgot all about me as he was forced to defend himself. He brought his truncheon up and back, aiming to drive it into the other man's face, but I jumped forward and wrapped myself around his forearm, twisting it further and further back until the baton dropped from his hand. Then the radio man finished the job, driving the back of Squarehead's skull against the wall repeatedly until his eyes rolled back in their orbits and he crumpled, sliding down the wall to the ground.

Gil stared at the last man standing, frightened awe showing on his face.

'What's the matter?' I asked him. 'You've never seen a five-hundred-year-old woman wearing a man's body before?'

'He's coarse, but he's strong,' Rosie said, examining the radio man's hairy, muscular hands and flexing his fingers slightly. The cadences of her voice were instantly recognisable despite the harsh basso burr of her vehicle's vocal apparatus. 'I like him.'

Jenna-Jane was probably well aware that by giving Rosie a different body to possess and inhabit every week, she was allowing an old ghost to develop a terrifying and dangerous skill-set. Rosie must have worked her way through three or four hundred volunteers in the years since I'd left the MOU. She knew the ins and outs of the human nervous system better than a London cabbie knows the way to Lullington Garth, and like the cabbie she was well past the point where she needed an *A to Z*.

I didn't need one either, come to that. From this close, I could have found the entrance to Jenna-Jane's underworld with a blindfold on and my hands tied behind my back – which was probably how a lot of its current inhabitants had arrived here. I picked up one of the fallen batons in a spirit of waste-not-want-not and led the way down the corridor, Rosie and then Gil falling in beside me.

'How are you doing this?' Gil asked Rosie, still staring at her in horrified fascination. 'How are you holding him when he doesn't want you there? It's not like it was with the volunteers. And you seemed to be getting weaker . . .'

'It's been a long time since I needed informed consent, my poppet,' Rosie pointed out with wicked amusement. 'And the weakness . . . well, a woman in my day learned the value of being underestimated.'

At another time I probably would have laughed at that. Asmodeus wasn't the only lion who could put on a convincing limp when the need arose.

We came to the door at last. There was a single guard on duty. Rosie dropped him with a devastating haymaker as he was opening his mouth to speak. He ricocheted off the doorframe, went down hard and didn't move.

Rosie flexed her fingers and gave a harsh, wincing moan. 'I've broken my hand,' she lamented.

'It's someone else's hand,' I reminded her. 'And he had it coming.'

I stepped through onto the steel platform at the head of the stairs leading down into the abyss. It was hard, as it had been the first time around, to cross that threshold, to walk into the screaming turmoil my death-sense was picking up from below, a hundred times more strident and painful than the monotone clamour of the fire alarm. But hard as it was for me, it was a lot harder for Rosie. She stopped dead in the doorway as though there was a solid barrier there, as though the steel door was locked and bolted instead of standing wide open. The wards again, the wards written on the door to keep the dead and the undead from breaking out. It kept them from breaking in too – and an axe wouldn't be much use against die-stamped steel.

'I can't come through here,' Rosie said.

'Then watch our backs,' I suggested. 'And wait for us.'

'Don't be long, Felix.'

'We'll either be quick or dead,' I muttered grimly. 'Give it ten minutes, Rosie. One way or another, it'll be over by then.'

She nodded tersely and set her back to the open door, a dragon in the gateway, stopping any reinforcements from the building's upper floors from crashing our party. Probably most of the rent-a-cops were in the basement already, but every little helps.

We ran down the metal stairs, the din of our booming footsteps drowned out by the general hubbub. Down here the fire alarm's shrill warning had to struggle to make itself heard in a chorus of bellowing and shrieking voices, metallic booms and echoes, weeping and wailing and – I strongly suspected – gnashing of teeth. The inmates of the basement Gulag seemed to be collectively going crazy.

'Any idea where she'll be?' I yelled to Gil. He couldn't hear me so I shrugged and gestured to indicate that I didn't know where to go.

He put his mouth close to my ear to answer. 'There's another lab down here. A big one. That's the room the professor was prepping this morning, so that's where she'll be.'

I let him take the lead again as we walked between the squat cement cell blocks. This place was terrifying even when looking down on it from above like the eye of God; when you were in the middle of it, it was indescribable.

As I think I mentioned earlier, to an exorcist every place is soaked in the residue of past emotions like the smells of old cooking. This place was saturated with fear and despair, an effluvium as rich and deep as the leaf mould in an ancient forest. Out of that rich substrate, something even more hysterical and insensate rose like some exotic bloom. I found myself breathing in shallow gulps as though that would somehow keep the emotional tsunami from entering into me.

Another patrol of three men crossed an intersection ahead of us. We flattened ourselves against the wall and they missed us in the dark.

Something was scrabbling near my ear, unnoticed in the clamour until I got right up close to it. I turned my head and saw the Judas window of one of the cell doors right beside me. I didn't have time for this. I was here for one thing and one thing only, and getting distracted could get a lot of people I cared about dead and worse than dead. But something moved me forward in spite of myself, and I pressed my eye to the hole.

The inside of the cell was even darker than it was out here: a single red emergency light in a far corner lit up the room no more brightly than a child's night light. The cell's inmate was clawing at the door, and the sound or maybe just the vibration had made it through the metal to me. He was a werewolf, a *loup-garou*. Wolves weren't in his genome though, so the word was a misnomer in this case. He looked more like a were-hare, ears hanging down like broken radio masts over his elongated face. A single huge eye rolled in his face; the other eye had been removed, and bare muscle twitched around the empty socket, making it expand and contract in lockstep with its neighbour.

I wanted to back away, but I just stayed there for an endless moment, staring into that sightless eye. Gil shook my shoulder. 'Come on,' he yelled. 'I think it's clear.'

Like a man coming out of a trance, I took a step back from the door, but I didn't move to follow him.

'Come on,' he said again. 'Castor, it's this way.'

'How do the doors open?' I asked him.

'On keypads,' he said pointing. 'What's that got to do with anything? The lab won't be locked. The professor will be in there now, working on your friend.'

'But there has to be a failsafe. Some way of opening all the doors in case the building catches fire or something.'

'I don't think so. That's not the way the professor's mind works.'

I shook my head to clear it, but that just made it hurt more. I knew I had to be right. This place might be a concentration camp, but it was a concentration camp built inside a hospital: the place had to be up to code, at least on the face of it. Somewhere there was a master switch that would open all these doors.

The fire alarm stopped ringing. The abrupt silence was a huge and shocking absence, a vacuum that extinguished all the other screams and yells and moans and bangs the way a wind tunnel sucks the flame from a candle. Soon there was just a single voice screaming, an inhuman ululation of pain and rage and madness.

A moment later the lights came on.

Gil gave me a frantic look, and I nodded, waving him on. In silence now, and more slowly, we rounded the corner of the cell block and found ourselves in yet another wide corridor. Ahead of us stood a pair of locked double doors labelled with NO ADMITTANCE notices that were both large and strident. Gil broke them down with the fire axe and we strode through.

Ten or maybe twenty yards ahead of us, there was one final door. This was where the screaming was coming from.

Other sounds from within, voices and footfalls and the clattering of instruments, made it clear that there was a party in progress, and that it hadn't stopped for the fire drill.

There was a guard on this door too, of course. He shouted out for us to halt, holding his sidewinder out in front of him in an *en garde* stance. I knocked it aside with a whirling parry, ducked and followed through, driving my own baton into his mouth with explosive force.

The poor sod went down like a sack of potatoes, his jaw in red ruin, and we walked over him into the room. For all I knew, he could have been poor bloody infantry – one of the newbies conscripted by J-J to fill the gaps in her ranks and keep anyone from bugging her while she dismantled Juliet. He might not know the first thing about the people who signed his pay cheque or what was going on a few feet behind him. On the other hand, he presumably wasn't deaf.

Sometimes it pays to ask the hard questions.

The room we walked into looked more like an operating theatre than anything else. Half a dozen men and women in white coats stood around a very fancy piece of apparatus – a flat surface, eight feet by four, mounted on a series of nested gimbals so that it could be adjusted to any height and any angle. The naked form strapped to it was instantly recognisable as Juliet. Her bone-white skin – right down to the absence of aureoles – and ink-black hair, the catastrophe curves of her impossibly perfect breasts, had haunted my dreams for so long I wasn't likely to mistake them when I saw them once again in the flesh.

At any other time, seeing Juliet naked would have fused my cerebral hemispheres into unusable slag and left me running on the default systems of animal lust. Now what I felt was very different.

She was twisting and writhing on the table. Tight leather restraints at neck and wrist and ankle held her in place, but from shoulder to coccyx her back rose and fell, filled out like a sail on winds of pure agony.

They were painting Asmodeus' wards onto her body, but Jenna-Jane loves to push the envelope – to extend her researches into different modalities. They were incising the designs into her skin with scalpels too, and something like a Zeiss engine set up directly over the operating table was projecting a light show of overlaid pentagrams directly onto her bare flesh.

The white-coated figures paused in their work and looked up as we entered, startled and affronted, but the projected images still slid over Juliet's skin, merging and dividing, and the high, inhuman screaming went on. One of them – not Jenna-Jane – came forward to block our path, all bluster and outrage. He was a little man, about forty or so, with the craggy authority of a senior consultant.

'This is a restricted area!' he stormed. 'You have no right to be here!'

'Are you right-handed or left-handed?' I asked him.

'What?' he blinked. 'What do you—'

Odds favoured the right. I remembered reading somewhere that a survey in America didn't find a single southpaw surgeon. I hit his right elbow with the sidewinder, using a figure-of-eight manoeuvre that Gary Coldwood had shown me once, the one that riot cops use when they want to do some real damage. There was an audible crack as the whip-thin wood connected. The little man gave a hoarse, choking cry. He staggered and fell, folding up around his now-useless arm.

'Anyone else here interested in practising medicine one-handed?' I asked politely.

The white coats retreated from the operating table and from their grisly work in a scared gaggle, like snow geese. All but one: Jenna-Jane pulled down her surgical mask, an affectation I hadn't even noticed until now, and skirted the table to stand right in front of me.

'Felix,' she said, more in sorrow than in anger. 'And Gilbert too. You've both gone mad. The succubus has no rights in law; the man you've just assaulted most definitely does. You'll both go to prison for this.'

'I'm not looking that far ahead, Professor,' McClennan said glumly. 'I don't think either of us is. You can take this as my letter of resignation, by the way.'

'One of you untie those restraints,' I called over Jenna-Jane's shoulder to the gaggle. 'Now.'

'The police!' The man I'd crippled moaned from the floor. 'Somebody call the police!'

Jenna-Jane shook her head in bewilderment. 'How can you even imagine you're going to get away with this?' she asked, in the same grieving tone. 'You're committing professional suicide. There'll be no coming back, I promise you that.'

'Swap?' I said to Gil. I held out the sidewinder. He took it and gave me the fire axe.

'Untie her,' I said again to the room at large, 'and turn that fucking projector off, or people are going to start losing large body parts. If you think I'm kidding, feel free to call my bluff.'

One of the geese hastily bent and flicked a switch low down on the wall. The luminous pentagrams sliding over Juliet's body faded to nothing over the space of about three seconds. She slumped against the table, her screams dying away to shuddering, panting breaths. Two more geese broke away from their comrades and started to loosen the leather straps that held Juliet down, shooting me wide-eyed looks from time to time as if they were afraid they hadn't shown willing enough.

Jenna-Jane tried again. 'Felix, this is the most significant breakthrough we've had in ten years of dealing with her kind. The implications are bigger than you can comprehend.'

'Don't worry, J-J,' I assured her. 'I think I've got the implications pretty much taped.'

Jenna-Jane's eyes narrowed, and she breathed out heavily through her nose. She made to walk past me, out into the corridor, and I held out my free hand to push her back. She touched my hand with her own, and a jolt of white lightning went through me. Suddenly I was down on the floor of the room, my elbows and knees stinging from where they'd hit the tiles, my head full of ringing after-tones as though somebody had decked me with a glockenspiel.

Jenna-Jane stood over me. The thing in her hand looked like a Stanley knife, black steel overlaid with yellow warning strips. She had it aimed squarely at Gil McClennan's chest. 'Please drop the baton, Gilbert,' she said, 'and then go and sit next to Felix on the floor. This is an M18 taser. It shoots a shock-charge of fifty thousand volts, and I can assure you that it's a great deal more pleasant to give than to receive.'

Gil weighed up his chances, which at that range were

pretty much non-existent. He let the sidewinder drop to the floor, where it bounced once and then rolled in a half-circle around the fulcrum of its own weighted end, coming to rest a good six or seven feet out of my reach.

Gil sat down.

'Now, if somebody would be good enough to call a security team,' Jenna-Jane said in her most schoolmarmish voice, 'perhaps we can proceed.'

Perhaps she expected a docile chorus of 'Yes, Professor Mulbridge' from the gaggle. Instead, the sound that met her pious request was a strangled wail from the white-coated woman who'd been untying Juliet's wrists. My gaze flicked in that direction, just as everyone else's did.

Juliet was on her feet. Admittedly she was leaning against the table for support, but her feet were planted firmly on the tiles. Vivid rivulets of blood marked her perfect, pigmentless skin in meandering lines, as though a butcher had marked her up for filleting. She had her hand on the throat of the lady doctor, her arm fully extended so that the other woman had to lean back from the waist. They were staring at each other, the lady doctor in abject terror, Juliet with the pained wonder of someone who's just scratched their pubes and come up with something small and wriggling.

'No,' she said very distinctly. 'Not you. Where? Where is she?'

Jenna-Jane swung the taser round, but she didn't have a clear line of fire. The moment that she hesitated was long enough for Gil to kick her legs out from under her.

There was a scramble for the taser. The doctor with the broken arm won it, but I'd gone for the fire axe. I took a wild swipe and knocked the weapon out of his hand with the flat of the axe blade, making him yelp in anguish. The way I was feeling right then, he was lucky he didn't get the sharp end.

As I lurched to my feet, the echoing tramp of booted feet in the corridor outside announced some late arrivals to the party. The security guards we'd passed among the cell blocks – or maybe a different group altogether – came charging through the door, only to come to a dead halt when they found that I had the axe blade pressed to Jenna-Jane's throat. I was still shaking violently from the taser zap, and it was all I could do to hold it steady, but I did my best to look like a man you wouldn't want to cross.

'Better think about this,' I advised the rent-a-cops, my voice a little more tremulous than I would have liked. 'If she dies, who's going to give you your Christmas bonus?'

'His name is Castor,' Jenna-Jane said quickly. 'Felix Castor. The other man on the floor there is Gilbert McClennan. Radio to someone outside the building and give out those names.'

'You don't want to do this, son,' one of the goons said, holding out his hand for the axe. Son? He was probably younger than me.

'Actually, Dad,' I told him, 'it would make my entire year. I'm aching for a little uncomplicated good news, you know?'

The man hesitated. A lot of thoughts were probably going through his mind, and I suspected it wasn't used to handling that volume of traffic. Axe blades are generally kept blunt, but you don't have to break skin to snap someone's throat, especially someone like Jenna-Jane, who was past the first flush of youth. Did I look like the sort of man who'd commit cold-blooded murder in front of a dozen witnesses? Did his desire to make me eat the fire axe offset the trouble he could get into if Jenna-Jane died and the company he worked for had to pay damages to the MOU? How would it play on the ten o'clock news?

I don't know exactly which argument swung the vote but finally the guy stepped aside. So did the men behind him, but they parted to both sides of the door so that I'd have to have my back to at least one of them as I went through.

'Over there, numb-nuts,' I said to the guy in charge, nodding toward the far corner of the room. 'Go play doctors and nurses with the doctors and nurses.' I returned my attention to Jenna-Jane. 'There was a note,' I said, 'at the house. A note from Asmodeus. Do you have it on you? Think carefully before you lie to me, J-J, because I'm a desperate man already. You wouldn't want to send me over the edge.'

'It's in my pocket,' Jenna-Jane said. 'On the left-hand side. There's no need for melodrama, Felix. I always intended to show it to you when you came back from Surrey.'

Holding the axe in place one-handed, I dipped into her pocket. There was a slip of paper there, folded into four. I took it out and glanced at it. All I could see were a few words, at random and upside down: 'only possible place'. It looked like the real deal though. Asmodeus formed his letters in a style that was almost pointillist, from myriads of straight lines no bigger than ink flecks. It would take a lot of effort to forge, and I couldn't see why she would have bothered. Despite that bland assurance, I was never meant to see this. I stuffed the note into my own pocket.

'McClennan,' I said, 'we're leaving. Bring Juliet.'

Juliet had been holding the throat of the lady doctor all this time, but she released her grip as Gil approached her. The woman staggered back from Juliet, her hands going to her bruised neck. That meant she backed into Gil, who steadied her with his hands around her shoulders.

'Take off your coat,' he told her, 'and give it to me.'

The woman did as she was told without argument. She'd stared into Juliet's black-on-black eyes at point-blank range. Juliet's inner fires were at a low ebb right then, but even so that had to have left her shaken to her psychosexual core. There was no fight left in her.

Gil draped the coat over Juliet's shoulders, very tentatively, being careful not to touch her. She stared at him with a feral intensity.

'We have to go,' he said.

For a few moments she seemed not to have understood, but finally she nodded and pushed herself away from the table. Her legs folded under her immediately and Gil caught her as she fell. His eyes widened. He must have been surprised, as I was when I carried her out of the Mount Grace crematorium, by how little she weighed. But it was more than that. He stared across the room at me, tense and alarmed. 'She's like ice,' he said, 'and she's barely breathing.'

I hesitated. I could swap places with McClennan, and have him take charge of the Mexican stand-off while I used my whistle to try to bring Juliet back to herself. I'd done it before with varying degrees of success, so I already knew the tune. But setting off the fire alarm would have alerted the emergency services too. They were probably already on their way, and getting out of the building would be complicated if it was surrounded by a ring of fire engines and police cars.

'She's stronger than she looks,' I said. 'And she only breathes for show. She'll make it.' I turned my attention back to the security guards, who'd all relocated to the corner of the room, behind the operating table. 'You stay there,' I said. 'If you follow us, I'll play who's-got-the-guillotine with the good professor here.'

We backed out of the room, Gil carrying Juliet. She seemed to have lapsed into a sort of waking dream state, muttering to herself and twitching fitfully in his arms.

'You're a marvel, Felix,' Jenna-Jane muttered tightly as we retraced our steps through the cell blocks. 'You came all this way to rescue a monster that's lived on human flesh and human souls for millennia. Broke in here, terrorised and assaulted my staff, caused untold damage to my systems. I've known for a long time that you were losing your bearings, but this goes beyond anything I could have expected.'

'Always more sinned against than sinning, J-J,' I said. 'But think about Mr Dicks before you throw the first stone. We had a deal, and I stuck to it until you tried to have me killed.'

Jenna-Jane laughed incredulously. 'Tried to have you killed? Is that what Gilbert told you? It's nonsense. I admit I wanted to delay you in Surrey. Of course I did. I simply didn't trust your objectivity when it came to the succubus — and I'd say your present actions provide ample evidence that I was right.'

'They're following us,' Gil muttered.

I glanced back over my shoulder. The myrmidons were

advancing from cell door to cell door, corner to corner, staying far enough back to be no immediate threat but clearly waiting for their chance. That might mean there was a flank party somewhere. I slowed down as we approached an intersection, but the ambush I was expecting didn't materialise.

We could see the metal stairs ahead of us now, and Gil accelerated toward them. The black uniforms came out from behind the stairwell when we were ten strides away from it. At the same time, the ones who'd been tailing us closed up the gap, trapping us neatly.

'No innocent bystanders here,' one of the guys in front of us said. He was an unprepossessing specimen, with lank black hair and a drooping Spanish-waiter moustache. He slapped his baton into the flat of his hand with a ringing *thwack*. 'Drop the girl and let the professor go. Otherwise I'm letting these men off the leash.'

'If you do, she dies,' I said.

The guy smiled unpleasantly. 'Better get on with it then,' he suggested. 'Because we're not moving. On my mark, gentlemen. Three . . . two . . . one—'

'Don't any of you move a muscle!' Jenna-Jane ground out, her voice deep and carrying. 'I forbid it! Do you under-stand?'

The rent-a-cops fell back a step out of pure reflex, responding to their master's voice. The leader looked nonplussed. 'Professor . . .' he began.

'The succubus is a valuable medical resource,' Jenna-Jane snarled caustically. 'By heaven, I will have the skin off the back of the man who harms her. Now, you will back off and you will allow these men to leave, unharmed.

Anyone who disobeys will answer to me. Doubt me not, you whoreson dogs.'

I'd already started to have my suspicions with 'by heaven', not to mention the flogging reference. By the time she got to 'whoreson', I knew damn well what I was dealing with. This wasn't Jenna-Jane; this was Rosie Crucis.

I moved towards the stairs, shifting to avoid turning my back on any of these sonsofbitches. 'You heard the lady,' I said. 'Come on, McClennan.' Gil was baffled but he wasn't stupid. He stayed with me as I shuffled round to the foot of the stairs and put my foot on the bottom step.

'Give them some ground!' Rosie bellowed, and the myrmidons fell back as one man.

'Did I ever tell you I loved you?' I muttered to Rosie.

'Often and often,' she chuckled. 'But don't ask me to kiss you with these lips, Felix. It would be a crime against nature.'

Gil was staring at us in a kind of existential horror, his eyes wide. Then the penny dropped, visibly. 'How did you break the wards?' he whispered.

'I didn't,' Rosie whispered. 'I went under them. There were no wards on the floor.'

At the top of the stairs we paused. I looked to the right of the door and found what I expected to find: a locked junction box. I let go of Rosie and took the fire axe to it, breaking off the lock with three clumsy strokes. Inside were two red buttons. The one on the left was labelled LOCK and the one on the right RELEASE.

'Any idea where you'll go from here?' I asked Rosie.

She shrugged, and an uncharacteristically wicked grin played across Jenna-Jane's features. 'I haven't had a tumble in five hundred years,' she said. 'I think I might remind myself what the sins of the flesh are actually like.'

'When that gets old,' I said, 'drop by and say hello.'

'Certainly, Felix,' she agreed. 'Perhaps even before.'

I hit RELEASE. There was a prolonged, ragged-edged *chunk-chunk-chunk* sound as hundreds of cell doors opened in near but not perfect simultaneity.

Rosie slipped away. Through my death-sense I felt her go, but even if I hadn't, I would have known it was the real Jenna-Jane I was now looking at as her face twisted into an expression of naked, almost berserk hatred.

'Castor!' she choked.

'I think you said three days' probation, J-J,' I reminded her. I held up thumb and forefinger, almost touching. 'I came this close to making the grade.'

I slammed the great steel door shut and threw the bolt.

19

We held our council of war at the Walthamstow Gaumont. Nicky wasn't exactly thrilled to host, but he was still feeling sheepish about missing the boat with the anagrams in Asmodeus' summonings, so I had a little leverage to work with.

He let us in off the street, giving the bundle in my arms – Juliet, now wrapped in my greatcoat and still more or less out of her head – a curious look.

Gil McClennan shivered as he stepped over the threshold. The change in temperature from the warmth of the air outside was sudden and marked.

'Place is as cold as a tomb,' he muttered.

'Well, shit!' Nicky sneered. 'Here I've been looking for a good analogy all this time, and it was right there in front of my face.'

Gil's face went through some interesting changes as he realised belatedly that he was talking to a dead man. 'No offence,' he offered at last.

'None taken,' said Nicky. 'To be offended, I'd have to give a fuck. Go on upstairs. Joan of Arc is already up there waiting for you.'

Trudie was pacing the floor of the projection room, wearing two jackets against the cold. Her arm was in a sling, her shoulder swathed in bulky bandages. She looked almost as pale as Nicky, but without his excuse of having been four years dead. In her free hand she carried a bright orange Sainsbury's bag.

'Castor!' She hurried over to us as we entered, then recoiled slightly when she realised what it was I was carrying. Her gaze went from Juliet's face to mine. 'I seem to have missed a lot,' she said. 'Can you bring me up to speed?'

Nicky cleared the table and we sat ourselves around it: a coalition of the willing, if that term includes people who've tried out all the other options and ended up painted into a corner. Juliet was on the other side of the room, lying on a camp bed under the projector. The mattress smelled of mildew and was unpleasantly damp, but it was the best we could do.

Asmodeus' note – item one on an agenda of one – sat in the centre of the table. It was short and to the point.

Castor

You and your demon bitch are invited to my farewell party. In case you need an incentive – they're alive, and they stay alive until you come. After that, it depends on how it plays.

Peckham. That little upstairs room you fitted out for me, remember? We had such good times there, it seemed like the only possible place to say goodbye.

A

'You've got nothing,' Nicky pointed out. 'Sorry. Thought I might as well start by stating the obvious. You've bumped into him twice, and both times you barely survived. You go in there now – with him actually waiting for you – and he'll kill you, sure as eggs is eggs.'

'We do have this,' Trudie said. 'It got broken when I went crazy back at the MOU, but it might still be usable.' She put the Sainsbury's bag on the table and shoved it across towards me. I knew what it was, so I didn't bother to open it. It made a grating rattle as I took it and put it down by my side.

'Incendiary grenades?' Nicky asked sardonically. 'White phosphorus? Depleted-uranium shells?'

'Something along those lines,' I allowed.

'Unless it's an A-bomb, he'll still kill you.'

I nodded. 'I wouldn't bet against it,' I agreed. 'But let's not kid ourselves, Nicky. Killing us isn't the cake, it's just the icing. Maybe not even that. Asmodeus has worked really hard on this, and we know now that he could have walked into Pen's house and ripped my head off any time he wanted to. The wards barely tickled him.'

'Then what?' Gil demanded. 'If there's a big picture, I'm not seeing it. This is all about revenge, surely? Ginny whatever-her-name-was – she helped out with the ritual that brought him to Earth in the first place, so he started out by killing her. Ditko performed the ritual, so he took out the last surviving member of Ditko's family. With you, he gets the hat trick.'

'Yeah,' I agreed. 'But no. I already made that mistake once – thinking this was all about me. That was why I was so slow off the mark in figuring out what those summonings were. He hates me, yeah, but he didn't go for me. Not really. He went for Juliet.' Juliet didn't stir at the mention of her name.

'She helped you put him back in the bottle the last time he got free,' Trudie said slowly. 'But so did a lot of other people.' She glanced across at Nicky, who shrugged irritably.

'I just provide a service,' he said.

'The effect of the wards was to confuse and enrage her,' Trudie went on. 'Isn't that what you said?'

I thought about that. 'It made her more volatile,' I said. 'Less in control of her actions. She did seem a little confused, at times, but mostly what she seemed was off the leash, all her responses quicker, more extreme, less considered.'

'Removing at a stroke the effect of two years' socialisation on Earth, and maybe a couple of millennia of experience down in Hell,' Trudie concluded.

'Yeah. More or less.'

'Then that's the clue, isn't it?' She tapped the note with an extended finger. 'He specifically tells you to bring her, because it's her that he needs. He wants her to do something for him, and he doesn't want her to be able to think too much about it.'

'What kind of something?' Gil demanded. 'She's just a venus fly trap. She draws people in and eats them. Are you saying Asmodeus wants to arrange a hit? He can hit anyone he wants to.'

'You're coming at this from the wrong end,' Nicky told us. 'Unsurprisingly. You should be asking yourself what he wants and then trying to figure out from that how he could use Juliet to get it.'

'He wants to be free,' I said. 'He wants to get out of Rafi's flesh and go home.'

'And he thinks he's done it,' Trudie pointed out. 'He says in the note that this is his farewell party. So he's found some way of—'

'Wait.' Nicky was waving his hands in a rewind gesture. 'Go back, Castor. What did you say?'

'He wants to go home.'

'No. You said he wants to get out of Ditko's flesh. Right?'

'Same thing, Nicky?'

'No,' he said emphatically. 'It's not. It's not the same thing at all. Tell me how the succubus works. I've read about it, but I've never seen it. You saw it, didn't you? On that boat.'

He meant the *Mercedes*, the floating home of Lucasz Damjohn, whoremaster, where Juliet had been summoned to kill me and had turned on her handlers instead. That seemed like a long time ago now, and actually I hadn't seen all that much because I'd kept my eyes closed for most of it.

'You know what she does,' I hedged.

'I know what the books say. In real life, how does it work?'

I cast my mind back, with some reluctance, to the events of that night, and to the other night, even earlier, when Juliet had come close to devouring me. 'She turns you on,' I said, tersely, inadequately. 'She makes you aroused – very, very aroused. Then she eats you.'

'Seriously? I mean, bones crack, blood spills, meat is chewed?'

Fuck. I took a deep, slightly shaky breath. 'There's no mess,' I said. 'When she took Damjohn, I didn't see any blood. Any remains.' Actually, it had been even more remarkable than that. He'd been bleeding from a gut wound before she embraced him. Afterwards, the blood that had been on the deck was gone, without even a stain on the woodwork to show where it had been.

'So we're talking about physical consumption,' Nicky insisted.

'Yeah. That, and . . . the other kind. Her nutritional needs are pretty complicated, Nicky. She needs the soul as well as the flesh. It's as though lust is a digestive enzyme for her. It's the magic ingredient that makes it possible for her to feed on us. On people. Otherwise it's like what happens when we eat grass: we can't break down the cell walls, so we can't get any nourishment from it. We could fill our stomachs . . . and still, you know . . . still starve to death.'

I wound down like a clock, because I'd suddenly seen what he was driving at. I could see that Trudie had too. She was shaking her head in sick amazement.

'What am I missing?' Gil asked the room at large.

For a moment or two nobody answered him, because we were all still trying to work out the implications. Then I explained, haltingly, aware as I said it how absurd and unlikely it sounded. Unlikely to the point of impossible. The only thing it had going for it was that no other theory explained everything that Asmodeus had done.

'That's insane,' Gil said, when I'd finished.

'I think it's fucking genius,' Nicky said, shaking his head in wonder. 'As prison breaks go, it makes digging a tunnel under Rita Hayworth look like nothing at all.'

'So the succubus is the key to Asmodeus' plan,' Trudie summarised. 'So we work without her, obviously.' She shrugged her good arm. 'She's probably too weak to move in any case. It's a pity, because she would have been our biggest gun, but we don't let her get near this thing.'

'And how . . .' said Juliet haltingly '. . . do you intend . . . to stop me?'

She was on her feet and limping towards us. She let the surgical gown fall from her shoulders. For Juliet, disrobing serves the same purpose that shrugging the hem of his poncho back to show his six-guns does for Clint Eastwood. But this time the magic failed to flow. Looking at the half-healed cuts that criss-crossed her body, I felt no arousal at all, just a sort of numb sadness. You know that feeling you get when you watch a movie you loved as a kid, and you find out it's nothing special? What I felt then was like that, only raised to the nth power. The true north of my libido was gone, and my disenfranchised dick had nothing to point to.

Juliet reached the table, but staggered when she got there and almost fell to her knees. Clutching its edge in both hands, she glared at me. 'He took Susan,' she said. Her voice had a terrible hollowness to it, as though she'd been cored out by the torture runes and was just an empty, walking skin.

There was no point in lying. 'Yeah,' I said, 'he did. Who told you?'

She wiped her sweat-beaded forehead with the back of her hand. 'The woman,' she said. 'The woman who was drawing on me, with knives and paint. She taunted me with that knowledge. Is that woman still alive, Castor? I'd be happy to know that she was still alive.'

I made a could-go-either-way gesture. 'She might be,' I said. 'Jenna-Jane is a tough old bird. Juliet, sit down before you fall down.'

Nicky pushed a vacant chair in behind her, unexpectedly solicitous. Juliet had given him his one and only post-mortem erection, so maybe his feelings were running along the same lines as mine. Juliet sank down, her arms visibly shaking from having supported her weight for those few seconds.

'Okay,' I said. 'You'll admit that there isn't a lot you're good for right now.'

'We heal quickly.'

'Quick enough to get up to fighting strength in less than an hour?' I demanded. 'Listen, I promised you I'd keep Sue safe.'

'And you broke that promise.'

'The day's not over yet.'

Juliet bared her teeth in a snarl, and however weak her body might have been right then, she spat out the next four words with the full, scary strength of her will.

'I'm coming with you.'

I was prepared to argue some more, But Nicky spoke up before I could. 'Why are you even arguing about this?' he demanded. 'Asmodeus' plan depends on her being there, right? He might not even let you in through the door without her. And he's likely to let her get in real close to him for the same reason. She can be your Trojan Horse.'

Juliet turned her head to stare at Nicky with cold ferocity. She said something in her own demonic tongue that was probably very insulting and – I was willing to bet – physically impossible.

Nicky leaned back from her sudden, unsettling anger and tensed, looking like he was about to bolt. Being dead, he hates physical confrontation. When you're running on empty, your body doesn't heal, and every wound is irreversible.

Trudie stepped in to take some of the heat. 'Maybe he's right,' she said. 'Forget what I just said. Asmodeus is too strong for any of us. If he wants us dead, we're dead. We've only got a chance at all because he needs Juliet alive.'

Gil laughed sardonically. 'Until he finds out that she can't do the mojo any more. That's not going to give us much of a window, is it?'

Trudie looked at me expectantly. I hefted the Sainsbury's bag and carefully poured the jagged pieces of broken glass out onto the table. Juliet, Nicky and Gil stared at it, their faces registering all the many flavours of nonplussed.

'Fortunately,' I said, 'we have a secret weapon.'

Gil cleared his throat, looking a little awkward. 'Actually, we have two,' he said. He reached into his pocket and took out a slim rectangular case, which he cracked open to display the shiny silver disc inside. 'A little present from Davey Nathan, Castor. He gave it to me this morning, but with everything that's happened . . .'

'Is that my anti-Asmodeus lullaby?' I asked.

'The extended disco remix.'

'Thank Christ,' Nicky said glumly. 'We're saved.'

20

Imelda Probert had lived – and died – in an otherwise abandoned low-rise block in a grubby little cul-de-sac in Peckham, south London. Long ago scheduled for demolition, the building hung on like most of Imelda's clientele in a sort of limbo state between life and death. The front door was nailed up with plywood boards, across which someone had sprayed the word WU-TANG CLAN inside a stylised W logo that looked like spread wings of a bird. More inexplicably, someone had painted the entire frontage of the block matt black, although red brick showed like raw flesh in places where the paint had cracked and fallen away. From the outside the building looked not just dead but already decayed.

Imelda hadn't minded that at all: it just guaranteed her the quiet and privacy she needed to work. Her third-floor flat had been like the spark of life in a zombie's cooling brain. That was until I brought Asmodeus here for the first time, and shifted the balance in favour of death. Everything that had happened since stemmed from that one stupendously bad decision.

Now here I was again to put things right – with Wayne Coyne singing 'Too Heavy for Superman' in a dirgy adagio inside my head.

We drove up and parked right in front of the house, the four of us, like the horsemen of some B-movie apocalypse, except we were riding in a high-sided Fiat Ducato which Nicky had appropriated from God knew where. It had been modified for use in the first London mayoral election, and for some inexplicable reason had never been touched since. Its customised sides were emblazoned with Frank Dobson's gormless, what-me-worry face along with the worst election slogan in the history of the civilised world: FRANK AND TO THE POINT. In the middle of Peckham's genteel Georgian slum district, the van was about as inconspicuous as President Ahmed Ahmedinajad at a Village People concert.

Gil slid over and let Trudie take his place in the driver's seat. She shot me a glance, troubled and unhappy.

'I'd rather be in there with you,' she said.

I touched the thick mass of bandage on her upper arm, like an American football player's shoulder pad. 'You can't fight,' I pointed out gently, 'and you can't perform an exorcism. But you can do this. It makes sense.'

'I know it makes sense.' Her voice was tight. 'But I've been in on this hunt from the very start. And I've got the feeling tonight might be it for me. The last time I ever do this. It's hard when it's your last time and all you're good for is back-up.'

'You're not back-up,' Gil said. 'You and Heath, you're our long-range artillery.'

Trudie grinned at that, a little sourly. 'And I suppose the three of you are the cavalry?' she said. 'Great metaphor, Gil. You can take turns being General Custer.'

I jumped out of the van and went round to the back, where I opened the doors. Juliet was slumped among the boxes there – probably full of old campaign fliers and I'M BACKING FRANK badges – but she climbed to her feet and stepped down, the wobble in her stride barely noticeable. She was wearing a black tracksuit that Trudie had picked up from the Oxfam shop on High Street; a pair of black boots with tall heels, likewise. For once, I felt no compulsion to imagine what she was wearing underneath. No electricity came from her. Even her scent had gone. She smelled of nothing but new leather.

'You'll need to hang back,' I told her, for the tenth or maybe the twentieth time. 'If you go in too fast, he'll figure it out. And if he figures it out, we're all dead. The only reason he won't just kill us all outright is because he still needs you to do him that one last favour.'

'I'll eat his face right off his skull,' Juliet growled.

'A sentiment we can all get behind,' I agreed. 'But for the love of God, Juliet, hang back. Don't take the lead.'

'For the love of *who*, Castor?'

Another good point. I let it stand.

We synchronised watches, mostly for Trudie's benefit: ten to midnight.

'Luck, Castor,' she said.

'Yeah, and you. We'll have a pint afterwards, yeah? I think it's my round next.'

'Do you even have any money?'

'No. But I like to keep track of my debts.'

I led the way, the point of a triangular battle formation that had Juliet and Gil McClennan as its other two vertices. My skin prickled as an invisible wave of pressure swept across it, the feeling an exorcist gets when the dead or the undead are watching him.

Asmodeus knew we were coming. He'd known we were coming even before we did.

Ignoring the front door, we circled around the left-hand flank of the building. A little way along, the black brick-work gave way to a spavined wooden fence with a door set into it. The door had a Yale lock, but it had never been locked as long as I'd known it. It wasn't even bolted: the warped wood was all that kept it from swinging open by itself. It yielded to my push and we stepped through into a backyard so thick with brambles and thistles that it looked like the set of *Day of the Triffids*.

The side door was open too, and the hall inside was completely dark. I tiptoed to the foot of the stairs and listened for a moment or two in silence, throwing out my arm to hold Juliet back in case she tried to step past me. Nothing seemed to be moving in the gulf of air above us.

Slowly, I began to climb the stairs, with Juliet right at my back. They creaked and shifted under us, appallingly loud in the echoing emptiness. Ridiculously, even though I knew there was no point in stealth, I couldn't keep myself from moving softly, trying to minimise the noise.

I also couldn't stop watching the shadows, but that was a whole lot more rational. The room that Imelda and I had kitted out for Rafi was up on the second floor, but there was no reason at all why Asmodeus would feel obliged to play by the rules. He could be anywhere in the building.

But he *was* in the building, at least I knew that. The sense of him was everywhere, so pervasive that I could only pick up the barest hint of a direction. Above us some-where, and watching, even now, because there was that prickling, itchy pressure again, across my shoulder blades.

We got to the first landing, turned onto the second flight of stairs. Juliet was crowding me from behind, filled with a desperate urgency that wouldn't let her slow down even though she knew how this was meant to work. No good. No good at all. If we kept on climbing, we'd run into the demon in the dark, on his terms, and everything would accelerate out of control.

'Are we really taking this to the wire?' I asked aloud, in a conversational tone. 'It's late, and I'm tired, and we all know what you want, you grandstanding prick. Send the women down, and Juliet comes up.'

'No,' said the demon's voice, echoing down the stairwell. He sounded relaxed and amused. 'This isn't a hostage situation, Castor. I said I'd keep them alive until you got here, that's all.'

'So where are they?' I demanded. Impossible to get a fix on him in the pitch dark. He sounded close, but the stairwell was four storeys high. Close could mean ten feet, twenty, even thirty. There's nothing worse than a valiant charge that turns into a long-distance slog.

'They're here,' Asmodeus assured me. 'They're not in very good condition, but they're here. Still breathing. More or less. If I were a man, I'd be a man of my word.'

'You fucking . . .' The words caught in my throat. 'If you've done anything to them . . .'

'I did a few things, at first. Then I discovered it was more interesting to make them do things to each other. It's like they say, Castor. Fear eats the soul. Get someone scared enough, and civilisation flies right out the window.' He chuckled softly, the sound falling like aeons-old dust through the dark. 'You'll have to watch your step when you come up here. It's a little slippery underfoot.'

Juliet gave a wordless cry. I knew what was coming and

I lunged to stop her, but her headlong rush knocked me sprawling against the banister, which cracked and gave ominously under my weight.

Too soon. Way too soon. I threw out my arm and caught her ankle just before she got out of reach, tripping her so that she fell full-length on the stairs.

'Don't!' I shouted desperately. 'Juliet, don't!'

She kicked me on the point of the jaw. At any other time that would probably have killed me, but she wasn't herself right then. Blood filled my mouth as my teeth were driven into my tongue, but I somehow managed to catch hold of her leg again, dragging her back down the stairs and clambering up in her place.

'We don't even know what you've got,' I yelled up into the dark. 'This is all bullshit until we see them.'

A hollow click sounded from above, and the stairwell was flooded with stark, shadowless light from a 150-watt bulb hanging directly over our heads. Asmodeus, up on the second-floor balcony, took his hand off the switch and let it fall back onto the banister rail. He was obviously alone.

'I rest my fucking case,' I said, sounding far less tough and uncompromising than I would have liked.

The demon just smiled. 'Do you need to see them?' he asked, speaking past me towards Juliet, who was only then struggling to her feet.

'No,' she whispered. I don't know how Asmodeus heard her. Standing right next to her, I could barely make out the word.

'No,' the demon agreed, almost gently. 'Because you can smell her. You can smell her flesh, her blood and her breath, even from way down there. You know she's still alive, but you don't know how long that might last. And the only way you're going to get to her, and find out how bad it is, is to go through me. You, fuck-doll. Just you. Anybody else who comes up here goes down again in pieces.' He shrugged theatrically. 'So what are you waiting for?'

Juliet pushed me aside. I raised an arm to halt her again, because I knew we still had time to kill before zero hour, but her hand moved in a flicker of speed, and she caught my wrist in a grip so tight I cried aloud. Evidently her strength was coming back. So was the crackling erotic aura that normally surrounded her. Her touch made the breath catch in my throat.

'Mine now,' she growled.

And she threw me aside so that I tumbled and rolled back down the stairs, coming to a jarring halt on the warped boards of the first-floor landing. The wood was so dry and worm-eaten that I almost went through them.

I rolled onto my side so that at least I was facing the right way to see what was happening above me, but there was no way I could stop it now. Juliet was taking the steps two at a time, her long-legged stride indicative in itself of the renewed energy and potency that was pouring into her – at the worst possible time.

I clambered up, a jolt of agony shooting through my right knee. Maybe I shouted out her name again, but I really don't remember. She was face to face with Asmodeus now, and he was spreading his arms to receive her. The smile of welcome that broke across his face was the most terrifying thing I'd ever seen.

*   *   *

'What part of this are you not getting?' Nicky demanded, exasperated.

'All of it,' Gil admitted. 'You're saying he actually wants the succubus to devour him?'

'No, he wants her to devour Rafi,' I said. 'Think about it, Gil. Think about everything he's done since he got free. First of all, he contacts the satanists—'

'Castor!' Trudie warned, but I had no intention of giving away professional secrets, and anyway it was all on the point of not mattering very much. I ignored her and went on. 'They were meant to do an encore of their number from last time – carry out a sacrifice on a child who'd been born and raised and prayed over in all the right ways, and set him free. But they blew it. They couldn't deliver.

'That's when he starts in on the murders. I think they're a crude improvisation – trying to shake Rafi loose by making him despair. Certainly they weaken him. They keep him on the defensive. Maybe they loosen his hold on the body they both share.

'But it's plan C that Asmodeus is putting his money on. If Juliet can be made to devour Rafi – body and soul together – what will be left?'

Gil shrugged. 'A greasy stain?'

'The demon,' Trudie said. 'Just him, in some bodiless form. It has to be that. He wouldn't respond to Juliet's spell – he'd feel no lust for her, because it's human lust she's adapted herself to arouse. So he'd be indigestible. When she was finished, he'd still be there. It would just be Ditko who'd be gone.'

'That's insane,' Gil objected.

'I think it's fucking genius,' Nicky said. 'As prison breaks go, it makes digging a tunnel under Rita Hayworth look like nothing at all.'

*   *   *

Juliet put one soft, caressing hand behind Asmodeus' head, drawing his face in close to hers. Their lips met.

Presumably, on a psychic level, some vast ethereal centrifuge began to turn, slowly at first but with gathering speed and irresistible momentum. Being a man, Rafi was drawn to Juliet. There was nothing he could do to stop it. I'd been there and I knew how it felt: the desire that was so like despair that you poured your heart and soul and lungs and liver and lights into its welcoming emptiness, wanting nothing but to penetrate, to be accepted, to be swallowed up.

Asmodeus, being a demon, would stand out of that vortex, immune to its pull. He would watch Rafi succumb, experiencing the immense satisfaction of a long and complicated chain of events drawing to its inevitable conclusion. He had turned his enemies into the moving parts of a machine which would deliver him from his bondage; there couldn't be many pleasures more visceral than that.

I heard a whimper come from Rafi's lips, and I knew who it belonged to. On a different level entirely, I heard the whispering echo of the demon's laugh.

And then, louder than either, I heard the liquescent, insinuating crunch as Juliet drove her makeshift blade home into Asmodeus' chest.

His eyes widened and he drew in a shuddering, unsteady breath. He winced, almost in slow motion. It was as though he fought against the recognition of that pain, with all that it implied.

He took a single step back, staring down at his chest. The irregular triangle of glass, like a flattened icicle, protruded from the left side of his body, high up, more or less where you'd expect his heart to be. Blood welled up around it and poured down, saturating his shirt in an instant and spilling out across the fabric with the suddenness of the paint-bucket effect in Photoshop.

If it had been a knife, Asmodeus would have torn it out of his own flesh and cut Juliet's throat with it. But it wasn't a knife.

'I thought silver was what you were supposed to use against demons and the undead,' Gil said, with the tone of someone letting us down gently.

'That's the rule of silver,' Trudie pointed out. 'This is the rule of names.'

'I'm . . . not seeing a name,' Nicky interjected into the profound silence. 'Should I be?'

'It's Rafi's communion photo, Nicky.' I held up the biggest piece to show him: an isosceles triangle, three inches wide at the blunt end and eight inches long, with half of Rafi's twelve-year-old face visible close to the tip. 'Printed onto the glass instead of onto paper. It's a real big thing in Macedonia. Trust me.'

Nicky raised his eyebrows. 'I'm sure. So the question is . . . ?'

I spelled it out. 'Exactly how does this work? Do names have power because of their mystical correspondence with the thing they name? And if they do, would that correspondence be stronger or weaker for an actual image of the thing?'

'What Martin Moulson did,' Trudie mused, 'was to inject himself – by means of his name – as an antibody into his own system, to drive the demon out of him. We want to drive Asmodeus out—'

'With a Polaroid. Yeah. Pretty much.'

* * *

Asmodeus screamed.

It was a sound born out of anger as much as pain. He had it all worked out, and we weren't playing by the rules.

But if having Rafi's smiling face rammed into his left ventricle was an unpleasant surprise, it wasn't the coup de grace I was hoping for. His arm came around like a scythe, smashing Juliet to her knees. Then he caught her as she fell with a swivel kick that lifted her into the air.

The wood of the banister exploded into jagged splinters, and Juliet pitched headlong into the stairwell. She fell past me, and there was a liquescent thud as she hit the tiles below.

And then there was one. But this was all about misdirection, and I hadn't been a kids' party magician for nothing. If you can make a roomful of six-year-olds watch your left hand while you slip the rabbit into the hat with your right, then a ten-thousand-year-old demon is nothing much. That's what I told myself, anyway, as I advanced up the last flight of stairs, drawing my whistle and setting it to my lips like a sniper finding the spot weld.

Asmodeus snarled and stepped up to meet me – then stiffened, eyes wide, as Gil hit him from behind with the taser.

'I'm going to be fuck-all use in all this,' Gil commented sourly. 'The one thing we're not throwing against the sonofabitch is an actual exorcism.'

'Can you climb a drainpipe?' I asked him, producing Jenna-Jane's M18 with a certain sense of occasion.

Fifty thousand volts isn't a lot, when you come to think

about it. That's manufacturer's spec, too, so you're probably talking forty-eight thousand and some small change, if anyone bothered to check. A bolt of lightning can get you up into the millions, no trouble.

But Asmodeus was hurting already – in his dignity, as much as anywhere. He was pumping arterial blood, he had a razor-edged smiley face in his heart that was making him feel anything but happy, and his meticulously laid plans were turning into a Whitehall farce. So I'm willing to bet the effect in this case was out of all proportion to what it said on the label.

Again, it might have ended there. He could have folded up into nothing, and left Rafi in charge of a body that was leaking precious fluids faster than they could be replaced.

He didn't. He grabbed hold of the taser's conductive wire and hauled hard. Instinctively, Gil tightened his grip on the taser, so he was yanked forward, off balance. Asmodeus' fist met him halfway, catching Gil at the junction of neck and shoulder, so that he fell to the ground as heavily as a bag of hammers. It had all happened so fast that the echoing boom reached me a second afterwards.

But as the echoes of that unlovely sound died, we both heard something new and worse coming in from the street, sickening the air. It was like the skirling call of an infernal ice cream van, playing at a hundred and some decibels, summoning ghosts and ghouls and damned souls to stop me and buy one.

'We'll need a way of playing this,' I said, turning Nathan's disc

in my fingers with the gingerly care of the technologically challenged. 'I mean . . . aloud.'

'I think I can cut you a deal there,' Nicky ruminated. 'You remember the first mayoral elections? When Red Ken beat friendly Frank by a country mile? I know a guy who bought up some of the leftovers. Including one of those fucking trucks with all the loudspeakers that drives by at six in the morning and tells you that the candidate won't come inside you . . .'

'What do you know?' I said, as I finally reached the upper landing. 'They're playing our tune.'

I drove my fist full into Asmodeus' face. The satisfaction I took from that was tempered by the fact that the face actually belonged to Rafi, but it still felt pretty good, all things considered.

His head snapped back, but he didn't lose his footing even for a second, and his riposte was swift and terrible. His arm swept round in an elliptical arc, the air cracked like a whip, and the world exploded.

There are two or three seconds here that I can't account for. The next thing I was aware of was a pressure against my back, and a sensation around my mouth and chin as though someone was drinking from me through a straw of enormously wide bore.

Not knowing if I was standing on my feet or sprawling on my arse, I twitched my limbs in random combinations in the hope of getting good reports. But my eyes were definitely at floor level, and canted at ninety degrees.

The demon flickered in my blurred vision, getting closer and then receding. I steeled myself for the blow that would end everything, shut me down for good, but it didn't come. I blinked furiously to clear my sight, and saw something I didn't understand.

Asmodeus was dancing. Or at least that was what it looked like. The light from a street lamp, shining in through a window just off to our left, picked him out like a spotlight.

It was finally zero hour, and everything was kicking in. The bastard was writhing on an invisible cross as big as the world. But would that be big enough?

'It's not enough to hurt him,' I said, with absolute certainty. 'Not nearly enough. Moulson drove in fifteen hundred nails. He punctuated his body at microscopic intervals . . .'

'You want something to pull him in a lot of different directions,' Gil said.

'Yes.'

'With your glass dagger pinned in his chest. So he's stretched out taut and he can't get away from the pain.'

'Fuck! Yes! If you've got something, McClennan, spit it out.'

Gil gave us a guileless look. 'Vote early,' he said, 'and vote often. Heath, how many friends have you got on all your conspiracy-of-the-month websites?'

'A million,' Nicky said. 'Give or take. Why?'

'How many of them can do a summoning?'

Asmodeus staggered, fell, scrambled to his feet. He baulked, and blood spurted between his clenched teeth in a pressurised stream.

His searchlight gaze found me across the width of the landing. His eyes narrowed.

'Very clever,' he bubbled. 'Castor, I love you. I never expected for a moment that you'd make a fight of this.'

He slumped against the wall, his eyelids flickering like those of an epileptic in the grip of a grand mal seizure. He was on the ropes. The very mechanism he'd chosen for his escape – using Juliet's guaranteed fatal attraction to separate out the human from the the demonic parts of the amalgam he'd become – gave us our window of opportunity. If there was ever a time when Asmodeus' grip on Rafi's soul could be prized free, it was now. The demon had done the groundwork for me. All I had to do was to bring it home.

As though God loved me, I found my whistle ready to hand. It had fallen only a few feet away, and it hadn't broken. I took it in my hands and raised it, my fingers finding the stops by automatic reflex. I pursed my lips.

Where were my lips?

I couldn't even feel the mouthpiece where it pressed against my mouth. I tried to blow a note, and red froth sprayed the metal. The tingling, sucking absence in the lower part of my face made sudden, sickening sense, and I moaned aloud.

Reeling like a drunk, Asmodeus wheeled about.

'But everything's relative,' he growled. 'Isn't it? You feel like playing me another of your lazy little 'tudes? No?' He kicked something across the floor at me – something red and wet that looked as though it belonged in the little plastic bag you find up a chicken's arse and throw away before you cook it. Part of my jawbone; I could tell by the fact that it still had three teeth embedded in it.

'Then let's shut that fucking PA up,' Asmodeus slurred.

He crouched low on his haunches and leaped into the stairwell.

There's a moment in the execution of any plan when you realise that you're just not as good as you think you are, that you've done everything you could and it isn't enough. You got the angle right, and you gunned the engine like a maniac, but your bike isn't going to make it to the other side of the canyon.

That moment fell on my shoulders now. I struggled to my feet, trying it on for size. It felt like it belonged, like I'd been wearing it, more or less, ever since the night when I sat down in Rafi's cramped bathroom and performed the one, crappy piece of improv that was destined to encapsulate my life.

I flexed my legs to see if they were going to give. Then I charged the window and kicked it out of its rotten frame in one piece. It fell and shattered on the pavement below me with a crash that could be heard even above the screaming discords of the demon lullaby. Climbing up onto the ragged ledge of splintered plasterboard where the window had been, I launched myself after it into the street.

Two storeys isn't even twenty feet, but it's enough to snap your legs like a couple of twigs unless you're either a professional stuntman or very lucky. I'm not either of those things, but I was aiming for the Ducato, which stands eight feet high on its wheelbase. My feet staved in the roof and part of the near-side panel, turning Frank Dobson's slick smile into a leering grimace, and no doubt taking Trudie to the brink of a heart attack.

A second later the front door of the building was ripped

off its hinges from the inside and tossed negligently away through the air.

Asmodeus stepped out into the night, shaking his head the way a dog shakes itself off after diving into ice-cold water. His gaze tracked from side to side, seeming to miss the van first time round even though it was right in front of him, but then catching it on the next pass.

He walked towards us, the glass dagger protruding obscenely from his chest. Fresh blood gouted from it with each step.

I banged on the roof of the van to get Trudie's attention. 'Give me the gun,' I shouted, but what she would have heard was 'WUFF-uffa-FUH!' I didn't really have a working vocal apparatus any more, and in a wistful, just-about-to-go-into-shock kind of way, I was starting to miss it.

Asmodeus was maybe three strides away from us when Juliet plunged through the doorway behind him and tackled him from behind. They went down together and rolled almost under the van's wheels. Juliet's hands were locked around Asmodeus' throat, but he had his own hands – which looked much bigger than Rafi's right then, the muscles in his forearms standing out like ropes – clamped to either side of her head. He forced her head further and further back, trying to snap her spine.

I dropped off the roof of the van, falling on all fours but scrambling to my feet again quickly. Trudie was fumbling with the shotgun, but she only had one hand and she couldn't seem to find the safety. Nicky had only demonstrated it once, and things can slip your mind in the heat of the moment. Right then, the moment felt hot enough to scald.

She blanched when she saw me, and almost dropped the gun. 'Oh shit!' she exclaimed. 'Oh, Castor!' I held out my hand, and she put the shotgun into it without a word. Probably just as well. The conversation was likely to be pretty one-sided in any case.

Asmodeus had rolled over on top of Juliet. He drove her face hard into the pavement and lurched to his feet. He turned to face me, his agonised features rippling like water.

'Now . . .' he snarled.

'Fifteen hundred nails,' I'd said. Actually, they were tiny metal discs, which sounds a lot less dramatic, but that doesn't lessen what Moulson did. Inch by inch, he had waterproofed the house of his own flesh against the bad weather coming from Hell, and when it was all over the house was still standing. Fifteen hundred surgically precise incisions. Fifteen hundred grinding ordeals as he forced the metal deep enough for it to stay. He said it had taken most of a day.

A shotgun doesn't score quite as high on accuracy, but it's a fuck of a lot faster.

I fired the first barrel.

Glass. Glass ground up as fine as birdshot. It was such a light load that at twenty yards or so it probably wouldn't even sting. But this was six feet.

Asmodeus' jacket and shirt were flecked, ripped, stripped away by the multiple, stinging impacts. The demon flinched, drawing in a harsh, astonished breath, and then he bellowed in agony as our purpose-built payload started to work on him.

*   *   *

We'd selected three pieces of glass from Rafi's photograph for Juliet to use as knives: we thought overkill was advisable under the circumstances. That still left a whole lot of fragments that were too small to have any viable use in hand-to-hand combat. A little bit of Rafi's arm here, the other half of his face there. It seemed a shame to let them go to waste. Nicky carefully unpacked the shot he normally kept in the gun, looking thoughtfully at the little pile of glass shards. Then he went away from the table and came back with a hammer.

Asmodeus stared at his hands with a sort of numb fascination. Blood from a dozen lacerations welled out onto his palms, between his fingers, down over his wrists.

'Fuck,' he said distantly.

With terrible deliberation, he focused his will on his raised hand, trying to exert the same authority over that tortured flesh that he had enjoyed by right of conquest from the night when he moved in right up until now.

The flesh didn't obey. Didn't even answer. Asmodeus started towards me. Anger and consternation crossed his face, but what finally stood out there was fear.

'When you die,' he grated hoarsely. 'When you die, Castor . . .'

That was as far as he got. He fell a few feet away from me, twitching. I followed him maybe a second later, unable to hold myself upright any more. I was staring directly into his eyes, so I saw when they filmed over, and then cleared again.

'Fix . . .' Rafi whispered.

The street was alive with noise suddenly, as black cars and vans and at least one eight-wheeled truck rolled into the small cul-de-sac and screeched to a precipitous halt that left the asphalt streaked with burned-rubber spoor. Doors slammed open, men and woman in black stealth gear jumped down and deployed themselves in blunt wedge formations, looking in all directions for an enemy who wasn't there.

Thomas Gwillam stepped out of one of the cars and surveyed the carnage. His cold, appraising gaze started up high, at the broken window, and ended with the bodies on the pavement, lingering on Rafi before finally coming to rest on me.

'I came as soon as you called,' he said. 'But of course you didn't call until you could be sure I'd arrive late. I warned you against false pride, Castor. What good is back-up that arrives when the battle's over?'

He had a point. Astutely, I lost consciousness before I could be made to admit that. Glad to be out of it, to tell you the truth. My jaw was starting to sting like a bastard.

21

There's a lot to be said for fainting dead away at the awkward moment when the action is over and done with and the cleaning up has to start. Other people can bear your wounded body from the field and take care of all the messy stuff, while you cavort with pastel-coloured bunny rabbits in a magic garden where marshmallows and bottles of single malt whisky hang like fruit among the trees.

In this case though, the ancillary staff weren't up to the job. Gwillam and his people were only interested in Rafi, and apart from them the only one who was even capable of standing on her own two feet was Trudie Pax. The first thing she did – since she knew a thing or two about clinical shock – was to slap me awake again.

That was something of a blow, to be honest. I would have preferred to wake up in a hospital bed, with all my missing parts sewn back into place and a gentle novocaine high percolating through my body. Instead I found myself still on the pavement, aching in every limb, joint and organ, and with some sort of agonising neural fireworks display going off in what was left of the lower part of my face.

Trudie had torn off my shirt and wadded it up under my chin to staunch the worst of the bleeding. That was as much as she could do, right then. She'd called 999 and an ambulance was on its way; in the meantime, there were a lot of other people to check in on.

Rafi seemed to be alive. At least, Gwillam reported, he had a pulse, although it was weak and irregular. The wound in his chest had all but stopped bleeding, so Trudie saw no point trying to pack it. The shotgun wounds were too many and too small for her to do anything about them.

Juliet didn't have a pulse and she wasn't breathing, but when Trudie muttered a blessing over her, she sat up and swore in some guttural language whose inhuman consonants made Trudie's eyes water. Leaving Gwillam conferring with his chiefs of staff, the three of us went into the building together to get the final count and find out whether we'd won or lost that night.

Gil seemed the least damaged of all of us, but he was only stirring into consciousness when we arrived on the second-floor landing. He climbed groggily to his feet, only to sit back down again hurriedly. The left side of his face was a single bruise, the eye swollen shut. He stared in fascinated horror at my bemonstered face, then made a thumb-up, thumb-down gesture: a question.

I shrugged: jury still out.

Juliet led the way because Juliet could find them by smell alone. She went into a room next to the one where we'd kept Rafi confined after we took him from the Stanger, less than two months before. The only piece of furniture in the room was a tall free-standing wardrobe. Juliet tried the doors, found them locked.

I offered the stock of the shotgun, but Juliet broke the lock with her bare hands and threw the door open.

Pen and Sue were standing side by side in the wardrobe, their hands and legs tied, kept on their feet by crude nooses slung around the clothes rail above their heads. If they'd

fallen asleep or stumbled, they would have hanged themselves.

They hadn't been touched. Not a wound, not a bruise.

Even now, that's the part I find hardest to understand.
Asmodeus needed them alive because he needed to be sure
that Juliet would come to him. But he wanted her angry,
and what would drive her more berserk than the broken
body of her lover, waved in her face?

It's possible that he'd promised himself their degrad-
ation and death after all this was over, that he put it off
as an epicure might put off a fine meal, sharpening the
pleasure by prolonging the anticipation. But that kind of
logic only gets you so far with a demon; mostly they just
take what they want when they want it, and in this case
our reactions – meaning mine and Juliet's – would have
been a big part of the fun for him.

So I'm wondering, crazy as it sounds, whether it might
have been Rafi who spared them rather than Asmodeus.
Maybe he saved his strength for one final rebellion, and
fought down the demon's hands whenever they tried to
consummate that part of the plan.

The bottom line is that I don't know. And there's nobody
I can ask.

Rafi doesn't remember one damned thing after the night
he drew that fucking magic circle and said, '*Surgat mihi
Asmodeus.*'

22

About a month after the dust settled on all this, I went back to the Whittington one last time. I slipped in quietly, late in the evening.

Nobody had ever come round to question me in connection with the mayhem at the MOU, or the physical and psychological dismantling of two security guards last seen in my company down in Surrey, but that just made me more uneasy. Sooner or later, somehow, the axe was going to fall.

It had been impossible even for Nicky to find out how things had turned out after I slammed the door on Jenna-Jane and her staff and walked away. The embargo on that information went both very high and very deep, which left me with the unnerving conviction that she must somehow have survived. If she'd died, then what was left of her operation would surely have been in more disarray.

I came dressed in overalls and carrying a plastic bucket. That was enough to stop anyone from challenging me as I slipped into the pediatric ward in the wake of a visiting family.

Once in Lisa Probert's room, I locked the door and took out my whistle. Closing my eyes, I started to move my fingers on the stops, imagining the tune, low and fast; letting it play in my head, because it would take another three months for the bone graft to be stable enough to allow the steel pins to be removed from my jaw.

It was a tune I knew really well, easy enough to visualise

in its entirety. I held one end of it in my mind, cast the other end like a hook out into the dark. It seemed like no time at all before a telltale prickle of pressure on the skin of my face and hands told me I was being watched.

The four little girls stood in a ragged horseshoe formation, staring at me impatiently. They never liked to have their city-wide games of hide-and-seek interrupted.

'Abbie,' I said, sounding like a bad ventriloquist because my mouth wouldn't open wider than half an inch. 'Good to see you. Good to see you all.' I could never remember the names of Charles Stanger's three victims, and I never wanted to go back to the records to refresh my memory. 'I hate to bug you, but I was hoping you could do me a favour.'

I pointed to the still, barely breathing figure in the bed.

'Find her,' I said. 'Find where her spirit is hiding. Bring her home, if you can, back to this body. And if you can't . . . then maybe she can hang out with you, for a while, until she decides what she wants to do.'

'All right, Mr Castor,' Abbie whispered, her voice not stirring the air. 'We'll see what we can do.'

I left as quietly as I'd arrived, and nobody even knew I'd been there.

Come to think of it, that's pretty much how I felt when I dropped in on Juliet and Sue later that same night. The two of them were so wrapped up in each other, they scarcely knew the world existed.

Somehow the power dynamic in the relationship had shifted, and it was a strange thing to see. Juliet had come back to her full strength, but to look at them together you'd think that it was Sue who had the whip hand and the ineluctable magnetism. Juliet was as attentive to her, as solicitous for her, as quietly, ubiquitously there for her, as a Victorian butler. She kept touching Sue's hand, or her cheek, or her shoulder, as though she had to reassure herself constantly that she was still there.

It was because she'd been back to Hell, or at least that was my best guess. Because Asmodeus' wards had dragged her back against her will into her own past, and she'd seen with sudden, terrible clarity what it had been like: what she'd gained and what she'd lost, and what she might be again if she let herself slip. She held onto Sue because Sue was the embodiment and the anchor of her new life. Sue was the mnemonic that let her remember who she was.

I excused myself as soon as I found a decent opening, using some mumbled bullshit about Nicky inviting me over for a screening. He hadn't, but I dropped in on him anyway. As it turned out, he was busy pricing up stock for his new enterprise down the market and had no time to spare for socialising, but he had one quick question for me before he shut the door in my face.

'One of the original prints of *A Matter of Life and Death*,' he said, hefting the heavy silver canister, like a thick discus, so I could see it. 'Shit-awful condition. Breaks. Burns. Splices. Not really playable, but still . . . an original print. How much?'

'A tenner?'

'I was thinking a couple of thousand.'

'High Street Market? You want to attract the casual impulse buyer, Nicky, not the cruising millionaires.'

'It's a piece of fucking history.'

'Cut it into three-inch pieces. Sell them for a tenner each.'

He tried the idea on for size and decided that – besides increasing his profit margin substantially – it made a lot of sense. 'I guess people only want as much history as they can easily carry around, right?'

'That's always been my personal preference.'

'Yours feeling any lighter?'

'Yeah,' I admitted. 'A little. But I'm benching three and a half decades, Nicky. A month here, a year there . . . it makes less difference than you'd think.'

He nodded philosophically. 'Sure, sure. Well, I'm up to my neck here, and tomorrow is the grand opening. Stop by if you're in the neighbourhood.'

I headed back out into the night, the heavy steel doors echoing behind me.

I could have taken in a late-night movie, or caught the last couple of rounds at a bar where the music and the beer were more or less bearable. I could even have gone back home and slept. But Pen and Rafi were renovating both the house and their relationship right then. I never knew which room they were going to turn up in, so the less time I spent at home, the less chance I had of accidentally walking in on some of the wilder stretches of the Kama Sutra.

I caught the last Tube out of Walthamstow Central back into town, and walking on autopilot I found my steps taking me through Somers Town again. To my amazement, I bumped into a familiar group of zombies sitting around a familiar fire, although they had it banked a little higher now that the nights had started to turn.

There was a Londis open nearby, with a small but not too shabby selection of booze behind the counter. I bought a couple of bottles this time, one of whisky and one of rum, and a packet of plastic cups. Then I went and sat with the dead men for a while, fulfilling a promise I'd all but forgotten I'd made.

They were surprisingly good company, once you stopped registering the smell. They'd been through everything the world had to throw at them and earned their philosophical detachment the hard way. It made for a sort of fatalistic good humour: life's a bitch, and then you die, and then . . .

The levels in the bottles sank inch by inch, the sky started to lighten around the horizon, and I was about to call it a night when a newcomer joined the circle around the fire, crowding me a little close. She brought her own warmth with her, noticeable in this company because most of the regular crowd were at the ambient temperature.

I turned round to see who it was.

'Private party?' Trudie Pax asked.

'Limited to the living, the dead and the pending file,' I told her.

'Good enough. Any of that booze left?'

I poured her a generous measure of Scotch. 'How did you track me down?' I asked.

She held up her hands, both of which were wound around with many loops of multicoloured string. 'A little stiff,' she said, 'but I'm right back in the game. You wouldn't believe what I can do with these babies now.'

'I'd love to find out.'

It was the kind of mildly off-colour remark I throw out by reflex, and I expected an equally perfunctory put-down. Instead, Trudie slipped her hand into mine.

When the dawn filled half the sky, the zombies headed

off to pastures new – an ownerless shed round the back of Camden Lock where they could lie low until the unruly sun stopped poking at them. Hand in hand with Trudie, I walked through Euston Square and watched the morning get its kit on.

'I heard that Imelda Probert's daughter made a full recovery,' Trudie said, her tone guardedly neutral.

'Yeah,' I agreed. 'I heard that, too.'

'Any idea where she'll go now?'

'She got a job,' I said. 'At a market stall in Walthamstow. It'll pay the rent.' My tone was even more off-hand than Trudie's, but that was because the subject was one that still hurt too much to dwell on for long. I'd given Lisa back her life: I didn't believe for a moment that in doing that I'd settled the debt between us.

'You ever wish you were part of this?' Trudie asked, indicating with a toss of her head the scuttling commuters, the street cleaners, the shopkeepers taking down their shutters on the station concourse.

'Of life, you mean?' I asked, surprised by the question. 'No. Not much. I'd rather be an ironic commentator.' But it was a flip answer, and from the tone of her voice she'd meant the question seriously. 'I suppose when I think of it at all, I feel like Janis Joplin in the Chelsea Hotel song. "We may be ugly, but at least we've got the music." I wouldn't want to give up what I've got for what they've got.'

'No,' Trudie agreed. 'Me neither.'

We walked along together in silence for a while.

'So how religious are you feeling today, Ms Pax?' I asked at last.

'Very. Very devout. How about you, Mr Castor?'

'Atheistic. Blasphemous. Practically satanic.'

She leaned her head on my shoulder.

'Let's form an inter-faith study group,' she suggested.

extras

www.orbitbooks.net

about the author

Mike Carey is the acclaimed writer of *Lucifer* and *Hellblazer* (now filmed as *Constantine*). He has also written extended runs for Marvel's fan-favourite titles *X-Men* and *Ultimate Fantastic Four*, the comic book adaptation of Neil Gaiman's *Neverwhere*, and a movie screenplay, *Frost Flowers*, soon to be produced by Hadaly/Bluestar Pictures. He lives in London with his wife, Linda, also a novelist and screenwriter, their three children and a cat named Tasha.

For more information about Mike Carey visit www.mikecarey.net

Find out more about other Orbit authors by registering for the free monthly newsletter at www.orbitbooks.net

if you enjoyed
THE NAMING OF
THE BEASTS
look out for

A MADNESS OF
ANGELS

by

Kate Griffin

Prelude: The Trouble with Telephones

In which a summoning is almost (but not quite) perfect, some new friends are made, and some old enemies remembered.

Not how it should have been.

Too long, this awakening, floor warm beneath my fingers, itchy carpet, thick, a prickling across my skin, turning rapidly into the red-hot feeling of burrowing ants; too long without sensation, everything weak, like the legs of a baby. I said twitch, and my toes twitched, and the rest of my body shuddered at the effort. I said blink, and my eyes were two half-sucked toffees, uneven, sticky, heavy, pushing back against the passage of my eyelids like I was trying to lift weights before a marathon.

All this, I felt, would pass. As the static blue shock of my wakening, if that is the word, passed, little worms of it digging away into the floor or crawling along the ceiling back into the telephone lines, the hot blanket of their protection faded from my body. The cold intruded like a great hungry worm into every joint and inch of skin, my bones suddenly too long for my flesh, my muscles suddenly too tense in their relaxed form to tense ever again, every part starting to quiver as the full shock of sensation returned.

I lay on the floor naked as a shedding snake, and we contemplated our situation.

runrunrunrunrunRUNRUNRUNRUN! hissed the panicked voice inside me, the one that saw the bed legs an inch from my nose as the feet of an ogre, heard the odd swish of traffic through the rain outside as the spitting of venom down a forked tongue, felt the thin neon light drifting through the familiar dirty window pane as hot as noonday glare through a hole in the ozone layer.

I tried moving my leg and found the action oddly giddying, as if this was the ultimate achievement for which my life so far had been spent in training, the fulfilment of all ambition. Or perhaps it was simply that we had pins and needles and, not entirely knowing how to deal with pain, we laughed through it, turning my head to stick my nose into the dust of the carpet to muffle my own inane giggling as I brought my knee up towards my chin, and tears dribbled around the edge of my mouth. We tasted them, curious, and found the saltiness pleasurable, like the first, tongue-clenching, moisture-eating bite of hot, crispy bacon. At that moment finding a plate of crispy bacon became my one guiding motivation in life, the thing that overwhelmed all others, and so, with a mighty heave and this light to guide me, I pulled myself up, crawling across the end of the bed and leaning against the chest of drawers while waiting for the world to decide which way down would be for the duration.

It wasn't quite my room, this place I found myself in. The inaccuracies were gentle, superficial. It was still my paint on the wall, a pale, inoffensive yellow; it was still my window with its view out onto the little parade of shops on the other side of the road, unmistakable: the newsagent, the off-licence, the cobbler and all-round domestic supplier, the launderette, and, red lantern still burning cheerfully in the window, Mrs Lee Po's famous Chinese takeaway. My window, my view; not my room. The bed was new, an ugly, polished thing trying to pretend to be part of a medieval bridal chamber for a princess in a pointy hat. The mattress, when I sat on it, was so hard I ached within a minute from being in contact with it; on the wall hung a huge, gold-framed mirror in which I could picture Marie Antoinette having her curls perfected; in the corner there were two wardrobes, not one. I waddled across to them, and leant against the nearest to recover my breath from the epic distance covered. Seeing by the light seeping under the door, and the neon glow from outside, I opened the first one and surveyed jackets of rough tweed, long dresses in silk, white and cream-coloured shirts distinctively tailored, pointed black leather shoes, high-heeled sandals composed almost entirely of straps and no real protective substance, and a handbag the size of a feather pillow, suspended with a heavy, thick gold chain. I opened the handbag and rifled through the contents. A purse, containing £50, which I took, a couple of credit cards, a library membership to the local Dulwich Portakabin, and a small but orderly handful of thick white business cards. I pulled one out and in the dull light read the name – 'Laura Linbard, Business Associate, KSP'. I put it on the bed and opened the other wardrobe.

This one contained trousers, shirts, jackets and, to my surprise, a large pair of thick yellow fisherman's oils and sailing boots. There was a small, important-looking box at the bottom of the wardrobe. I opened it and found a stethoscope, a small first-aid kit, a thermometer and several special and painful-looking metal tools whose nature I dared not speculate on. I pulled a white cotton shirt off its hanger and a pair of grey trousers. In a drawer I found underpants which didn't quite fit comfortably, and a pair of thick black socks.

Dressing, I felt cautiously around my left shoulder and ribcage, probing for damage, and finding that every bone was properly set, every inch of skin correctly healed, not even a scar, not a trace of dry blood.

The shirt cuff reached roughly to the point where my thumb joint aligned with the rest of my hand; the trousers dangled around the balls of my feet. The socks fitted perfectly, as always seems the way. The shoes were several sizes too small; that perplexed me. How is it possible for someone to have such long arms and legs, and yet wear shoes for feet that you'd think would have to have been bound? Feeling I might regret it later, I left the shoes.

I put the business card and the £50 in my trouser pockets and headed for the door. On the way out, we caught sight of our reflection in the big mirror and stopped, stared, fascinated. Was this now us? Dark brown hair heading for the disreputable side of uncared for – not long enough to be a bohemian statement, not short enough to be stylish. Pale face that freckled in the sun, slightly over-large nose for the compact features that surrounded it, head plonked as if by accident on top of a body made all the more sticklike by the ridiculous oversized clothes it wore. It was not the flesh we would have chosen, but I had long since given up dreams of resembling anyone from the movies and, with the pragmatism of the perfectly average, come to realise that this was me and that was fine.

And this was me, looking back out of the mirror.

Not quite me.

I leant in, turning my head this way and that, running my fingers through my hair – greasy and unwashed – in search of blood, bumps, splits. Turning my face this way and that, searching for bruises and scars. An almost perfect wakening, but there was still something wrong with this picture.

I leant right in close until my breath condensed in a little grey puff on the glass, and stared deep into my own eyes. As a teenager it had bothered me how round my eyes had been, somehow always imagining that small eyes = great intelligence, until one day at school the thirteen-year-old Max Borton had pointed out that round dark eyes were a great way to get the girls. I blinked and the reflection in the mirror blinked back, the bright irises reflecting cat-like the orange glow of the washed-out street lamps. My eyes, which, when I had last had cause to look at them, had been brown. Now they were the pale, brilliant albino blue of the cloudless winter sky, and I was no longer the only creature that watched from behind their lens.

*runrunrunrunrunrun*RUNRUNRUNRUNRUNRUN RUNRUN!

I put my head against the cold glass of the mirror, fighting the sudden terror that threatened to knock us back to the floor. The trick was to keep breathing, to keep moving. Nothing else mattered. Run long and hard enough, and perhaps while you're running you might actually come up with a plan. But nothing mattered if you were already dead.

My legs thought better than my brain, walked me out of the room. My fingers eased back the door and I blinked in the shocking light of the hundred-watt bulb in the corridor outside. The carpet here was thick and new, the banisters polished, but it was a painting on the wall, a print of a Picasso I'd picked up for a fiver – too many years ago – all colour and strange, scattered proportions – which stole our attention. It still hung exactly where I'd left it. I felt almost offended. We were fascinated: an explosion of visual wonder right there for the same price as a cheap Thai meal, in full glory. Was everything like this? I found it hard to remember. I licked my lips and tasted blood, dry and old. Thoughts and memories were still too tangled to make clear sense of them. All that mattered was moving, staying alive long enough to get a plan together, find some answers.

From downstairs I heard laughter, voices, the chink of glasses, and a door being opened. Footsteps on the tiles that led from living room to kitchen, a *clink* where they still hadn't cemented in the loose white one in the centre of the diamond pattern; the sound of plates; the roar of the oven fan as it pumped out hot air.

I started walking down. The voices grew louder, a sound of polite gossipy chit-chat, dominated by one woman with a penetrating voice and a laugh that started at the back of her nose before travelling down to the lungs and back up again, and who I instinctively disliked. I glanced down the corridor to the kitchen and saw a man's back turned to me, bent over something that steamed and smelt of pie. The urge to eat anything, everything, briefly drowned out the taste of blood in my mouth. Like a bewildered ghost who can't understand that it has died, I walked past the kitchen and pushed at the half-open door to the living room.

There were three of them, with a fourth place set for the absent cook, drinking wine over the remnants of a salad, around a table whose top was made of frosted glass. As I came in, nobody seemed to notice me, all attention on the one woman there with the tone and look of someone in the middle of a witty address. But when she turned in my direction with 'George, the pie!' already half-escaped from her lips, the sound of her dropped wineglass shattering on the table quickly redirected the others' attention.

They stared at me, I stared at them. There was an embarrassed silence that only the English can do so well, and that probably lasted less than a second, but felt like a dozen ticks of the clock. Then, as she had to, as things probably must be, one of the women screamed.

The sound sent a shudder down my spine, smashed through the horror and incomprehension in my brain, and at last let me understand, let me finally realise that this was no longer my house, that I had been gone too long, and that to these people I was the intruder, they the rightful owners. The scream slammed into my brain like a train hitting the buffers and tore a path through my consciousness that let everything else begin to flood in: the true realisation that if my house was not mine, my job, my friends, my old life would not be mine, nor my possessions, my money, my debts, my clothes, my shoes, my films, my music, all gone in a second, things I had owned since a scrawny teenager, the electric toothbrush my father had given me in a fit of concern for my health, the photos of my friends and the places I'd been, the copy of *Calvin and Hobbes* my first girlfriend had given me as a sign of enduring friendship the Christmas after we'd split up, my favourite pair of slippers, the holiday I was planning to the mountains of northern Spain, all, everything I had worked for, everything I had owned and wanted to achieve, vanished in that scream.

I ran. We didn't run from the sound, that wasn't what frightened us. I ran to become lost, and wished I had never woken in the first place, but stayed drifting in the blue.

* * *

Once upon a time, a not-so-long time ago, I had sat with my mad old gran on a bench beside a patch of cigarette-butt grass that the local council had designated 'community green area', watching the distant flashes of the planes overhead, and the turning of the orange-stained clouds across a sullen yellow moon. She'd worn a duffel coat, a faded blue night-dress and big pink slippers. I'd worn my school uniform and my dad's big blue jacket, that Mum had unearthed one day from a cardboard box and had been about to burn. I'd cried, an eleven-year-old kid not sure why I cared, until she'd saved it for me.

We'd sat together, my gran and me, and the pigeons had clustered in the gutters and on the walls, hopped around my gran's slippered feet, wobbled on half a torn-off leg, flapped with broken, torn-feathered wings, peered with round orange unblinking eyes, like glass sockets in their tiny heads, unafraid. I had maths homework which I had no intention of doing, and a belly full of frozen peas and tomato ketchup. Winter was coming, but tonight the air was a clean, dry cold, sharp, not heavy, and the lights were on in all the houses of the estate. I was a secret spy, a boy sitting in the darkness of the bench, watching Mr Paswalah in number 27 ironing his shirts, Jessica and Al in number 32 rowing over the cleaning, old Mrs Gregory in 21 flicking through 300 TV channels in search of something loud and violent that when her husband had been alive she had felt too ashamed to watch, it not being correct for a lady raised in the 1940s to enjoy the *Die Hard* films.

So I sat, my gran by my side, as we sat many nights on this bench; just her, me, the pigeons and our stolen world of secret windows.

My gran was silent a long while. Sitting here on this bench, with the pigeons, was almost the only time she seemed content. Then she turned to me, looked me straight in the eye and said, 'Boy?'

'Yes, Gran?' I mumbled.

Her lips were folded in over her bright pink gums, her false teeth inside the house beside her little single bed. She chewed on the inward turn of them a long while, head turning to the sky, then back to the ground, and then slowly round to me. 'You sing beautiful in the choir, boy?'

'Yes, Gran,' I lied. I may have cried to save my father's coat, but I had enough teenage self-respect to not be caught dead singing in the school choir.

'Boy?'

'Yes, Gran?'

'You cheat at tests?'

'Yes, Gran.'

'I told 'em, I told 'em, but the old ladies all said . . . Angelina has a problem with her left ear, you know? You cheat at tests, boy?'

'No, Gran.'

'Always gotta keep your pencils sharp before the ink runs dry!'

'Yes, Gran.'

Silence a long, long while. I remember staring at my gran's legs, where they stuck out beneath the nightdress. They were grey, riddled with bright blue veins, large and splayed, like some sort of squashed rotting cheese grown from the mould inside a pair of slippers.

'Boy?' she said at last.

'Yes, Gran?'

'The shadow's coming, boy,' she sighed, fumbling at her jacket pockets for a tissue to wipe her running nose. 'The shadow's coming. Not here yet. Not for a while. But it's coming. It's going to eat you up, boy.'

'Yes, Gran.'

She hit me around the ear then, a quick slap like being hit with a thin slice of uncooked meat. 'You listen!' she snapped. 'The pigeons seen it! They seen it all! The shadow's coming. Young people never listen. He's coming for you, boy. Not yet, not yet . . . you'll have to sing like the angels to keep him away.'

'Yes, Gran.'

I looked into her fading, thick-covered eyes then, and saw, to my surprise, that tears were building up in them. I took her hand in sudden, real concern, and said, 'Gran? You all right?'

'I ain't mad,' she mumbled, wiping her nose and eyes on a great length of snot-stained sleeve. 'I ain't crazy. They seen it coming. The pigeons know best. They seen it coming.' Then she grinned, all gum spiked with the tiny remains of hanging flesh where teeth had once been. She stood up, wobbling on her feet a moment, the pigeons scattering from around her. She pulled me up, my hands in hers, and started to dance, pushing me ungainly back and forth as, with the grace and ease of a drunken camel, we waltzed beneath the sodium light of the city. All the time she sang in a little tuneless, weedy voice, 'We be light, we be life, we be fire, te-dum, te-dum! We sing electric flame te-dum, we rumble underground wind te-dum, we dance heaven! Come be we and be free . . .'

Then she stopped, so suddenly that I bounced into her, sinking into the great roll of her curved shoulders. 'Too early to sing,' she sighed, staring into my eyes. 'You ain't ready yet, boy. Not yet. A while. Then you'll sing like an angel. The pigeons don't have the brains to lie.'

And then she kept right on dancing, a hunched singing sprite in the night, until Mum called us in for bed.

Looking back, I realise now that the problem wasn't that my gran knew more than she was saying. The truth of the matter was, she said exactly and honestly what it was she knew, and I just didn't have the brains to see it.

I stopped running when my feet began to bleed. I didn't know where I was, nor what route I'd taken to get there. I knew only what I saw: the edge of a common or a small public park, a dark night in what felt like early spring or late autumn. Leaves falling from the giant plane trees round the edge of the green – autumn, then. It was drizzling, that strange London drizzle that is at once cold and wet, yet somehow imperceptible against the background of the pink-orange street lights, more of a heavy fog drifting through the air than an actual rain. I couldn't think in coherent words; it was too early for that. Instead, as my brain registered all my losses, panic immersed it like the splashing of a hot shower, preventing any reasoning of where I might go next or what I might do.

I found a dim, neon-lit passage leading under a railway line, that no beggar or homeless wanderer had colonised for that night, and sank down against the cold, dry paving with my knees against my chin. For a long while I did no more, but shivered and cowered and tried to seize control of my own thoughts. The taste of blood in my mouth was maddening, like the lingering dryness of cough medicine that couldn't be washed away. I played again the bright blue eyes of a stranger reflected in my reflection, tried to put those eyes in my face. The memories didn't bring physical pain; the mind is good at forgetting what it doesn't want to recall. But each thought brought with it the fear of pain, a recollection of things that had been and which I would move to some uninhabited rock away from all sodium lamps and men to escape again.

For a brief moment, I contemplated this idea, telling myself that the loss of everything was in fact a liberation in disguise. What would the Buddha do? Walk barefoot through the mud of an unploughed field and rejoice at rebirth, probably. I thought of worms between my toes, fat wriggling pink-grey bodies, cold as the rain that fed them, and we changed our mind. We would run, but not so far.

Instinctively, as it had always been when afraid, I let my senses drift. It was an automatic reflex, imparted as almost the first lesson of my training, the first time my teacher had . . .

. . . my teacher had . . .

Give me life!

. . . *a shadow is coming . . .*
runrunrunrunrunRUNRUNRUNRUNRUNRUNRUN
RUNRUN

Breathing was strength, the wall was safety. I pressed my spine into it, my head against it. Fingers would not grow out of the wall, claws would not sprout from the shadows. The more of me was in contact with something solid, the fewer places there were for the darkness to crawl, the better it would be. I imagined a great barking dog, all teeth and slobber, squatting by my side to keep me safe, a loyal pet to stand guard when I grew too tired. There were things which could be done, almost as good as a guard dog; but I didn't know if they would attract too much attention.

And so, again, as my breathing slowed, my senses wandered, gathering information. Smell of electricity from the railway overhead, of urine being washed away by the rain, of spilt beer and dry mortar dust. Sound of the distant clatter of a late-night commuter train, carrying sleepy one-a-row passengers to the suburbs and beyond. A bus splashing through a puddle swollen around a blocked drain, somewhere in the distance. A door slamming in the night. The distant wail of a police siren. As a child, the sound of sirens had comforted me. I had thought of them as proof that we were being protected, by guardians all in blue out to keep us safe from the night. I had never made the connection between protection and something we had to be protected *from*. Now the sirens sang again, and I wondered if they sang for me.

My clothes were too thin for the night. The drizzle made them soggy, clinging, itchy and cold to my skin. I could feel damp goose bumps up the length of my arms. We were fascinated by them, rolling up our sleeve to stare at the distortion of our flesh, and the little hairs standing to attention as if they were stiff with static. Even the cold interested us, how disproportionate it made our senses, our freezing feet too large for the space they inhabited, our numbed fingers huge pumpkin splatters across our thoughts; and it occurred to us that the human body was a very unreliable tool indeed.

Crispy bacon.

The smell of pie.

Taste of blood.

Memories of . . .

. . . *of* . . .

Half-close your eyes and it'll be there, all yellow teeth and blue eyes, looking down at you; press your eyes shut all the way and the blood will roll once again over your skin, pool and crackle across your back and sides, tickle against the sole of your foot, thicken in the lining of your socks.

You really want to remember all that?

Didn't think so.

Don't close your eyes.

I rolled my sleeve back down, tucked my chin deeper into my knees, wrapped my hands around myself, folded my feet one on top of the other.

There were other senses waiting to report in.

A little look, a quick gander, where was the harm? No one would ever know; breathe it in and maybe it will be all right, despite the shadows?

I inhaled, let the air of the place wash deep into my lungs, play its revelations through my blood and brain. Here it comes . . .

The feel of that place where I huddled like a child had a sharp, biting quality, thin on the ground, not so heavy as in other places where life moves more often and more densely, but carrying traces of other areas drifting in the air, snatched across the city in tendrils that clung to the commuter trains rattling overhead. What power and texture I could feel had a strong smell, but a slippery touch, retreating from too firm a command like a frightened bird. It gave me comfort, and a little warmth.

I pulled myself up and looked at the white-painted walls, examining the graffiti on them. Most of it was the usual stuff – 'J IS GAY!' or 'P § N FOR EVER' – but there was across one wall an orange swish of paint, all loops and sudden turns, that I recognised. It felt warm when I pressed my fingers to it, and tingled to the touch like slow-moving sand. A beggar's mark, delineating the edge of a clan's territory. It was good to find my senses still sensitive to such things – or even, I had to wonder, more sensitive than they'd been before? Though we could see the advantages, the thought did not comfort me.

I staggered down the tunnel, examining now in careful detail each splash of paint and scratch across the white-washed walls. Messages like:

DON'T LET THE SYSTEM GET YOU DOWN

or:

⊠⊠ULTRAS⊠⊠

or:

Don't lick the brushes

melted into each other over the cemented, painted surface of the bricks.

One splash of paint at the far end of the tunnel caught my attention, and held it. It had none of the usual trappings of protection that most who understood such things used to defend their territory, but was written in crude capital letters across the wall in simple black spray-paint. It said: 'MAK ME SHADOW ON DA WAL'.

It made me uneasy, but other things that evening were taking priority on my list of concerns, so I ignored it. I had no paint, but dribbled my fingers in the sharp sense of that place and, in the middle of the tunnel, started to draw my own mark on the wall, feeling even that slight movement give me comfort as I made the long shape of the protection symbol, my own ward against evil and harm. Not quite a guard dog; but close enough.

When I had finished, my head ached, and my fingers shook. Even something so small took too much out of me, the last vestige of strength left in my limbs. A warmth inside me suggested a hollowness that time, perhaps, might repair, and the weakness was not so much one of exhaustion, but of inexperience, as if every finger was freshly grown, the muscle untested, not yet conditioned to its former use. I slumped against the opposite wall and waited.

It took only a few seconds before the shape I'd drawn started to burn and hiss on the wall, its lines emerging in thin black swirls. I slid back onto the paving stones, tucked my knees up to my chin and shivered. The white strip lights overhead buzzed quietly; I could taste the electricity in them. Lesson one for anyone in my profession was always about electricity.

I took a risk, and with the tips of my fingers snatched a little warmth and light out of one of them, which died into darkness as I drew its energy to myself. The pea-sized ball of light and heat I managed to drag from it was like a match held between two fingers – shockingly hot when I brought my skin close to it, but not enough on which to sustain life. Uncertain which was likely to cause more pain, the cold or the failure of my own strength, I risked pulling down more light, and a few degrees more heat, caressing it into the sphere between my fingers, until almost all the lights overhead were extinguished, leaving just one at either end of the tunnel. The effort left me in a cold sweat, breathless and with a nasty case of tinnitus, but it also left me clutching a fat bubble of white light the size of a small, immaterial football. I lay down and curled myself around it like it was a bag of pure gold, feeling it warm me through and drive some of the wetness out of my clothes, and closed my eyes.

We did not want to sleep – our thoughts raced, our senses strayed out as far as we could reach, into the scuttling of a rat's claws under the street, the snuffling nose of a ragged-tailed urban fox, while we tried to pick out every shape and sense of life around us. But I was tired – too tired – and regardless of what we wanted, I had to sleep. I felt my eyes sink like an executioner's blade.

Taste of blood.

Yellow teeth and watery, weak blue eyes.

Give me life give me life give me life give me life GIVE ME . . .

Not quite sleep.

Distant siren, distant cars. Someone was out tonight looking for someone else; crawling through the gutters, talking to the pigeons, stealing the nose of the orange fox seeking its hamburger supper.

We did not enjoy sleep. Our dreams were mixed in with our reality, the world seen through a haze of blue. I had always loved nights like this, when the rain bubbled in the gutter. It gave everything a clean, clear quality, and allowed the mind to roam far and easily without becoming obstructed by the haze of crowded life and busy sense that too often obscures the wandering vision. Thoughts without words.

I couldn't have slept for more than a few hours. When I woke, the warmth in my hands had slipped away back into the lights, which glowed with their earlier harsh whiteness. On the edge of my senses I was distracted by a faint *drip drip drip drip.*

At one end of the tunnel, the beggars' orange-painted

mark was running down the wall in trickles, like blood from a nosebleed. It caught on a chip in the wall, pooled, then overflowed, dripping with a tiny, regular rhythm into a sad stain on the ground. I looked over at my own protective mark, the swirl of burnt paint at the other end of the tunnel, and saw that it too was starting to wobble round the edges, the lines of its power shimmering as if caught in a heat haze, the very bottom of the sign starting to liquefy.

I pulled myself up onto my feet, which immediately reported that they wanted nothing to do with the rest of me, and throbbed with a dull ache to prove the point. Blood and dirt had mixed into a dull brown stain. Hobbling to the end of the tunnel, I looked out into the dark. It was still night, or at least that dead time of morning before the dwindling gloom can muster any outline on the horizon. The rain was giving its all, pocking the ground with tiny silver craters, and turning the pavement into a reflective sheen of ebony blackness, pink-orange neon and flashing puddles.

I let my senses wander, and felt uneasy, a shuddering across my skin more than just the cold. There was a smell cutting through the rain, a blunt assault on the senses, a taste as much as a stench, that forced itself to the back of the nose and activated every receptor at once so that the brain was overwhelmed with so much information it couldn't even begin to decipher the component parts of the smell to say that this is orange peel and that wet cardboard. It was the smell of warm, wet rubbish, left to rot and moulder in interesting ways in a tight, dark, compressed area, before being let out into the air. And it was getting stronger.

I listened for dustbin trucks, scavengers and thieves. Nothing.

Just the slow hiss of melting paint and the pattering of the rain.

I am not given to paranoia, but recent experience had altered my perspective. It seemed unlikely that paint could melt and the air smell of litter – no, of something *more* than litter, a bite sharper than disgust – without there being some direct and unpleasant connection. I turned away from the stench and started walking as quickly as my battered feet would allow me, down the tunnel and out into the rain, letting it wash over me and enjoying the shock as it ran into my eyes and washed out the sleep; even as the rest of my senses came up to scratch and reported. . . .

. . . the smell of rubbish . . .

. . . taste of mould . . .

. . . touch of rain . . .

. . . empty street of strange shadows . . .

. . . sound of footsteps . . .

. . . edge of dry, hot ozone, getting closer, getting stronger . . .

I started jogging, uncomfortably, each landing on the soles of my feet a reminder that the human form actually weighed a lot, and that this burden was supported by a very small area relative to the mass. What a ridiculous form our flesh took, we decided. What a ridiculous species to have conquered the world.

There was a sound in the road behind me like newspaper blowing across sand. I broke into a run, suddenly not caring about the pain, but overwhelmed by a desire to be somewhere else, fast. The noise behind me grew louder, and so did the smell, and with it came a strange, low rumble, like the engine of a very old diesel car just before it explodes in a cloud of steam.

I saw an alley between two houses, full of dirty rubbish bags and oily puddles, and turned into it, racing for the wall at the end. Somehow being hemmed in comforted me – I had no way out, but whatever was behind me had only one way in, and I could face it properly, my back safe from claws and yellow teeth. I reached the wall at the far end and turned, pressing against a high wooden gate that presumably led into someone's back garden. I stretched my fingers out on either side of me, braced myself against the reassurance of a solid surface behind and started dragging power to me. It was slow, too slow, too long since I had last tried this – I hadn't had need for so many years! Still I pulled, thickening the air with it until the walls either side seemed to ripple with the pressure I was building up, cocooning myself inside a wall of force, ready to throw it at anyone or anything that might be looking for me. No such thing as coincidence. Not tonight.

At the end of the alley, nothing. I strained and heard a faint *cling cling*, and then a noise like the slurping of thick cake mixture being slopped up from the bottom of the bowl. Then that too stopped, and there was only my breathing, and the madman's certain feeling of being watched.

I didn't move. If it was going to come down to a battle of wills between me and whatever was out there, I was more than prepared to stay exactly like this, at the end of the alley until dawn or dusk, rather than expose myself to an unknown danger.

My head snapped up as a pair of pigeons exploded up from a nearby roof gutter. For a moment I considered borrowing their eyes and looking down on the world, but decided against it. Staying upright was demanding enough; multitasking was out of the question.

I waited.

It could have been a minute, it could have been ten; I didn't know, didn't care, and the adrenalin in my system wasn't about to let me judge.

I heard a can rattling on the alley floor. I looked across at the bin bags thrown against a wall. One of them was split, and its contents had poured out, into the stagnant puddle I'd waded through to reach the safety of the rear wall. Lank, torn crisp packets and broken banana skins floated in it; dead tissues, toilet-roll tubes, cardboard boxes for ready-cook meals, stained kitchen cloths, the broken handle of a cup, ripped foil, scrunched cling film, compressed orange-juice cartons and bent pints of semi-skimmed milk, all had spilt out of the bag, and all were, very gently, and without any explanation, starting to shake like popcorn in the pan.

The small, pale finger of dread levelled its tip in my direction and offered a suggestion. I knew what this was. It had been too easy.

Old plastic bags, torn-up junk mail, broken CD cases, they bounced through the tear in the bag, ripping it further, to let more rubbish spill out. They shook on the floor of the alley, and then, the lightest first, shopping bags caught in the breeze, remnants of ham packages, the sleeve that had held some piece of cheese, started to rise, straight upwards as if gravity were just some passing fad. Then the heavier pieces of rubbish – the cardboard box that had held a new portable radio, the remnants of a half-gutted lemon, a pile of orange peel that unwound upwards like a stretching snake in one unbroken piece. I watched them drift up from the torn rubbish bag in a slow, leisurely fashion, sheets of cling film each unscrunching and spreading as they ascended, bread sacks inflating like hot-air balloons and rising, bottom down, nothing rushed, nothing dramatic, all to a gentle hissing and rustling of old litter.

They rose towards a single spot, a shadow on the edge of one of the houses, clinging to the corner where wall met drainpipe, and as it all rose, it seemed to mingle with the shadow's form, a crisp packet reflecting with silver foil off what might have been an arm, a silver of cardboard coating what could perhaps be described as a belly. It looked like some sort of organic gargoyle, dripping strange thick liquid waste from one of its clinging limbs, still, patient, lumpen.

Then it turned its head, and its eyes glowed with the dying embers of two cigarette stubs. When it exhaled, its nose, the broken end of a car exhaust pipe, gouted smoke; when it raised one arm off the wall it clung to, its paw came away with the suction sound of well-chewed gum sticking, and its claws gleamed with the shattered razor-edges of old Coke cans and soup tins. Its thighs were composed of old hosepipe left in the street by some builders after a water-main repair job, its middle was covered over with old pieces of tin and card, bent traffic signs and abandoned boxes, to create an armoured underbelly beneath its hulked form, under which I could smell, and through cracks between its surface skin, see, a squelching heart of dead fruit, apple cores, chips, half-eaten hamburgers and abandoned Chinese takeaway, all crunched together into a brown mass beneath its surface armour, like a belly without the skin. Its teeth, when it opened its mouth, were reflective green glass from a broken bottle, its face was covered over with old newsprint and abandoned magazines, its arms shone with the reflective coat of foil, its wings were two translucent thin spreads of cling film that rose up behind it with a thin, sharp snap across the air, the joins woven together with fuse wire spun like tendons throughout its body. As it clung with its gummed paws to the wall of the house above me, the rubbish from the split bag settled into its flesh, spread itself across its arched back, wrapped itself around the backward-jointed bend of its knee. If it had been a living creature, I would have said it resembled a giant hyena, larger than a man, but hunched and feral, the shape its body made was arched and ready for a strike. But since it was not living, and its very breath was hot with the power that sustained it, I took it for what it was: a litterbug.

It had all been too easy.

I should have guessed that something like this would have to happen sooner or later. I'd just been counting a little too optimistically on later.

It stretched its jaw of green glass and rotting sandpaper tongue wide and hissed a tumbling gout of black exhaust into the air. The last broken plastic straw and burnt-out light bulb drifted up from the alley floor, settling into the litterbug's flesh, making it bigger, stronger. I saw its back arch, cling-film wings shimmering with the rainwater running across their surface, as with the hiss of a dying carburettor it stretched its razor-tin claws for my face, opened its mouth to emit a gout of fumes, kicked off with its back legs and tried to take my head off.

Instinct rather than conscious decision saved my life.

I let go the wall of force I had been building. It slammed into the litterbug mid-leap, propelled it backwards, threw it up against the wall, sending an explosion of dirty newspaper and mouldy organic spatter out from its flesh, and dropped it into the alley in a pile of torn foil and cling film. I had no interest in seeing whether this was going to stop it, I was pretty sure that it wouldn't, so without further ado I turned, slammed my shoulder into the high wooden gate until the lock tore away from the door, and ran into the garden beyond. Behind me, the litterbug pulled itself onto its hind legs, the torn remnants of its skin flowing back into its flesh, and advanced after me, snorting loudly through its rusting nose.

I ran across the soggy garden lawn, climbed over the back wall without looking back and slipped down the long drop to the railway line below on my backside, which, compared to my feet, had had an easy time so far. Bracken and broken shopping trolleys, which always seemed to find their way into railway cuttings, tore at my skin and clothes, nettles stung me, and a family of rats scuttled for cover in the destructive wake of my passage. I hit the hard ballast of the railway line with a bang and sprawled across it, catching myself on one of the railway tracks, smooth and silver on the top surface, rusted thick brown on the sides. Getting back on my feet was perhaps worse than the descent down the embankment: every muscle screamed indignation, every inch of skin featured a cut or a bruise or a stung bubble of inflamed flesh. I hobbled along the side of the railway track in that dry muddy space where ballast met slope, not caring where I was going, so long as it was somewhere else. Litterbugs did not just randomly stalk the streets of Dulwich; they had purpose, direction, intent, and it didn't take any thought to know that tonight, it wanted us. Behind me, I could hear the low wailing hunting-cry of the creature, a sound like the shriek of ancient bus brakes. I didn't have the courage to look back, but kept on hobbling along the railway line.

* * *

It was hard to say how far I went. I stopped only when I reached a station: North Dulwich. It was locked, the lights on its high yellow-brick walls casting odd shadows. I crawled onto the platform close by the safety of its heavy doors, and didn't care that the CCTV camera was watching. I lay down on my back and shook and felt in pain and generally sorry for myself.

When I had my breathing under control and some of the fire in my skin had died down to just a dull ache, we cast our awareness into every inch of ourself, feeling the shape and pressure of every cut and bruise. We were oddly fascinated by it, by the reality of it, even though we were surprised and appalled at the indignity of pain. We lay, and felt the cold rough surface of the concrete beneath us, and the cold rain drying on our face in the breeze that drifted along the railway track. For a moment, the overwhelming torrent of sense from every inch of our body, from every nerve in our skin, the coldness of the rain, the hotness of our muscles, the dryness of our tongue, the wetness of our hair, the gentle bleeding of our scratches and the tightness in our bruising, was fascinating, real, alive. For a moment, we wanted to laugh, although I wasn't sure if it mightn't be wiser to cry.

Then I smelt the rubbish.

Getting up on my feet was a triumphant act of will – staggering to the closed exit a shocking realisation of weakness, leaning against it a second of reprieve. I whispered imploring words to the lock and caressed it with my fingertips until it gave up and clicked; pulled back the heavy door even as, beyond the circle of neon light on the platform, I saw the glowing reddish embers of the litterbug's eyes. It slunk out of the dark, taller than ever, its skin now glowing with pieces of broken glass snatched up from the railway embankment, mosaicked across its flesh like royal jewellery.

I staggered out of the station, and it followed. The moment of reprieve had given me time to think, remember; I knew what I needed. It didn't take me long to find it as I ran through the tight uphill streets. The first was the lid of a black dustbin, painted with 'Flat 5' in yellow letters. The second was a bank of green wheelie bins, left by the local council outside a chemist on a small shopping parade, and thank all the powers in the heavens, they weren't too full. The litterbug was not far behind me, but it was too big to run as fast as the fear could carry us; not that it would give up for such a simple reason.

I opened all the lids on the wheelie bins, checking that there weren't any containing split rubbish bags – and tonight my luck held: every bin looked clean. I held the black dustbin lid I had taken from Flat 5 like a shield, pushing my right hand as far as I could through its handle, until it rested just above my wrist, wedged onto my arm. But by the time I was ready the creature was in sight, padding up the middle of the road and wading through the rainwater that poured downhill, with the slow, laborious and inevitable purpose of a sidewinder crossing the desert.

Here, the rain pouring off my face and seeping into my clothes, and, I hoped, washing some of the stench away, I turned and faced the monster.

We regarded its approach curiously, watching the care with which it advanced towards us, and with what single-minded purpose. It seemed almost a pity to destroy it, since we could probably have learned a lot from its structure, its form of life, but the preservation of ourself took priority.

As it came on, I stood my ground, hefting my dustbin lid in front of me, waiting. It advanced more cautiously than I expected, and before reaching me it stopped, raised its snout and emitted a strange shriek, like the scrape of old tyres skidding on a wet road. It did this three times and then sunk onto all fours, eyeing me up with its unblinking red embers. I felt that if I blinked it would pounce, and was immediately aware of my own eyes and the need to blink, as if, by thinking about it, the unconscious part of me that controlled this action could no longer function, and every blink and every breath had to be a deliberate, demanding thought-process. Still the monster didn't attack, and it took me too long – embarrassingly so – to work out why. The shrill call wasn't a challenge or an expression of pain – it was a call for reinforcements.

So much for this.

I looked around the street for a source of heat and found a fragment clinging to the wet surface of the chemist's bright green and white shop sign. Raising my left hand, I dragged it into my fingertips, crunching it down into a small penny shape between my fingers. The light, sucked dry of its energy, flickered and whined in indignation. I turned to the litterbug. It sensed my intentions, shifted uneasily, rose up a little, flexing the metal shards of one of its paws and emitting puffs of smoke. I pinched the penny of heat between my thumb and forefinger, and it winked out. For a second, nothing happened. Then the cigarette embers in the creature's eyes glowed brighter, burnt yellow, and exploded into flame. The spitting fire caught the newspaper of its head and burrowed into the soggy mass, sparks digging down through its skull to the dry ash and paper that formed the bulk of its long, snoutish head.

It screamed with the sound of a thousand screeching brakes as flames burst up through the mesh of wire and old laundry line that had spun a frame around its head, gouts leaping out through its nose, mouth, eyes and ears, spreading down the dry rope of its spine and melting the thin fuse wire of its wings, turning their cling-film sheen black and liquid, dripping hot plastic onto the ground. The flames burst out between the metal plates of its belly, glowed red-hot in the joints at its knees and elbows, spat out angry sparks between its clawlike fingers, made the chewing-gum pads of its paws dribble and smoke with a sickly smell, sent gouts of steam exploding off its surface—

But didn't kill it.

Instead, with a furious roar, it drew itself back on its hind legs, tensed its blazing back, and sprang.

I dropped onto one knee as it leapt, raising the dustbin lid up over my head to protect myself, and braced for the impact. Its bulk blocked out the light; its smell made my eyes run, twisted a knot in my stomach and sent a shudder through my belly. When it hit, it was like bricks falling in an earthquake. I tucked my chin into my chest, hunched my shoulders towards my stomach and put my arms, with the bin lid across them, over my head. Around me, rubbish showered down, and a thin gout of smoke stretched into the darkness. I heard a low moaning sound and peeked up from under my makeshift shield. The litterbug lay on one side, half an arm missing and a small hole gouged in the side of its chest. Around it litter drifted, displaced by the impact with my shield. I staggered upright, head spinning from the shock, and raised the dustbin lid against it. It rolled over and stood, moving awkwardly, its mass now off balance, belched smoke and ash, and threw itself at me. This time I raised the shield high over my head and willed what was left of my strength into it, until the plastic burnt against my skin. As the litterbug drew up to its full height, towering overhead, almost as high as the upper windows of the houses around us, I shoved the bin lid up towards it.

It roared with the blare of a hundred car horns, and smashed one claw down towards the bin lid with the weight of a wrecking ball. The force of the collision nearly knocked me off my feet. Around my shield a shower of bright orange sparks flew out in an umbrella shape, and litter rained down. The monster reared back in agony, clinging to the remnants of its shattered paw. As it did, distracted by whatever it was that counted for pain in such a creature, I threw my shield aside and leapt at it. I punched through a piece of cardboard that made up its loose underbelly, into the sticky, hot, rotten mass of its chest, while it flailed at me with shattered, stumpy arms. Fire snapped at my sleeve as I drove my arm into its middle, up to the shoulder; jagged metal parts, that seemed to float inside the foul core of mouldering food and other remains, slashed at my skin. My fingers closed over something small, that felt frozen, at the exact same moment that the litterbug, swaying precariously, wobbled onto one foot and with the other delivered a clawed kick that threw me backwards across the pavement, spraying organic spattered remains and soggy cardboard as I went.

The litterbug stood, its insides dripping, its head steaming as the rainwater competed with the smouldering flames of its eyes, and looked confused. Its gaze settled on my hands, where, with the creature's slime dripping off it in a thick black sludge, I held a single scrunched-up ball of paper, ice-cold to the touch. I unfolded it. Underneath the scrawl of symbols, summonings and incantations drawn in black felt-tip pen, I saw the words:

... local borough initiative ...

... recycling boxes provided ...

... collection Monday, Thursday *...*

... glass, tin, paper and all organic ...

... making a BETTER *environment ...*

... for the people of ...

The ink started to run in the rain. The litterbug screeched, with its strange, mechanical, metal voice. I crawled onto my feet. My eyes fell on the open, waiting wheelie bins. So did the monster's. It started to run, ready to throw itself into my path. I began to run too, slipping onto the pavement and reaching out for the bins, the icy piece of paper growing soggy in my fingers. Just as I reached the nearest bin, the litterbug reached out to slam its lid, and I was suddenly trapped between the bin and the monster's on-coming burning bulk. I closed my eyes instinctively, ready for the life to be crushed out of me, and dropped the piece of paper into the bin.

There was a bang, and I felt a sudden warm, enveloping sensation. I heard the sound of the rain, and a rustle of falling paper, felt the gentle passage of sticky rotting goo run down the back of my legs and the tickling brush of old newsprint and bits of plastic floating down around me as, without a sound, the litterbug collapsed. Its cardboard skin slid off its rotting flesh with a great wet *splat*, its wings drifted like angels' feathers to the floor, bits of hosepipe slid out of its mass like the splattering of intestines falling from a gutted fish. The embers in its eyes went out, the cigarette butts falling with sad little *plop plops* onto the soaking ground.

I pressed myself against the wheelie bins, forgetting to breathe as the drifts of rubbish settled around me. A few loose plastic bags caught in the wind and floated down the street. A ball of compressed newspaper rolled into the gutter and got stuck between the bars of a drain. A few embers were burning out in a puddle, a crunched Coke can bounced loudly against the wall. I opened the wheelie bin's lid an inch and peered inside. The inscribings on the piece of paper, the symbols of invocation and command that were the core of any construct and the heart of the creature, were gently burning themselves into ash inside the bin, powerless and contained.

I dropped the lid and turned, rubbish shifting at knee height all around me. Back down the hill, a few hundred yards away, a car was parked directly across the middle of the street. It hadn't been there before. A man got out of the passenger door. Then two more climbed out of the back, and a fourth, probably a woman, it was hard to tell in the light, got out of the driver's door. They started walking towards me. Reinforcements, I guessed. They'd heard the litterbug's wail.

I leant against the wheelie bin and half-closed my eyes, struggling to retain control. We were tired, in pain, and angry. We had not come here for this, this was not how things were meant to be, the wrong kind of living. Everything, we realised, but everything, was wrong.

I was too tired to care.

We opened our eyes. The world was bright blue in our vision, electric fire.

We stepped forward through the swirling remnants of dirt

and monster. We opened our arms and let the blue fire spread between our fingers. It was so good, so easy! We thrilled in it.

'Do you wish to fight us?' we yelled towards the advancing men. 'Do you think you will live so long?'

They stopped, hesitated, drew back in the middle of the road, and I could have just sat down in the filth of the street, stopped, could have, but that the fire was now burning behind my eyes. Beautiful, brilliant blue fire. 'Do you not relish what life you have?' we called, letting the flames burn across our skin. 'Do you not live for every breath, dance every moment to the rhythm of your own heartbeat, have you not seen the fire that burns in every sight?'

We tightened our fingers, ever so slightly, pulling them into the shape of a fist. Above us, the neon lights of the street lamps exploded, the burglar alarms on the sides of the shops popped, spraying metal, the water in the gutter bubbled, twisted, turned, like it was being sucked down into a vortex. 'If all you see in life is its end,' we called, 'then join us!'

It was so easy, now we were willing to try, the power felt so good, that brilliant, sacred word we hadn't dared to whisper since I had first reopened my eyes, the magic of the streets, *my* streets, our magic . . .

Lights started turning on; there were voices in the houses; car alarms started to wail in the street. I didn't want to be caught, I so badly didn't want that to deal with on top of everything else now, please not now. I wanted to sleep. We wanted them gone.

Neither, it seemed, were they prepared to stay. They started backing away; then turned and ran, scuttling into their car, and firing the engine. We let the power slip from our fingers, although I knew, so easily, I knew that just a thought could burst their brakes or shatter their windows or twist their pipes or burn their fuel, we knew we still had that strength inside us, so simple, so easy to just . . .

I let the power go, let the built-up magic between my fingers slip away; and it hurt. There was so much of it, just letting it go without bursting into flame made my head ache and my heart pound. Inside, I knew that we loved it. We loved that fire in our fingers, we loved that victory against the monster, we loved the rain and the rubbish and the night and the noise, and we would never, entirely, let it go.

As the first person started shouting from their window, 'What the fuck is . . .'

. . . I turned, and walked away, into the night.